The Power of 2

By

John Holding

Book 1

2s

First Edition

ISBN -13: 978-1461143673

ISBN-10: 1461143675

Copyright © John Holding 2011

Cover design by Emma Will and Nicole Leask

For Chick and Elma

God Bless

PRAISE FOR THE POWER OF 2

The Power of 2 is an example of why first time novelists should wait before publishing. Its author has all the technical skill a new talent commands but he has also lived his life and to John Holding's fiction this brings a depth and substance. This is a dimension often lost in speedy examples of the thriller genre, written by clever young minds adept at plot turns. This is a story that will have you turning the page late at night and putting off sleep, its premise is gripping but its characters are more than plot vehicles. What is the power of 2? The power between a man and a woman, a master and servant, the power of living life and facing death? This is a story of brothers and brothers in arms; it's a story of graves and digging your own one. It's a story of lovers. It will leave you breathless and better informed about human nature and its machinations.

Susanne Power – author of The Lost Souls' Reunion and Angel Journey.

ACKNOWLEDGMENTS

Many people helped me bring this idea to fruition and I'd like to record my thanks to them here. Firstly, grateful thanks go to Lancaster University. Their Creative Writing Courses helped me gain confidence in producing short stories and built steadily toward an idea that ultimately became *The Power of 2*. Latterly, in the midst of studying technique and craft with Manchester Metropolitan University's Writing School, the novel took shape. Grateful thanks are due to the various course tutors for their patience and careful guidance and, of course, to all my fellow fledgling writers - a great bunch - who together made the shared process such a valuable and enjoyable experience.

In particular, special thanks go to my *writing buddy*, Sarah Harding, who – from various locations in Europe and the USA – was always available with endless encouragement and who provided feedback on each chapter of *The Power of 2* from start to finish. Thanks buddy!

Chapter 1 ~ Somebody has to do it ~

~ Adam ~

I work with an energetic rhythm, my lips silently mouthing the words of the songs that play in my head. And that's how it goes, that's my plan. Perspiration gathers on my brow and I wipe it away with my sleeve. But after a while the sweat runs in rivulets down the hollow of my chest and the crevice of my back. Under my thin, standard allocation council jacket, my vest clings to me like a second skin.

After over an hour's labour I'm happy with the depth. These days I don't have to check, I just know. I straighten, lean my spade against the sidewall and with the palms of my hands pressed on my lower back I thrust my chest out and push my elbows together, teasing the kinks from my spine. A small involuntary gasp escapes my mouth. I tug at my clothing and peel the vest from my body.

Now that I'm standing upright the rays of the mid-morning sun are warm on the back of my neck, and this despite the fever of my own efforts. I look down at my work; those same rays will have burned the morning dew from the grass above, but the heat doesn't penetrate more than a few inches into the soil. I glance at the dark surrounding walls, their clawing dampness drawing the fire from me, swallowing it whole. A shudder runs through me. Not for the first time I wonder what I'm doing in a job like this.

Of course, there's more to it than meets the eye; if there weren't I'd not have had to attend all those training courses. In some respects I can argue that what I've acquired is a skill, but I don't; at least not with anyone other than big Nigel at pay review time. It began as a means to an end, a job like any other, at the time the only one I could get. But I soon realised it was something of a conversation stopper. People look at me differently when they find out and keep me at a distance thereafter, as though I'm marked through association. I'm used to it but I learned it was a no-go area when I was out on the pull with Colin and Ferris. If a girl asked what I did for a living I told her I was a Council worker in Tannock Bar. If pressed further I'd go as far as to say I worked in the Parks and Gardens sector. It wasn't a lie; it just wasn't specific.

My breather over, I look at my watch then turn my attention to levelling out the base, heaving out the last few shovelfuls of soil onto the surrounding tarpaulin. These last scoops are always the worst. With the ground above head height the effort has to be that bit steadier, more deliberate and the shovel feels heavier in my hands than when I laid it down because my muscles ache and protest all the more with the renewed effort.

Finally I'm satisfied that the base is level so I take my spade in both hands and carefully push it out onto the grass. Then, with my cheek pressed into the cold face of the dirt wall I raise my right arm and feel along the grave's edge until my fingers find the handle of the trimming blade. I gather the tool in and run it down each of the four corners in turn taking out any rough edges, any hang-up points, squaring them off. I'm on my hands and knees trimming the final six inches of the last two corners when it happens. It dawns on me that I'm not sticking to the plan; I'm letting the music wash over me, letting myself think, no longer mouthing the lyrics. The thought alone forces me to re-focus on the track that's playing but the up-tempo beat has been replaced by something slower, something soulful, almost haunting. Too late, I realise my mistake, Annie bloody Lennox is in my head singing 'I've Got a Life'.

In the chilling depths of the pit my mind's eye conjures an image. My mother's face swims before me, her expression serious, questioning. But almost as quickly as it formed, it is gone, though the lilting voice continues. I feel my jaw drop; my breaths quicken. Another vision forms in the mists of my exhaled breath. I make out Colin's eyes, the bridge of his nose... this is too much. My fingers let go of the trimming blade. I fumble at the cord at my neck wrenching the ipod from beneath my jacket and the headphones from my ears. I launch them up and out.

"Everything okay, Adam?"

I reclaim the trimming blade and scramble across to run it down the remaining corners.

"Sure boss, I'm all done."

"Good," he says, reaching the grave and peering down at me. "You're gonna need all your time. I'll have someone else prepare the graveside as we agreed. You get yourself gone."

The foreman passes down a small ladder purposely laid adjacent to the graveside excavations and I climb out. His eyes linger on the grave. He lays a hand on my shoulder, "Good job, son, I know that can't have been easy."

Half an hour later I'm standing under the shower in my one-bedroom flat letting the steaming water cleanse me. Everyone gets wrapped up in the job's cringing, uncomfortable association with death; I almost laugh as I recall myself telling Colin and Ferris that the gruesome aspect didn't bother me. It's not like I'm handling the bodies, like an undertaker or a mortician, or dissecting them like a pathologist. Now that would be morbid. But few people really appreciate how physically demanding and downright filthy my job can be. I mean, dirt and dust get up my nose and in my ears. More than that, it lies in the creases of my skin, in the furrows of my brow, even under the thin folds of my eyelids. I keep my fingernails well trimmed, but at the end of each day they too are caked in grime. The thought unnerves me; I reach for the shower gel and soap myself for a third time. With my eyes closed I roll my head in a slow circle first one way then the other, hearing the light creak of muscle and tendon stretching at the same time as the warm jets pummel my skin. I sigh; however much the dirt and smell of the graveyard clings to me I know I can wash it all away. This thought always makes the shower at the end of my shift the best part of my day.

I pass into the bedroom in the final throws of towelling my hair dry then pick up my watch from the top of the dresser. "Fuck," I say, noticing the time as I slip it on. I throw the towel on the floor and dress quickly; a fresh pair of boxers, my smart black trousers and socks; a crisp white shirt - short sleeved but then I don't have another, at least not a white one. And, of course, the black tie I bought specially. I use the mirror above the dresser to check that the knot looks okay then reach into the cluster of bottles that sit on the left hand corner of the dresser. A squirt of aftershave; a little gel run through my hair and I'm done. I set the gel back down and my eyes fall onto the framed, yellowing photograph peeking out from behind the bottles. I pick it up. Her fair hair glistens, falling straight like a waterfall to spill across her shoulders and, like the shine in her bright eyes; it belies her otherwise pallid complexion. Hers is the first picture my mind had conjured in the depths of the grave earlier in the day. Those eyes burn into me. "You looking at me like that doesn't make it any easier, Ma. Things don't always work out the way we want." I set the picture back onto the dresser, face down.

The intercom sounds and I walk to the hall to lift the receiver. "Hello?"

"You right then?" the voice asks.

"Sure, Ferris, keep the engine running on that rust bucket of yours. I'll be right down."

I step into a pair of black shoes. On the way out I grab my wallet, keys and finally a black raincoat from the hallway closet. On the landing I've got the key in the door ready to turn the lock when I hesitate. Five seconds later I'm back in the bedroom, wiping the glass photo frame with the face of my new tie before setting it back upright in its place on the dresser.

In the street I spot Ferris in a grey suit twenty yards away leaning with his backside against the passenger door of his aged Capri, its engine idling. I call out as I get within earshot. "Hey, where did you get the suit, Ferris? Did Mothercare have a sale on?"

"Ha, fucking ha," he yells back.

"The car had a scrub too then has it?"

Ferris shoots up and cranes his neck over his shoulder trying to look at the seat of his trousers. "Bastard suit's just out the cleaners too. Is it bad?" he asks, turning his backside to me.

"Bad? It's the scrawniest little arse I've seen in months; like a knot in a hankie."

"Very funny, I'll need to remember that one," he says dusting himself down.

We climb into the car and once we've got going he asks how we're doing for time, so I look at my watch. "We should just about make it."

"How did it go this morning?" Ferris asks. "Must've been bleedin' weird." He glances at me for a second then looks back at the road. Then he removes a hand from the wheel to run a finger between his neck and shirt collar. He's made an effort and I know it.

I turn away and stare absently out of the passenger window then exhale noisily. "It was strange; you've heard the phrase 'whistle while you work,' well I updated it. I wore my ipod and drowned my thoughts with music just so I could get through it without thinking too much." My thoughts pass to the vision of Colin's face I'd brought to mind in the grave. I'm about to tell Ferris, then, I think better of it. Instead I say, "Not every day you dig a grave for a mate is it?"

"At least you were able to do something for him; he'd have been pleased about that."

"C'mon, Ferris, it's Colin we're talking about. We both know he wouldn't give a toss for sentimentality." I watch Ferris's lips tighten, biting back further comment – he knows I'm right.

We drive on until Ferris finally breaks the silence. "Anyway, how come it's a church service and a burial? I mean Colin wasn't religious."

"Colin's sister made the arrangements. I suspect she pulled a few strings to get him a plot. I think she's a church elder or something, not here but wherever it is she lives. It's who you know that makes the difference – even in death."

"Colin's sister? I didn't even know he had a sister."

"Hmm, Barbara," I tell him. "They didn't get on, haven't…hadn't," I correct myself, "spoken in years apparently."

"You've met her then?" Ferris asks.

"I met them both in the care home. Colin was a bit of a tearaway. Barbara thought I was a bad influence on him."

Ferris raises his eyebrows and his jaw visibly slackens. "You; a bad influence on Colin? You've got to be bleedin' kidding. He didn't need help from anyone there."

"Well," I tell him, "you can understand it. He was her brother; she's bound to think the best of him."

Small stones thud off the underside of the car as the tyres churn the gravel at Tannock Bar Parish Church. Ferris draws the Capri to a halt and we climb out.

"Well, it got us here," I say nodding at the Capri.

Ferris looks up with a hurt expression on his face. "She's a classic," he announces, in a higher pitch than normal. "I'll have you know there are plenty of people who'd want this beauty."

"Yeah," I tell him, "and all of them scrap merchants." I raise a half-hearted smile, but even that seems out of place.

I look around whilst Ferris hauls at the waist of his trousers and dusts his backside again. "Less than half a dozen cars and one of those'll be the Minister's. It's a small turnout, Ferris. Let's get it over with."

"Least he's got a nice day for it," Ferris says looking skyward.

I lead the way and we walk up the path to the church. At the door Ferris taps me on the arm and points to my shoes. They're dull; I've forgotten to polish them. I rest both hands on Ferris's shoulders for balance and rub the face of my right shoe down the calf of my left trouser leg. I do likewise to obtain a shine on the left. Ferris gives me the thumbs up. I get the feeling that I'm making such an arse of showing proper respect that somehow Colin would be pleased.

Inside the organist plays something sombre and I'm hit by a wave of disappointment. It's indicative of the mood but, for me, it doesn't reflect Colin's attitude to life. Three men and a woman sit together in a pew midway down the aisle; they speak in whispers that seem to bounce off all the walls intensifying the attempted private discussion yet leaving it an unintelligible garble. We walk past them and sit two pews in front. Ahead, in the foremost pew two women sit alone.

Ferris groans and leans in towards me. "Jesus," he whispers, "it brings it home seeing it sitting there, eh?"

I nod. The coffin sits out front bedecked in wreaths, the largest of which sits lengthways along the coffin itself. I've seen them often enough. Indeed, I often have to clear them from the gravesides myself after funerals. This one is a fusion of yellow and white flowers teased through a wire frame to form the word 'Brother'. As the Minister appears from his vestry we make to stand and I glance behind me. The mourners number precisely eight. I ask myself if this is the sum total of Colin's life. Were these people really the only lives he touched? The thought leaves me cold.

The Minister clears his throat and we rise in unison. He conducts a simple service, speaks of sorrow at the loss of a life in tragic circumstances, of promise lost and hopes unfulfilled. Whilst this is all true it's also generic. It's obvious that the Minister knows nothing of Colin; the sermon holds nothing of 'him'. I find myself switching off, delving into memory to recall the freckle-faced fourteen-year-old who'd befriended me on my first day at the care home; a time when I really believed my stay there was only a blip in an otherwise normal childhood. Of course, I'm ignoring the fact that my mother was a single parent. But what I mean is that until that point I missed out on nothing for the lack of a father.

On a signal from the Minister half a dozen men appear from the wings and proceed with admirable regard to first raise then carry the coffin from the church. The mourners, all eight of us, fall in behind the Minister. As the two women from the front pew pass I recognise one as Barbara. Her eyes, reddened with tears and the tiredness of loss, meet mine and immediately cut away. In that moment I know there is to be no reconciliation between us.

As the mourners gather at the graveside and watch the coffin being lowered into its final resting place I stand a yard or two further back, Ferris beside me. Ferris hasn't spoken for a while but chooses this moment to break his silence.

"I take it you don't want to get any closer?"

"You could say I've been too close already, Ferris, but you go nearer if you want." I just wanted to give Barbara her moment without interference; she was, after all, Colin's blood.

"I'm fine here if you are," Ferris says.

The Minister says a few brief words over the grave, Barbara casts the obligatory sprinkling of earth onto the coffin and it's over. She shakes the Minister's hand, thanks him for his service and brusquely brushes past Ferris and I on her way out of the cemetery leaving the friend who had accompanied her trailing in her wake.

"Don't tell me," Ferris says watching her stride away with her friend scurrying to make up the ground between them. "That was Barbara, huh?"

"Yes."

"Jesus, I wouldn't count on a Christmas card from her if I were you," he says.

We exchange solemn nods with the Minister and the remaining mourners as each makes to depart. Finally, we are alone at the graveside. I squat down, grab a handful of earth, sprinkle it onto the coffin and whisper *God Bless*. Then I stand, walk to the floral tributes that have been brought out from the church and bend to read the cards. There is one from Bob, Donna and the boys, another from Mike and Sadie – both, I surmise, might be neighbours or perhaps friends of Barbara's. Leaving Barbara's tribute aside, that leaves just two others, one simply reads 'R.I.P.' initialled JM, the other 'Missing you,' from Anne-Marie, Mark, Jeff, Steve and all at Trondby. I smile and walk back to the graveside.

Ferris stands, hands in trouser pockets, staring into the grave. I lay a hand on the nape of his neck. "C'mon, they'll want to fill the grave, let's leave them to get it done."

"Are we heading back to the hotel for a drink with the rest of the mourners?" Ferris asks.

"Nah, let's head off on our own. Those people didn't know Colin, or most of them didn't."

"I didn't recognise anyone," Ferris says. "I didn't even know Colin had a sister until five minutes before we buried the poor bastard. Who were they all anyway?"

"Well, now you know who Barbara is. My guess is that the lady with her was a friend, maybe a neighbour offering support." We reach the Capri and speak across the car roof. "I looked at the cards that came with the flowers; there was one from a JM." Ferris's face remains blank. "You know Colin had big ideas, just bluster for the most part, but maybe he was making some connections."

"How do you mean?" Ferris asks.

"It's a bit of a leap but maybe JM is Jack Muldoon."

Ferris squints. "Hasn't he got a bit of a reputation?"

I motion that we should get into the car and wait as Ferris first climbs in then reaches across to unlock my door from the inside. "I've not met anyone who knows him either – but I've heard whispers. He's bad news, Ferris. Thing is, I just can't think of a 'JM' who might have sent Colin a wreath. I could be way off base here."

"Shit, but what if you're right?" Ferris says. "The crash was an accident, wasn't it? I mean Colin wouldn't have pissed this Muldoon guy off or something?"

I smile. "No, let's not get carried away. All I'm saying is that I think Colin was setting his sights higher than the next job and he'd started making himself known. Maybe we went along with this for too long. Now is a good time for us to get out."

Ferris stays silent; he stares out of the window. "There was another wreath there too," I tell him, "from all at Trondby's. I reckon the other four mourners were his workmates from Trondby."

Ferris purses his lips and blows out a long, slow breath. "You read my mind. I was worried that he'd screwed up and dropped us in it. So they've no idea that he took the job just so we could turn 'em over?"

I shake my head, "None at all."

Ferris guns the engine. "Great, we're in the clear then. Let's go have a drink and give Colin a proper send off."

****

Chapter 2 ~ *Safety in numbers* ~

~ *Mo* ~

Me and Harvey are in the first floor snooker room of Moods, Cornelius's place. Downstairs, the nightclub is closed; the punters won't arrive for hours, yet the muted strains of a disco beat filter up through the ducting and every now and then, when the bass or the treble are high, you can feel the vibrations through the soles of your shoes. Harvey thinks I'm stalling and tells me to get on with it; they're trying out a new DJ is all. But I'm not bothered, after all, the club is none of our concern; Cornelius has other guys looking after that side of his little empire. No, now, is my time; mine and Harvey's and this game's for me.

My head's been pounding for a while but I reckon I've stuck it out maybe fifteen minutes more than last time. I take a pace to the left and bend low to look at the angle from behind the cue ball. Harsh light from the fluorescent tube illuminating the table shoots back at me from the polished surface of the balls. It's like my eyes are being punctured by a hundred tiny needles, stinging as they enter then exploding in heat behind my eyeballs. The suffering builds upon itself growing ever more insistent. I know the pattern only too well, my temples throb, a bastard of a headache settles behind my eyes then a constant hum, like that from an overhead power cable, reverberates in my head growing in intensity until I relieve the pressure.

I stand again and, not for the first time, wipe my weeping eyes with the back of my hand. I feel my left fist unconsciously tighten around the cue and see my knuckles whitening. I'm fighting an urge to lash out; bearing the pain in an effort to overcome this thing, a 'stultifying weakness' the doctors called it, and I know I'm reaching my limit. I've always thought the discomfort strange; searing at the start, it becomes a dull and creeping nag. I curse albinism and photophobia. If they lived and breathed I'd take pleasure in their slow and tortuous murder.

Across the room I sense Harvey shifting uneasily in his chair, the miserable git wants to win so much he forgets why we're doing this. These games began as an exercise to help me fight photophobia. When it didn't work as planned it became about building my concentration, turning my mind off to the gnawing irritation and the blinding headaches. Lately though Harvey has tired of it all, he's given up on me, needs the side bet to keep him interested enough to play at all. *The preening bastard.* I want to smash this fucking cue into the smug, perfect face he takes so much pride in. It'd serve him right. *Calm down, Maurice,* I tell myself. *He wants you to lose it, but it isn't gonna happen. Take a deep breath, ignore him.* It's at times like now that I realise my own brother's just like all the rest. He thinks he's the one with the fancy words – mister articulate – and that because I've little to say, my head's full of violence and not much else. But I'm not violent due to some derangement or stupidity – if I were I wouldn't see his actions for what they are. No, I might be quiet but I'm always thinking and I'm violent because it frees me and because it frees me, I love it.

From his seat in the soothing shadows Harvey clears his throat. "For fuck's sake, Mo, put your effing shades on or we'll be here all bloody night."

I glare at him; he draws deeply on his cigarette then exhales a long, thin line of smoke. He returns my stare, his lips curling into a grin, then he winks at me. Anger boils in my gut, but I keep the lid on it. I look at the table once more. My options are few; in fact I'm pretty sure I'm screwed, but again I bend over the table and settle into my shot. Harvey moves into my line of vision, pinches the dying embers of his cigarette between thumb and forefinger then casts the smouldering butt three feet across the room to land in an ashtray. Its passage through the air leaves a thin, wispy arc. I straighten and feel the heat of anger pass through me.

Harvey has his hands held up, palms open. "C'mon, bruv, you've been needing snookers for the last ten minutes." He strides forward and flutters his fingers over the two fifty pound notes under the chalk at the table's edge, but his eyes never leave mine. "This game's as dead as last Sunday's roast beef, and we both know it. Let's call it a day. I'll take the cash now, eh?"

I raise my cue like an accusing finger and level it at him. "Sit down you skinny fuck, I can make this shot."

Harvey pulls his hand away from the money, "Sure you can," he says, then returns to his chair, still smiling.

My eyes remain fixed on him. It occurs to me that I've said the wrong thing and I wish I could take it back. Not the insult, he's asked for as much. But this isn't and shouldn't be about money and Harvey would do well to remember that. I shake my head in annoyance then lean over the table and stare down the length of my cue, determined to concentrate. I linger; allowing my breathing to slow, *let the bastard wait*. I'm preparing to strike the cue ball when the door rattles and falls open spilling light from the corridor across the room.

"Aw, for fuck's sake, what now?" Harvey yells. "We're trying to finish a game here."

In the doorway stands the figure of a slightly built man in a dark blouson leather jacket, the pockets baggy with overuse. His face seems to glow with sweat and his hair is drawn tightly into a ponytail that curls back onto his shoulder. It takes me longer than it should to register who this is, but when I do, I realise it isn't sweat that covers his face: or at least none due to prolonged effort. No, Rats seems to wear a permanently greasy complexion over a badly pockmarked face; and, with him, it somehow sort of fits.

"Sorry to interrupt," Rats says.

Harvey sighs. "I might have guessed it'd be you. What do you want, Rats?"

Rats shuffles his feet, thrusts his hands into his pockets and pulls his jacket more tightly around himself – an action which makes his shoulders appear more rounded than they are. "I don't like you calling me that."

Harvey straightens in his chair and Rats takes a half step back. "I don't give a flying fuck what you like or don't like." He lets the words echo around the room then in a calmer voice says, "Besides, it's kinda stuck now."

Rats changes the subject. "Cornelius sent me to find you… needs to see you both."

Harvey turns to look at me, his eyebrows raised. "Think you could stretch to maybe playing out this frame before whatever job Con has for us grows legs and walks away?"

"I think it's about money," Rats says.

Harvey shoots up from his seat and takes a step forward. "It was a fucking rhetorical question you git and it wasn't even addressed to you. You've delivered the message, now piss off."

Rats lets his gaze drop to the floor and backs out pulling the door closed behind him. I feel the merest twinge of sympathy for Rats – he's an ugly fuck, like me. "Why do you give the little shit such a hard time?" I ask.

"Dunno. I think he's wound too tight somewhere, the voice is a little on the precious side. And he wanders around like he's wearing bloody slippers. Gives me the creeps."

"Why did Cornelius take him on?" I ask.

Harvey scratches at his stubbled goatee. "Fucked if I know. Take your shot." He grabs his jacket, shoots his cuffs and settles it onto his slim frame. Then he runs both hands backwards through his dark hair and returns his attention to the table.

I strike the cue ball. It squeezes past the brown and glances off the side cushion but misses the remaining red by several inches. "Bastard," I yell.

Harvey snatches up the cash and beams back at me. He rubs the crisp notes between his fingers and brings them to his lips; kisses them with a loud, exaggerated smack, then stuffs them into his pocket.

I feel the fury rising in me again causing the small hairs all over my body to stand tall. My hands are clammy and begin to twitch. Without warning my eyes roll and in a burst of frantic motion I take the cue in both hands, lift it into the air then bring it down over my raised thigh at speed. It breaks with a sickly, splintered snap. For a few seconds I stare into space, the cue ends quivering in my balled, trembling fists.

"Feel better?" Harvey asks from the doorway.

"Uhuh." I let the cue pieces fall to the floor and tug on my jacket. "I imagined it was your bloody neck."

"There's gratitude."

I pull a stylish pair of slim, square-framed glasses from my top pocket and slip them on. The lenses are dark and the thick legs act as side shields tapering to a thin bar above my ears. Immediately the harsh light loses its venom though my head still aches. I follow Harvey out of the door and we head toward the stairwell at the end of the corridor.

When we reach Cornelius's office we find Rats leant against the wall opposite the door. He straightens as we draw near.

"Sorry, he's still busy," Rats says.

Harvey casts his eyes to the ceiling as if to suggest that for loose change he'd strangle this little prick.

Rats tilts his head to the side and looks up at Harvey through narrowed eyes. "So how come you two always wear those three piece suits?"

"It makes a statement, like presence and style. But don't worry…" Harvey runs his eyes over Rats from head to toe and back again, "…it's not something that's likely to trouble you."

"You don't like me… do you?" Rats says, and, for an instant, I catch a grin flickering across his face.

I can see the question has surprised Harvey as much as it has me. In the last five minutes Rats has said more in backchat than we've heard him say in all of the ten days he's been here. Is he mocking us or is it just nerves? After all, people are always a little nervous around me; I make them uncomfortable just by being in the same room. I can't let it pass; my fist clenches and I take a step toward him but Harvey's arm holds me off.

Harvey smiles, "Oh, I wouldn't say that. I mean, I don't know who the fuck you are or what you're doing here.

Cornelius wants you in… so you're in." He taps the centre of his chest with his fingers, "But that doesn't mean I trust you, you'll have to earn that."

"So it's just 'cos I'm new," Rats says with a straight face.

Cornelius's office door opens. Mickey Fisher, who runs Cornelius's money lending business, walks out. He appears deep in thought but acknowledges us, holding the door and gesturing us in.

Harvey leans toward Rats and lowers his voice. "Sure, 'cos you're new, but I'll be keeping an eye on you… and if you don't measure up I'll cut your fucking head off. Understand?"

I follow Harvey into the office eyeballing Rats over my shoulder just long enough to see the smile die on his face and the colour drain from his cheeks. Inside, Cornelius sits behind a large walnut desk in his familiar leather chair, the window at his back. The blinds though are shut; a solitary lamp spills a soft light across the table and illuminates the two empty chairs opposite. A cigar rests between his chubby fingers and my attention is taken by the smoke that rises from it like skeletal fingers feeling their way to the darkened corners. I like the dark, it soothes me.

"Ah, lads, pull up a chair won't you, that's grand so," Cornelius says.

We sit. Behind us Rats shuts the door and stands with his back to it. I remove my shades; my head still throbs but the subdued light makes me sufficiently comfortable without them.

Cornelius seems to puzzle over some numbers on the papers in front of him; he raises his head and peers over the top of his glasses. We follow his gaze over our shoulders;

he's looking at Rats. "I'll be shouting on you when I need you. Go get yourself a coffee," he says.

"But, Boss, I thought…"

Cornelius raises his voice, "I said you can fuck off, this doesn't concern you."

A glow of satisfaction lights up Harvey's face. Rats leaves the room like a scolded pup, his shoulders hunched, his head held low.

Cornelius's pallor is as grey as his thinning hair. He pushes up his glasses, closes his eyes and massages the reddened bridge of his nose. The top button of his shirt is undone; his tie is slack and sits askew. He lurches to one side and his free hand digs deep into his trouser pocket. It emerges with a white linen handkerchief which he runs around the nape of his neck then dabs across his forehead. He gives a cursory glance at the residue in the cloth before tossing it onto the desk.

"Okay, lads," Cornelius says. "Here's the situation. I've got a deal going down, a cash investment – a big one. I've weighed in with everything…all the ready cash I can lay my hands on but I'm still going to come up shy."

Beside me, Harvey rakes his fingers through his goatee. "That explains the heat these past few weeks. I thought we were in trouble but you were squeezing extra cash to fund this deal?"

Cornelius nods. "The businesses are fine, Harvey, lad. I just needed a bit more from them or we'd lose this opportunity. And you know me, I've wrung from them every penny… and I've called in favours." He rests an elbow on the desk and brings his thumb and forefinger together until they are almost touching, "…we're that close."

"So how much is shy?" Harvey asks.

"I'm short fifty grand."

Any sense of tension leaves Harvey's face and he throws up his hands. "Okay, so Mo and I crack a few heads, we'll soon rustle up some donations."

I allow myself a grin but Cornelius isn't smiling.

Cornelius raises a hand halting the enthusiasm. "Sure that's grand so, but there are restrictions. This is…" he pauses as if looking for the right word, "…delicate. What needs done we'll do quickly and quietly, no loose ends."

I glance at Harvey, normally I'm happy to let him do the talking when it comes to business; he has ambitions in that direction whereas I have none. But I need only catch his eye to alert him if I have a concern. This occasion proves no different. Harvey picks up on it right away.

"What's the deal?" Harvey asks.

Cornelius taps the side of his nose. "All in good time, lad."

"Okay," Harvey says, "then what do we *need* to know?"

Cornelius sits back in his chair. He stares hard at us both, but says nothing. The silence weighs heavy. He breaks eye contact, sucks on his cigar then raises his head to blow smoke towards the room's darkened ceiling. Finally, he settles the cigar in his ashtray and raises a finger and then his voice, "I'm telling you this because then you'll appreciate the importance of doing it right. But I want you to use your heads. Am I clear?"

I tense up, Cornelius has given this too much of a build up. What is already crystal clear to me, even through the fog of an aching head, is that I'm not going to like what comes next.

Cornelius speaks softly now into the table, almost carelessly, "Carnie's onto something big. So big even he can't handle it alone. I've agreed a deal to buy us a slice of the action."

My mouth hangs open, the dull hum in my head seems to spike; *Carnie? Surely I misheard.* I look at Harvey and see that he is staring at the floor; his right hand cradling his jaw whilst he bites into the flesh of his forefinger. I can't hold back, I stand, scraping the legs of my chair across the linoleum floor. "Con, Sholto Carnie doesn't do deals with anyone. He'd slit his own kid's throat if it was worth his while, you know this."

Cornelius sucks on his lower lip then suggests I retake my seat. "Carnie can't handle this deal alone; there could be as many as a dozen others buying in… safety in numbers if you like."

Harvey sighs. "Whatever the deal is, he's not to be trusted, boss."

"There are no second chances with him, that I'll grant you," Cornelius says. "That's exactly why I need you to be careful – no fuck ups, no undue attention. Besides, this deal will set us all up for life and I've worked too hard to let a poxy fifty grand cost us our shot."

"So what do we do?" Harvey asks.

Cornelius sits forward to rest his elbows on the desk. "I've had Mickey Fisher run a check on the punters we've loaned cash to over the last five years. We've come up with a couple whose businesses have really turned the corner. We loaned them cash when no-one else would so I'm hoping that you two can persuade them to part with a little dividend for us." He takes a puff on his cigar. "Between the two of them we should get what we need. I want you to get with Mickey; he'll give you the details. We've picked these guys carefully; they're unlikely to cause a fuss." He dips his cigar toward me. "You can have a bit of fun if it's necessary just don't go too far." Cornelius lets his gaze fall back upon the sheaf of papers on his desk and the room falls silent. I make to get up; it seems the meeting is over.

"Do we have a fallback, Con?" Harvey asks.

Cornelius raises his head but says nothing.

"I mean just in case these guys don't come through," Harvey adds.

"No reason why they shouldn't. Did you have someone in mind?"

"Remember, Colin Strath?" Harvey asks. Cornelius's expression remains blank. Harvey continues. "He's small time; approached us a while back to okay a robbery on our patch."

"Ah, cocky little bastard, we agreed a cut didn't we?" Cornelius says.

Harvey nods. "He croaked and the job went tits up but he wasn't alone. A couple of phone calls are all it'll take to come up with some names."

"You want to make them cough up our cut anyway?"

"Why not? You could've let someone else pull the job. I reckon we press 'em, it might get us a few thou."

"Grand, so. Make the calls. Then the pair of you can pay them a visit too." Cornelius again bites into the butt of his cigar and returns his attention to his papers.

We catch up with Mickey downstairs in Moods main bar. He's seated at a table with his back to the wall. I grudgingly give him credit for this, though in truth I'm not certain he sat there with any greater purpose in mind than resting his bones. Mickey looks up as we approach, a weak smile momentarily pushing up the corners of his thin lips. Harvey bypasses the table and carries on to the bar. Mickey shifts in his seat to make space for me to sit alongside him but I remain standing; I know we won't be staying. Mickey's gaze drops back to the table. He raises his glass to eye level, tilts it and swirls the contents around. He seems lost staring into the glass before he pulls it down to breathe in the aroma. I can make it out from where I stand; a sort of mixture of peat and sawdust. It's Mickey's way; he seems to enjoy the smell as much as the taste. I've known him to nurse a whisky for half an hour without a drop passing his lips. A laugh from another table catches my attention, I glance around the bar. In the far corner a couple of men sit a few feet from one another, each with a drink in hand as they watch the early evening news programme playing from the plasma TV screen. In the centre of the room, cut adrift amid a sea of empty tables, people huddle in groups of twos and threes making quiet conversation. I shake my head, customers barely reach double figures. Harvey returns from the bar with two glasses of fresh orange juice and hands one to me. I take it and stare beyond Harvey. Rats has just walked in; the barman is busy but Rats steps behind the bar pulls a glass from the overhead rack and helps himself to a short at one of the optics.

"No wonder the old man's got a sweat on if this is all he's taking in," Mickey says.

"Hmm," I say. "I was thinking the same and look who's keeping an eye on us."

"Well, it's just gone six," Harvey puts in. "This is just the 'quick drink between work and home' crowd. It's Friday night for fuck's sake, the place will be heaving in a few hours. Anyway, it's not quiet enough for our needs. C'mon, we can chat next door."

Harvey has the barman open the partition gaining us access to the dance hall and function suite. It's empty again after the new DJ's try out; it isn't normally opened until seven thirty and only then for the DJ to warm up. The clubbers won't begin to drift in until after nine.

We throw the switch but have paced several yards into the room before the lights splutter into life revealing a large, rectangular hall. A raised stage lies far to the right set-out with what I know to be twin mixing decks, an array of speakers and coloured lights that match those hanging from the ceiling. The tables are set around a polished wooden dance floor, we select one far enough from the partition to ensure we'll not be overheard.

Harvey sits forward, his elbows propping clasped hands like a bridge over his fresh orange. "So, Mickey, Cornelius says you've fingered a couple of punters we need to squeeze."

"Sure," Mickey says. "He's desperate for ready cash as I'm sure he's told you by now. And we trawled through records and crossed a few palms before we were sure the profiles were right, I can tell you."

"Profiles?" I ask.

Mickey is biting into the coarse skin of his thumb but breaks off to answer. "No point trying to squeeze money from someone if they don't have it to give, or if they'll scream from the bleedin' rooftops when you take it. Cornelius can't afford a ruckus."

Harvey sips from his glass then sits back in his seat. "Level with us, Mickey, you're a money man, how much do you know about this investment Con's involved in?"

Mickey swirls the whisky in his glass again and speaks with an assured voice. "You guys know Cornelius as well as I do, he plays his cards close to his chest. I've known he was working on something for weeks. But even then he only told me at all because he was transferring funds out of the loan business for some 'new venture'. He's effectively shut *Loan Solutions* off to new business – we've no money left to lend, but I didn't find out about Sholto Carnie until today."

Even the mention of the name upsets me. I shake my head and slam a balled fist into the table, making all three glasses jump. "I can't believe we're even talking about a deal with Carnie. We can't trust him. He'll screw us over, Harvey, and you know it."

Mickey shrinks back into his seat, plunges both hands into the pockets of his leather jacket and draws it tightly around himself. Harvey though leans forward again; his eyes wide and fixed on me. "You done now?" he says.

"Fine," I spit, "but you know what Sholto's like, whatever Cornelius has in mind it better work ... or we're all fucked."

A nervous grin flickers across Mickey's face. "You two aren't comfortable with this deal, are you?"

Harvey sucks his teeth. "Mo's right, Mickey. If Sholto's relying on our stake money and we don't produce," Harvey raises his index finger and taps the air. "...and to the last penny mind, then he'll consider it a loss of face. And if he feels he's lost face then we're as good as dead, nothing surer."

In the ensuing silence Mickey draws a hand from his pocket and sweeps it back across his bald head. Finally, he reaches for his whisky. "Then I suppose we'd best make sure we get Cornelius the bleedin' money." He knocks it back and winces.

I dry wash my face with both hands pushing my fingers under my shades to rub my eyes. "It could be worse," I say. "I mean, fifty grand's fuck all really, it shouldn't be too hard to come by. Tell us about the punters, Mickey, then we can get tooled up and get this over with."

Mickey sets his glass down again. "Nah, we can't do this tonight, it has to be tomorrow."

"I thought this was urgent," Harvey says.

"It is," Mickey agrees, "but listen, Cornelius has to have the cash inside ten days and as long as he does – no problem. The guy we're gonna squeeze is up north just now anyway, he doesn't fly back until tomorrow and when he does, we'll be waiting."

"Cornelius mentioned two punters; can't we hit the other one tonight?" I ask.

Mickey shakes his head. "Nah, we only hit the second punter if the first can't give us the whole fifty. It's neater that way."

I'm disappointed and let my head drop, I could do with relieving some of the pressure I've built up. I can feel my nostrils flaring and rub the back of my neck whilst the fingers of my right hand clench to make a fist, spring open, and clench again repeating and repeating.

"That makes perfect sense, Mickey," Harvey says while watching me. "But, Mo, here is a little tense and wants to make a start. If you don't need us until tomorrow then there's an insurance job we can probably do later tonight instead. But as we're not pushed for time how about we grab something to eat and you can tell us about the guy we meet tomorrow?"

"Good idea," Mickey says smiling, "I'm so hungry I could eat a scabby horse."

Harvey pulls his cell phone from an inside breast pocket and makes two calls. The first is brief and secures us a table at The Olive Grove. The second lasts only moments longer; Harvey tells the recipient to find out who Colin Strath pulled jobs with then call him back with the names and where he'll find them tonight.

During the first course at the restaurant Harvey's mobile rings and he's given the names he'd asked for. The caller can't say where to find them but says he's working on it and promises to call back. At five past ten Harvey gets the second call. He smiles as he returns the phone to his pocket. "One of them's turned up at Danny Allison's place, The White Hart. It's only about twenty minutes away. Danny's gonna make sure our friend doesn't leave before we get there." My bother is once again back in my good books. He stands, "want to come along for the ride, Mickey?"

"Not me, I'm knackered. I'll push off home; we can meet up at noon tomorrow."

After a short walk in the still bright evening we climb into Harvey's black Jaguar XJS.

"So, who we after?" I ask.

"A sticky-fingered nobody called Adam Rosewood."

"Never heard of him," I say.

Harvey nudges the XJS into the flow of traffic, "There's no reason you would have. How's your head?"

"Thumping, but it'll settle after this."

"Good," Harvey says. "Just remember, not too heavy, eh. The likes of this guy won't have the cash we need. So we have to make him believe we're serious while leaving him fit enough to go find it. He's no good to us in hospital, yeah?"

I reach for a thin pair of leather gloves from the back seat. I push my hand into one then caress it with the other, pushing down on each finger, allowing the heat from my hands to mould and smooth the leather until it's tight to the skin. "I'll be gentle," I tell him and make to pull on the second glove.

****

Chapter 3 ~ Let's dance ~

~Adam ~

By 10pm I'm sitting on a barstool at The White Hart, I've ditched the tie and the raincoat having left them in the back of Ferris's Capri earlier in the day. We'd seen out the afternoon with a couple of drinks in The Trojan Horse then a few more in The Bat in the Belfry, both had been favourites of Colin's. We played darts at The Trojan and talked at length. We'd even made a fruitless attempt to defeat the quiz machine in the Belfry; the one Colin endlessly pumped coins into only to berate us for our inability to help him when he was stumped by the obscure question it inevitably threw out. Then we talked some more. By the time we headed off for a curry in the early evening I think I felt more sober than when we'd started out.

At The White Hart Ferris had made straight for the toilets leaving me to get the round in. A pint of Golden is set before me, the bubbles within racing from bottom to top forming a frothy head. I ordered the same for Ferris and look over my shoulder for any sign of him as the barman sets it down. The rest rooms are close to what passes for the dance floor and I suspect Ferris is using the opportunity to check out the talent. Friday at The White Hart is live band night. It brings an influx of girls anxious to dance and a steady stream of predatory males looking to pull. Not so long ago Ferris, Colin and I had considered these nights as the highlight of the week. Friday nights were the start of the weekend, better than Saturday when somehow dull Sunday loomed large and Monday morning cast a stifling shadow over the remainder of the weekend. We'd compete to see who could score first. Desperate pulls didn't count; ugly birds weren't an option. When I think about it I suppose each of us had fallen into a pattern, for my own part it'd been a different girl every few weeks for as long as I could remember. We didn't let them get close to us, though I doubt it was a conscious decision. None of us were ready for anything serious, we were only having fun, just lads really, too young for ties. Thirty isn't old these days. Though maybe recent events suggest it's later than any of us know.

"You're doing it again," Ferris says, edging his way into the bar to retrieve his drink.

"Doing what?"

"Staring into your beer like there's an answer in there somewhere."

"Sorry, I was just thinking."

"Look, we've been through this. Colin's gone. The funeral's past. It's sad and it's bleedin' unfair but it's time to move on. He wouldn't want you to turn into a morbid git. You know, I've been waiting for you to open up about it since the accident but maybe it was…" he pauses for a second trying to find the right phrase, "just meant to be."

I take a drink then set it back on the bar giving a light shake of my head. "Nah, nobody deserves to go out like that, Ferris. That can't be part of the plan. But you're right that Colin wouldn't want me to dwell on it and I am trying, honest."

"He was my buddy too you know."

"I know, maybe it's just that Colin and I go way back. He was probably as close to family as I had. The whole thing's just made me think a bit, that's all."

Ferris slaps me lightly across the shoulder blades, "Okay, mate, but you can't change it. You're still alive, so live." He lets me chew on that for a few seconds then his tone changes. "Now there's a little redhead that I've had my eye on since we got here and I think it's time I made my move. Want to check out her friend or am I flying solo?"

"Nah, I'm not the best of company tonight, you go for it. I'm going to finish my beer and call it a day."

"You sure?"

"Yeah, I'll give you a shout tomorrow."

I watch Ferris wander off into the throng, his slim frame cutting a path through the milling bodies. He sets his drink down at the redhead's table and makes his pitch. I smile and turn back to the bar, I've witnessed this a hundred times and know just how it'll turn out. The little redhead doesn't stand a chance; it's impossible to get upset with Ferris. He'll make her laugh; his endless patter will wear her down and win her over.

A whisky sits beside my half empty pint glass. A few feet away one of the barmen is drying glasses. He sees my confusion and calls over, then seems to realise he can't make himself heard in the din. He makes up the distance between us and leans across the bar to shout in my ear. "It's on the house…for Colin," he says.

I acknowledge the thoughtful gesture and sip the whisky. In fact I'm feeling quite guilty. As barmen go, I'd thought those in The White Hart to be as grim as they come. They weren't particularly friendly, had never even acknowledged Colin, Ferris or myself as regulars let alone partake in any banter or repartee with us. On occasion, they could even be a little heavy handed, appearing too ready to throw out any poor bloke who was edging towards having had one too many. I decide I've perhaps been too harsh, maybe they appear that way because customers are more fleeting in this type of bar. After all, none of Colin's other favoured haunts had made such a gesture. I drain my glass and climb down from the barstool.

"Get you another?" the barman asks.

"One for the road, I'll be back in a minute." I head for the gents, my eyes seeking out Ferris as I pass through the crowds but both he and the redhead are gone from the table. The band plays 'La Bamba' and the place is heaving. A few steps further on I spot Ferris and the redhead on the outer edges of the dance floor and have to fight hard to suppress a laugh. Poor Ferris has never been known for his sense of rhythm but his petite redhead is quite some mover. Whilst her tiny hips swivel and shake to the beat, Ferris, one moment flaps like a fish out of water and the next swirls his grey jacket above his head like a stilted and monochrome Travolta. The look of horror on the redhead's face is priceless. He'll have his work cut out from this point on and no mistake.

The music dies away, muffled as the door of the gents closes behind me. I join a couple of others at the urinals, empty my bladder and then linger at the washbasins catching sight of my reflection in the mirror. Colin's death has left me deflated, I'm not sure if it's my imagination or not but the lines around my eyes appear to have deepened and I can see grey flecks in my hair where there'd been none before. No doubt they've been there all along and my demeanour has somehow heightened my awareness of them.

The hairs on the back of my neck prickle as a draft blows in and the final strains of 'La Bamba' first rise then are once again snuffed out.

"Fancy yourself as a bit of a ladies man then?"

I turn to see a tall man by the doorway. His dark hair is slicked back and his stubbled goatee owes more to a designer look than a sudden reluctance to shave. He wears a charcoal three-piece suit under an open three quarter length cashmere overcoat. If I'd seen him before I felt sure I'd recognise him, but I don't. That said the two guys either side of me at the washbasins make a hasty exit, they all but cower as they pass this guy taking a much wider path than strictly necessary. I sense the tension in their bodies melt away as they reach the door. Out of the corner of my eye I see the last guy at the urinals look over his shoulder, sway a little, then return his attention to passing water.

The stranger takes a couple of steps forward and wags a finger at me as though chastising a child. "You don't know who I am? I'm hurt, of course, but no matter. The point is that I know you."

The voice is confident and steady. If it's intended to

convey menace then I'll admit it's succeeding. I'm feeling confused yet strangely alert. "Should I know you?" I ask, stepping away from the washbasins. As I speak a second figure comes through the doorway. He wears a grey three-piece suit; his shirt is open at the neck but he doesn't have an overcoat. His short hair is peroxide white, matching his goatee. As if in contrast he sports square-shaped dark glasses and black driving gloves. He glances around then moves down the line of toilet cubicles snapping open each door in turn, thundering it back into the frame.

"Let's just say we had a mutual acquaintance in Mr. Strath," the stranger continues.

"You knew, Colin?" I ask.

"Yes. But, before we discuss business I must ask the gentleman behind you to leave. Now!" I turn as the guy at the urinals yells that he's nearly finished. Having established that the cubicles are unoccupied the grey-suited man strides toward the urinals and raises his unsuspecting quarry into the air by his shirt collar and trouser belt. The poor bloke's feet barely touch the ground as he's marched toward the exit then thrown through the doors. He'd been in mid flow and leaves a trail of urine before surprise and fear interrupt nature.

The two converge on me. I back away until I feel the washbasins prod into the base of my back. The grey-suited hulk clamps a hand to my left shoulder then presses his forearm into my chest pinning me over the washbasins. Then he rips the wallet from my back pocket and throws it to his partner who flicks through it, and pulls out what he's looking for.

The dark-haired guy gives my driving licence a cursory glance then stuffs it back into the wallet. "I'm Harvey Scallion," he says, "and this here is my brother, Mo. Ring any bells?" I shake my head. He continues. "A little over six months ago your friend, Colin, agreed a deal with my employer – Cornelius Callaghan. You were part of Colin's light-fingered little trio and I'm here to collect what's due. I take it you recall the arrangement?"

A vague light of recognition flickers to life. "Yes…" I say, "but we passed the news down the line. The job never went ahead, there's no money to split. Colin was our inside man. When he died, so did the job."

"That's as may be, but a deal's a deal. Mr Callaghan kept his part of the bargain; no one else was given leeway to hit upon your target, he expects his money."

Beside him, the white-haired guy, Mo, raises a hand, removes his shades and folds them into his breast pocket. My mouth hangs open. This guy hasn't coloured his hair and goatee in any peroxide dye. His skin gives it away, it's creamy, his eyebrows are white and his eyes, God, his eyes. They're creepy; a pale, neon blue. Mo is an albino. If that were all, in someone with his build, it'd be scary enough but his face is blank, expressionless, like there's no one behind those cold eyes. I realise I'm staring and turn to look again at Harvey.

"I don't have it," I say.

"Well, let's see," Harvey says, "Mr. Callaghan's original cut was to be twenty grand wasn't it? But he's not an unreasonable man. Under the circumstances if you pay him, say, ten grand within seven days we'll consider the debt paid. Understand?"

"But I still don't…"

Mo unleashes a right-handed punch that catches me in the centre of my midriff. My legs crumple beneath me and I sink to the floor. My eyes water and I fight for breath without success. I can feel my face and neck bloat and redden, my mind runs on in panic, I'm suffocating. The smiling face of Harvey Scallion looms over me, it's going to be the last image I'll see.

Harvey kneels down and jerks my head back by the hair. Pain registers in my scalp but I don't care, I'm worried that I still can't get a breath. Harvey brings his face to within two inches of mine and speaks softly, almost in a whisper. It's like I'm feeling things with abnormally high sensitivity. My oxygen-starved brain is straining to experience the maximum in my final moments. I watch Harvey's lips form the words and each one flows into me.

"One blow and your diaphragm has gone into spasm, you're fighting for breath. Uncomfortable, isn't it? You'll be able to breathe again in about twenty seconds - once the diaphragm relaxes, but those seconds can seem like an eternity, huh?" Harvey releases me and stands. The spasm relents. I gulp air greedily and exhale in rasps, coughing spittle down my chin. "I did you a favour, there," Harvey says, his voice no longer quiet. "You see, it can take me two or three tries to do that, but Mo, he hits the button every time. And believe me; you don't want to find out how inventive he can be in administering pain. Now, Mr. Callaghan has a reputation to maintain. We can't allow you to walk away from our agreement, what message would that send out? You'll pay Mr. Callaghan ten grand within one week and thank him for his generosity and compassion. Otherwise you can draw lots with Mo to decide which parts of your anatomy he'll hack off with a dull and rusty blade. Understand?"

"Yeah," I splutter.

"Good, it's not healthy to disappoint us." He drops my wallet on the floor, rakes his fingers through his hair and checks his look in the mirror. "We'll be in touch, get the money."

I see Mo slip his shades back on before the brothers turn and walk out. Only once the doors have stopped rattling in their hinges do I feel it's safe to move. My chest is on fire and my throat feels red raw. I reach out to gather in my wallet then crawl into one of the cubicles. I'm still retching into the toilet bowl when I hear the outer doors burst open and a commotion of voices. Then Ferris is beside me.

"Are you okay, Adam? I'm sorry mate; the bouncers wouldn't let anybody in."

"Don't be daft, Ferris, you couldn't have done anything." I clamber to my feet and realise I'm wet. I look down at my clothes. In my haste to get to the cubicle I've crawled through the piss on the floor.

****

Chapter 4 ~ Self help ~

~ Mo ~

Me and Harvey get back to our end terraced house in Harlesden shortly before 3am. I watch him unlock his door then make for the side entrance to my own. He's my brother but it's been a frustrating day and I'm glad to see the back of him. The house belonged to our mother; we helped her buy it from the council long ago. It's a working class area with a large immigrant community and an undeserved reputation. We had the house converted into self contained maisonettes after she died, Harvey taking the ground floor and me the upper. It means we can stay close but also gives us each a little privacy. I like my own space, my own company and my own things. Harvey says my preference in décor is matched only by my choice in cinematic entertainment. I once overheard him tell someone that I don't clutter my place with the usual stylistic niceties in which most owners take questionable pride. You won't find any flamboyant mirrors or fancy glass-covered pictures in my place, though you might see the odd cult movie poster hanging where the light can't find it – Donnie Darko and Dark City are current. Of course, when Harvey makes these comments he thinks he's being smart but he's really just being a prick. I avoid things with reflective surfaces and it suits me that the rooms are a little dark and plain; my house is a sanctuary from a world that's all too bright.

Once in the living room I hit the switch and the place is bathed in soft, low light. This used to be two rooms but I had them knocked into one turning it into an expansive bed-sit. I wander over to the leather sofa easing off my jacket and folding it over the arm, my shades are in the breast pocket. I unbutton my waistcoat before sitting. It's been a difficult evening and a long time to have borne a nagging headache. I clasp my hands behind my head, push back in the seat and rest my feet on the wooden panelled coffee table. In the silence I hear the clink of glassware from below. Harvey has opened his drinks cabinet and is serving himself up a nightcap. I'm reminded of how different we are and gaze around my room, from the widescreen home cinema system in front of me to my running machine and weights in the other half of the room. I can't be bothered looking but I know that over my left shoulder my heavy duty punch-bag hangs suspended from the ceiling on a chain, and if I glance behind and to my right I'll see my king size bed made up with black satin sheets with its unrestricted view of the TV. Down the hallway, separate doorways lead first to the small room where I hang my clothes, then to the bathroom and finally to a small kitchen - the least used room in my flat.

Harvey, on the other hand, skips practicality in favour of delicate and ornate things, the same pretentious clap-trap he claims I avoid. Some would say he covets class he'll never have. He owns hand-painted figurines worth thousands; persists in listening to classical music, sometimes opera, has the best of sound systems and occasionally likes to entertain lady friends. Appearances can lie and I'm far from stupid; I know that he needs to be with a woman from time to time. It's different for me, it's an urge I've managed to suppress, but I'm careful to give him space knowing that, for all our differences, it is in all likelihood the single most important reason for the independence I enjoy.

I slip a DVD into the mouth of the player, collect my jacket from the sofa and head first for the changing room and then to the bathroom. I shower and return to the living room to rest naked outwith the covers on the bed of the now darkened room. I gaze at the ceiling. In the corner, the TV plays my favourite film. I've watched it a dozen times or more, but tonight the irritating buzz inside my head wont rest. It drowns the dialogue and the flickering shadows that the changing scenes cast upon the ceiling fight for my attention. I look at the clock at the side of the bed; the luminous hands tell me it's almost 4am. I sigh and reach for the remote. The DVD player opens and spits out the disc. I return 'The Crow' to its case and place it back on the shelf between 'Nosferatu' and 'Edward Scissorhands'.

Once more I lie on the bed and stare into the darkness above me. I won't sleep while my head buzzes though the gloom itself offers something in the way of comfort. I find my thoughts returning briefly to events earlier in the evening. Out of courtesy, we'd spent twenty minutes with Danny Allison in the back room at The White Hart. It gave Danny the opportunity to make the usual noises; enquire after Cornelius's health and ask to be remembered to him. And strangely, rather than despising Danny for his fawning show of weakness, I found myself almost grateful for the small semblance of normality it provided – the thought of Cornelius dealing with the likes of Sholto Carnie was upsetting. I'm suspicious of change; things are fine as they are.

Afterwards, we returned to Moods; the solitary punch I'd landed on the guy in the toilets may have pleased Harvey, but alone it provided little discharge for the thumping pressure that droned inside my head. We thought that if anyone stepped out of line at Moods then I'd be on hand to sort it and the release would clear my head at the same time. As it was though there had been no trouble and Harvey insisted we come away early as we have a lunchtime meeting with Mickey. With no release I know now what I must do. Just thinking of it pushes my thoughts deeper, back to the first time, to Aunt Margaret. Even then I thought she was a bit weird. There was an aniseed smell to her; it clung to my clothes days after she'd gone. I was still a teenager when the doctors told Mam that their tests showed me differentiated in mind as well as body. Hair and eyes marked me and then Hare's test showed me psychologically damaged too. I likened it to the tales we learned in history class, Burke and Hare, monsters and ghouls. And that was what they were saying I was. Ma wept whereas I felt only that same rage and need to lash out that had brought about the tests to begin with. But no more doctors, no more tests and, for me, no more schooling. Ma almost pulled Harvey out too. She'd let no one call her boy a psychopath. Family rallied round, Aunt Margaret taught me what she knew and my violent outbursts diminished, until we found a use for them.

The veins at my temples pulse and the dull nag behind my eyeballs surges as if to remind me of the here and now and that sleep is not yet an option. I know what I have to do. I take a deep breath then exhale noisily through pursed lips. At the same time I shake out my arms and flex my fingers before resting them at my sides. I target a point in the darkness above and concentrate – the way Aunt Margaret taught me.

I close my eyes and listen to the sounds of my own body. The hum inside my head becomes a rhythmic aid to my focus; its relentless pulse beating out the pace at which I retreat to an inner fortress where no one can harm me. Minutes go by. When I feel ready, when I feel calm, I let myself go. I imagine the sinuous fibres of my being untethering themselves from bone and gristle. Those slow to unwind wrenching and tearing but yielding nonetheless to the strength of my will, freeing me to rise out of myself and float steadily from the bed and above my living body. I sense myself almost weightless, rising without effort until I know I've reached that dark space beneath the ceiling. My eyes spring open and I turn to gaze upon the pathetic wretch below. The body is toned and the muscles taut but the best of physiques can't detract from the shocking coldness of the pale skin and that inhuman stare.

I hover over my prostrate form and with a scalpel slice open the chest from north to south, ribcage to abdomen. Then I force my fingertips into the seeping, pencil-slim wound and tug at the blubbery skin until the thin red line becomes a gaping pit. A festering stench leaks from the bloodied hole; I hold my breath, turn my face away lest it infect me and then push my arm in up to my elbow. My fingers probe between ribs and behind organs. I touch something cold, inorganic. I tear at it but it holds fast. My fingers find better purchase and again I pull. The body strains as though unwilling to give up whatever is buried within it, as though glad of it, as though having it somehow makes it more. But my will is stronger and with a sucking rasp the resistance is broken. I grip the heart-shaped stone like a trophy, allowing the blood to drain from it. My fingertips run across the face, made smooth under nurture and caress; at its centre is carved a word but I can't make it out. I tilt the stone this way and that but the inscription remains illusive, ill-formed and unfathomable. Eventually I tire of it and hurl it to the furthest corner of the room, then with renewed vigour thrust my arm into the wound again. My fingers search blindly but latch onto an inert and frigid object amid what seems a tepid sludge inside my chest. This time I withdraw a cosh and it too bears some lettering, but in a tongue that's not my own. I cast it aside and delve in again not stopping until I sense there are no more foreign bodies to find. I recover five items in all but each expedition has the same result; the item retrieved bears a mark I can feel with my fingers or see with my eyes, but I can never quite grasp its meaning. I seal the gaping maw, drawing a zipper from the base of the abdomen to the top of the ribcage. My inanimate self lies open-eyed beneath me, nothing more than an empty vessel until I sink back into it. But I'm not ready for that yet. Instead, confident as never before, I consider whether my inner self has a reflection. I pass effortlessly to the hallway then into the room beyond.

The only mirror in my flat is fitted over the bathroom sink. My inner self stands before it; my own face stares back, pale skinned, with white hair, eyebrows and goatee. But the eyes, well they are different. Bloodied tears stream down my cheeks and protruding from the eye-sockets is the cause - the stalks of two pencils. I recall telling Harvey that the pain of photophobia was at first sharp, then dull and grating. Crisp, as though my head had suddenly been impaled upon something razor edged, then sluggish and scraping as though I were slowly sinking further onto the impaling object. I can't decide whether my subconscious has picked up on that description and presented me with an image I can identify with or whether it's something with a less savoury meaning: like my subconscious stabbing at that part of me which makes the whole so abhorrent. I return to the prone body on the bed and through gritted teeth lower myself back into its confines. Fibrous tissues, like tendrils, wrap themselves around bone and gristle locking me into place to the sound of tightening cartilage and the slosh of displaced fluids. Once more I exist in a world of weight, I always have. I'm no nutter; I know I don't physically leave my body. Aunt Margaret maintained I didn't have to believe it, just think it. And briefly, as my mind registers the absence of the pounding in my head I know again that she's right. Then I slip from consciousness into a deep and dreamless sleep.

****

Chapter 5 ~ The morning after ~

~ Adam ~

Be-beep! Be-beep! Be-beep!

How I ended up with a clock with such an irritating alarm I'll never know. Hang on though, that's not strictly true. But I suppose it's one of those imponderables, you recognise you need an alarm clock and you search for one that looks the part and has the function built-in – but you don't physically check what it sounds like, or at least I didn't think to. So now I'm stuck with it and on any given morning its mechanical high-pitched chirp sings out too cheerily to be healthy. Is anyone ever grateful to be dragged from a warm bed and much needed sleep? I know I'm not. Bleary-eyed I throw my right arm across my chest to shut off its damn racket. This is a mistake. The sharp pain that rips through my chest tells me as much. I suck air in shocked surprise and my hand shoots back automatically, as though I'd just touched the hot ring on the cooker. A dull memory of my run-in with the Scallion brothers at The White Hart swims to the surface of my thoughts. I push it back; I'm not ready to go there yet. I lie motionless for a few seconds; my eyes, for no reason that I can fathom, picking out the hairline cracks in the jaded paintwork on the ceiling above my bed, reminding me that at some point I really should do the place up a bit. Yeah, another time, I think. I raise myself up on my elbows and, pushing down on each in turn, *walk* back up the bed a little until my shoulders rest on the headboard. I peel back the duvet and gawp at a blue-black bruise that spreads from the centre of my ribcage; its hard edges already fading, hinting at a more colourful memento to come. Actually I'm disappointed; it's only about two inches across and wholly disproportionate to the level of discomfort I've just experienced.

In the shower I let the jets play across the discolouration and watch as a red heat blotch encircles the blemish and spreads outward across my chest. Then I massage the offending area with the heel of my hand. It's tender but it eases, changing from a sharp and stabbing hurt to become dull and tingling, almost pleasurable. The thought has me ill at ease and I shake my head as if to dislodge it. My neck feels stiff, I tease out the kinks before slowly becoming aware of the dry, sandpaper-like quality to the inside of my mouth. Without turning off the shower I slide the door open and step out into the bathroom for a second to grab my toothbrush and paste. A small puddle forms on the floor but it can wait 'til later.

Brushing your teeth in the shower isn't a particularly endearing habit, I know. But I can never seem to get my electric toothbrush behind my front teeth – the way my dental hygienist insists I should - without a foaming, spluttering mess cascading down my chin and onto whatever I'm wearing. Brushing in the shower then resolves two problems for me; I don't wander around with toothpaste stains down my front and my sadistic hygienist has tangible evidence that some effort has been made and is forced, however grudgingly, to show some restraint.

I'm cheerful, congratulating myself on the application of simple male, bachelor logic. If I'm honest, somewhere in the mix too is the realisation that this act could also be said to refute that earlier flash of masochism. I smile broadly; I've got enough faults without adding that to the list. But just the act of smiling is a trigger. Suddenly I picture myself writhing on the floor, Harvey Scallion's grinning face hovering over me; sincerity and certainty evident in his calm voice as he explains what will happen if I don't pay him ten grand inside seven days. The toothbrush slips from my grasp. The hollow sound it makes as it bounces on the plastic shower base mirrors the emptiness I feel. "Jesus, where the hell am I going to find ten grand?"

I skip breakfast. That information alone would be enough to tell either Colin or Ferris that something wasn't right with me. I never miss breakfast, not even with a hangover. I've got to have my cornflakes and a slice of toast or the day's just not set right. But instead, I let the memory of the night before weigh heavily on me and it throws me out of my routine. As I dress I lose minutes staring into space thinking how quickly it all went down. At the time it seemed like an age but in reality the whole thing was probably over in three minutes, maybe less. I go over it again and again in my mind and several things strike me. I recall how quickly the place emptied when Harvey spoke to me. A couple of guys had breezed past him, their heads low, careful not to look him in the eye. Now either that's unusual or perhaps Harvey was just lucky not to stumble across some young thug in the loos pumped with alcohol induced bravado and looking for a fight. But the more I think about it the more I'm convinced that the two guys who brushed past Harvey knew he was more trouble than they could handle. Then there's the albino - Mo wasn't it? He was strong; he'd raised some guy by the scruff of his neck and thrown him out as though his weight were nothing. Then he'd felled me with one blow and I was powerless. A shiver runs through me as another realisation hits. Mo had resisted going for the guy who lingered at the urinals until he'd first checked the cubicles near the door. As I replay it in my head it seems that he was making sure that there'd be no witnesses to what was going down and no possibility of anyone surprising him from behind. Viewed in retrospect the whole thing was premeditated, fast and, to my admittedly limited knowledge, quite professional. Not the sort of guys you want to be in debt to then. As I snap out of my thoughts I realise that I'm bathed in a clammy sweat and I'm running late for work.

By the time I reach the cemetery I'm fifteen minutes late for my shift and, unfortunately, it's Nigel Perryman's weekend as acting foreman to young Martin Currie and myself. Nigel's okay in small dozes but he can be a bit anal. That means he's not content just to dock my pay the standard half hour, I've got to listen to his sermon too.

"Saturday morning eight 'til noon one week in four," he crows in an affected, twee voice designed to provoke. When I don't respond he tries again. "Hardly a big ask is it?"

Nigel's a big lad, six two, dark haired and heavy set with a square jaw that carries a permanent five o'clock shadow. Under normal circumstances I'd give him some verbal just for the sake of it and he knows it. But in this instance he's in the right, and I can't muster the enthusiasm to spar with him. To be honest, my mind is elsewhere. I'm thinking that if forgetting you've had a kicking the night before qualifies as a mistake - and why wouldn't it given the discomfort that resulted - then arriving late for work is my second slip-up of the day, and it's not even gone eight-thirty. These things come in threes; I'm wondering what's next?

As it turns out though once big Nigel makes his point and realises I'm not going to add to his enjoyment by offering up an argument he tells me that there's not exactly a mountain of work that needs doing - no burials to make preparations for. It's hardly a surprise; after all, Tannock Bar's a small village, with only a few burials a month. So, the morning's work consists purely of routine maintenance. I get the impression a little verbal sparring would have been the highlight of Nigel's morning, I leave him disappointed.

I busy myself with a general tidying of the cemetery borders: gathering the ever-present sweetie wrappers; foils from cigarette packets or fish and chip papers that the wind blows in from the surrounding streets. After that there's the removal of dead flowers from the gravesides. That said I pull rank on Martin so I can consign myself to duties within the long established part of the cemetery staying a safe distance from Colin's grave. It doesn't seem right to pass by in work mode quite yet, it's all *too fresh*. I force thoughts of Colin from my mind and consider the bridges. The lads call the grassy rows between headstone and path 'bridges' because we trim them so often we imagine it must be like painting the Severn Bridge; by the time we've trimmed the last row the first is ready to be cut again. I take the diesel mower to the four rows by the west wall, cut the borders with trimming shears before painstakingly gathering the clippings, taking care to avoid sudden twists and turns lest I receive a cursory reminder as to the tenderness of my chest. But as I work my mind turns back to Colin. Can I really work here every day, walk past his headstone and not let it bother me? Sure it's difficult just now I tell myself but deep down I know the answer – of course I can. But the events of last night make things much more complex, maybe I could use a few days away?

When I'm done with the grass cutting, I clean down and re-oil both the mower and the shears. It's gone noon when I finish up and return them to their places in the maintenance shed. Martin has already gone but Nigel hovers at an old desk in the corner that the foremen use for writing up the timesheets and job cards. I ask him if I can have a word.

"If you make it quick," he says, "I'm getting set to go."

I hesitate for a second, "I want some time off."

"Jesus. Turn up late then put in a holiday request. Got a bit of a neck haven't you?"

"I was late and I apologise. But you've docked my timesheet and I've made sure I'm making this request in my own time, not the council's."

Nigel glances at his watch, sees it's almost ten after noon and sighs. "Well that's true, I'll grant you that much. So when d'you want 'em and for how long?"

"Two weeks starting Monday."

"What, right away?" Nigel says. He pulls a pencil slim diary from his breast pocket, licks the tip of his forefinger and uses it to skip through the pages. His eyes narrow.

"I've built up the time," I add.

"Sure," Nigel says, "but two whole weeks on top of the fixed summer dates, that's gonna wipe out your entitlement." A frown settles upon his brow. "Besides, I'd appreciate some bloody notice. This place doesn't run without a bit of planning you know."

I see this is heading the wrong way. Nigel's got a point about the lack of notice. It'd be just his style to go off on one and start talking about the setting of precedents and the like. It feels a bit underhand but I play my trump card. "Look, Nigel, I fully understand about the notice and you're right, no question. But yesterday has hit me a bit harder than I expected. I can't get my head around the fact that my best mate's lying in a hole that I dug out for him. I'm not sure if I can walk past every day – at least not so soon after. I need a break." I shut up; let the silence work on him. His frown lines soften and he stares at the pages of his little diary again.

"Well, it's not clashing with anybody I suppose," he says, "but I can't be seen to let you take vacation with next to no notice. How about you work on Monday and take vacation from the Tuesday? I'll even make sure we fix you up with something offsite to give you some distance from this place."

Again I hesitate. As I anticipated, the bugger's done me up with the precedent thing. The wonder is he managed to do it without even mentioning the word. It is a reasonable compromise though and I suppose he is being fair. "Okay," I say. "Thanks, Nigel, I appreciate it."

"Good," he says. "Go to the Laplin Street Depot on Monday morning, Davie Armitage will sort you out with something for the day, I'll tell him to expect you." I nod and make for the door. "Hang on, there's paperwork to fill in for your vacation," Nigel says.

"That's okay, you do it, Nigel. I trust you." As I pull the door closed behind me I see his mouth hang open in disbelief. A small point back for me I think.

Back at the flat I change out of my work clothes then replace the bathroom towel and use the stale one to mop up what remains of the puddle I left on the bathroom floor this morning. The clothes and the towel go into the washing machine but it's not sufficiently full to merit turning it on. My stomach grumbles reminding me that I've not eaten and I rake through what little food I have in the cupboards. I settle for a tin of carrot and coriander soup that I can't remember buying when the doorbell rings. The flat has an intercom access system so if the doorbell goes then whoever is there has already bypassed the intercom and gained entry to the building. So either it's a resident from one of the other flats or someone who has gained access after being 'buzzed in' by a neighbour. Mrs. Harper on the ground floor can be a little guilty of that. The poor old dear's going deaf and struggles to pick up voices over the intercom. During the winter months some local teenagers stumbled across her habit of just hitting the entry buzzer when her flat was called. For weeks, until we discovered how they were getting in, the rest of us would get home in the dark evenings and find kids using the stairwells as somewhere to screw.

I squint into the fisheye peephole at the front door realising at the same time that before last night I probably wouldn't have bothered with it. Barry, a fuzzy-haired lad from the first floor flat below stands outside. He dangles a brown jiffy bag bearing a familiar logo from one hand whilst his other scratches at his crotch. I unlock the door and shout for him to come in while I wander back toward the kitchen.

"Your stuff arrived in this morning's post," he breezes.

"I know," I tell him as I open the tin of soup and empty the contents into a bowl.

"You mean you presume that's why I'm here," he says with a confident swagger.

I place the bowl in the microwave and give it two minutes. "No, Barry. I saw you through the peephole before I opened the door, swinging the Autobitz package and clawing at your balls; so I know." His cheeks begin to burn, he's a good kid though and I shouldn't tease him, he's done me a favour. He's a bit of a computer nerd and gets me some good deals on original Japanese spares for my Sportrak. I know he adds on a few quid for his trouble, I insist upon it, and it's still a good deal for me. He hands me the package and I rip it open. "Yeah, that's the business; Barry, you've solved the problem of how I was going fill my afternoon. Now, in a few hours, I can have the jeep back on the road."

"Why do you insist on calling it a Jeep?" he asks. "It's a Daihatsu."

"I'm referring to the original meaning of 'jeep' – no capital 'J'."

"As in *just enough essential parts*?" he asks.

"Right," I tell him, "and what's more 'just enough' than a Sportrak these days?"

"Fair point," he says.

I take my wallet from my back pocket and pull out a few notes for him. It's more than we agreed but I'm feeling guilty.

"I don't have change," he says.

"I don't want any. I'd have spent more than that in the pub this afternoon with nothing else to do."

After lunch I change again, some old clothes this time that a bit of oil and grease will add character to as opposed to spoiling. My green Daihatsu is parked a little way down the street. A 1997 'P' registration, it's covered a few miles – over 114,000 of them – but that's the beauty of it, being Japanese it runs forever and there's not a spot of rust on it. It carries its age well. Of course, it's a prime target for Ferris; he loves to have a dig at me about it. His Capri is, or was, all curves and acceleration. The Sporty has no curves, it's unpretentiously square inside and out. To use Ferris's analogy it's butt ugly. It'll last longer than Ferris's Capri though; at least I hope it will. That said it has been off the road for the last couple of weeks. It began to overheat and emit a little smoke - the head gasket had gone. I had a mechanic replace the gasket, skim the head and reseat the valves. As belt and braces I had him replace the cam belt and tensioner as well. But he said I ought to change the thermostat too as it might have caused the head to leak in the first place. And now, finally, I have the new thermostat.

It's not a big job, if it was I'd leave it to the experts; I'm not especially handy. I'm following explicit instructions given me by the mechanic. It's a pleasant afternoon, I take my time and it all goes smoothly. When I'm done I sit behind the large steering wheel and turn the ignition; she starts first time. I let her idle for a full ten minutes to warm up then take her for a spin around the block. So, the Sporty is back on the road and maybe it's no bad thing. The way things are shaping up I may need it.

Once I'm back inside the flat I head for the bedroom with the intention of changing back into something more appropriate for a casual Saturday night out. But the flashing red light on the telephone draws me across first, I hit the message button.

Ferris's voice is hesitant. "Adam, you there? Shit, you know I hate speaking to these bleedin' machines. Listen, I'm sorry but I've gotta let you down tonight mate. Tina, that's the little redhead to you, she's asked me to go to a wedding reception. It's too good a chance to miss; it's in Luton so we'll be stopping over. I'll give you a shout, yeah?" The phone lets out a mechanical whir as the tape rewinds and the red light goes out. It's not as though I haven't got a lot to think about but now I've got all weekend to do it too.

****

Chapter 6 (Part I) ~ Long Tall Sally ~

~ Mo ~

I awake to the sound of passing traffic and voices in the streets outside. It's twenty past ten on Saturday morning. Although I could probably do with another hour's sleep I feel quite refreshed; my head is as clear as the bottled water in Harvey's fridge. I stumble out from beneath the sheets, wander through to the kitchen and pull a carton of orange juice from the fridge. It's tangy and sharp passing over my throat and I feel sharp too. In fact, I feel brand new. Between gulps I tip the carton appreciatively to an absent Aunt Margaret, a mad old bag but she knew what she was about. Aside from kicking the living shit out of someone her method is the only thing that's ever cleared my head when I've had a buzz on. I take a piss then brush my teeth. The mint on my tongue doesn't taste right after orange juice but what the hell. Five minutes later I'm in shorts and trainers pounding out a few miles on the running machine.

It's no joke; running is boring, especially when your surroundings are static. I've tried music but it just doesn't work for me, it can't hold my attention. I prefer to think; about anything really but mostly about the day to come or the one that's past. In this case I can't dwell too much on what's to come because there's so little to go on – Mickey gave us the bare bones. Instead my mind returns to how this job's come about. A bloated image of Sholto Carnie comes to mind but I push it away; I can use it later but not now when my efforts have to be constant and steady. I shift the gradient setting to steep and increase my efforts for a final ten minute stint. My thoughts return the early hours, to the things I imagined buried deep within my chest. It's been months since I had to resort to using Aunt Margaret's teachings, a state of higher consciousness she called it. Whatever it is, I do it twice, maybe three times a year tops. She told me to picture myself taking out what was bad, but from past experience there seems little connection or relevance to the objects I dig out from my guts. There are only two constants; first, whatever I find bears marks of some kind and second, I can never read them anyway. I can't say it bothers me; as long as it clears my head that's all that matters.

When I've finished running I slow the pace and cool down a bit with some work on the weights; nothing much just alternate single arm curls with the dumbbells then a few presses with some heavier stuff. When I'm done I make sure I set them down carefully on the rubber mat – Harvey gets pissed off if they clank off the floor, says he expects them to burst through his ceiling one day. I finish off with some bag work, saving the best 'til last, it's my favourite. I pull on a pair of brown, leather gloves with the fingers cut away between knuckle and finger joint. They're well worn, the leather is faded over the knuckles and the finger holes curl over into the shape of my clenched fist. They're comfortably stale; coated with hours of my sweat and toil. Their job is simple; they stop me bruising my knuckles. The bag itself is a patchwork torso; the patches replicate organ shape, size and location - my own idea. It twists and turns suspended on the chain, bobbing and weaving like an opponent. I call up Sholto's image; throw a few punches building up rhythm and tempo, rolling my shoulders and opening up with rights and lefts. The bag spins and turns away but that's the beauty of the patchwork. No matter which way it spins there's always a target to aim for and I can make every blow count. I lick my lips, following the bag's gyrations. I throw a right hook and sink into the kidneys, follow up with a combination taking out first an upper then a lower rib. Adrenalin courses through me, I love this. When it's real I can play with a guy and have him suffer, or I can take him out cold. A strike to the solar plexus, like last night, is always a thrill. The guy goes down like you've pulled his plug from the mains - always thinks he's hurt more than he is – and it gets attention. The bastard of it is I don't always get to choose.

A knock at the door brings me to a halt, it's Harvey yelling that it's 11 o'clock and reminding me that we need to meet Mickey at noon. I tell him I'll be down in fifteen and he clears off – he's worse than our old Ma.

I shower and shave taking care to trim my goatee, then select a fresh shirt from the rail, but yesterday's suit will do – no point in changing when chances are that it could be heading for the dry cleaners if things turn nasty today. I leave the bed unmade; Harvey and I share a cleaner, Mrs. Winstanley, who does that for us and keeps on top of our washing and ironing. Harvey gives Mrs. W. a hard time, he likes things just so. Me, I couldn't give a shit. I slip on my shades and meet Harvey out front.

It's gone five past twelve when we arrive at the offices of Loan Solutions in Horton Square. Mickey is sitting behind his desk running through some files. "Hi guys," he says, "the insurance job go all right then?"

"Sweet as a nut," Harvey answers.

"Good," Mickey says, "let's hope today brings the same result. I dug out some file details on our guy so we could go over them. I've even got a photo. It wasn't part of the original file you understand – Cornelius had it taken a week ago when we were putting all this together."

Harvey takes the photo, looks the guy over then hands it to me.

The bloke is pictured looking over his right shoulder as he's about to get into his car. It's a clear shot and whoever took it caught him well. He's about sixty, of slim build with a craggy, well lived-in face.

"This is Salvador Alonso, an antiques dealer," Mickey says.

"Salvador?" I ask.

"Yeah, he's Spanish," Mickey says. "He has a small shop and not much stock tucked away in Tannock Bar. I saw his books a year or so back when he came to us for money and know what sort of state his business was in. You wouldn't set up in a small village and expect to do a roaring trade in antiques would you? He told us he planned to do business over the internet and offer a service acquiring pieces on behalf of well-to-do clients. He now does a fair bit of importing. But we reckon he's got to be running a scam to have turned things around so quickly. Either he's creaming off more than his percentage as a go-between or he's importing more than what's on the manifest."

"We're not bothered about what he's doing though are we?" Harvey asks.

Mickey shakes his head. "Couldn't care less. We're only interested in a one off payment. Then we leave him to do as he pleases."

Harvey scratches at his goatee. "So what's the plan?"

"He's been making regular jaunts up north; we think these trips are paydays. He's due back into Luton later this afternoon, hopefully bringing some ill-gotten gains with him. Con said to take two cars, tail him from the airport and follow him back here. We either pull him over at a quiet spot on the outskirts of the village or lift him as he gets home."

"Why tail him from Luton? Why not just wait for him at his house?" Harvey asks.

Mickey shrugs. "We could do that, but we don't know that he won't stop off somewhere on the way home, or even if he'll go home at all."

"Okay," Harvey says, "so we tail him from Luton then take him. But leave Mo and I to deal with when and how."

"Hey, it's your show," Mickey says, "I'm only here to pick him out."

"Anywhere set aside to take him assuming he heads home?" Harvey asks.

Mickey opens s drawer and removes a set of keys.

"The lockup?" Harvey asks.

Mickey nods.

Me and Harvey grab a sandwich to eat in the car. When we park up at the airport it's around 3pm. I let Harvey and Mickey head towards the arrivals area after first relieving Mickey of his car keys and Alonso's photograph - I know better than to ask Harvey for the keys to his Jag. We still have half an hour until Alonso's flight is due in so I take a walk around the long-stay car park. It takes me a good fifteen minutes but I find what I'm looking for. A dark blue Range Rover bearing the same plate as the one in the picture. I move Mickey's car to the long stay car park, a few bays from the Rover, then call Harvey on his mobile and tell him what I've done.

"Good thinking," Harvey says, "but you'd best come in anyway. Alonso's flight's been delayed. We could be sitting for another hour yet."

It's almost 4:15pm when they announce the arrival of Alonso's flight. Mickey heads off to his car leaving me and Harvey to tail Alonso from arrivals. We pick him up without much trouble. He's much taller than the photograph suggests, about six four if he stood straight, but his shoulders are a little hunched and he has a stoop that loses him a couple of inches. He's wearing the same grey raincoat as in the photo and carries a small briefcase. But, if anything, the picture flattered him; his face is gaunt, his skin lined and loose, like a man who's lost two stones he could ill afford. He stops two feet outside the airport entrance doors, pulls a cigarette packet from his inside pocket and lights up. Then he marches at pace in the direction of the long stay car park.

Traffic's pretty heavy but we're never far behind him. We run into occasional queues as the carriageways merge and I watch him. He's a chain smoker, never without a ciggie between either his lips or his fingers; he drives with the window a few inches down flicking out ash like it's a nervous routine. When we hit the slipway a few miles short of Tannock Bar our three cars are all but alone on the road. On the long straight, before the lights at the bridge, Harvey signals for Mickey to overtake Alonso while we settle in behind him. Mickey times it to perfection arriving at the lights as they change to red and Harvey pulls up inches from the Rover's bumper. I slip out and half a second later I'm climbing into Alonso's passenger seat. He's so wrapped up in watching the lights and tapping his fingers to Classic FM that he doesn't realise what's going on.

When he turns, shock is etched into his wizened face, he mouths *what the fuck*…

I put a finger to my lips. "Shush and you won't get hurt. When the lights change, follow the car in front across the bridge then pull up in the first side street on your left."

He's staring at me, between his parted lips his tongue darts from side to side; he's weighing up his alternatives. His eyes flick to the door, perhaps for a second contemplating making a run for it but reasoning that he couldn't hope to outrun me. The lights change; I lift my shades and glare at him. The effect is instantaneous; he moves the automatic from neutral to drive and follows Mickey across the bridge.

When we've parked I grip the old man's arm and cup my left hand. He takes the keys from the ignition and drops them into my palm. Harvey draws the Jag alongside and I pull the briefcase from the back seat. I help Alonso into the back of the Jag then climb in beside him. He jabbers non-stop until I tell him to shut the fuck up.

Some time later we pull up outside Cornelius's lock-up under the railway bridge. The laminate black on white signage has lasted longer than the original occupants. But Paxton's name is still visible beneath red graffiti swirls, together with their slogan *'You're safe with us'*. Mickey unlocks and raises the rollover door and Harvey drives the Jag straight in. When the door shuts behind us there's no escape for Alonso, he's ours. We sit in the dark for a moment until daylight spills from the single door as Mickey enters. Seconds later overhead lights splutter into life and me and Harvey climb out. Alonso is reluctant to leave the Jag; I have to haul him out.

The lock-up garage housed a security business long since defunct. There were several such businesses set up in the railway arches; garages, taxi firms, small engineering works and the like. But it's neither a busy nor a choice part of town and ultimately they dwindled away.

These days Cornelius retains his lock-up as just that, somewhere to store his cars safely if he's overseas or out of town for a while. But the place is cold, dank and a little isolated - all of which make it ideal for our present purposes. I take the briefcase to the workbench; it's locked so I search for something to open it with. Mickey joins me and comes up with a scissor-sized set of strong jawed bolt cutters. Not what I had in mind but they'll cut the case in half if needs be. I hang onto them; Alonso may yet open it freely.

Harvey sits Alonso in a squeaky wooden chair and takes the lead. "You are Salvador Alonso?"

All at once the old man opens his hands, draws in his shoulders and pulls a face. Then he's jabbering again. "Yes, I'm a respected businessman. What do you people want with me?" His English doesn't suggest he's foreign; his body language does, he can't speak without using his hands.

Harvey leans against the bonnet of the Jag and pushes his fingers through his hair before lighting himself a cigarette. "You did some business with my employer a while back, Mr. Alonso. He helped you when no one else would. But you weren't straight with him. What you're doing attracts a higher rate of interest. So you owe us a little dividend."

Alonso's eyes narrow, he looks perplexed. "I deal in antiques; ask anyone about Sali Alonso, they will tell you."

"Spare us the bullshit then, Sali," Harvey says, smiling. "Cornelius Callaghan was a friend to you once and now you can be a friend to him. You do remember how Mr. Callaghan helped you don't you?"

Alonso gasps, his nostrils flare and he shoots up from his seat tapping furiously at his chest. "I am a respectable businessman…" Then turning his bony finger towards Harvey he takes a step forward, "…whereas you people are nothing more than common criminals. You abduct me, bring me to a place such as this, then ask me to be a friend?"

I drop the case and rush to restrain the old man. The reaction isn't quite what any of us expected, but Harvey is calm. "Oh, come now, Mr. Alonso, there's no need to get upset. We know what you're up to and we're prepared to turn a blind eye once we've had our cut. A one-off payment. Fifty big ones buys you Mr. Callaghan's seal of approval. We'll let you on your way and no-one else will touch you."

I'm behind Alonso gripping him by the shoulders, bolt cutters in hand. I feel his body relax as he listens to Harvey. But in the blink of an eye he tenses up and starts yelling again. Maybe being rumbled has panicked him, either that or Harvey asking for fifty thou. Whichever, he'll not be calmed. He shrugs and it dawns on me that I have more of his jacket than I have of him. He jabs a nicotine-stained, index finger toward Harvey again and again, telling him he can fuck off, he'll not get a penny from him. I pull his hand back but he wrenches it away, spittle spilling from his mouth. I'm struggling to control the old man. He's fighting when he should show respect. The heat rises in my gut; I have the bolt cutters in my hand and as Alonso points at Harvey once more I reach out, grip his finger between the steel jaws and squeeze. It takes no effort. The finger, severed below the joint, falls into a puddle of condensation on the floor with a thin, dull slap.

Silence. Alonso, Harvey, Mickey and me; all of us looking at the finger on the floor. Then the blood shoots from Alonso's wound and he screams. I pull a cotton handkerchief from my trouser pocket, force it around the bloodied stump and clasp Alonso's left hand to it. Now I'm in front of him I push him down into his seat. "Shut your noise or I'll put an end to you."

Alonso is quiet; staring blankly into my chest, rocking back and forth. I toss the cutters away and ask Mickey to hand me the briefcase. Then I get down on my hunches, raise my shades and look into the old man's eyes.

"What's the combination?" He almost cries me the numbers.

Harvey takes the briefcase to the workbench light. As the tumblers fall into place it clicks open and he flicks through sheaves of papers in the base, auction house listings and brochures. A thick brown envelope peeks out from a foldaway section. He pulls it out. "Jackpot. Twenties, fifties and hundreds," he calls.

Mickey takes the cash and begins to count while Harvey and I load the still rocking Sali Alonso into the back of the Jag.

Harvey lights another cigarette and passes it to me over the open car door. "Here give him a fag."

I lean in; Alonso's lips open to receive it. He draws on it and for a moment releases the pressure on his wound. The handkerchief falls away and he raises his hand to his face to pinch the cigarette between index and middle finger – but, of course, he can't.

"Left hand from now on," I tell him. I pick up the handkerchief, fold the sodden sections to the inside then wrap the still oozing stump so that he can grip it in the ball of his fist.

"There's exactly twenty-six 'k'," Mickey yells.

"Hear that, Sali?" Harvey asks. "You're twenty-four short. Any more at your gaff?"

Alonso stares into the rear of the diver's seat. "Gone," he murmurs. "Gone, and all for nothing." The stupid bastard is gripping his upper arm trying to staunch the blood loss. Harvey closes the door.

"Let's leave it at that for now," Mickey says quietly. "It's a good start. We can move onto number two on the list and get back to Sali if we need to."

I walk over to look at the finger on the floor. "Harvey, gimme your handkerchief."

Harvey scowls at me as if insulted. "No chance."

"C'mon," I tell him, "the old man's got mine." But Mickey throws me his instead and I gather it up. I stuff it into the stow section to the rear of the passenger seat when I climb in beside old Sali.

We drop Alonso a couple of streets short of his car. Mickey mentions that spots of blood are dripping onto the seat and Harvey gets agitated about the mess on his upholstery. He decides we're close enough so I bundle the old man out of the car. He's still gripping his upper arm so I shove his car keys in his pocket and tuck his briefcase under his arm. He looks every year of his age and more. His eyes plead pity, but I liked him better when he showed some guts.

****

Chapter 6 (Part II) ~Prop ~

~ Mo ~

The three of us sit at a large round table in one of the upstairs banquet rooms at The China Garden. Earlier, I'd let Harvey and Mickey hand the cash over to Cornelius and explain how things went down with Alonso. At the time I preferred to have a bottle of sparkling water in Moods; it didn't need three of us to tell the tale. Mickey came back saying despite getting only half what was needed Con was actually pleased, so much so that he booked us a private room at a restaurant where he holds an account. Saturday's evening meal is on him. But he'd insisted we move to secure the rest of the cash after we'd eaten.

I remove my shades and tuck them into my top pocket. As it happens I'm quite impressed by The China Garden, it seems an inspired choice. The lighting is low; flower troughs are set off neatly along the walls, the tall grasses and green foliage standing out against a dark background. On the main wall, above the plants, hang two vertical, decorative banners depicting Chinese writing in a blood-red hue; separated by a dragon headdress. The colours and the lighting are soothing. Harvey likes the place too; I watch him pick up and admire the crockery then summon a waiter. I hear him mention Liu Fang and moments later the distinctive sounds of oriental lute music float in the background. It completes the mood; he knows it and smirks at me. I nod back, impressed; but then I've long since accepted that my bother's a pretentious wanker.

The banquet room's focal point is a circular table that would probably seat six, but I like plenty of elbow room so we sit with space between us. A glass turntable at the table's heart allows us to pick from the various dishes. Above all, the room provides privacy from other guests, and the Chinese waitresses, dressed in fire-red silk with green garden motif, are nothing if not respectful. I like that.

No-one raises the subject of the next job until the main course selections are on the table. Harvey ladles some rice into his bowl then adds slivers of canton beef and spicy vegetables.

"I suppose you'd best tell us where we're off to next then, Mickey."

Mickey draws the turntable around with the tip of his finger and the dishes journey between us. He helps himself to rice and king prawns. "Redbridge. This guy's bit of a whiz kid."

"Redbridge," Harvey mutters almost approvingly.

The lemon chicken is in front of me as Mickey continues to fill his bowl. I scoop a few pieces into my mouth while I wait for my turn at the rice.

Harvey glowers at me.

"What?" I ask. But he says nothing and instead turns to Mickey.

"What do you mean by whiz kid?" he asks. "Don't tell me this is some spotty teenager?"

Mickey sets a prawn husk on his side plate and wipes the juices from the corners of his mouth. "No, he must be in his late twenties. What I mean is I suppose he's what's called a young entrepreneur. You know the type: sees a gap in the market, sets up to exploit it then flogs the business as a going concern and moves on."

Harvey tilts his head to the side and raises his eyebrows; his turn to be impressed; I've always said he'd never make a decent poker player.

"We lent him a few quid when the banks weren't keen," Mickey continues. "Now he's going from strength to strength, winning a lot of foreign business."

I spin the turntable, get the rice at last then add beef and vegetables on top. "He won't be working on a Saturday night, Mickey, so do we pick him up at some club or other?"

"You'd think so given his age wouldn't you?" Mickey says. "But he works from home. His companies are all web based."

"I knew it. He's a sad prick forever stuck in front of a computer, isn't he?" Harvey asks, his eyes narrowing and nose crinkling.

"More than likely," Mickey replies.

Harvey shakes his head and digs into his food. The geek will never know it but he had Harvey's respect – for all of thirty seconds.

Mickey scrapes the last of the king prawns onto his plate. I can't help myself. "Hey, you gonna eat all the fucking prawns, Mickey? No-one else is getting a look-in."

Harvey throws me that look again, but Mickey just looks fucking guilty.

Harvey catches the eye of a waitress, whispers as she leans over his shoulder. A few minutes later more king prawns are served up. Harvey pays no attention but I feel his eyes watching me and catch the slight shake of his head as I dig in.

Mickey and I finish up a little ahead of Harvey; possibly because Harvey insisted on using the chop sticks. When we're all done Mickey pushes his chair back and mops the sweat from his bald head, "Jeez, those vegetables were spicy, huh?"

I nod in agreement as the waiters and waitresses begin clearing the debris. Cornelius may be picking up the tab but I leave a twenty on the table and make sure Harvey leaves ahead of me. It'd be just like him to pocket it on the way out.

There's no need for us to use two cars; the three of us can go in the Jag. As we near the car Mickey's gibbering something about directions and makes a show of pulling some scribbled notes from his inside pocket. Harvey throws me a look. Mickey getting the directions out is a subtle way of suggesting that he should be sitting up front in the passenger seat. I couldn't care less, but I head for the passenger door all the same and Mickey doesn't breathe a word. All it'd have taken was a little bottle, but Mickey's not like us, he's a money man.

We drive in silence for a few miles then Harvey says, "What's the guy's name, Mickey?"

"Does it matter?" I ask. "More to the point, is there gonna be anyone else in there?"

"It's important 'cos I need to know how to address him," Harvey says tersely, then adds, "but you're right. Can we be sure he'll be alone, Mickey?"

"His name's James Pinchbeck." Mickey stifles a laugh at something that's occurred to him. "We had one of the guys call him last week posing as someone from Redbridge Borough Council. Said he was checking whether Pinchbeck had declared the house was used for business purposes. Pinchbeck threw a strop, so our guy calms him by coming clean about some clerical errors caused by an incompetent council employee who'd since left. Said he'd make sure he amended the records so Pinchbeck wouldn't be inconvenienced again."

"Is it a council house?" Harvey interrupts.

"Haven't a clue," Mickey says.

"Surely the council can't stop him running a business if it was a private housing estate?" Harvey asks.

Mickey waves the question away. "There's bound to be a by-law, otherwise your neighbours could set up as a haulage contractor running trucks down your street at all hours. The guy would've ad-libbed if Pinchbeck came at him with that."

Harvey considers, then shrugs acceptance.

"Anyway," Mickey continues, "our guy says he'd best check nothing else was screwed up and asks him to confirm how many people live there. When Pinchbeck says he lives alone, our guy acts surprised and Pinchbeck goes on to tell him that his girlfriend's finishing her PhD at Loughborough and won't join him until the summer."

"Good story," Harvey says, "but it doesn't mean that he won't be tucked up with some tart, and we don't want any unnecessary complications. Let's just play it safe. We can watch the house for a bit before we make our move."

It takes us about forty minutes to get to Redbridge then another twenty going round in circles. All the while Mickey is perched on the edge of the back seat craning his head between the front seats so he can gawp at the names of the streets as we approach. In the end where we need to be is some leafy street lined with bungalows.

Harvey pulls up away from the street lights and peers down its length, giving it the once over. "This doesn't look too shabby now, does it?" Once again he shows a grudging admiration.

We watch the house for no more than five minutes and as each minute goes by Harvey re-adjusts the air con as it fights to prevent the windows from steaming up. The lights are on at Pinchbeck's house but the blinds are shut, there's no movement and we're learning nothing.

Harvey is restless, the quarter moon and lack of cloud cover look to have him on edge. "The longer we sit here the more likely we are to draw attention," he says. "I'm expecting to see some old bag's curtains twitching at any second. How about Mickey and I go to the front door while you take the rear, Mo? Give him long enough to answer then get inside."

"Works for me," I say. "Give me a head start so I can figure out how to get in." I pull my leather gloves from their hideaway in the front dash and step out quietly. Just thinking about the job reminds me of Alonso's finger. I open the rear door and pull the now dry-bloodied bundle from its' rear seat stow. I stuff it into my jacket pocket; I have an idea.

The street itself is quiet, it's dry and the clear sky gives the night a chilling freshness. I hurry up the stone steps leading to Pinchbeck's house, bypass the path branching off to the front door and disappear instead into the shadows at the side of the house where the path continues to the back garden. At the end of the path is a full-size wooden gate. The latch is on the other side but a circular hand hole allows me to raise it from the front. I slip into the garden and close the gate behind me. Two rooms overlook the back garden; one either side of the back door. A light shines in the one to the right whereas the small, single window to the left is in darkness – probably a store cupboard. I hear the doorbell ring, Harvey's impatience has him at the door before I've determined how best to get in. I hear voices; Pinchbeck has answered so I try the handle on the back door. It yields, I halt to slip my shades on then step inside. I'm aware of a dark shadow for the briefest of seconds before a powerful blow to my upper chest bowls me over and all hell breaks loose. A large Alsatian is on top of me barking and snapping. Instinctively, I pull my right forearm across to shield my face but the dog fastens its jaws around it and bites down until its teeth puncture the skin. A mistake; and now I have it. I clamp my left hand to the back of its head and force my right arm deeper into its throat. My sleeve is shredded in the process, my arm with it but the dog releases it grip and backs off, now wary of me.

"Walter, Walter, what's going on?" A man with short cropped hair stands at the entrance to the kitchen and grabs the dog by the collar. His mouth hangs open as he tries to make sense of the scene before him. As I get up I can see Harvey and Mickey coming down the hallway behind him.

"Ah, this gentleman is a colleague of ours," Harvey says.

Pinchbeck turns. "Wait, you can't just come barging into my home."

Harvey wears a menacing smile. "Oh, this is a very delicate matter, Mr. Pinchbeck. I think, later, you'll be glad we discussed this out of earshot of your neighbours. Now, leave Walter in the kitchen and show us to somewhere we can talk."

After five minutes I join Harvey, Mickey and Pinchbeck down the hall in what appears to be a room converted into a somewhat sparse office. Pinchbeck sits in a seat by his computer whilst Harvey and Mickey remain standing, it being more imposing that way.

Pinchbeck looks the nervous type. "What have you done to Walter?"

I hold out my right arm. Torn threads dangle from my mangled and blood-stained sleeve. "Walter can look after himself, but my suit and shirt are ruined. I helped myself to a bandage from your first aid box in the kitchen."

"Walter's never this quiet with strangers in the house, what have you done to him?"

"Relax," I tell him. "I just fed him whatever you had cooking in the oven. Right now all he's interested in is eating."

"Never mind the dog; we have more important matters to attend to," Harvey says. "Cornelius Callaghan helped hoist your business off its knees a while back. We reckon now you're doing so well you're due him a little dividend. Let's call it twenty five thousand."

Pinchbeck glowers at Mickey. "I paid my loan back with interest and you know it."

Mickey holds his hands up. "James, how often will you get the chance to do someone like Mr. Callaghan a favour? It's an investment; he's a powerful friend to have."

"No!" Pinchbeck says.

Harvey sighs. "Are you sure that's the attitude you want to take? I wonder if your pretty little girlfriend would say the same if we asked her?"

"Leave her out of this," Pinchbeck says.

"Glad to," Harvey says, "but that depends on you. See, I have friends in Leicester who owe me a favour but I hesitate to ask 'cos they're not too strong on subtlety. So maybe you're right, best if we can find a way to keep her out of it. Mr. Callaghan needs Twenty-five grand."

"I can't do it and I won't do it," Pinchbeck says.

I reach into my pocket, remove the bloodstained handkerchief containing Alonso's finger and open it up in front of Pinchbeck.

Harvey sees where I'm going with this. "The guy who owned that said no. Understand?"

Pinchbeck looks as though he's about to puke. He spins his chair round to face his computer desk, rests his elbows on the table and cradles his head. "But the business isn't doing well," he says. "I don't have twenty-five thousand."

"Bollocks," Mickey chip in. "The broadsheets quote new orders and contracts."

Pinchbeck sits back in his seat and sighs. "All lies," he says. "It's a set-up."

"What d'you mean?" Mickey asks. "You've been winning orders from all over the place; it's been in the business press and the company records show money coming in."

"That's how it's meant to look," Pinchbeck says. "The business wins contracts from all over the world and I squeeze as much publicity out of it as I can. Money comes in but it's the same money being wired around the world - my money, sent in from dummy satellite companies I've set up to make the company appear to be worth more than it is. Don't you get it? There are no orders, no contracts. None!"

Harvey rubs his goatee, stares at Mickey and shakes his head.

"Show me," Mickey says. "Prove it to me on the computer or so help me I'll cut your fucking fingers off myself."

While Mickey and Pinchbeck pour over computer records I wrap the finger and return it to my jacket pocket. Then I pull Harvey into the corner. "This is a crock of shit," I whisper. "I could've had my head torn off by a crazed fucking dog that Mickey, dozy bastard that he is, should have known about and now there's no cash. What do we do?"

Harvey runs a hand through his hair. "Yeah, somebody fucked up. Let's wait and see what Mickey says. Maybe the kid's trying to pull a fast one."

After ten minutes Mickey has seen enough and turns to face us. "Okay, if the kid pulls his resources from this bloody money-go-round then he's in credit by about twenty grand."

"So what's the point of all this?" I ask.

Mickey sighs. "To a mug punter the company looks as though it's winning lots of orders with money coming in from various places – the same money. Boy wonder here then sells the firm for way more than it's worth."

"Well, James," Harvey says. "How do you think Mr. Callaghan is going to react to being taken for a mug punter when he put so much faith in you?"

Pinchbeck still looks as if he's going to puke. He shakes his head and looks to the floor.

"Tell you what," Harvey says. "We'll take fifteen, leave you with your fingers intact and try to smooth things over with Mr. Callaghan. You'll still have five to carry on with. Call it a business down-sizing if you like."

Pinchbeck says nothing.

"Do we have a deal?" Harvey asks.

Silence.

"Or shall we find out if Walter has room to squeeze down a finger?" Harvey adds.

"Take the money," Pinchbeck says.

"Very wise," Harvey says. "Now how do we get it?"

"Easy," Mickey pipes up, "he's got access via his computer, he can transfer it to Loan Solutions right now; I can give him our account number."

~

The journey back is quiet until I ask what we're going to do about the nine grand we're short. Mickey looks up and shrugs, and that's all it takes. I edge further around in my seat. "That was your fucking mess back there. You make sure you tell that funny story to *the guys*."

"What do you mean?" Mickey says, sinking back into his seat.

"I'm talking about doing your bloody homework. About a fucking big dog none of us knew was there. About scrambling for cash from a prospect you'd checked out, that's what."

"Okay, okay, calm down," Harvey says. "The whole thing was a complete fuck-up but let's move on. We've nine grand to find. I suggest we pick up where we left off with Alonso and see if there's anything left to squeeze out of him."

"Pinchbeck had twenty, why'd didn't we take it all?" I ask.

"We could have done and he knows it," Harvey says. "This way he'll concentrate on that rather than on making waves. Remember what Con said about drawing undue attention?"

I see the logic. "But what if Alonso was telling the truth and hasn't got more cash?"

It's Harvey's turn to shrug. "That's what our insurance job is for. Either that or Mickey can suggest that Con sell one of his motors." Mickey gives a nervous smile. "Anyway," Harvey continues, "there's nothing more we can do tonight so let's put it behind us. I fancy going to Benny's; had my eye on one of the lap dancers for weeks, they're supposed to be horny as hell at the end of their shift, you know. How about it? Benny tells me that Myrna took a shine to you, Mo, asked him who the shy hunk was; I think you might be in there."

It's a long time since I've been with a woman and for a moment the idea holds some appeal, but I know too well the anxiety that comes with it. Harvey takes his eyes from the road. He's grinning, knowing he's made me uncomfortable.

"Another time," I tell him; but I don't let him know how close I got to saying yes.

"Aren't you even going ask what Myrna looks like then?"

"Like it matters to someone like me," I say. Now perhaps I've spoiled his chances of splitting a pair or maybe he just wanted a sideshow but either way he loses the grin.

"You might want to get that arm seen to, then. Can't you get lockjaw or something from dog bites?"

"My tetanus shots are up-to-date, it'll be fine. The insurance job?" I ask, "You mentioned a team, but we hit on just the one bloke."

"One was enough," Harvey says. "We can get the other guy anytime we need to."

"Maybe I'll look him up while you're busy, put some extra pressure on them now we need them to come through."

"It's not necessary," Harvey says.

"I'll feel better for it," I tell him, and I will, but what I mean is that I'll feel better to be out of the house and not have to suffer the cooing of some tart as he sweats and grunts above her.

****

Chapter 7 (Part I) ~ Morbidity ~

~ Adam ~

Sunday has been something of a non-event. I've spent hours over things I normally do piecemeal throughout the course of a week so that their impact on my time is minimal. I'm talking about domestic chores; vacuuming and dusting. Added to that I changed the bed sheets, washed what was in the linen basket, even did some ironing; all necessities, but hardly things any of us look forward to. By late afternoon I'm as caught up as it's possible to be. Since then I've been alone with my thoughts and it's been depressing to say the least. I can't remember such a dull weekend and I think, subconsciously, I looked for things to fill my time and postpone the reality that faces me now. It's never really struck me that I'd become reliant on Colin and Ferris for company, but I have and I am.

Now I sprawl on the settee in front of the TV with a cold beer from the fridge. My eyes take in some channel four movie but I can't concentrate on it, instead I'm thinking how it's come to this; how I've allowed my circle of friends to erode over the years. What was a significant number whittled away in ones and twos, with no discernable pattern, not as you might expect by order of age, looks or perceived intelligence. There's no great mischief or mystery involved though, just the passing of time, people growing older, their interests changing; a growing apart if you like. Some progressed at work and moved away. Others moved on in different respects. And by that I mean into permanent relationships. A thing that - no matter how strong the initial intent to stay in touch - seemed to chip away at camaraderie under the guise of expanding responsibility, an inevitable reduction in free time, and ultimately a changing set of values that meant one fewer of us on the weekend pub and club circuit.

It didn't actually seem so bad when it finally got to be just the three of us. On the positive side it meant we never had to exclude anyone in order to talk about any of the little jobs Colin found for us on the sly. The money was never big but always welcome. The Council don't pay well and I saw it all as a bit of fun and a little payback. After all, life and authority have done nothing but take from me. Now that it's just Ferris and I though, I sense it's the end of the line, things have to change. Once again, my mother comes to mind, she likes to prick my conscience.

I sigh and tear my eyes away from the TV screen. From my seated position, I glance around my front room as the walls close in around me. It feels like I've imprisoned myself in a small, tight space; that I need merely stretch out either arm to touch these dreary walls. Eight years I've lived here, yet if you packed away the things that are truly mine, like maybe my clothes, my CD collection and Annie's photo from the bedroom dresser, then even Ferris would be hard pushed to find anything of me left in what remains. Okay, I decorated when I moved in but what went on the walls and floors had more to do with what was 'on special' than any personal preference. The furniture came with the flat, the bed's mine but, if truth be told, I'd see it skipped before I'd take it to another place. The flat's rented, but even if that weren't so it's never really felt mine. I've happened to this place in much the same way that I've allowed life to happen to me; randomly, lightly, making little or no impression whatsoever. Maybe this time Annie's got a point; it's time to grow up and move on.

The thought sets me off. I give up on the film and root among the drawers until I find an old scribble pad and a biro. Then I fetch Annie's photo from the bedroom dresser and set it down on the table beside my beer. The paper's lined, but it doesn't matter, it's not as if I can ever send this. I look at my mother's yellowed photograph, the corners turning up where the sun has bleached it; at least the glass holds it back from curling in on itself completely. I remember being with her when it was taken; it's a head and shoulders shot but in my mind I can pull back from that and see the rest of the hospital ward around her. I know now that she'd made a special effort in preparing for it, knowing before I did that it'd be the last she'd ever have taken. She'd been lecturing me before the nurse arrived to take it, telling me that I had to work harder at my schoolwork, that I'd been strong in growing up without a father and that these things all had purpose. But she was abnormally severe with me that day and try as she might to shake off that stern frame of mind it's always there when I look at her picture. Of course, I understand now that she'd have been frustrated at being unable to explain to me quite why these things would be so important and I marvel at her courage in thinking of me with what lay ahead for her. But the feeling that she was disappointed with my efforts has stayed with me, I've never shaken it and I've not deserved to. Maybe it'd have been different if there'd been a grave to visit; something other than a photograph. I lift my pen and begin to write. I don't think I've ever written a letter in my life and in truth I don't know why I'm doing it now, it just seems right.

I surprise myself and for twenty minutes my pen is lifted from the page only as I turn to begin another. It pours from me; I'm telling her how much I've missed her, asking why it had to be like this; admitting that I blamed her for abandoning me - a revelation to myself if not to her - and asking for her forgiveness. Colin, as my closest friend for the last eighteen years, had replaced her and his death was like losing her all over again. I confide in her, tell her of the thieving and the cheating we had done, as though she hasn't been watching all these years from over my shoulder. I explain how my sense of insecurity and injustice had eaten away at me and made me lose touch with all she'd stood for. In essence, I come clean, unburden myself but make no excuses. Every day, I tell her, I look at her picture and feel her disappointment and my own shame; I know that I'm letting her down, know that I'm breaking the last promise I'd ever made to her. I'm not the son she'd hoped for, certainly not the son she deserves.

In the early years I argued it wasn't fair. I'd promised not knowing what she knew – that I'd be alone in the world and I hadn't fully understood what she'd said, but the arrogance of youth made me too stubborn to admit it. I understand now of course, I just don't believe it. But if Colin's death has shown me anything it's that we can't wait around for life to take off. We have to live life as though the moment is all there is.

When my thoughts finally dry up I find I've written four pages. I stare blankly at the TV screen folding them over and over until I can't make them any smaller, then I toss them into the corner of the sofa and grab my beer.

****

Chapter 7 (Part II) ~ Laplin Road ~

~ Adam ~

Another Monday. Early, cold and crisp; I'm almost excited. I can't decide whether the relative inactivity of the weekend makes getting out of the flat more appealing. I push aside any thoughts of why the break is necessary. I prefer to think it's because I've admitted that Annie is right. Deep down, I know it. But for now it's enough that I've decided to change.

The feel-good factor continues on the journey; the Laplin Road Depot is on the outskirts of town so I take the jeep. I could sit behind its wheel all day and still come out smiling. The traffic is light, the tarmac dry and Capital Radio has my fingers drumming on the steering wheel. As I swing through the depot's open gates I realise I can't recall the detail of the journey. Ordinarily, such a lack of awareness wouldn't cause me to smile but it does now. It's like a final affirmation. I've shaken off the doom and gloom of Sunday and taken heed of Ferris's warning about turning into a morbid git. Today I'm ready for anything.

After a couple of false starts I find Davie Armitage sitting in a portacabin inside one of the two depot warehouses. He's the stocky sort; sleeves rolled up past his elbows, probably in his early fifties with ruddy, weather-beaten cheeks that glow beneath thick eyebrows and a shock of wavy grey hair that adds maybe an inch to his height. His eyes light up as I tell him my name and mention Nigel Perryman.

"Great," he says. "I managed to rope in a couple of the new apprentices. You can imagine what it's like getting any bugger to volunteer around here. It's been a flaming struggle until you came forward, I don't mind telling you."

I'm silent a second too long as Davie's comments register. Nigel never did tell me what the job was and I was so keen to have him approve my holidays that I never asked. Davie rises and moves out from behind his desk. His grin tells me he's sussed it. "Got to hand it to big Nigel," he says. "It never occurred to me I could fill the slots without actually telling folk what they'd be doing."

"He's tucked me up, hasn't he?"

"Aah, it's not as bad as it sounds. C'mon, we'll find the apprentices and get changed."

Davie leads me out of the portacabin and across the yard into the second warehouse. Two young lads sit in the far corner in a section given over to metal lockers and wooden benches. He introduces me to a skinny bloke named Paul, then to Darren, a black, muscle-bound kid with shoulders almost as wide as Davie is tall. He opens a large cabinet beside the lockers. "Your feet, Paul. What size?"

"Eh, eights."

"And you, Darren?"

"Elevens."

Davie traces a finger along a set of pigeon holes before pulling out a pair of heavy-duty Wellington boots for each of them - the leg of one stuffed into the other so the boot appears two-footed as he hands them over. Then he turns to me and I say eight to his unasked question. We stumble into our boots as he lays out rubber gloves, cloth sacks, a round metal tin not unlike those used for storing coffee and a set of belts each holstering a leather pouch and a spear-stick.

"Okay," he says. "We're gonna be clearing the brook just across the street. It runs the full length of Laplin Road and it'll take us most of the day. Here's how it's done.

Adam works down from the north end, I'll work my way up from the south and you two lads start in the middle with Darren working toward me at the south end and Paul working north toward Adam. Got it?"

We nod in unison and he continues. "The brook's about six feet at its widest point and probably only six inches deep. You each take a sack, a pouch and a stick for the rubbish. Branches overhang in places and stop you getting at some of the debris, that's when you use this." He picks up a spear-stick and glares at the two apprentices. "Let's be clear, this ain't a fucking light sabre, nor is it for stabbing at the odd rat you might happen across neither. We had some clown do that a couple of years back; daft prat managed to put it clean through his own foot. But apparently that didn't hurt as much as the tetanus jabs in the arse that came afterwards. Be warned; I say this every year without fail and every flaming year we have an incident, not this year though, eh?"

"What are the pouches for?" I ask.

"Ah, good point, I nearly forgot. I ain't saying you'll see any mind, but if you find any needles or syringes, then they go in the leather pouch. Handle them carefully because if they stick you, then you're talking AIDS tests and more flaming jabs. We'll transfer them to the metal tin here at the finish for proper disposal, and by the way, there'll be extra sacks left here for when you need 'em and you will need 'em, okay?"

No one says anything. The two kids don't quite know what's hit them. I wonder who set *them* up. I can't think that they'd have volunteered for this; no-one would be that stupid. Then again, who was I to speak; I thought I'd put one over on Nigel, leaving him to complete my holiday forms, when all the time he was setting me up for this. *Sneaky bastard is our Nigel.*

We set off together, walking the short distance toward the midpoint to get the boys started first. I watch the lads as they chat to one another and I twig why they're here. Darren has a slight stutter, nothing bad but enough to set him apart and Paul has a protruding lower jaw which sees his lower lip jut out. I remember a kid like that from my time in care. We gave him a terrible time, wouldn't let him join in anything we did claiming he drown in a shower of rain. Kids like him grow up and move from that to this, nothing changes.

Laplin Road didn't actually seem that long whenever I'd had occasion to drive down it in the past. It's set out a little differently, the council depot giving way to plush housing on one side of the road with the green fairways of the local golf course visible through the trees on the other. It's maybe four hundred metres long, so a mere hundred apiece for each of us to clear, yet Davie was sure it'd take us most of the day. Even allowing for break times and a half-hour stop for lunch, it seems to me like no more than a few hours' work. It's not until I get my first proper look at it that I begin to understand. From the footpath that runs parallel to the brook I take the few short steps across the grass and peer down a steep grassy bank. It's maybe a two-metre drop to the water below and, for the most part, the trees and bushes lie on the opposite bank. All of which make it a near-perfect fly-tipping site. I watch the young lads scramble down the embankment into the water and once Davie has them working back to back, edging slowly away from each other, we leave them to it.

"It should be about break time when you've filled your first sack," Davie says. "Pick Paul up on the way and you can take a short break at the depot, then crack on."

"No problem," I tell him before we head off in different directions. But it's the same old supervisor stuff; when we're thinking 'rest', he's thinking 'lost time'.

It's hard work and slow going. I lose count of how many plastic fizzy drinks bottles and discarded, disintegrating cigarette packets I collect. It's awkward too; although the water is shallow the bed is uneven, strewn with a minefield of algae-coated boulders ready to upend the unwary. Twice I'm saved from a soaking when overhanging branches arrest my fall, the second at the cost of a small branch whipping across my cheek. But that's not the worst of it. There's a strange, sweet smell to the brook I'd not noticed before; it's as though I kick it up as I wade, the odour of dirt and decay. As the sun burns off the crispness of the morning, clouds of flies and midges begin to hover in patches. I disturb them as I move forward and they pick up on my sweat, settling in my hair and irritating the back of my neck. My hands, too, are sticky to the point of itching inside the rubber gloves and I realise I'll emerge from this little job no cleaner than if I'd been digging another grave in the bowels of the earth.

After about an hour and a half I've probably only gone about twenty metres but my bag is already heavy and unwieldy. Ahead of me a tree leans across the brook blocking my path. I have to get out and go around it, so it's a good point at which to stop. I swing my sack up onto the bank, unhook the belt complete with spear-stick and pouch and heave it out too. Unhindered, I clamber up the grassy bank.

It's a relief to be out, but after a few short breaths I hitch the belt around my waist again, sling the sack over my shoulder and walk back toward the depot. We'll probably be in ahead of proper break time but I'm thinking of how good it'll be to give a quick swill of water to my face and neck and how a cup of milky tea will clear my throat and nostrils of that pungent, over-ripe smell. I'm looking out for Paul when I hear a cry. It's maybe ten metres ahead and elicits that momentary tingle of elation in my gut; that devilish enjoyment we take at another's misfortune. For a split second I imagine him losing his balance, ending up sitting square on his backside in the stinking water. Then it comes again, a strangled, angst-filled yell, but this time pleading for help. I drop my sack and run but the spear-stick bounces at my hip and I have to stop, unbuckle and drop the belt. I call out to him to let him know I'm coming.

Paul staggers up the bank a short way ahead of me. His face is white; he's breathing heavily and spittle drools from that protruding lower lip.

"What's wrong, Paul, are you okay?"

He fixes me with watery eyes. "A body," he says, pointing back down the embankment. "A dead body!"

"My arse," I tell him. But the little bastard's face stays fish-belly white. I brush past him, slide down the embankment passing his discarded sack, and ease myself into the water. A few metres ahead, tucked into the side of the bank and half hidden by grass overhanging the edge is a large dark mass. A smile crosses my face, I was right the little shit's taking the piss. This'll turn out to be a dead rat lying beside an old golf bag. I wade forward but long before I reach it the outlines become clear and I slow. The lurch in my gut tells me this is no joke. It's a large body, the face submerged in the shallow water. I hunker down and try to turn it over but make heavy weather of it; water has saturated the clothing and I'm being unnecessarily gentle. I swallow hard, get myself tight to the body then bundle it over. The up-turned head lolls to the side but there's no point in checking for a pulse; this guy's long gone. His lifeless eyes bulge in their sockets, his face is ashen and bloated and his mouth is frozen in a contorted grimace. It looks as though he died in some discomfort. *Poor old sod.*

Paul peers over the embankment. "You gonna give him the kiss of life?"

"He's beyond that, Paul. We'll let the police deal with it. There's an attaché case here too; he must have been lying on it." I leave both case and body where they are and climb out.

I gather up Paul's sack and hand it to him once I'm on the footpath. "C'mon, let's get the rubbish back to the depot and we'll make the call."

"You just gonna leave him?" Paul asks.

"Why not? He's not going anywhere and the police will want to see him as we found him. You want to stay?"

"No way," Paul says.

"I thought not."

I retrace my steps to collect my own gear and then head back to the depot, Paul scampering along beside me, his mouth flapping with incessant questions. Will the police want to speak to him? Will he get into trouble? If we left the body shouldn't we at least have taken the attaché case? Will it be on the telly or in the papers?

If the depot had been any further away there might have been two bodies to report.

~

Police Constable Wormer sits in the chair where Davie Armitage first spoke to me earlier in the morning. He tells me he'll be speaking to all four of the brook clearance team, as he refers to us, but he'll need official statements from just Paul and me. He's quite matter of fact in taking my statement. No doubt he's seen this before. He goes through the formalities of taking my name, address, how long I've worked for the council and then asks me to explain the nature of the job we were involved in. Finally he asks me to tell him, in my own words, how I found the body. All standard stuff, I suppose but I'm edgy about giving out personal information to the police for obvious reasons and I wonder if it shows.

"So you weren't actually first to see the body?" Wormer asks.

"No, Paul was."

"But Paul didn't see the attaché case, did he?"

"I don't know for sure but I doubt it. I only saw it myself after I'd managed to roll the guy over. It was underneath him."

Wormer taps his pencil on his notebook. "And you didn't check for a pulse?"

"He looked long dead. Are you saying he might still have been alive?"

"God no! The white coats reckon he's been dead for somewhere between twelve and twenty-four hours. I just wondered what made you so sure."

"I suppose it was the colour of him."

Wormer opens his hands and cocks his head to one side. "Hmm." He stares into space for a moment as though weighing my answer then looks back at me. "Anything peculiar about the body d'you think?"

"Like what?"

"Like anything unusual?" he asks.

"He was bloated, but I put that down to him having been face-down in the water and maybe taking some of it in." I'm about to leave it at that when I recall the twisted mouth. "He did have a bit of a grimace."

"Yes," Wormer says, "but I wasn't thinking of that. I was rather hoping you could tell me about his hands."

"I never looked at his hands."

"Hmm, he's lost a finger, recent by the looks. My sergeant thinks someone might have taken a liking to a ring or suchlike and been unable to prize it off; what with the body becoming bloated. But you wouldn't know anything about that?"

I shake my head and for once the incredulous look on my face is genuine.

Wormer snaps his notebook shut. "Thought not, it's a long shot on the sarge's part."

"You don't really think this bloke was killed for a ring do you?" I ask.

"You're missing the point. We're not suggesting he was killed, more that someone might have relieved him of some jewellery after finding him in the brook. Between you and me," Wormer says, tapping the side of his nose, "that grimace says a lot. It'll be a heart attack. Post mortem will confirm it, you mark my words."

I rise to leave. It strikes me that Wormer, not his sergeant, is probably the one hoping to make something from this that isn't there; maybe that's why he's still a constable. Before I get to the door Wormer stops me and tells me to send Davie in.

I find Davie sitting with the apprentices on the wooden benches by the changing lockers and tell him he's in next but he casts me a black look. He's listening as Paul talks about the corpse being missing a finger and speculating that this could be the murderer's signature, the thing that marks his victims as 'his'.

Davie shakes his head and turns to me. "You realise they've put a halt to the clearing operation, don't you?"

"I suppose they have to," I tell him.

"Fourteen years I've run the brook clearing exercise and this'll be the first time we won't finish the same day. Not even when that little shit speared himself did we fail to complete."

"Hey don't beat yourself up over it, Davie; it's not your fault."

He gets up from his seat. "My fault? How could it be my fault? You're the one who brought the circus to town. Nigel said you were trouble and he was right, the job's knackered. We'll be lucky if we get back to it this week with all this nonsense going on. So you can clear off. I want you off my flaming site, okay?" He spins away crossing the concourse towards the portacabin.

Even as I change out of my gear I can't take it in. How the hell did I end up being the bad guy?

~

Noonan's is only a ten-minute stroll away from my flat. It's one of those places that fall between the cracks. In trying to meet the needs of those who either thirst or hunger it's neither one thing nor the other; not a pub or even a boozer, not a fast food joint and certainly not a restaurant. It picks up passing trade and thrives on its convenience, but it isn't somewhere you stay for particularly long, the beer is overpriced and the décor's synthetic. You know the type; all bright walls and easy-wipe furniture. It has no soul, no character; but if you catch it on a good day the food's decent enough.

I've arranged to meet Ferris here after he's finished work but I'm landed with more free time than I expected so I decide to grab a bite to eat before he arrives. I didn't actually speak to him; we exchanged text messages in the standard shorthand, though he did manage to give me the impression he had something to tell me. I'm bracing myself for news on how his weekend with Tina panned out. It can't have gotten serious already, that's not Ferris's style, but I suppose you never know.

I order a pint at the bar; skim-read the menu and settle for the seafood platter. I glance around before picking a table; there are less than a dozen people in the place. A group of five men in tired business suits stand further down the bar, discussing the merits of various pubs in the high street and which should be their next port of call. Three girls sit amid the empty tables enjoying a drink and a snack with an array of shopping bags nestling at their feet. In the furthest corner an elderly man sits alone pretending to read a newspaper, but failing to ever turn a page. I take up a seat at the window and watch the last of the Monday shoppers wander by.

Ferris arrives early; I'm almost ready for another pint but only half way through my platter. I catch the barmaid's attention and order two more pints.

"Sorry," I tell Ferris, "I ordered food thinking I'd be done before you got here. Are you hungry?"

He looks at my plate and I know what's coming. "Couldn't face it, mate," he says. "You know how I feel about seafood. God made those things ugly for a reason." The barmaid sets the drinks down and Ferris scoops his up. "I've been gagging for this, though."

Between mouthfuls I ask him how things went with Tina. He's a little skittish, casting odd, furtive glances over his shoulders, and I notice for the first time that he's a little grey around the gills.

"Oh," he says, smiling for a second, "she's a doll, a real doll. We had a great time."

"What, that's it? *We had a great time*. I thought you had something to tell me, you can't just leave it at that."

Ferris takes a long drink, sets his glass down and wipes his mouth with the back of his hand. He gives a little laugh, but it's the nervous kind. "Oh, I've got news all right."

I know something's very wrong and set down my knife and fork. "What's up, Ferris?"

He leans forward, his arms on the table and his shoulders hunched. "I got home really late on Sunday, maybe two am. I let myself in and there he was, sitting in my front room, calm as you like. I nearly crapped myself."

"Who we talking about?"

"Scary Santa," Ferris answers. "The big fucker with the white hair and half a beard."

"What?"

"My landlady stops me going down the stairs this morning and says some bloke's been looking for me. Seems he'd been hanging round in the small hours of Saturday too. Poor mare thought she was doin' me a turn. I could hardly tell her he'd bust in and collared me the night before."

"Did he threaten you?"

"Not in so many words, no. He said he knew I was a mate of yours and that I was to pass on a message."

"But why come to you? If he could find out where you live, he could have found me just as easily."

Ferris nods. "I've been thinking about that. The way I see it he's already hurt you. Maybe it makes more impact to show us he can get to us both."

"So what did he say?"

"He said we weren't the only guys who owed them but that we had to understand they were serious." Again Ferris glances over his shoulder then he lowers his voice. "The bastard gave me something. Grabbed my arm, forced it into my palm and folded my fingers around it. Said it would help us focus our minds."

I'm beginning to sweat, unsure if I want to know but I ask anyway. "Did you bring it?"

Ferris reaches into his jacket pocket and withdraws a folded tissue. He sets it down on the table and gives an involuntary shiver, as if the beer on his pallet had gone sour on him. He shakes his head. "Don't open it here."

I consider for a second, take a deep breath and peel back a corner. But the paper has stuck to what's inside and catapults it out onto the table. I feel the colour drain from me. It's a finger, icicle white but for a yellow edge and a pink frill of tissue spilling from its end like entrails from a gutted fish. I smother it with the complementary serviette and look around to see if anyone noticed, but it seems we're okay.

"Well, say something," Ferris says.

It's my turn to shrug my shoulders. "Looks like I'm well and truly fucked, doesn't it?" We sit in silence for a few seconds before I pull a few notes from my wallet and catch the waitress's eye. She nods in acknowledgement and I slip the notes under the salt cellar, lifting the serviette and what it covers at the same time.

We head off in the direction of my flat; it's the closest place that we can talk in private. On the way I step into the gutter and bend down to let the finger slip through the grating of a street drain. Ferris looks at me, his lips parted as though about to say something. "Did you want to hang onto it?" I ask.

It's only as I fumble for my keys outside the flat that it hits me we might be walking into these thugs again. I look at Ferris and know the same thought is in his head. My eyes scan the doorframe and lock, no tell-tale jemmy marks, it looks normal. I press my ear to the panel. Silence; and if that's good how come I don't feel any better? I ease the key home and turn it until I feel the lock disengage. Then I push the door inward, just an inch, and slide the key back out. I glance at Ferris; he's taken a step back toward the stairway. He nods and I give the door a shove. It arcs back and bounces off the door stop, but the hallway is empty.

"Who's there?" I call out. There's no reply. I raise a hand suggesting Ferris stay put and I step inside. I wander through each room, it's as I left it and I feel a complete mug. I tell Ferris to come in.

In the living room I turn on the TV just to have some noise and hand Ferris a beer I took from the fridge.

"So what do we do?" Ferris asks.

"I don't know, but I can't go through that every time I come home." I take a slurp from my can and sit down. "There's something else, you'd better sit down to hear this."

"Oh, shit, it can't get any worse," Ferris says.

"I got sent home early today and I've taken some time off." He looks at me, awaiting the detail. "We were clearing rubbish from the brook in Laplin Road and we found a body."

Ferris almost spits out his beer. "Jeez."

"Just some old geezer. The cops reckon it was a heart attack."

"Then I don't understand," he says. "Where's the relevance?"

"You said Scallion told you I wasn't the only guy who owed them." Ferris purses his lips then nods. "Then he gave you that finger," I add.

"Yeah."

"The copper who took my statement said the old guy had recently lost a finger."

Ferris sets down his beer. "Either that's one hell of a coincidence or no coincidence at all."

"Exactly. These guys are serious. I arranged time off to think about how I could raise the ten grand but now I think we need to get out of here."

Ferris leans forward, elbows resting on his knees, his palms rubbing together. "Where would we go and for how long? I mean, I can't just up and leave."

"For fuck's sake, these guys aren't messing around, Ferris. I've got a few hundred quid in the bank; enough to catch a ferry and lay low in the north of France until the deadline passes."

Ferris bites his lower lip. "And then what? If they'll risk killing people they're not gonna forget about it 'cos you're not around for a few days."

I know he's right but I don't know what else to suggest. In desperation I ask if there's a job we could pull.

"I don't know of anything," Ferris says. "And I can't go anywhere just now. I couldn't get the time off work and I blew what little dosh I had over the weekend with Tina. But I'll tell you what. I think it's best that you get away. I can afford to hang back a bit yet. They're not likely to get nasty until the deadline passes. That'll give me time to ask around about possible jobs and maybe get a few quid together."

"They'll come after you though."

He shakes his head. "I can stay with Tina; it'll be as safe as being abroad."

"You sure you won't come with me?"

"I can't. Listen, the only way to get them off our backs is to give them what they want. And we can do that from here if I come up with a job."

And that's how we leave it. We finish the few cans I have left in the fridge and avoid the subject. Neither of us wants to think about it any more.

****

Chapter 8 (Part I) ~ Gorilla ~

~ Mo ~

When we told Cornelius that Pinchbeck's business success was a front he blew his stack. Said that between us we had him stumbling towards his deadline now a ridiculous nine grand short and that he'd be the fool for none of us. So while he and Harvey try to squeeze another few grand from the businesses here I am, sat in a blue Vauxhall Astra a little down the street from Sali Alonso's gaff in all that remains of Tuesday afternoon. Harvey said I might appreciate a spell behind the wheel. A sly reference to the regular checks I need to pass to ensure my eyesight is good enough to retain a licence. The car isn't mine; it's from Cornelius's pool of run-arounds. It's a decent enough runner, but it stinks to high heaven and the radio slips off station so often I've given up on it. I'm bored out of my skull with inactivity having spent part of Sunday and Monday in much the same way outside Sali's antiques business while Mickey sat where I'm at now.

For my part it all seems so desperate, all this hassle for nine grand? Harvey said it to wind Mickey up but he has a point: Con could sell his Beamer, his X5; he'd get twenty-five 'k' for it tomorrow if he was that desperate. That would put an end to all this pissing around. Maybe he can't afford to be seen struggling; maybe he's worried about loss of face? I don't know; but all this grief over nine grand; and for what? To hand it over to Sholto Carnie and claim it's a great investment? Do me a favour. Carnie's a disaster waiting to happen, and in his heart of hearts Con knows it. If you ask me, Con won't sell his Beamer 'cos he knows it might be all he has left after this deal. That said, Cornelius has my respect, he's always done all right by me.

I close my eyes, push the fingers of both hands under my glasses, massage my eyeballs and let out a sigh. All this sitting around isn't good, too much time on my hands, too much negativity creeping in. I jump, startled by the ring tone of my own mobile in my breast pocket. It's Harvey telling me I've got to get back to Moods. I ask if he's arranging for cover at Sali's but he ignores the question and tells me just to get my arse in gear. His tone suggests this is no celebratory get together.

At Moods I take a shortcut through the bar giving a cursory nod to the barman as I make for the corridor and the back stairs. Again it crosses my mind that if only the barman were too busy to make eye contact then none of this nonsense would be necessary. Harvey would no doubt whine at me saying *it's a Tuesday for fuck's sake what do you expect?* In the corridor I glance left, Rats is standing by the main door. He has one hand thrust into the pocket of his tired leather jacket while the other is thrown over his shoulder playing with his ponytail. He turns in time to spot me cutting through and rushes after me.

"Hey, I was sent down to look for you."

"Well done, you found me," I tell him, then take the stairs two at a time, but he's anxious to keep up.

"Cornelius is really pissed. What's going on?"

I ignore the little shit's question and carry on until I reach the upper floor. "Are they in Con's office?"

He slows now that I've stopped and takes the last few steps casually, shaking his head and tutting. "You've fucked up haven't you? What's happened? Maybe I can help."

The effort of climbing the stairs puts me in mind of my exercise routine but what's running through my mind might not be the best course of action. He's looking at me wide eyed, his lips parted in an expectant grin, like I'm about to tell him some great secret. The stairwell's fluorescent lighting bounces off his pitted, oily cheeks and for the second time inside a minute I wonder if anyone would really care if I thumped him, just one right hander. But instead I reach out and grab a fistful of his shirt, balling it tight in my hand and yank him toward me. I raise my shades with my other hand and look down into his eyes, "Con's office?" He nods, his grin remains fixed but that's not what gets me. I've had a lifetime of reading reactions in people's eyes and the fear I expect to see in his just isn't there. I toss him away like some screwed up newspaper I've no more use for and he collapses in a tangle of limbs against the stairway railing.

"Aw don't get upset, Mo," he says sarcastically, "I'm only trying to be your buddy."

I tug my glasses back down and go through the double doors leaving Rats struggling to get up from the floor. But midway down the corridor I stop and strain to listen. I can't quite believe it but he's laughing, the little bastard's laughing.

At Cornelius's office I knock and enter without waiting for a reply. The room is thick with cigar smoke and Con is sat behind his walnut desk hunched over the table all tight and humourless. Harvey and Mickey sit facing him but the look on their faces as they turn toward me tells me that right now they'd kill to get out of there.

Cornelius beckons me in then fixes me with a glare. "Mo, it's the dog's fekken tail that you are, but at least we can get things moving now you're here."

He doesn't speak to me like this unless he's in a foul

temper and only then if I've fucked up. I cast a quizzical glance toward Harvey but he's giving nothing away. After the experience with Rats things are just too weird, so I speak up. "I don't get it, what's going on?"

Cornelius throws me a disgusted look then turns to Harvey. "He doesn't get it." But he's no sooner glanced at Harvey's than he's spinning back in my direction, shooting up from his chair so its legs rasp across the linoleum floor. "No loose ends! Do it right! Did I not say that?"

I'm still lost and stare back at him blankly.

"It's what I said now, wasn't it?" he yells.

"Sure, boss."

"That much we're agreed on then, grand so. But tell me why it is that you and Mickey here wasted the last two fekken days watching Alonso's home and work when the poor bastard was roasting in hell not ten minutes after you left him?"

"The old man's dead?"

Con's face is scarlet; the veins at his temples pulse. "Isn't that what I'm just after telling you? You snipped his fekken finger off and the bastard keeled into a ditch not five hundred yards from where you left him. They found his body yesterday, cold as a witch's tit. Cutting his bloody finger off might have got us what he had on him but it's slammed the fekken door to anything else he had stashed. Now if either you or Mickey had just checked if his car had moved we wouldn't have lost a few days, I wouldn't owe some slimy sergeant a favour and we might have covered our tracks a bit better. As it is we're in the lap of the fekken Gods."

There's nothing I can come back with I just stand there, head bowed, and take my licks. When Cornelius is on a roll it's best to let him get it over with. My chin is all but resting on my chest and I notice my three piece suit is in bit of a state; my waistcoat resembles a concertina and my trousers are no better. That's what happens when you sit in a car for the best part of two days. An image of Alonso jumps into my head; he's in his suit in the back of the car gripping his forearm when he should be gripping his hand. The old bastard was having a heart attack and none of us realised. No point in saying now.

I raise my head in time to see Con run a hand through his thinning hair and sit down. There aren't any free seats so I remain standing, not that it'll be an advantage in any further discussions, it's impossible to talk down to anyone when you've been made to feel two inches tall. Now I know why Harvey offered no clues, Mickey probably copped his blast earlier and Harvey didn't want any of the smelly stuff sticking to him. Can't say I blame him.

"So," Con says. "Nine grand short and the final payment is due next week; any suggestions?"

An early chance to redeem myself and for a brief second I think of the X5, but just as quickly I dismiss the idea. Then I remember what Con and Harvey were meant to be doing while Mickey and I were sat on our backsides. "Can we get any more from the businesses?"

Con doesn't lift his eyes from his desk; his tone is resigned and tired, like he's been over this a hundred times with Mickey. "Loan Solutions has no funds to bring in business just now, there's nothing it can offer. Moods has been running promotions for weeks to get bodies through the doors; but we're at the point where doing more is likely to cost as much as it'll bring in. The only scope we have is at Calendar Girls. Benny's already had the girls working double shifts and though we said to ease off we've had to renege on that today and ask him to keep them going. Even so, all that's likely to bring in is an extra grand, two at most – nowhere near what we need."

Harvey shifts in his seat. "Looks like we'll need our insurance fallback after all."

"Colin Strath's little caper ?" Con asks.

"Hmm," Harvey nods. "Mo and I tracked down one of the gang and said we'd settle for ten grand by the end of the week. It'll work out nicely assuming they come through."

Cornelius frowns. "Just how likely is that though?"

Harvey purses his lips and exhales with a loud whoosh. "It's hard to say, boss, we did enough to scare him without going too far but these guys are small time. They may have to sell something or pull off another job to come up with the cash."

Con stares into space pulling at his bottom lip while Harvey hangs on his next words. Mickey hasn't said a word since I came in and he doesn't look as though he's going to add anything now. Then Con tilts his head to the side; his eyes narrow behind the thick frames of his glasses. "There were three of them until Strath croaked, am I right?"

"Right," Harvey says.

"And you only got to the one guy, you say?"

"Rosewood," Harvey says folding his arms. "All we could manage in the time, boss."

Cornelius sighs. "Pity, if they both felt threatened they might be more likely to pull resources to come up with the money."

Harvey sits back in his seat, breaks his folded arms to cradle his jaw and scratch his goatee as he speaks. "Well, I did give Mo the address so he could look the other guy up after we'd finished with Pinchbeck but it seems he didn't go home that night. Could be that he's already done a runner."

Cornelius gives a disparaging shake of his head.

"That's not quite right," I hear myself saying. All three heads turn in my direction. "I broke into his place on Sunday night. I thought it was worth another try and sure enough he turned up."

"You never told me," Harvey says.

"Well, I should've been outside Alonso's antiques place in case *he* showed."

"Never mind that now," Con says. "Fair play to you, you've shown some initiative, so. Are these two working on getting our cash together or what?"

"I didn't ask questions, boss, just made it clear we know who they are and where to find them."

"Fair enough, a further reminder might nudge things along then," Con says, the tension easing out of his frame.

"I gave them a nudge all right," I say. Again, all three faces stare back at me, so I continue. "He all but puked when I forced Alonso's finger into his hand and left it with him. I said it would help focus their minds." I was pretty pleased with that sentence at the time and felt sure Con too would see how apt it had been.

But in the snap of a finger the tension returns to Con's body as he plants his elbows on the desk and buries his face into his clenched fists. "Holy Mary Mother of God, what the fekken hell did you do that for?"

I can't see the problem and glancing at Harvey and Mickey there's no help from them this time either. I'm confused, my head starts to nip – there's a headache on the way. I raise my voice perhaps a little more than is respectful. "All I did was up the anti; let 'em know we mean business. You just said yourself they needed to understand."

For the second time Con gets onto his feet. He rests his clenched fists on his desk and leans forward on them. "Yes, lad," he shouts through gritted teeth. "But I didn't say give them the evidence that connects us to the death of Sali fekken Alonso, did I?" He holds his position, his face purple with bubbles of saliva oozing from the corners of his mouth. The room falls silent and I hang my head. Another fuck-up, but I wasn't to know Sali was dead was I?

"Okay," Harvey says, "let's think about this." Con retakes his seat, dabs at the back of his neck with his handkerchief then mops his sweating brow.

"On the plus side," Harvey continues, "these guys haven't scarpered and they'll realise we're not messing about. On the other hand they've now got something which could tie us to Alonso's death, but only if they they've heard about Alonso and we don't know that it's public knowledge yet or even if the fact that he's missing a finger will be mentioned." From either side of the desk both Con and Mickey nod in the face of Harvey's logic. "We should also consider," Harvey says, "just how likely it is that these guys would go to the police. They'd need to be pretty scared; the police would want to know why they were being threatened. They'd need to come clean about the job they were going to pull."

Con stares into his desk, weighing it up for a moment or two. "You're probably right at that, Harvey lad. But all the same we can't take the chance. Rosewood's the one you tackled first and agreed the sum with, am I right?"

"Yes."

"Then it's decided," Con says. "Catch up with this other guy; he can be our guest until Rosewood makes good with the cash. And don't be hanging onto that ruddy keepsake. If the little bastard's still got it then you get rid of the fekken thing, am I clear?"

Harvey nods. "Where do we take him?"

"You'll think of somewhere," Con says. Then he extends an arm, and points at me. "Just make sure *he* doesn't screw up again." He looks me in the face, his eyes drop to his arm then to his own wagging finger and the irony hits him. He pulls it back quicker than a kid caught shoving a hand through the monkey cage at the zoo. And that's how he's makes me feel right now, like some mindless gorilla he can't trust to do anything right, one with the strength to rip his arm clean out of its socket.

I trudge downstairs to Moods bar. I'm going to pick up an OJ and then hit the snooker room. But when I turn into the bar Rats is there again, picking a glass from the overhead rack and turning back to the optics. Where does Con get off giving me a bollocking like that when he has a shifty little bastard like Rats doing sweet FA and helping himself to his booze at the same time? I spin around and head back upstairs.

****

Chapter 8 ~ (Part II) ~Blood matters ~

~ Mo ~

I'm half way though a frame in the snooker room when Harvey sticks his head around the door. His eyes fall across the table, the spread of the balls enough to tell him that power, not finesse, has been my game play.

"You okay?" he asks.

"I've a headache. I'm taking it out on the balls."

He takes a couple of paces in and lets the door close behind him. "Listen, Cornelius was a bit hard on you but you can see how stressed he is."

The cue balances in the palm my right hand; I let it spill across my fingers as though I'm about to let it drop and at the last moment flick my finger tips sending it spinning in a small arc back into my palm. "Sure," I tell him.

"I got him to drop Mickey."

The news seems to bounce off the insides of my skull before I grasp it. I straighten up and face him. "What for?"

"Alonso and Pinchbeck were Mickey's prospects; they're not in the picture any more so he needn't be either. The play's on our turf now." He forces a laugh, "Con's gonna give him some hard sums to do, it'll keep him out of our hair. Next bit's just you and me, we'll sort it."

"So what's the plan?"

He closes the gap between us and throws his arm around my shoulder pulling me into him. "We snatch the guy tomorrow. Pick him off on his way to work, I've got the details."

"Why not now? I could use the release."

He relaxes his grip, lets his arm drop. "Cos we're gonna take him to the lockup, but you've seen it; it's not up to holding someone for days. Needs a few home comforts first."

"So we ready it tonight and lift the guy tomorrow?"

Harvey purses his lips. "Someone else will see to the lockup. We've some unwinding to do. Con's idea; all work, no play and all that. He reckons it's taken the edge off our game. I've reserved us a table at nine - Giuseppe's."

I feel his arm on my shoulder again and he begins walking me to the door. I drop my cue on the table and glance at my watch. "It's not even half seven?"

"Yeah, but we need to get changed. We can't arrive at Giuseppe's stinking of cigarette smoke and cat piss."

"Eh?"

"Those old cars of Con's; you never know who or what was last in 'em. And look at the state of your suit. Any longer getting it to the laundry and it'll be stiff enough to walk there on its own."

He's lost me but I'm not going to argue with him. Giuseppe's Restaurante Italiano is his personal favourite and he makes an occasion out of each and every visit. It won't hurt to humour him and already I'm planning to squeeze in five minutes at home on the punch ball to clear my head of this nagging ache.

In the car he slips on a Vivaldi CD but immediately begins to talk over it, prattling on about the importance of image, how the way we carry ourselves and behave in public says everything about who we are. How belief in our authority is self fulfilling, or something like that. He's on his soap box; I nod every now and then. I've heard it so often it's become supermarket music playing in the background to a disinterested audience. But I can overlook that and all the other shit too. The moment he said the edge was off *our* game I knew he'd stood up for me. Harvey can be a tosser, but he's blood to me.

I'd concede that Giuseppe's is all that Harvey makes it out to be. He jabbers on about its little touches of class, like the complementary aperitifs and the unhurried ambiance. But once the plates are cleared away and the waiters leave us undisturbed, the grin that's been on Harvey's lips all night tires and he gets all serious on me.

"You are okay aren't you, Mo? You'd tell me if something changed, right?"

"What d'you mean?"

"That business with the finger..," he says, frowning, as if the word itself now has a stigma.

I keep my voice low. "The guy was being disrespectful, Harvey. It's not like I planned it or anything."

"Not Alonso," he says. "I mean leaving the bloody thing with the guy from our insurance job. What were you thinking?"

I shrug. "It was just an impulse. It worked with Pinchbeck."

"Yeah, but you didn't leave it with him."

I glare at him, squinting behind my shades. "You're saying it was stupid?"

His eyes avoid me; he runs his fingers back through his hair. "I'm saying it wasn't one of your better decisions." He lets it hang for a second, takes a sip of his Rioja. "You'd tell me if you were taking anything again?"

"Now hold on. Do you think I want to feed more money to that bastard Carnie?"

"No," he says and hurries another sip from his glass. "But I could understand your frustration. After all, trying to build a tolerance to your sensitivity just hasn't worked."

I straighten in my seat. I wasn't expecting any of this. I'm unprepared.

He leans across the table. "You think I don't see it when we play a frame? Sure, you hold out a little longer each time but that's just you being bullish. I can spot it kicking in; can see you twitch as it bites deeper. It backs you into a corner until you make a rash decision." He sets his glass down and leans back in his seat. "I'm just voicing a little concern, bruv."

I rest my elbows on the table, lean into my hands and massage my temples. "Look, we've been through this. Using was a mistake. It just made things worse."

"A lot worse," he says. "When you came down you complained the headaches were more intense than they'd been to start off with. If not for that he'd have had you hooked."

"Don't think I don't know that."

"I asked around, Mo. Drugs and photophobia are a bad mix."

"I found out for myself, thanks. Look, I'm clean, okay, and it's got nothing to do with what's happening now. I'm impetuous, always have been. Don't make more of it than that."

"Are you sure?"

I raise my shades; let him see I'm looking him in the eye and tell him, yeah.

"Then I believe you," he says. "Now, we need to go. Don't want your treat getting cold."

"What treat?"

"Well you didn't think just grabbing a meal was us unwinding did you? C'mon, we're going to Benny's, there's a girl you've just got to meet."

I watch him stand, slip into his jacket and shoot his cuffs to settle it across his shoulders. I'm not sure I'm up for this. But as he runs his hands back through this hair again I can see how considerate he's been. He's looked out for me more than I realised. Blood means something to him too, and if this is how he wants us to unwind, so be it.

****

Chapter 9 ~ Mountebridge ~

~ Adam ~

I'm stuck in three lanes of motorway queues; caught up in the onset of rush hour traffic wondering why I'm snarled up like this when I had all day to get organised. Of course, I'm surrounded by the whys and wherefores and my thoughts jump back and forth weighing time well spent, and not. Folded on the passenger seat are a couple of casual jackets, one light the other padded. In the back, with the rear seats folded forward to make room, are a couple of pairs of shoes sitting on top of my canvas holdall. I'm travelling light with perhaps only four or five changes of clothes. It took me an eternity to decide what to take and what to leave. To be fair an unreasonable chunk of space is given over to shampoos, deodorants, aftershave and hair gel - a consequence of my job I suppose, or more accurately my fixation with scrubbing myself clean of it. Then there are essentials like the chargers for my shaver, mobile and ipod. I need to remember to pick up an adaptor at the ferry port terminal or all three will die on me and I'll need to change my sterling into euros too.

The morning timetable included a trip to the bank to withdraw what was left in my account - I asked for euros, but they need notice – so I continued on and paid my rent. My thinking being that, whatever happened, I'd not overspend to the point where I daren't return to the flat for fear of bumping into the landlord. But after that, when I looked at just what I was left with, I knew I'd be struggling to cope for a couple of weeks, even if I found a cheap B&B. Hence the unplanned expedition in the high street resulting in the clutter of equipment that now sits behind me. I've become the completely underwhelmed owner of a dome tent, sleeping bag, primus stove and various other apparently indispensable camping accessories. Despite never having spent so much as a single night under canvas there have to be at least two positives. Firstly, my money will go further at campsites than at hotels or B&B's. Secondly, and maybe more importantly, if I didn't know I was heading for a French campsite until two hours ago then no-one else will either. If it comes to it, I don't even know which site I'm going to – I'll just drive until I find one.

The queues edge forwards, twenty yards every other minute, or so it seems. My eyes shift to the clock in the centre of the dashboard, it's ten after five. I didn't even get around to checking the ferry departure times but I expect the crossings will be pretty regular and even if I need to get my head down in the jeep for a few hours it'll be no real hardship. I flick on the radio and scan the stations until I find something soulful, resigned now to the journey taking as long as it takes.

After a further half hour of stop-start driving I'm past the worst of it and once again moving at motorway speeds, or as close as is comfortable for my aged Daihatsu. A car blasts past in the outside lane tooting its horn. I look on, frowning, I don't know what his problem is, but then maybe it wasn't meant for me. Moments later, in the rear view mirror, I see the car behind flash me before pulling out to pass and that's when I feel the tremor in the steering. He draws alongside and the passenger jabs a finger repeatedly toward my offside rear wheel.

I park up on the hard shoulder and climb out. Traffic screams past, the draught rocking the jeep, forcing me to squint. But the damage is plain enough; it's almost pancake flat and the tyre wall itself is lined and cracked, completely wrecked. I'm surprised I didn't feel the jeep pulling earlier. If anything it looks worse once I've broken out the jack and removed the wheel. I need to find a garage and have it replaced. It'd be asking for trouble to catch the ferry without a reliable spare.

Twenty minutes later I'm easing back into the traffic; on the radio Sheryl Crow belts out 'Run Baby Run' – a reminder I can do without. I switch stations and find something that's soothing without being catchy, more background music than sing-along, the kind you can almost forget is there at all. Soon my thoughts slip into automatic and I imagine how I'd have coped had my mishap happened on French roads. I dredge my memory for old schoolboy French and settle on – *Pardon, monsieur. Mon pneu est en casse.* I surprise myself believing this is close enough to make myself understood. I've a smile on my face as the first fifty yards of an exit slipway passes by. I'm toying with the idea of pressing on, just finding a garage in Ramsgate. But as the slipway nears its end I think *what the heck* and swerve across the chevrons to make the turn. It earns me a blast from the guy behind and I give him a middle finger response before realising that he's got a point. I slow into the wide left hand turn that leads me back onto a single lane carriageway. A road sign lists a few place names I've never heard of and I'm just four miles outside the first, Lower Weaton – wherever that is.

It's a relentlessly dull stretch of road. Hedges rise on either side allowing mere flashes of the open fields that lie behind them. Within a minute or two the strangest feeling overtakes me. Black tarmac stretches unbending into the distance, its end lost in a copse of trees low on the horizon. The hedgerows are green walls skipping past my side windows and the way ahead narrows until it feels like I'm in a long, tapering funnel, being drawn forward, about to spill over the edge of some vast chasm of … nothingness.

Before I reach the trees a signpost on the left rushes to meet me, shaking me from lethargy; it's festooned in coloured ribbons and reads - Welcome to Lower Weaton ~

Twinned with Ville De Paix. A few yards further there's another, a home-made placard this time proclaiming The Five Villages Spring Festival.

The hedgerows give way to trees then the road banks to the right, cutting into the copse, and the village it enshrouds opens up before me. Small timber-clad bungalows are scattered along the outer edges. But ahead stands an imposing red brick hotel with a crush of people gathered outside and overflowing into the road. The crowd parts as I slow and it becomes clear that the way ahead is blocked, cordoned off by makeshift barriers; the streets have been pedestrianised for the festival. I brake to a stop, searching for somewhere to pull over. For the first time I notice cars straddling the grass verges, it seems normal parking restrictions have been relaxed; I edge the Sportrak onto the pavement and crawl onto the verge alongside a rather splendid silver Lexus.

I tug on the light casual jacket from the passenger seat and walk towards what appears to be the main street, glancing first at The Weaton Arms Hotel on the right. It's not short on custom, tables in the concrete 'beer garden' out front are fully occupied and the bar doors are wedged open allowing the strains of country and western music to filter out. I'm unlikely to resolve my tyre problem before morning but already I know I won't be lodging at The Weaton Arms.

The main street runs diagonally left of the hotel exposing only its barricaded tail end to view. Tiles inlayed into the red brickwork of the final house identify the street as Hope Road. The buildings are terraced and much older than the timber-clad homes I passed at the village boundary. But only once I'm on Hope Road can I look down its length and take in the multitude of sights, sounds and activity. Bunting criss-crosses the street from upper window to upper window and the roadway is given over to a street market. There can't be a soul in the village that remains indoors for the thoroughfare is a mass of shifting bodies. Voices ring out from all directions as stallholders and street musicians vie for attention. It makes The Weaton Arms look like a peaceful retreat after all.

Once more I find myself queuing as I shuffle from stall to stall and I regret pulling on my jacket. The slight chill in the evening air is unnoticed in the heat generated by the sheer numbers converging in such a small area.

The stalls themselves seem fairly typical selling bric-a-brac, crafts, home made preserves and hot food and drink but the side streets hold much more interest. I wander along munching on toasted sandwiches and watch children and adults pay to fire arrows at a target in an alleyway between houses. It's maybe a sick indulgence on my part as I can't help wondering whether anyone will try to enter the alleyway from the rear of the houses while the contest continues. In time I move on to another side street where some unfortunate creature has been locked in a set of stocks while people pay to throw wet sponges at him. I linger, watching a teenager pay her money and dip her first sponge in the bucket of water.

"Give it yer best shot," the man in the stocks yells.

The young girl steps up to the mark - some eight feet distant - takes aim and throws. But the dripping sponge sails high and wide. The assembled throng give a collective howl of disappointment. She takes a second sponge from the pile, dips it and tries again. Another miss and another low moan from the gathered multitude.

"Last chance," shouts the man in the stocks. "You couldn't smack your own backside."

This raises a few laughs amongst the onlookers. The girl prepares to dip her sponge but instead grabs the bucket and sprints the short distance to heave the contents into the face of the trapped man. The crowd erupt in laughter and it brings a broad smile to my face too.

Enjoyable as this is I realise I'm not making any progress on finding a garage so I pick up my pace side stepping bodies and squeezing past queuing numbers at the stalls. I'm concentrating so hard on moving forward that as space opens up I move into it without thinking. It doesn't occur to me that people are parting like the pages of a book for a reason. I step past someone and I'm almost knocked to the ground by a young lad skipping through the crowds at speed. My arms enfold him in an automatic reaction, but he's more interested in what's over his shoulder than in meeting my eyes. I look past to see his three teenage pursuers come to a halt an arm's length away.

"Is there a problem?" I ask.

They look at each other, back to me then finally at the boy. "He's not from here, he's a Mounty."

"So? I'm not from here either," I tell them.

"But he was spying. And that ain't fair," one says. But they don't wait to explain, disappearing back into the crowd instead.

The youngster turns round to face me and I get a proper look at him. He's thin but in a wiry sort of way. His mousey brown hair is a little too long at the fringe and he gives a casual shake of his head to flick it aside revealing bright blue eyes that dance across my face, weighing me in an instant. He's probably in his early teens and looks full of mischief: the type of kid who has boundless energy and is hard to tie down; maybe a bit like I was myself.

"Thanks, that was cool," he says.

"What was?"

"Saying you weren't from here."

"But I'm not," I tell him.

"Yeah, it spooked 'em."

I smile, "I'm really not from here. I pulled off the motorway looking for a garage to repair a damaged tyre. Is there one here?"

"There's a petrol station," he says, "but they don't fix things. If you want that you'll need to go to a proper village."

"Such as?"

"Mounty, of course. We've got a garage."

"Is it far?"

"Only three miles, I can show you if you like."

We pick our way through the masses until we're at the end of Hope Road and across from The Weaton Arms.

"I'm parked on the grass verge along from the hotel. So what road do I take to find Mounty?"

He looks at me through narrowed eyes. "Aren't you giving me a lift back then? And it's Mountebridge, Mounty is just what we call it."

I hadn't realised he wanted a lift and I'm sure it shows on my face. I'd assumed all he'd intended was to point the way to Mounty, or Mountebridge as it seems it's called. Giving him a lift is something else all together.

"Aren't you here with your parents?"

"No, I came down on the bus. You can save me the fare back and I can show you the garage. Everybody wins."

I'm struggling. How do I put this? "What I'm saying is that you don't know me and getting into a car with…"

"You're not a weirdo or something, are you?"

"Of course not, but that doesn't make it right."

"What's your name?" he asks.

"Adam."

"I'm Joel. So you know who I am, I know who you are and…"

"Just a minute," I tell him. "It's not that simple, that's not nearly enough these days."

He lets out a deep sigh and reaches into his pocket. "Okay, will you give me a lift if my Ma says it's all right?"

I don't answer but he takes my silence as acceptance. He knows his mind this kid. He stabs at a button on his mobile and then waits. I have to admit I'm not exactly comfortable with the whole idea and maybe that's because I'm just not used to dealing with kids. Joel seems sufficiently streetwise and I'm sure he knows what I'm getting at, but right now he's the one coming up with plausible alternatives. After a moment his call is answered and I hear him make his play. He starts by saying that he's met a bloke at the Weaton festival who's looking for a garage. Says he can take him to Buckley's if it's okay for him to get a lift. There's a pause while he listens to the response, but when it comes it can't be positive as he launches into a stream of *but this* and *but that's* the gist of which suggest he's always been encouraged to bring people to the village. I let him get on with it and turn away feeling a slight tension lift from my shoulders.

When I turn back he's saying he can see him from here, then he hands me the phone. I stare at it blankly, he flicks his wrist a couple of times as if to say *hurry up, take it*. He waves across the street as I raise the mobile to my ear and say hello.

"Hello," the voice answers. "Sorry, who am I talking to?"

"My name's Adam."

"I'm so sorry, Mr. Adam. Has Joel foisted himself upon you?"

It's a sweet voice and full of concern, and she makes me feel that concern's for me rather than for Joel. I imagine she's been through every conceivable parenting worry so often that she's developed a second sense for these things.

"Not at all," I tell her, "he's been very helpful and I'd be happy to give him a lift. He's doing me a favour, after all, it's just that... well young kids and strangers, you can't be too careful."

"You're quite right. He knows better and I appreciate you having him call me. Has he got hold of Dave?"

I'm momentarily lost at her meaning but I turn to see that we've been joined by an overweight, shaven-headed guy wearing a black short-sleeved shirt *with* 'The Weaton Arms Hotel' embroidered in gold lettering over the breast pocket.

"Yes, this must be him now," I tell her. "Shall I pass you over?"

"No, there's no need. Dave lives here in Mountebridge but works in Lower Weaton. I know his shift ends soon but he'll knock off early and come with you as a favour to me. Not that you're untrustworthy, Mr. Adam. It's just how people in small places look out for one another."

I hand the phone back to Joel and smile at Dave but all the while I'm thinking about that *people in small places* comment, she made it sound like the Mafia in miniature; village size.

After throwing my padded jacket into the back Dave slides into the passenger seat; he doesn't seem the talkative kind. As I've folded up the rear seats I have to rearrange things so I can pull one of the seats back down to let Joel sit. He clambers in through the rear door and it perhaps provides some novelty value for him. As we hit the road Joel peers over my shoulder eyeing up the square dash and I can tell he's a little less than impressed with the Sportrak. He crinkles his nose like it gives off a bad smell though he's more than taken with the clinometer.

"That's for when it's off-road," Dave says, seeing Joel's eyes settle on it; then to me. "You do take it off-road, don't you?"

"Actually, I don't." I can almost pluck their disappointment from the air and try to recover. "It's great to know that I can if I need to though." But it's too late; any lingering chance of their being impressed by the Sportrak is gone and Dave has turned to look out of the passenger window. So before they hit me with anything else I go on a little offensive of my own.

"Tell me, Joel, what did you mean when you said I'd spooked those other kids?"

He looks at me as if I'm stupid. "The competition is judged by an outsider each year. It might have been you."

I'm none the wiser. "What competition would that be?"

Joel's nose crinkles again and I'm even dumber now. "The Five Villages Festival, of course."

"Oh, so why were they chasing you?"

He shrugs his shoulders. "I suppose they don't like us knowing what we've got to beat."

Dave sighs. "Same every bloody year."

"When's your festival then?"

"They change the order each year," Joel says. "Lower Weaton is first this year, Wingate's next, then Chillinghill, Foxburn and Mountebridge."

It's a winding road but one they've no doubt travelled often and like most kids Joel's attention span is short. He fidgets in his seat and with no interest in the view he's soon twisting round and squinting in the back.

"Hey, is that a tent? Are you going camping?"

"I was planning to before I had the flat."

"Cool," Joel says. "Where you going?"

I hesitate for a second. It's an innocent enough question but there's comfort for me in no-one knowing my plans. "I've nowhere special in mind. I just thought I'd drive until I found somewhere that took my fancy."

"We have a site. You could stay there," Joel says.

"You make it sound like it's the centre of the universe," I tell him. Joel smiles back at me, his sense of pride evident and I'm all at once ashamed for my sarcasm.

We pass the 'Welcome to Mountebridge' signpost – not twinned with anywhere by the looks – and I slow to pass over a hump-backed bridge fording a small stream. There's a steep incline before we turn sharp left into what I assume must be the main street. Shops, with living accommodation above, stretch out along the right-hand side while opposite them the full length of the street is given over to a large expanse of grassy lawn trimmed with a footpath. We trundle on in second gear. Wooden benches are spread evenly apart stretching into the distance; empty now but doubtless used by locals to watch life go by on warmer evenings than this. Behind the lawn, tall trees and the steep hill form a natural barrier between the village and the stream that I now know runs below. It seems to me that this area is intended to be the heart of the village but it's deserted. I'm about to say as much to Joel when there's some movement ahead.

"You can drop me here," Dave says. "You too, Joel, your mates are out front."

Looking forward, there's a large outdoor chess board set into the grass where a group of youngsters are gathered. I pull up and Dave climbs out then draws his seat forward so Joel too can scramble out. He makes to run off toward his mates then stops to yell back.

"Buckley's Garage is at the end of the street. It'll be closed now but if you need to stay over follow the road around and you'll find The Huntsman."

"Thanks for your help," I yell, but he's already gone. Dave closes the door, gives me a nod then crosses the street, content that his favour is done.

I watch Joel join the group of lads then pull away still casting an eye over the place. Beyond the outdoor chess board is a rather rickety-looking village hall, and further on a bowling green and then a bandstand that's seen better days.

At the end of the street the road banks to the right and I see Buckley's facing me across a little square. It's long closed, as Joel said it would be, but I pull up outside and climb out. Before I've even reached the pavement I see what I'm looking for. White lettering on a transfer stuck to the inside of the glass frontage; Tyres, Batteries and Exhausts – I'm in the right place.

The Huntsman is set off the road on the edge of what appears to be a residential area. I swing into its gravel car park and give it the once over. I don't know what I was expecting, perhaps the name suggests more character than is evident, but it's pretty nondescript, a grey building in a grey, backwater village. I retrieve my holdall from the back of the 4x4. There's not even a rustle from the leaves on the trees, the only sound the crunch beneath my feet as I make my way in. If I'd not seen the boys at the park I'd swear there was no-one alive in this place.

The reception area is brightly lit and I surprise the aged night porter poring over the crossword in his newspaper. He hastily folds it away and I tell him I need a room for the night, nothing fancy. When nothing fancy comes in at sixty quid I give serious thought to just getting my head down in the jeep in some lay-by. The porter, though, can see me wavering and softens the blow saying I won't find anything cheaper hereabouts and it includes the best 'Full English' for miles around. I relent and once I've registered he hands me my room key and says the bar through the back is busy but good for a nightcap. I thank him, I'm almost tempted to wander through just to see what passes for busy here.

Once in my room I let my holdall fall to the floor and sit on the edge of the bed bouncing lightly in the ridiculous way you do to test the mattress. I don't know what I'm expecting but it seems fine and the room itself is okay if a little musty-smelling. I walk over to the window and peer out. It's a front-facing room overlooking the car park, nothing moves. I draw the curtains and switch the TV on, more for the sake of background noise than anything else. I realise I've not had an evening meal. I'm not particularly hungry having had something from the stalls at Lower Weaton, but maybe I could pick at something. The room has no mini bar, but there's a kettle with tea, coffee and some cellophane-wrapped biscuits. I step into the bathroom; it's clean, uniform white with plenty of towels. The tub has an overhead shower – but I fit the stopper in the plughole and turn on the taps deciding a hot soak would make a nice change. I settle for a hot bath to be followed by coffee, dry biscuits and bed.

Maybe it's the country air, the effects of a relaxing soak, my subconscious thinking too deeply about the situation I'm in or a combination of all three; but as I drift off to sleep I feel myself slipping into a familiar dream as easily as an old pair of trainers. A dream, a memory – the distinction is lost on me. It used to haunt me, but there's no longer any shock value; it holds no surprises. I'm twelve years old and like every other day for the preceding five weeks Mrs. Thornton from the care home has picked me up from school and trailed me to the hospital to visit my mother. It's the last time I'll see her alive – my mother knows it, I sense that now, but no matter how many times it plays out in my head my twelve-year-old self never does.

****

Chapter 10 ~ Showtime ~

~ Mo ~

It's gone midnight when the taxi drops us off. Light drizzle hangs in the air like a mist, visible in the glow of the shimmering sign that advertises Calendar Girls as a Gentleman's Club. It strikes me that I've never seen any of those inside and I almost smile, enjoying my own joke. A few glasses of wine have mellowed me; this doesn't feel like such a bad idea any more. I hurry the short distance to the entrance, step inside and hold the door for Harvey. He walks at normal pace; he'll take a light dusting of rain in preference to anyone seeing him run.

In the foyer I nod to the girl in the booth who takes money at the door. I don't come often enough to recall her name but she knows who we are. She waves us through, suggesting we sit at the bar while she gets hold of Benny. Harvey dabs at his face with his handkerchief then runs a hand through his hair, his grin is back. I follow his lead and wipe the drizzle from my shades. The girl in the booth mouths *fuck me*; but it's not a request. Unable to turn away she knows I've caught her staring. Normally I'd be riled, but tonight I let it pass.

Beyond the foyer the building opens out. We move off to the left and climb half a dozen steps to the bar area. Here, men stand in clusters with drinks in hand; most are laughing and joking but one or two eye us with suspicion, perhaps deciding if the new arrivals might recognise them. Near-naked girls slide between the groups, eager to sell them a dance. We pick a table and sit.

"Shouldn't we order a drink?" I ask.

Harvey's craning his neck checking out each of the girls in turn. "No, let's not mix our drinks. I'll have Benny get us a bottle of wine when he comes down."

"Which one is she, then?"

"Myrna? She doesn't flash her backside out here; she's more like the cabaret. You'll see."

Together we watch a high cheek-boned brunette leading some bloke to a cubicle for a private dance as Benny McGinn slips into the seat beside us.

Benny follows our gaze. "That's Katya; she's from Warsaw, fabulous body." He extends his hand to each of us in turn. A squat guy, Benny's in his early fifties with an earthy rasp to his voice; probably the legacy of a lifetime spent in smoke-filled rooms. He's run everything from topless bars to escort agencies and strip clubs for Con over the last twelve years.

"Business picking up, or shouldn't I ask?" Harvey says.

Benny's eyes scan the bar area like he's suggesting we take a good look around. "We can only do what we can. Put it this way. I don't want another month like the last one."

Harvey nods. "It's been hard on us all."

"Anyway, aren't you guys having a drink?" Benny asks.

"Yeah, we're gonna party a little as long as you don't rip us off," Harvey says.

"As if?" Benny says and calls a barman while Harvey tells him any Rioja will do.

"Are Myrna and Faith around?" Harvey asks.

Benny winks, "revved up and ready to blow your socks off. C'mon, I've put you in the pole room. We don't normally allow drinks in there but as it's just the two of you it should be okay. I'll have the barman bring you the wine."

We follow Benny down the stairs, past the foyer into a small anteroom. A pink stage runs down the middle from a circular, curtained doorway; like a fat tongue spat from a gaping mouth. There are maybe ten seats scattered either side of the stage. It's only when he sits us beside it that I notice the glitter-clad pole rising from stage to ceiling at the tip of the tongue, so-to-speak.

"This new, Benny?" I ask.

"Shit, Mo, you need to get out more. Been like this for eight months. Anyway, what did you do to get Myrna so fired up? The randy bitch has been rattling my cage about you this last week."

Harvey and Benny look at me, expecting an answer. "I dunno, I've never met her."

Benny shrugs. "Well, the girls' shift is finished after this so they'll be free to have a few drinks with you if you wish. Enjoy."

Benny leaves us and a moment later the barman arrives with a small folding table tucked under his arm. He balances a tray in his other hand and puts it on the stage. Then he sets the table up between us and finally moves the bottle and glasses to it. Harvey finishes pouring as music filters from the speakers concealed in the side of the stage and in the ceiling above.

"Showtime," he says, beaming.

A silver-haired girl pirouettes through the curtained doorway to a shower of sparks. Her silver boots finish above the knee and she's dressed in what looks to be a tin-foil strip. It's wound around her from the tops of her thighs to the tip of her left shoulder, alternately encasing then exposing strips of naked, pink flesh. She gyrates to the beat of the music, moving ever closer to the pole. She's a pencil-slim, wisp of a girl, but tall; elegant yet leggy. Harvey lets out a low groan.

"Is this her?" He's too involved to answer.

As the tempo climbs she spins around the pole, rubbing her body up and down its length. Then, from a position at the base of the pole, she reaches up, grabs it with both hands and upends herself to wrap her legs around it. She inches up until she's able to lock her ankles around the uppermost part and release her hands to drape herself upside down, her arms and upper body still swaying to the beat. I realise I'm holding my breath.

The music changes and she rights herself, dropping to spread face-down on the stage floor. She stretches out her arms, raises herself using only her stomach muscles and writhes to the rhythm, carefully peeling the foil from her shoulder. Face-down again she traps the foil between her left hand and the stage then rolls slowly to her right unwrapping herself. She continues, trap and roll, spinning away, arching her body up at each turn, revealing her increasing nakedness. I feel a stirring in my groin; she's good, more than good. When she heads through the curtains Harvey is already on his feet applauding.

He turns to me. "What about that? Pretty fucking fantastic, eh?"

"Fantastic," I agree. "Was that her?"

"That was Faith. Myrna will be next." He drains his

glass and pours himself another. He looks at me and smirks. "They'll give us a couple of minutes to let us calm down."

"She must practise a lot. You need strong stomach muscles to do that."

"Sod her stomach muscles. I just want to fuck her. Have since I laid eyes on her."

"I was right then? She won't play ball unless you find someone for her friend."

Harvey throws me a look, like I should be grateful. "Don't worry, you won't be disappointed, bruv."

The music picks up again and Myrna steps out from behind the curtain. Blonde curls spill out from the neat hat she wears. Not nearly as tall as Faith, she's dressed in a tight nurse's tunic that halts just above the tops of her white stockings. She's a busty girl; her breasts strain at the front of her uniform and when she draws her arms together, pushing them forward, it's almost too much for the thin material; she has us both on the edge of our seats. In no time at all she's spinning around the pole every bit as energetically as Faith before her. Her eyes find me; leaving me only as she turns, but locking onto me as she comes around again. She lowers herself to the floor until she's doing the splits just inches away from me. Then she rolls flat onto her front, feet toward me, and draws her knees in until she's face down on the floor with her buttocks raised high in the air. She tilts her head around to watch me ogling the cheeks of her arse, then pouts at me; all but daring me to caress it. It's almost more than I can stand.

I feel the heat of Harvey's eyes too and turn to look at him. He's watching me, a broad smile on his face. He can see the effect Myrna's having on me; can see his plans falling into place. When I look back to Myrna she's standing facing me, her tunic on the floor. The pace of the music has slowed and she kneels, moves both hands behind her back and undoes her bra and then slides her arms out from the straps. She leans forward; cupping her hands over her breasts and teases the material away. Her heavy breasts spill free and she discards the bra, stretches out and lifts the shades from my face. I catch my breath, but I let her do this. She dons them herself and stares back at me, swaying. I wait for a reaction, but there is none. Instead she moves elegantly into a sitting position, lies flat on her back at right angles to us and raises her legs. Her hands slip into her panties and she slides them from her hips, lifting her buttocks to ease them past and rolling them down her stockinged thighs; all the time looking at me rather than at what she's doing. I swallow hard. She frees first one leg then the other as the music dies away. When she stands, she's no more than two feet from me wearing only stockings, heels, my shades and a smile. She dips forward to throw something and I look down as her knickers land in my lap like a tangle of bootlaces. But when I look up she's gone and Harvey again is on his feet clapping, but I'm so hard I daren't stand.

"What do you think?" Harvey asks. "Is she a treat or what?"

"She's terrific and she's got my fucking shades."

"Yeah, clever bitch doesn't want you to go before she can give 'em back to you."

"You think so?"

"Are you kidding?" Harvey asks. "She didn't take her eyes off you the whole time and then threw you her biffs. How green does the light need to be?"

I'm sure he's right but he takes my silence to mean I'm not convinced.

"Look, these girls work odd hours, they don't get to socialize much. To regular punters they're like untouchable, unapproachable. But they're human. They get as horny watching our reactions as we get watching them. They're gagging for it. What d'you say?"

I look him in the eye, "I say yes, please."

Harvey doesn't mess about. He heads off to square the drinks and the show with Benny, and to arrange a taxi. I wait in the pole room alone and rub my tired eyes.

"I've got something for you."

The voice catches me by surprise. When I look up Myrna stands before me, Faith a step behind. They're in their street clothes but are none the less startling. Faith looks slightly different, it's probably her short dark hair after the silver wig; Myrna I'd recognise anywhere now. She's even prettier close-up, fresh-faced, a little rouge bringing colour to her cheeks - not overdone like some I've seen. I'd say she was mid-twenties, maybe less.

I'd stuffed her panties in the inside pocket of my jacket; I dig them out and offer them to her. "Want to swap?" I ask.

She smiles, places the folded shades in my outstretched hand and folds the panties into the small clutch bag she carries. "Thank-you," she says. Her nose crinkles as she speaks, it's sort of cute. She pulls up a chair as I slip my shades back on.

Faith leans against the stage. "Where's Harvey?" she asks.

"He's gone to pay Benny for the show."

"Did you enjoy it?" Myrna asks.

"Very much." An awkward silence follows. My answer doesn't feel enough somehow. I turn to Faith. "I mean, I said to Harvey, that bit where you raised yourself off the floor. You must have worked on your stomach muscles to do that, it's not easy."

She smiles at Myrna. "See, I told you."

"Told you what?" I ask.

Myrna leans toward me, places the palm of her hand on my chest and lightly traces a figure of eight. "She knows I have a thing for muscle-bound men. Do you work out, Mo?"

My chest tingles at the lightness of her touch. I make to answer but she leans in and kisses me, her sweet lips covering mine and her tongue slipping into my mouth. I kiss back pushing my own tongue into her mouth but she pulls back, sucking my tongue before releasing me.

"Oh, you'll do," she says.

The door opens and each of us turn to see Harvey march in. His face lights up. "Girls, fabulous show. I've got a taxi outside, do you fancy a club or maybe you'd prefer just to have a few drinks back at our place?"

Barely a word is spoken in the seven-seater taxi. From over my shoulder Faith has her tongue so far down Harvey's throat it's like she's sucking the life from him. Myrna reclaims my attention, shushes my attempts at small talk and runs her hands across my chest then inside the sleeves of my jacket running down to my biceps. I'll give him his due; it seems Harvey has never been more right, these girls are on heat. When we arrive at our end-terrace maisonette any pretence at drinks as a foursome is forgotten. Harvey and Faith close the door of his ground floor flat leaving us to take the stairs at the side to my own one above. I lead Myrna by the hand, not that she needs encouragement.

Myrna looks around the living room while I fetch us some drinks. When I return she's relaxing on the sofa. I hand her a glass. "Vodka and lemonade, all right?"

"Fine," she says, "what's that you've got?"

I feel almost embarrassed as I set it on the table. "It's an OJ, I'm afraid I've had enough."

"Don't apologise for knowing your limit." She smiles, and pats the seat. "Come and sit with me."

I set my glass on the table, slide out of my jacket and lay it aside before sitting. I move to take off my shades too then falter, no longer sure how I should act in my own house. "Do you mind if I..."

"Of course not," she interrupts, her free hand touching my wrist for a moment. "I don't mind your eyes, really. I've had my share of good-looking guys, Mo, and you know what — they're conceited and boring as hell. But I've a good feeling about you, you're different."

Her touch is like an electric charge, the hairs on my arm and neck are standing on end. I should say something, but what? I'm still thinking when she speaks again.

"Are you into Gothic?"

"No, I just find the dark colours easier on my eyes."

"Not the décor," she says. "Your DVDs. They're all a bit dark and sinister."

"I prefer unlikely heroes, anti-heroes I suppose you'd call them." She smiles, and again I'm lost, desperate to move things forward without quite knowing how. "Look, Myrna, I really like you but I'm not used to this kind of situation. My condition puts people off."

She drains her glass and puts it on the table. Then she leans across and kisses me; her tongue forcing my lips apart and invading my mouth. When we come up for air she pulls back, and glances over at the bed. She takes my hand, stands and leads me across. My mouth is dry and there's an ache in my groin. We kiss again by the bed and when we surface again I tell her how much I want to fuck her.

She shoves me firmly in the chest and I stumble back onto the bed. "That's not how it works with me."

I raise myself off the bed digging my elbows into the satin sheets. "What do you mean?"

"Take your clothes off. You'll see," she says, spinning back towards the sofa. She delves into her clutch bag and for a second I feel exposed, but when she turns she holds a small bottle. She tosses it onto the bed and begins to undress. "What are you waiting for? Strip!"

I lie on the bed and she climbs on top of me, sitting astride my thighs. She runs her hands from my shoulders to my groin, slowly building a rhythm. Then she splashes me with liniment from the bottle and oils me up, concentrating in turn on my shoulders, biceps, pectorals and the solid muscle at my stomach.

"Enjoying it?" she asks.

"Sure."

"Then take some oil, you can rub it into me too."

I coat my hands with a few drops of liniment and massage her breasts and she squirms and pushes herself into my hands. She begins to groan and leans forward until she can whisper in my ear.

"I don't want you to fuck me, Mo. It only works for

me if I fuck you." She edges forwards, reaches back and guides me into her, then arches back.

I watch her for minute upon minute; her eyes shut tight, her hands roving over my chest and biceps, her face contorted in ecstasy. She grinds down on me until finally her nails dig into the flesh at my shoulders, riding me frantically until I explode into her.

When we're done, she rolls off and flops down beside me, breathing heavily. It's easily the most incredible sex I've ever had. Perhaps I should feel used. I think I realise why my condition doesn't bother her. She gets off on muscle and control, maybe even the smell of the liniment; it could be anyone underneath her closed eyes. It doesn't matter to me. I don't care, I just want more.

"Do you have anything?" She asks.

"Any what?"

She rolls back into me and kisses my neck. "Pills, hash, weed. Sometimes, when the sex is really good, I like to get high afterwards."

"I'm sorry, I don't have any."

She comes around quick, as though I've made some sort of judgement of her. "I'm not a user, not really, if that's what you're thinking?"

"I'm not thinking anything," I tell her but I can see she's not convinced. "I don't have anything so that I'm not tempted." I gesture to my face, "it makes me worse."

"Oh." She settles back but I can see she's thinking. "It is okay if I stay, isn't it? You don't want me to go now?"

"Stay," I tell her. "I want you to stay."

Chapter 11 ~ Fate ~

~ Adam ~

Wednesday and I take breakfast at 8am. The dining room is relatively quiet, no great surprise since all I've seen of Mountebridge 'til now suggests nothing ever happens here. The waitress - a middle-aged lady dressed in black skirt and waistcoat with a white blouse beneath - notes my room number and asks whether I'd like the 'Full English' or the Continental breakfast. After the recommendation there can only be one choice. She disappears back into the kitchen after I've selected coffee over tea, white toast over brown. I glance around at the other guests. There are five of us scattered in a room that could seat thirty. The three guys furthest away wear collar and tie, sit together and talk quietly. I suspect they're probably Reps of some sort. They're close to a breakfast bar I hadn't noticed before. It's laid out with juices, fruits, cereals and various breads, croissants and the like. It seems the Continental breakfast is self service. There's an older gentleman sitting three tables away. He's alone but at least he has a paper to read while he sips his coffee. The rich roast aroma has filled my nostrils for the past few minutes, it swayed my earlier decision.

The sound of heels on a polished wooden floor draws me back to my own table. I half expect to see the waitress returning with my breakfast but the click-clacking comes from just beyond the breakfast room. The reception area is screened by a couple of swing-doors covering three quarters of the door frame. They obscure whoever is responsible but tantalisingly afford sight of plain black heels, a pair of shapely calves rising from them. She moves out of view, the click-clack returns, now literally staccato but suggesting, to me at any rate, a measured and confident stride. I let my imagination decide her age, consider whether her skirt sits upon or below the knee, wonder at the shape of her face, the colour of her eyes and the length of her neck; whether she's blonde, brunette or redhead. My mind's eye pictures the sway of her hips in time to the click of those heels across the floor and I see someone with poise and purpose. My coffee and toast arrives and still I play the game in my head, long after she's gone from the doorway; long after her echo has died away. Minutes go by, she must have left – a pity, now I'll never know how close my imagination got me. I'm left looking at the empty seat across from me; the triangular paper-napkin at its place setting, which will remain unused. I'm a lonely person in a lonely place until my 'Full English' arrives to break the spell.

I finish up just after 8:30. Part of me didn't want it to live up to its billing so I'd have cause to feel hard done by. But I have to admit it was excellent, the kind of breakfast that sets you up for the day. I don't need to check out until lunchtime so I decide to get the car fixed first. I drop it off at Buckley's and a cheery guy in blue-overalls promises me he'll have it sorted for me if I give him an hour.

I think about buying a newspaper and just going back to The Huntsman to wait it out. But it's a bright morning with a warming sun breaking over the rooftops so I take a stroll instead and follow the footpath along the grassy embankment eyeing the shops in the main street as they come to life. In a few short minutes I find myself at the point where I last saw Joel, by the chess board inlaid into the lawn. Standing over it provides a vastly different perspective than that which I'd gleaned from the 4x4 in the deteriorating light of the previous evening. Close-up its condition is poor, the black and white squares are blistered and peeling. Two oversized wooden box seats are positioned adjacent to the road, facing each other across the board. They are seats for the game's participants but moreover provide storage for the chess pieces. A couple poke out from the open end but it's readily apparent that the board has fallen into disuse - only a few of the pieces remain. I turn to head back but wander first down the path that leads to the frosted-windowed village hall, itself in dire need of a lick or two of paint. There's a notice board a few feet from the hall; it's so crammed that at first it appears almost like wallpaper, something seen once and thereafter forgotten, now too busy to catch the attention. But I force my eyes to settle and take in the detail placed evenly apart beneath the glass. There are ads for various clubs all meeting routinely in the hall. The Reading Circle hold sessions on Mondays, then there's Bingo on Tuesdays and Thursdays, whilst on Wednesdays Mountebridge Roundtable meet. And there's something called a Beetle Drive on Fridays. In addition there's information on Bell Ringing – held at the Church - Band Practice at Mountebridge Primary School and details on the upcoming Mountebridge Spring Festival. I work my way to the column on the far right. A thermometer charts the progress of the Mountebridge Fighting Fund. A thin line shows an undisclosed target some two thirds achieved but the thermometer's red strip is dull and faded; this is no new objective. From the village hall I move on to take in the bowling green and the bandstand. And while the former looks pristine if perhaps a little worn for so early in the season the latter is roped off in a state of rot and disrepair. I decide to head back and pick up that newspaper; the centre of the universe has lost its sparkle.

Back at the square I've still got some fifteen minutes to kill before I can go back to Buckley's. I pass a phone box on the corner, one of those characterless perspex types and then stop outside the Post Office, a few doors down from the newsagent. The notices on the board behind the grilled window catch my eye; then I realise there's something missing. There are no posters for Post Office Savings Accounts, nothing advertising Premium Bonds or TV Licence Stamps or even the range of insurances they try to sell these days. Instead it's that same Mountebridge Fighting Fund with the dull red line three quarters way up the thermometer and then I see something else, another home-made poster emblazoned *Save Our Post Office – sign our petition*. It too has dulled from its time behind the glass, its edges curling around the pins at its corners. I'm still looking at the poster when I take a step toward the newsagents and I'm almost knocked over by a security guard. He brushes past me without a word, the visor on his helmet down, a large metal box in his gloved right hand. He pushes open the Post Office door and for a fleeting second I see a man behind the counter at the far end raise his grey head to greet the new arrival before the closing door snuffs both from sight. In the road behind me the armoured security van's engine idles; the driver, pen in hand, attending to his roster while his partner makes the delivery. I walk into the newsagents wondering what a closing Post Office would need with a delivery from a security van. I'm still thinking about it as I search for a paper.

"You all right there?" I look up. The shopkeeper smiles back at me from behind his counter. "You look a little pale. Not quite here, if you know what I mean."

It feels as if it must be written on my face, but I recover quickly. "Oh, sorry. I'm still in a bit of a daze. I was almost knocked over by the security guard delivering a few doors down." I pick a newspaper and pass him a coin.

"Ah, busiest day of the week this is. For me and for the postmaster, though not for much longer I dare say." He hands me some change. "The old buggers will have to go to Chillinghill or Lower Weaton to cash their pensions soon."

****

Chapter 12 ~ The runt of the litter ~

~ Mo ~

I can't remember the last time I broke my morning exercise routine. But instead I shower, dress and then sip an orange juice in the chair I've turned to face the bed so I can stare at the sleeping form and the mop of blonde hair peeking out above the sheets. She lies on her stomach with her head turned to the side. I let my eyes slide down her outline, the black satin clinging to her, intensifying the curve of her backside, the turn of her thigh.

I can count the number of sexual partners I've had on the fingers of both hands. With most I paid for the privilege, others were a payment in kind. But I repeated the experience with none: for every one of them made me feel their part in the coupling was something ugly; something done hastily and best forgotten; something endured rather than enjoyed. Myrna may not have looked at me, but I know it wasn't because she was repulsed. She was lost within herself, closing her eyes to better concentrate on the sensations within her. She's the only woman I've wanted and want again.

I hear Harvey moving around downstairs and feel a surge of disappointment. I realise how at peace I am just watching Myrna. The doorbell sounds and I leap from my chair. I should have gone early to avoid him ringing, but Myrna doesn't react. The front door is closed with the kind of care I've not given it before. I slip my shades on. Harvey is in the Jag with the engine purring.

We're underway when he breaks the silence, a broad grin on his face. "So how'd it go?"

"Good," I tell him.

"Just good? You must be doing something wrong, bruv. Those girls are so fit and the positions... I mean, Faith was just amazing, she does this thing where …"

"Whoa," I tell him. "I don't want to hear what you got up to and I won't be giving you any details either, so don't ask. It was good. Okay? That's all you need to know."

Harvey turns away from the road for a moment and throws me that cheesy grin again. "Okay," he says.

"Was Faith awake when you left?"

"Are you kidding?" Harvey asks. "After the work-out I gave her she'll be asleep 'til this afternoon."

I don't bite. But he's read my mind and says they'll be all right and will let themselves out when they're ready.

In less than half an hour we're back in Tannock Bar, where we last saw Sali and where I wasted hour upon hour outside Sali's house and business. I hate the place already. Harvey takes it slow and weaves through the streets following some pre-planned route in his head. We draw up midway down some side street and find a space in a line of parked cars on the right. He switches the engine off, checks the clock on the dash and then his rear-view mirror before pushing himself back into his seat. He grimaces, staring ahead and scratching at his goatee.

"Five minutes walk down that way," he says.

"What is?"

"The DIY store where this guy works. He lives here and has a five minute walk to and from work each day."

I'm not sure what Harvey's point is but I nod as if I'm interested.

"I couldn't do that," he continues. "Could you do that? I'd need more than five minutes travelling time to get my head together." Then he shushes me, although I'd not so much as drawn breath to join the meaningless discussion. His eyes are locked on the driver's wing mirror.

I glance over my right shoulder and see a slight figure ambling along the pavement, hands-in-pockets, a canvas rucksack bouncing at his hip and his head downcast as though scanning the paving for the spilt change of others.

"That's him," I murmur, "the runt of the litter. Doesn't exactly look happy to be heading to work, does he?"

"Gives me a warm fuzzy feeling inside knowing we're about to add a little excitement to his life," Harvey adds.

I wait until he's a few paces away from the car then throw my door open and step out. He doesn't raise his head, he hasn't seen me yet. I walk around the front of the car, and stand facing him. If he runs I'll catch him with ease but he's walking toward me, his head still low. I open the Jag's rear door as he nears it. Either the sound or the movement alerts him, he raises his head and his body stiffens in recognition.

"Get in," I tell him.

He hesitates, a common enough reaction and one I'm ready for. In the time he takes to weigh up what's happening I move forward, help him into the back seat and climb in beside him. We have him, it's over in seconds and no-one witnessing it would give it a thought, not that there's anyone around anyway. Harvey pulls away from the kerb; our white-faced guest hasn't uttered a word.

"Did you deliver the message?" I ask him.

He nods.

"Still got the finger?"

He shakes his head, his eyes not meeting mine. I get a real sense that we've scared the little bastard shitless.

"Where is it then?" Harvey asks from the front, his eyes flicking from the road to the rear view mirror and back again.

The little runt finds his voice at last. "We didn't want to hang onto it, we threw it."

"Where?" I ask.

"We dropped it down a street drain."

I check Harvey's look in the mirror, he nods and I know he's happy with that.

"So can I get out now?"

"Now why would you think that?" Harvey asks.

He squirms. "Well, I delivered the message, so…"

"No! No! No!" Harvey says, interrupting him. "You see there's the little matter of the money that's due. We want it and until we get it you're going to stay with us. Now doesn't that sound nice?"

The runt edges forward in his seat. "You can't do that, I've got work."

I pull him back and tell him not any more he doesn't. His lips part to say something, but he appears to think better of it. He's quiet until the journey's end and we're safely installed inside the lock-up at the railway arches.

Harvey opens up then returns to the car to drive in under the rollup door. He flicks on the overhead lights and lowers the roller-door before I climb out of the car. I take my shades off and fold them into my top pocket. The lock-up looks different; the whole place has been swept and the workbench looks to have been dusted down and tidied too. A few essential items have been brought in; a portable TV, a mini fridge and a gas space-heater – important if we're going to be halfway comfortable minding this little git. The rickety wooden chair is still here but someone's located its twin and added a table. At the far wall, near the wash room and toilet, there's even a double bed and duvet cover. God knows where Con pulled that in from. But all the sweeping and the dusting and the few added comforts can't hide the mustiness of the place. It's still just a forty by sixty bricked off hole under the railway.

Harvey runs a hand backwards through his hair and looks around. "Not bad eh?"

"Not exactly the Ritz though, is it?" I answer. He shakes his head as though dismayed and tells me to get our guest out of the Jag.

"Introductions," Harvey says, rolling his shoulders beneath his jacket to re-settle it on his frame. "I'm Harvey Scallion and I believe you know my brother, Mo."

I relieve our guest of his rucksack. "And who is this little fuck anyway?"

Harvey looks at me, his eyes narrowing. I remind him that all he gave me before was this guy's address, not his name. "Ah," he says, "this is Ferris. Ferris Dick."

The little guy looks sheepish. "You're kidding aren't you?" I say, smiling. "With a name like that you must be a first born."

"What d'you mean?" The runt pipes up.

"You know. The unexpected arrival who condemns his parents to a life together they weren't quite ready to choose. I bet you've had the piss ripped out of you since first day at school. F. Dick."

"Fuck you too, arsehole," he says.

It's the excuse I've been looking for. In a flash I drop the rucksack and throw out a right hand catching the little bastard on the left side of the chest. The air is forced out of him in a wheeze and he drops to one knee. It'll teach him to think first and speak second.

Harvey shrugs his shoulders; he knows this helps our cause. He gets Ferris to his feet. The little guy winces, his eyes fill with water. I can tell he doesn't want me to see how much I've hurt him. He grits his teeth against it, but a tear or two escapes down his cheek. He clutches his arm to his side in support. He'll learn to take shallow breaths and avoid sudden movements. Cracked ribs will do that for you.

"You ready to be polite?" Harvey asks him. But without waiting for a response he launches into the do's and don'ts telling him there's only one way in or out – not strictly correct, but it avoids complications to let him think as much. Harvey makes it clear that one way or another Ferris will be staying put until we get our cash.

The rucksack doesn't hold much; a newspaper, a lunchbox and a shiny silver mobile.

"Bingo," Harvey says. "I bet we've got a mutual friend listed among your stored numbers."

Chapter 13 ~ The warmth of the sun ~

~ Adam ~

I collect the Sportrak from Buckley's, part with yet more cash and head back to the hotel to check out. The sooner I get going the better. Reception is manned by a girl I've not seen previously, I drop by to ask her to make up my bill so it'll be ready by the time I've thrown my stuff together upstairs. But when I reach the desk I realise she's on a call.

She acknowledges me, flashes me a radiant smile, covers the mouthpiece and whispers, "Won't keep you a moment, sir."

I turn my head to scan the reception area, looking needlessly at the ceiling rose and light shade, the pictures on the wall, then every so often letting my eyes fall back on the receptionist as though to check she's still busy on the call, but lingering a little longer than necessary. There's something about her, something smoulderingly attractive. Her brown hair is pulled tightly back from her forehead and gathered with a plastic scrunchy high at the back of her head to arch out an inch or two before dropping to shoulder height. It seems to swish like a horse's tail as she looks from desk to computer screen and I imagine if I ran my fingers through it they'd not snag, so straight and so fine it looks. Her eyes are dark, hazel I think, she's mid to late twenties and has a clear, though slightly pale complexion. A name badge on her white blouse identifies her as Shelley, nice name too, different. I realise this is the first time in almost two months that I've looked at a woman this way. A sign that the spin my head's been in is finally unwinding. A good thing then; perhaps I should follow it and try to lighten up. After all, this is a vacation; well, of sorts.

She ends her phone conversation and looks up catching me staring and like a kid caught pinching loose change from his mother's purse, I jump in a little too quickly and my reasoning doesn't offer adequate explanation. "I want to check out of room 106, please. Could you make up my bill and I'll be down in five minutes?"

She smiles. "Of course, sir, and the name is?"

"Rosewood."

"I'll have it ready when you come down, Mr. Rosewood."

I head for the lift thinking what a complete arse I've just made of myself.

In my room I splash on a little aftershave, throw my kit into my holdall - the newspaper too, I'll save that for the ferry. Then it's a last check to ensure I've not left anything and I'm off.

I hear him even as the lift doors are opening, his young voice bounces off the walls. Even then, it takes me a stride or two to recognise it as Joel's, but as I turn the corner into the reception area I'm already looking for him. He's halfway out of the door with one of his mates. "Hey, Joel," I shout.

He turns, recognises me and comes back, his mate trailing in too. "Hi," he says, his eyebrows a little furrowed. "Did you not stay in your tent then?"

"Well, no, you told me The Huntsman, so I took a room here."

"You two know each other?" The receptionist asks, rising from her desk.

"Yeah," Joel says. "This is the guy who gave me a lift last night, so I could show him where to find Buckley's."

The receptionist marches out from behind the desk closing the distance between us. And in those few short strides I hear the click-clack again. I can't help myself, my eyes drop to take in her plain black heels as though confirmation were needed. By the time I raise them it's like I've been ogling her from head to toe and back again. I meet her hazel eyes and see a twinkle that suggests not only that I've been caught, but given my earlier misdemeanour, I've immediately been found guilty.

"I thought you said your name was Adam?"

"It is," I answer. "It's my Christian name. You made an assumption and I didn't feel the need to correct you."

"I see," she says, smiling. "Well, thank-you again for helping Joel and I hope it caused no imposition to have Dave travel with him?"

It's there, I can hear it now that the formal tone has dropped; that sweetness in her voice. "It was no problem. As I said, Joel was doing me the favour."

She turns and heads back to reception giving a split second glance over her shoulder that implicitly requires that I follow. "Joel told me you intervened when he was being chased."

"Ah." I turn back to wink at Joel. "I think he was showing them a clean pair of heels until I got in his way."

Joel grins. "But why didn't you put your tent up? I told you we had a campsite."

"Here?"

"We have a Certificated Site in a field around back," the receptionist says. "You were looking at the sign this morning." She nods at the wall and I look across. Sure enough the 'pictures' aren't pictures at all; they're framed certificates: Investors In People, an AA Good Hotel Guide Recommendation and a green Certificated Site testimony from The Camping and Caravanning Club.

I let out a sigh. "Ever looked at something without really taking it in?"

"I suppose I must have," she says, handing me my bill. "But I think in the main it's a male thing."

I smile, purse my lips and suck in air. "Harsh." I pull my wallet from my back pocket and hand her the cash.

Joel's friend is impatient to be away and says something to Joel I can't quite make out. Joel makes his excuses and says goodbye.

"Was everything okay during your stay?" Shelley asks in her business voice.

"Fine, thanks; and it was a great breakfast."

"Well," she says, smiling, "the campsite is basic but competitively priced and guests can still get breakfast in the hotel."

Is that veiled encouragement? I want to think so, but all I say is next time then.

~

I'm folding up the back seats in the Sportrak to regain some space for my gear when my mobile rings. The screen tells me it's Ferris. I push the green button with the handset-shaped icon. "Hi, Ferris. How are you?"

I'm suddenly cold: his voice shuts down the warmth of the sun. He tells me he wishes he could be more positive but that Ferris has had better days and will be staying with him until our business is concluded. He asks when he will get his money. I ask if Ferris is hurt. I'm told he is okay, for the moment. But the gap between 'okay' and 'for the moment' is as menacing as it's intended to be.

I glance around the car park to ensure I'm not overheard, then climb into the 4x4. "Look, I don't have it, but I'm looking at a job. I just need more time."

Silence. Then… "How much?"

"This time next week."

"Too long."

"Listen, I can get what you need, I saw it today. Next delivery, I'll be ready."

"Never mind next delivery, do it today."

"That's impossible and if you've got Ferris then I'll need help getting what I need."

"Okay, you got a pen? I'm going to give you a landline number."

I find a pen in the glove box and write the number he gives me on my hotel bill.

"Call at 3 o'clock," he says. "Have your list ready and keep it short."

****

Chapter 14 ~ Being professional ~

~ Mo ~

Harvey has stepped outside to use the runt's mobile. The runt himself sits in the wooden chair across the table from me nursing his busted ribs and sipping air as though it were hot enough to burn his mouth. He's a sorry-looking sight and avoids my gaze. The strip lighting in here isn't particularly bright, so I don't use my shades. But that's not why he won't look me in the eye. I have my own theory on that.

Harvey's already settled into calling him by name but I won't do that. Harvey knows why. Initially, I'll want to know who he is, but then I put it away, so he's nothing to me. I don't need him to like me and I don't want to know any more than I need to. In fact, I've always found it easier if I don't like the guy. So much so that I'll go out of my way early on to create friction between us and reason not to like him. Harvey says I try to hate them. But I don't see it that way, hate is too personal a word. The truth is I feel nothing for them. It's fairer on the guy anyway. He learns real quick that me and him won't be friends and that's why he avoids me now, he senses it. We know where we stand with each other, what can be fairer than that? Harvey on the other hand likes to play up his intellect so he can appear approachable and get the guy to open up. His argument in these situations has always been that both of us must command respect but one of us must represent fear and the other reason. I can appreciate that, why not? It always works.

The side door opens and Harvey comes back having made his call. He's scratching at his goatee, neither smiling nor grimacing, so I suspect it's mixed news.

"Did you get hold of him?" I ask. Out of the corner of my eye I see the little runt's head lift to take in the answer.

"Yeah," Harvey says. "He doesn't have the money, of course. But he's casing a job."

"And you believe him?"

"Sure. He was concerned enough. He won't do anything stupid."

"Well, if he's preparing a job that's got to be good, I suppose." I notice the runt is playing head tennis shifting between us as the conversation continues.

Harvey tilts his head to the left and runs a hand backwards through his hair. "Yes and no," he says.

"What d'you mean?" I ask; throwing a glance at the runt at the same time, enough to suggest his constant head jockeying is getting on my nerves.

"Well, it seems, Ferris, here is something of a scrounger and pulls together whatever hardware is needed for jobs. As we have him otherwise engaged we might need to help Rosewood out."

"What does he need?" I ask.

"I told him to make a list and call back."

I sense there's more and I can see the little runt's head turn toward me out of the corner of my eye. His lunch box sits on the table between us.

"And?" I ask of Harvey.

The runt's head turns back toward Harvey and that's enough. I grab the box and launch it at the little shit. "Will you give your head a fucking rest?"

He raises an arm to deflect the lunch box but it hits him and he howls in pain, though more at his own sudden movement than any damage the plastic box did him.

"Bastard," he yells.

I turn back to Harvey, his eyes are wide. I took him by surprise too, but he knows the drill and won't object.

"He needs seven days," Harvey says.

"You're kidding, there's no way I'm baby-sitting this little fuck that long. He's got a smart mouth. I'll have his head ripped off inside three."

Harvey spreads his arms and raises his shoulders suggesting there's little he can do about it. He looks to the runt. "You'll behave, won't you, Ferris?"

"You can't keep me here for a week, I'll be missed," he says quietly. "People will be looking for me."

"Who?" Harvey asks, adopting an appeasing tone. "Not your mate, he knows you're with us and knows what he has to do to get you back in one piece. Not your landlady either. Let's be honest, her kind don't give a shit whether they see you from one rent-due day to the next, as long as they get their money. And don't expect your work to rally to the cause, 'cos I called you in sick when I was outside. They won't be expecting to see you back any time soon."

I have to admit these calm little chats are a speciality of Harvey's. I could have screamed all that at the little runt and it wouldn't have made half the impact. A nice touch too saying he'd called him in sick. I know it's crap; Harvey's too lazy to have bothered, but the runt doesn't. The little bugger's face turns pale. I've seen it before, it's like hope leaches from them like the trickle from a pricked water balloon. They list their friends in their heads and one by one they fail to come through for them. And all the people they presumed they brought a little light to each day and who were sure to notice their absence, they just up and disappear. It's a wake-up call to how vulnerable and unimportant they are; how little they'll be missed. The weight of it crushes them, they sag in on themselves, take on a gaunt and wasted look. Here, the prospect of a week with us, and in this shithole, has the runt moving into that phase already. I can't say I'm too pleased at the idea either. A mixed bag sure enough. I've said it before; Harvey will never make a decent poker player.

Harvey checks his watch. "If you're up for the first shift I'll go check in with Con. I'll come back with some lunch."

"Fine," I tell him.

"Lunch, Ferris?" Harvey asks. "Sandwiches okay? Anything you don't like?"

"I've got my own," he says, nodding at the lunchbox.

"Oh," Harvey says, "of course you have."

Things are quiet after Harvey leaves, there's an atmosphere; the runt's wary of me and that's just fine. But after a few minutes he's shifting uneasily in his seat.

"Can I get up and walk around? Would that be okay?"

"What you can see from where you're at is all there is."

"I need to stretch my legs for a bit."

I make him wait for a second or two then let him get up to wander around, it'll break the monotony to see what he does. He goes first to the workbench on the left hand wall and looks it up and down. There's a vice at one end but nothing out on the work-surface other than the portable TV and the mini fridge, neither of which are plugged in yet. There are drawers and cupboards below the workbench that I bet he'd like to check out but he wisely leaves them alone.

"What was this place?" he asks.

"Didn't you see the sign outside?" He shakes his head. "A security firm. They supplied alarms, door entry systems and safes."

He splutters. "Ironic, huh?"

I don't answer.

"Was it your boss's firm?"

I ignore that too, I don't want to make conversation. He shuffles back past the table and across the empty floor-space, stopping to look at the dried-in oil stains on the concrete from the runabouts Con occasionally stores here. Then he continues as far as the right hand wall turning to walk its length until it meets up with the wall at the rear. Like a jailed man in his cell he's pacing the floor, finding the limits of his prison.

He bypasses the newly acquired bed and sticks his head in the door of the washroom. I always feel the washroom's stippled exterior finish makes it look more like a portacabin set against the back wall, rather than the purpose-build unit that it is. The runt won't be too excited by what he finds in there. There's no window to the outside world, just a sink, a kettle, a microwave and a door at the far end that leads to the loo. The ten feet or so between the washroom and the adjoining left-hand wall is taken up by heavy duty packing boxes piled deep and high against the back wall. He lingers there and I'm about to get up when he spins around to wander back.

He sits down and stares across at me. "What's in the boxes in the corner?"

I can't make up my mind about him; maybe he's sharper than he looks. I answer this one only to puncture his curiosity. "They're empty, just old boxes the security firm used."

"So why keep 'em?"

I lean forward. "Fingers we deliver personally, heads we box and send through the post."

It's a little after one thirty when Harvey gets back. He's a little flustered as he drops a bulging carrier bag on the table. "Sorry, I'm later than I intended. I threw in a few drinks and eats from the shelves at the petrol station. Pick what you want for now."

I'd let the runt eat the portion of leftover pizza from his lunchbox earlier but it doesn't stop him reaching into the bag first. He pulls out a carton of fresh orange juice and I grab him by the wrist and squeeze until he drops it. "The OJ is mine; you can have Coke, Sprite or whatever."

After we've eaten the runt says he needs to take a leak. I point him toward the washroom. "You've got two minutes. Don't make me come get you."

Harvey waits until he disappears then turns to me. "So how was it this morning?"

"Slow, time really drags and he asks too many questions. It's too intense. Can't we knock him out or something?"

"It can't be that bad," Harvey says. "Watch TV, play cards with him, the time will pass."

"It's not time well spent. And, we don't have cards."

Harvey pulls a pack from the carrier bag. "See, I thought of everything."

"Even so, you know I don't like to get close."

"What would you use?" Harvey asks. He sees he's lost me and continues. "To knock him out, I mean."

"I don't know, sleeping tablets or something. Boots would find us something."

"You still keep in touch with Boots?" Harvey asks.

"No, but I can find him if I have to."

"Tell you what, how about we take a day each, a twenty-four hour day?"

"I thought we were going to split each day?"

"Yeah," Harvey says. "But if it's as awkward as you say then maybe it'd be easier to take a whole day at a time, then, spend a whole day elsewhere."

It seems to me that if the little prick irritates me so much over the course of just a few hours then extending this to twenty-four, even with the next day away from him, won't make things any better. I'm about to suggest that having a word with Boots might be the way to go when Harvey continues.

"Of course, on your free day you'd have time to look in on Myrna, maybe catch another show. That is if you're still interested."

"Works for me," I tell him. "Today can be my shift, and then you cover from tomorrow morning. But maybe I'll get hold of Boots anyway; it won't do any harm to ask."

"Fair enough," Harvey says.

The cistern flushes and seconds later the runt emerges from the washroom, moving a little more freely than before, his left arm now tucked tight to his side. I like Harvey's idea. I want to see Myrna again and I'm sure Boots could give me a little something for her too.

****

Chapter 15 ~Looking after the little things~

~ Adam ~

"Either next time has come quickly or you've forgotten something," Shelley says, as I walk back into reception.

"Change of plans," I say. "Tell me more about this site you have."

Shelley reads from the pc screen. "It's four pounds a night for a basic pitch. Six if you want electricity."

I run it through my head, twenty-eight quid for the whole week, when I've just spent sixty on one night. What a boost to my ailing finances!

"There's a freshwater standpipe and foul water disposal on the tree side of the field and a shower and toilet block by the entrance. It's small but very clean."

I'm not entirely sure what all this means, but I nod as if I do. Shelley's hazel eyes stare back at me, I know it's my turn to speak but I've no idea what's expected. When she continues I can only assume she's taken my glazed expression as anticipation of more detail.

"Of course, the electric pitches are generally used by the caravanners," she says. "Whereas you lot in the tenting fraternity are happy to rough it a bit. You're also welcome to use the hotel for drinks and meals. So, what's it to be?"

I'm still nodding as if in agreement about us 'tenters' but I manage a, "Sorry?"

"How long do you intend to stay and do you need an electric pitch?" she asks.

I settle for a week on a standard pitch.

The rear of the hotel is laid out in gravel as an overflow car park. There's a bungalow to the left but on the right is a dirt road that leads to an open field. The concrete toilet and shower block - a key for which nestles in my pocket - is halfway down on the left-hand side. It's not a particularly large field but there's plenty of room, and what's more, I've got it all to myself. It slopes down slightly from left to right and is lined by trees along the top left. The side opposite boasts no trees but three white boxes stand in parallel, maybe half a metre tall and ten metres apart. Closer inspection shows them to bear lightening fork stickers; these are the electric pitches Shelley spoke of. I drive up towards the trees and draw the Sportrak to a halt.

I've got as far as laying everything out. The main body of the tent lies flat on the ground and the waterproof outer cover to the side, weighed down by the mallet and tent pegs, lest the light breeze pick it up. The five flexible poles have an elastic cord running through them and I've connected them together, but they are three different lengths and I'm not sure what goes where.

The sun is high in the sky when Joel joins me. "Ma said you decided to stay after all. Do you want a hand putting the tent up? I've got half an hour to kill before lunch."

"Sure. Where's your mate?"

"He's setting off with his folks now. Just about everyone disappears for the break but us."

"What break?"

"Mid term; stupid."

I sneak a look at the instructions that came with the tent. "Let's see if we can crack this in half an hour then."

I thread one of the longer poles diagonally through the outer loops of the tent frame and Joel slides another through from the opposite diagonal. Then we do the smaller side ones. Each pole overshoots the flattened tent by several feet on each side. The fun starts when we try to fit the ends of the poles into the connectors sewn in the tent frame. This flexes the poles and they arch up raising the thin lining from the tent floor and we can see at last how it will look. But the handling is awkward; I'm glad of the extra hands Joel provides. When all four poles are fully flexed and secured the tent looks large and airy. I move to throw the outer lining over the top when Joel shouts out. It's not secured to the ground yet and he hauls the whole thing a few feet away before setting it down again. I throw the lining over and he knocks in the pegs while I thread the final pole through the outer sheet to create the porch entrance.

We're done and I look at Joel; like me he's sweating with the effort. "I could do with a drink after that, how about you? Have you time before lunch?"

"Sure," he says, flicking his head to clear his fringe from his eyes.

"Okay, you unload the rest of the gear from the jeep into the tent and I'll grab us a couple of Cokes from the hotel bar."

I wander in past reception and tell Shelley that Joel has been helping me. She knows and I apologise if I've made him late. I tell her I'll get him a Coke for all his help then send him in for lunch. She smiles and looks set to say something but the phone rings and I let her get on.

The bar is surprisingly busy; pub lunches must draw in the locals. I catch the eye of the grey-haired barman, a tea towel draped over his shoulder. He brings me two chilled cans and drops the change in my hand with a wink. Then he's on to the next customer.

Back at the tent Joel has emptied the Sportrak and stacked the gear under canvas. He sits in the open rear door of the 4x4, his legs swinging back and forth.

I hand him his Coke and sit next to him. "Thanks for your help with the tent, you were really great."

He takes a gulp then wipes his lips with the back of his hand. "You've not done this before have you?"

"It's a brand new tent," I tell him. "I didn't really know what it looked like."

"You've not put one up before though, have you?"

I exhale loudly. He's a perceptive little bugger. "Well, actually, no I haven't. What gave it away?"

"You were going to set up under the trees," he says.

"I thought that was good, the trees will give shelter from the wind, won't they?"

"Yeah, but regular campers don't like to be under the trees, the tree sap and the bird droppings damage the tent's waterproofing."

"Ah, so a beginner's error tripped me up?"

"Hmm. That, plus I saw you peeking at the instructions." He squints at me out of the corners of his eyes and I burst out laughing. He's a sharp cookie.

We sit quietly for a moment letting the cola slide over our throats.

"So what made you decide on a camping holiday?" Joel asks.

I take a last long swig to drain my can. It's a hard question. I don't want to lie to the little guy but I can hardly tell him the whole truth either. So I fall somewhere in between. "I needed a break. Camping's not expensive and going somewhere off the beaten track appealed."

"Didn't your dad ever take you camping when you were young?"

"Younger you mean. I'm not quite a pensioner yet thanks." He smiles and makes it easy to share a simple truth with him. "My mother was a single parent. I never really had a dad."

"Me either," he says. "I know what that's like."

We sort of sit there for a minute or so, neither of us saying anything. In a way I suppose this revelation accounts for his apparent resourcefulness, maybe he's had to grow up quickly. I feel too that this shared experience, perhaps it's a shared absence of experience, cements the connection we've made.

Then he breaks the spell, jumps down from the back of the jeep, tilts his head back and finishes his drink. "I'd best be going for lunch now."

"Thanks for your help."

"No problem," he says. "See ya."

I don't bother with lunch. I'm not really hungry. I climb into the Sportrak and drive. I realise how much I've been enjoying myself; having a big breakfast, thinking about women again as if the past six weeks never happened and then having fun with some kid putting up a tent. And all the while the Scallion brothers have been doing God knows what to the last mate I've got in the world. Poor Ferris. I know he didn't want to come, but I should have made him. I should have insisted. And why did I jump straight in to assume I could rob the Post Office when Harvey called? Is it even possible? Perhaps I'm clutching at it because the situation demands I find something? I'm trying to talk myself out of it, but somehow I feel that's why it popped into my head so readily. Something within me knew that Post Office was ripe for the taking – it's not just the situation, there's a realisation deep within me that this is a job I can pull off.

I leave Mountebridge behind, Lower Weaton too. I get back to the point where I turned off the M2 and head back toward London, letting a few miles clock up before turning off in the direction of Faversham. I set the trip meter on the dash until I find what I'm looking for but I keep going until I've reached the outskirts of the town and pull up in the car park of the first Public House I find. Inside I order a soft drink and ask if they have a payphone. I call the number Harvey gave me and let it ring.

"Hello." The voice offers nothing more and I'm pretty sure it's not Harvey's.

"Harvey asked me to call," I say.

Silence.

"About getting the right tools for the job," I add.

"You're early. You were to call at three."

"Be grateful I found a payphone at all," I answer.

"What do you need?"

There's enough activity in the pub to make it difficult for me to be overheard but I turn my back to the throng anyway and lower my voice. And still I'm cautious. "Listen, there are a lot of people around, I need the obvious."

"A weapon?"

"Yes," I answer, glad that he's taken the initiative. "Get me something with visual impact."

"A shotgun?"

"A short barrel would be perfect. And I'll need a holdall."

"Anything else?"

"Wheels, reliable but unobtrusive."

"Okay. Where and when?"

"Next Tuesday night, say by 11pm. Turn off the M2 and head for Faversham. Set your trip metre and exactly 2.3 miles from the turnoff you'll find an unofficial lay-by on the left."

"Got it. The kit will be in the boot and the keys in the tail pipe. What about the uplift?"

"Same place, twelve hours later," I suggest.

"Good. Leave everything in the boot, keys in the exhaust. We'll torch the car afterwards."

There's a click on the line and he's gone. No going back now.

Chapter 16 ~ A thing of beauty ~

~ Mo ~

When I wake I've a crick in my neck. I check my watch; it's a little after 6am but without windows in this place it could be anytime. I slept in the chair with my jacket draped over me and left the overhead lights on all night; only switching the space heater off around two. The runt has the luxury of the bed, though I doubt he sees it that way. Late in the evening I'd slipped a plastic cable-tie around his wrist, fed another through it and pulled it tight around the frame of the bed. In the right hands cable ties are as good as handcuffs; they don't give once they're on and they'll chafe and bite into skin if the wearer tries to squirm out of them. Now he knows what we keep in the drawers beneath the workbench. I don't think the tie caused him much discomfort, but I noticed he whimpered in his sleep when he changed position and the pain in his ribs kicked in.

I take a piss, then give my stubbled face a wash and dab water at my tired eyes. The air in this place doesn't circulate, it's dry and stale and my eyes feel raw. If I don't get out of here soon I'll get a blinding headache. The runt's still sleeping; not that I've attempted to keep the noise down any. A quick look confirms his wrist is still securely tethered. I walk down to the single door and let myself out for some fresh air.

Outside light rain peppers the roller door with the dull drum of a thousand fingertips. Despite the rain it's bright and fresh, forcing me to squint until I manage to slip my shades back on. I close my eyes and raise my head to feel those fingertips dance upon my face and neck. Then I let my head loll around, first one way then the other, hearing the tendons creak and crack and feeling at once, looser. The sound of a milk float operating a few streets away makes me realise how dry my throat is. I go back inside, pull the milk from the fridge and drink from the carton. I leave enough to flavour our guest's morning tea.

The runt wakes just before seven. It takes him a few seconds to come around and to remember that his right arm is attached to the bed-frame. After a few curses he begins to whinge about how pointless this is, how it could lose him his job, and then he asks if he has to wear the same clothes all week. There's no pattern to what he comes out with. If he thought about it logically he'd put up with the inconveniences and try to endear himself a little in the hope that we'd get complacent. Naturally, I wouldn't let it happen, but he's adopted the wrong attitude for the situation he's in. I cut the cable ties to let him go to the toilet and freshen himself up. He stops bleating when I turn on the television and let him watch the news. But I'm convinced the stupid prick listens to the bulletins expecting to hear of his own abduction.

Harvey arrives at 8am with a warm breakfast in a paper bag and passes it to the runt.

"You're spoiling him," I tell him.

The runt hurries a bite from the filled roll as though it might be taken from him. Yellow egg yolk crumbs spill from the corners of his mouth onto the table top – these fast-food places always hard-boil the eggs.

"We need to have a chat outside," Harvey says.

I get the pack of cable ties out, march the runt and his egg roll back to the bed and secure him by the wrist again. He's not happy, but he knows not to argue.

There's no sign of the earlier rain. Harvey draws on his cigarette and blows smoke high into the air. "Everything go okay last night?"

"Let's just say I'm glad it's your turn today. I'll feel better after some proper sleep."

Harvey exhales another line of smoke, fishes a set of car keys from his pocket and tosses them to me. "For the Astra," he says. "It still smells of cat piss, but it's in the back somewhere so don't worry about it. It's parked on the corner two streets down."

I don't say it but I'm thinking it's past time for Con to replace the Astra.

"Rosewood called," Harvey continues. "There are a few jobs you can get on with once you've had a rest."

"What does he need?"

"A sawn-off, a hold-all and a set of wheels we'd be happy to torch afterwards."

"Could we give him the Astra?" I ask.

"I know what you mean," Harvey says. "But it's better if you nick something a few hours before the job."

"I know."

"I'll leave it to you. Anyway, go grab a few hours sleep before you get to it."

I'm only a few paces away when he calls out.

"Oh, and if you bring us a hot meal around six I'll tell you what Myrna had to say when I spoke to her at the club last night."

"You were there?"

He grins. "Tell you at six," and disappears inside.

He won't hear it but I say it anyway. "Bastard."

~

It takes me an age to make my way back to Harlesden, but then it doesn't help that I'm fighting rush hour traffic.

The flat is tidy; Mrs. Winstanley would have been in the previous afternoon and nothing's changed since then. I set my shades on the table, pull the drapes, then undress and leave out my creased suit so it can be properly laundered. The rest I throw into the washing basket, Mrs W. will see to it. In the bathroom I give my teeth a brush and at last get rid of the stale taste from my mouth, and then I step into the shower. I'm tired but not overly so. I did manage a few hours rest and just need to top up. But I know I'll sleep easier once I'm feeling clean and fresh. After I've towel dried I wander through to the bed and draw back the sheets. I'm about to climb in when I spot an envelope on the bedside table; an undersized envelope with my name on the front. It's not like Mrs W. to leave notes. I reach over for it and tear it open. Inside is a single piece of plain white card that's been pressed firmly against freshly painted lips. *Love Myrna* is scrawled beneath. She won't know it, but a mother's love aside, it's probably the only token of female affection I've ever had. And although I know I'd give short shrift to anyone else I saw softening to a note or card, somehow I don't care. Climbing into the side of the bed she lay in I draw the sheets over my head and breathe in deeply, hoping I can recapture something of her fragrance. But there's nothing. Maybe Mrs. W. changed the sheets. It doesn't matter; I don't need to wait for whatever Harvey has to say, Myrna found her own way to tell me.

By early afternoon I've had a light work out, trimmed my goatee and showered again. I've had fruit, cereal and an OJ for breakfast. Now I'm dressed in a clean suit and back in the Astra heading for Moods. There are no messages on my mobile so I can assume all is well with Harvey. He's probably been having a ball, playing cards and watching soaps all morning with the little prick. But that's his way, and if that's what he's doing then no doubt he's finding out things we can turn to our advantage.

At Moods I look in past Con's office just to let him know I'm around, but his chair is empty. I head for the spare office at the end of the corridor; it has a desk and a phone and I need to make a call. Cornelius's businesses are all above board; how he funds them might, at times, be open to question but there are never any guns on the premises. Most of the problems Harvey and I deal with can be sorted with a beating, the threat of a baseball bat or a tumble down a flight of stairs. Sometimes there might be a bit of trouble with some upstart keen to make a name for himself and if that's the case then we might get tooled up to meet fire with fire, but it seldom comes anywhere close. As to finding a gun for Rosewood, normally we wouldn't touch it. We take a cut if the job happens in our neck of the woods but the risk isn't ours and if it goes tits up there's never any come back on us. But Con's big investment makes this different; we need to make it happen without becoming implicated if Rosewood screws it up. I have a few options but I always try Gavin Marsden first. Gav's uncle has had a respectable gun shop for years, completely legitimate. But I'd guess Gav makes as good a living as his uncle by supplying under-the-counter stuff. No licences, no questions and no records.

I call Gav's number; it rings twice before he picks up.

"This is Gav."

"Gav, it's Mo Scallion."

"Hey, onion man, you have some business for me?"

I laugh like it's the first time I've heard this. "Beer money to you, my friend, just beer money. Can I come see you?"

"Sure, I ain't going anywhere. What should I look out?"

"Window dressing; something double barrelled to scare the birds. I'll be round in an hour." I set the phone down. No hellos and no goodbyes. Despite my earlier comment we're not mates, this is business.

I head back down the corridor and bump into Cornelius as he's coming out of the gents. His face lights up like he's not seen me for a week.

"Ah, Mo, it's yourself. Are you on top of that little acquisition we need to make?"

"I'm off to sort it now, boss."

"Good so. Walk me back to my office."

He raises an arm and as I turn he rests it lightly between my shoulder blades, overcompensating after chewing me up the other day.

"Who are you using?"

"Gav Marsden."

"Ah," he says, letting his arm fall from my shoulder. "Shake hands with that little gobshite and he'll have the ring off your finger. Watch him won't you."

"I will," I tell him. But I know I could have mentioned any one of half a dozen people and his comment would have been the same.

We reach his office and he pulls his wallet from his inside pocket, licks the back of his thumb and draws out a line of notes for me. "That's all that's in it for him. You know why."

Gav Marsden hits the entry button to let me into his block. He's on the first floor and is waiting to usher me in as I reach the top of the stairs. I take a couple of steps into his hallway and hear him throw the deadlocks on the door behind me. As I turn he gestures me into the living room beyond with a jut of his chin.

"Take a seat," he says, "I'll be with you in a minute."

Gav likes to operate out of his flat. He must have a lock-up close-by but it's probably too risky to lead anyone there. He takes what you want to the flat and usually has options.

I suppose his taste in furniture would be classed as modern. The living room is light and airy with the cream coloured walls and the polished wooden floor both reflecting light from the large window overlooking the street below. It's too bright for me to be comfortable without my shades, but having been through this before I know I'll be able to take them off shortly. A brown fabric suite sits in the centre of the room in an 'L' shape around a low coffee table. I sit and listen to him moving around in the next room. A moment later he stands in the doorway and gazes around until his eyes settle on what he's looking for. He lifts the remote from the seat, points it at the window and there's a mechanical hum as the blinds slide across the window to shut out the daylight. I fold my shades into my breast pocket. It might suit me but I know this isn't an act of courtesy; he's making sure we can't be observed from the building opposite.

I watch him bring in a couple of holdalls. He stops midway to wipe his nose. I'd offer to help him carry the bags but I know I'm expected to stay where I am. Gav himself is pencil thin with dark, wavy hair worn a little longer than is fashionable these days. His chin and nose are sharp and angular; there's a reddish tinge to his face around the eyes and each time we meet he seems to be nursing a cough or a cold. A year or so back I learned he suffers from Crohn's disease. He's never mentioned it and I've never asked: as I said, we're not friends. Whatever it does to him it hasn't affected his appetite for a deal. I've known him get hold of high spec stuff. And I'm not talking about the odd handgun used for a hold-up or a hit; I mean a shitload of AK47's, grenade launchers, mortars and landmines; enough for a small war. But, however that sounds, the reality is paydays like that won't happen often. Most of his trade is in one offs like the purchase I have in mind. And he won't be getting rich from this transaction.

Gav sits in the seat adjacent to me, opens the first holdall and pulls out a black lint cloth before placing it on the table in front of me. Then he reaches in again and draws out his first offering, unravelling it from its own cloth wrapping and placing it on the lint as though it were fragile. I lean forward, rest my elbows on my knees, steeple my hands and let my fingers rest on my chin as I look at it.

"A thing of beauty, isn't it?" Gav says.

"Nice, but not what I asked for."

"I know, I know," he says. "But this is a SIG-Pro, a semi-automatic. It's lightweight, good for up to fifteen shots and it's real quick to reload. It even comes with a barrel conversion so you can change calibre."

"Just the same, Gav, I need something that looks imposing; we're not dealing with someone who'll know by sight what this baby is capable of."

He gives a muted laugh. "This isn't imposing?"

When I don't answer, he sighs deeply. "I can make you a great deal?"

"No, thanks."

He re-wraps the SIG-Pro and brings out a short-barrelled shotgun with a walnut stock. It's broken to show two empty side-by-side barrels.

"This is more like it," I tell him.

Gav can't hide his disappointment. "You'd pick that over a semi-automatic? You don't get the luxury of a free hand using one of these you know."

"Maybe, but it's what was asked for. If it does what we need then it'll be beauty enough." I pick it up and give it a once over, snapping it closed, feeling its weight then breaking it open again. "What about shells and something to put it in?"

Gav digs into his holdall and pulls out a box of shells and a black drawstring bag. He drops them on the table and delves into the bag again bringing out more shells.

"One box is fine," I tell him. Then I stare at the bag. "Is this the best you can do?"

"You can sling it over your shoulder, it's easy to carry and relatively unobtrusive. What more do you need?"

I think about it for a second and decide he's right. I slide my shades on and hand him the notes Con gave me.

He counts them quickly. "I was hoping for more."

"Why? It's worth next to fuck all, Gav."

"I have overheads."

"We all do," I tell him. "Look, you know as well as I do that I can pick one of these up from any number of sources. But I came to you. It's your shout. Take it or leave it, but there's no more."

He wipes the drip from the end of his nose, thinks for a second or two more and then concedes with a dismissive wave of the back of his hand.

Beer money, didn't I say?

On the way back to the lock-up I stop off and pick-up a carry-out. It's after six when I wrap on the outer door of the defunct arches security firm. Harvey lets me in without a word and returns to his game of patience at the table. The TV is on in the background and the runt's lying on the bed staring up into the roof with his hands clasped under the back of his head. The air inside is stale and I can sense an atmosphere between them. I remove my shades, set the carrier bag on the worktop and tell them grub's up, but neither shows any enthusiasm.

I grab one of the brown paper bags from inside the carrier and turn to face them, leaning back against the worktop. The bag rustles as I unfold it and spread it open. I raise my voice a little to be sure I break into their individual sulks. "You two ladies had a tiff then, or what?"

Harvey lifts his head and I quickly pack a few French Fries into my mouth. Further away, the runt rises from the bed and makes his way across.

"What did you bring then?" Harvey asks. "It's already stinking the place up."

"I went in past the Chinese. Got us all a sweet and sour with a portion of fries."

Harvey curls his lip. "Wouldn't rice have made more sense?"

"The fries were ready; I didn't want to wait for the rice."

We eat in relative silence, the sound of chewing and the occasional belch aside. I watch the runt. His face is sullen. Unshaven and dishevelled, he looks a broken man. Once we've all finished the runt pushes his polystyrene carton toward the centre of the table, stands and asks if he can go to the loo. I tell him yes and watch him shuffle away.

"So what's been going on?" I ask.

"He's been doing my fucking head in," Harvey says. "He's hard work and no mistake."

"You should use the cable ties and keep him strapped to the bloody bed, especially if you have to answer the door, like earlier."

"Easier said than done; he's playing us, I'm sure of it. Ten minutes after I put the ties on this morning he wanted the toilet and I had to cut them to let him go. Half an hour later he complained of cramp and I had to cut him free of another set so that he could walk it off. And when he's not moaning he shuffles around staring at the walls. I'm sure he's up to something."

"You're too easy with him. If he wants the toilet too soon after the last visit, just tell him to piss himself. That or give him a poke in the ribs. He'll get the message."

"The air in this place is bad enough, thanks."

The runt comes out of the toilet then sits on his bed to watch TV. I get up to leave.

"What's the rush?" Harvey asks. "I've not even told you about Myrna yet."

"I'll see her soon enough," I tell him. "There's something I've got to do first."

"Rosewood's hardware?" Harvey asks.

"No. That's taken care of. I'm going to see Boots."

I half expected a flurry of questions, but they don't come. Instead Harvey seems lost in thought and it's like I interrupt when I remind him that I'll be back in the morning.

"Are you all right?" I ask.

"Sure," he says, walking to the mini fridge. "But I'm dry after that meal. I need a Coke or something to wash it down." He turns to the runt, "Ferris, d'you want a drink?"

I leave them to it.

****

Chapter 17 ~ Making it real ~

~ Adam ~

A break is all well and good but you have to know how to fill your time to get the most from it. By mid morning I've enjoyed a quiet stroll, breakfasted in the fresh air and read my newspaper, all blissfully undisturbed. But now, sad to say, I'm beginning to feel a little bored and more than a little awkward. What do I do next? I have the campsite to myself but presumably people come here not just to relax but to enjoy themselves. Given that I'll soon be the cause of some unwelcome excitement in the village I need to look like I'm here for the right reasons. I decide to pay a visit to reception. Most hotels usually have a few leaflets advertising what's on in the area. I can't recall seeing any but maybe Shelley can give me a few ideas.

Long before I reach the desk I can see it's not Shelley sitting there. I try to hide my disappointment as I ask the young girl for help. She looks over my shoulder and I follow the line of her eye until I see a set of upright, wall mounted trays almost obscured by the open door. I thank her and spend the next few minutes rifling through various colourful leaflets and guides that peek from the top of the trays. The majority refer to London itself, to the theatre shows, museums and galleries rather than the local area, but I pick up a leaflet on the Five Villages Spring Festival and something on fishing the stretch of river in Mountebridge. As I turn back toward reception I'm faced by Shelley and Joel.

Shelley's wearing a knee-length beige raincoat, unfastened. "Hello, again," she says.

Joel is a couple of steps behind but has already seen the leaflets I'm holding. "Are you going fishing, Adam?"

"Hi," I say to Shelley. Then to Joel, "I don't know, I've just picked these up. I was about to ask the receptionist about the fishing."

"You'll need a permit, but we sell them here," Shelley says. She looks in the direction of the young receptionist, "Katy can sort that out for you."

"Anywhere local where I can hire rod and tackle though? I don't have anything with me."

"Ah," she says, in a way that instantly conveys the answer.

I look at Joel and notice that he's staring at his mother, his eyes wide, imploring. "Granddad would let him use his spare rod; and I could show him the best spot."

"Joel," Shelley says, raising her voice slightly.

"I'll ask him," Joel says, and races back through the dining room before Shelley can stop him.

I catch Shelley's eye. "What's just happened?"

"Oh, nothing you've done," she says. "Summer and mid-term breaks are always the same. Most days we can find something to keep him occupied but today's my day off and I need to go into town. We're down a cellar man in the bar so everyone's busy. Joel has to come with me, whether he likes it or not. This is just a last ditch attempt to get out of it."

I don't appreciate the ins and outs, but it doesn't stop me saying, "I see."

Joel bounds back through from the dining area and beams at me. "Granddad says you can use his spare rod." Then he turns to Shelley. "And Granddad won't need to spend time digging it out, 'cos I know where it is." Then he shuts up and stands with his chest heaving from the effort of running.

Shelley frowns. "Joel, you're putting me in an impossible situation."

"Look, fishing or no fishing I don't mind hanging out with Joel for a while if it helps." Then I remember my first chat with Shelley and quickly add, "that is, if you're happy that you know me well enough." I realise immediately that it's a stupid thing to have said because, of course, she doesn't know me.

"C'mon, Mum. You talked him into camping here. I can show him where to fish and you get to shop without me holding you back. Everybody wins."

I've heard him make that statement before and now both of us are looking at Shelley, waiting for her next words.

"Are you sure?" she asks me.

"Joel and I get on fine; I enjoy his company, really. Do you have a mobile?"

Shelley rummages in her handbag and finds her cell phone.

"May I?" I say, taking it from her. I save my name and number and press call. My mobile rings. I end the call and hand her mobile back to her.

"Joel has his own mobile," she says with a grin.

I bite my lip and give a slightly embarrassed smile of my own. "Okay, I should have remembered that. But now you can get hold of either of us."

"I need to go," she says and turning to Joel. "You have to be home by five o'clock and you get one chance, mister. Don't make me regret this." Then she's gone.

Joel makes a fist and punches the air. "A day's fishing...yessss!"

~

We fish from a shaded bank a few hundred yards from the little bridge into town. We've cast our lines and allowed them to drift into the deep waters off the far bank. It's the kind of place only the locals would know, we passed several spots I'd have been keen to try and Joel said that's why most visitors miss this one, they never get this far. It's on a sharp bend where the river turns towards us. The water isn't particularly fast-flowing but it really gets hung up in the bend to the point of being almost still at the far side. According to Joel it's where the fish hold up to feed. He's come prepared with rubber boots, a lightweight cagoule and a bag he says holds all we'll need – though I threw in some crisps, sandwiches and fizzy drinks on the way down so we'd neither thirst nor starve.

It's obvious that Joel's done a fair bit of fishing, he casts as far as I do holding the rod with his hands spread apart, allowing his whole body to aid the swing. There's a visible change in him too. The brash teenager is replaced by a serious lad who understands this to be a sport that demands patience and a quiet calm.

We spend a while letting our lines drift, reeling them in to cast again and watch them drift into the far bank. But neither of us senses so much as a nibble. I'm enjoying myself though. The constant gush of the river has a soothing effect; it's beginning to feel like a real holiday.

Joel breaks the silence between us. "So what is it you do?"

"For a living you mean?"

"Yeah. For a living."

I give him the stock answer. "I work for the council in Tannock Bar."

"Doing what?"

I scrunch my face. "Nothing exciting I'm afraid. I work for the Parks and Gardens."

"Designing them?"

I turn to look at him. "Tidying them; trimming the hedgerows, turning over the soil, planting the flowers, that sort of thing."

"Aw," he says.

I find myself thinking back to the girls at the nightclubs. It's no different here; the truth – or the part of it I'm ready to share – is so uninspiring even a kid can't hide his disappointment in it. I'm reminded of how empty my job leaves me.

"Time to try a different tack," Joel says. He reels in his line, sets his rod down and holds the fly and spinner at eye level. As he unpicks them from the line his tongue flicks out to lick his upper lip. When he's done he returns the fly and spinner to his bait box.

"You do that very well," I tell him.

"My granddad taught me." He pulls a plastic container from his bag. "You carry on. I won't be long." With that he disappears into the trees lining the embankment.

About ten minutes pass and I'm beginning to get a little uneasy about letting him wander off. But just as I'm considering going after him he ambles back through the trees.

"Where did you get to?"

He raises the plastic container and rattles it. "I found us a change of bait. Reel your line in and we'll give 'em a go."

A few minutes later we're casting out again having baited our hooks with the earthworms Joel had dug up.

"Good idea," I tell him.

"You wouldn't believe the things me and granddad have tried. The fish are in there but sometimes they just don't go for the spinners and lures. Granddad says the light has a lot to do with it. Sometimes they'll go for the worms but we've even compacted the bread and filling from our sandwiches to use as bait."

"And that works?" I ask, smiling.

"Nah," he says, laughing. "But it's fun to try."

"It sounds as though your granddad is a bit of a character."

Joel nods. "I suppose, but he knows his stuff too. If he's determined to make a catch he'll make up hand-rolled balls of his own bait, using liquidised fish from the hotel. He says the keen course fishermen add dissolving bags to their line to give the fish a free feed and create a feeding frenzy. Then they bait up heavy hoping the bigger fish will be less wary, taking the bait whole to show their line in the pecking order. We don't do any of that stuff. We have fun but we don't take it too seriously."

Not for the first time I find myself thinking Joel is a pretty well-adjusted kid. We spend another hour casting and re-casting. Joel has one strike, a carp. His face lights up as he hauls it from the water and flicks his mousy brown fringe from his eyes. He frees it from the hook as though he's done it a thousand times before then places it back in the water and releases it. I tell him it's a good point at which to stop and grab a bite to eat.

Having set aside my rod I wash my hands at the river's edge as Joel watches and when I'm stuck for something to dry them with I wipe them on my trouser legs.

I smile. "Your mum said that the tenting fraternity like to rough it a bit, but I don't think they'd go as far as eating their sarnies after pulverising worms onto a bait hook."

He laughs, gives his own hands a wash and then rubs them down the front of his jeans. He peels off his cagoule and lays it down to sit on. I do likewise with my jacket and we break out the food.

"So what normally happens when your mum goes into town?" I ask between mouthfuls.

He grins. "It doesn't happen often; only on school breaks and only then if she needs to get away. I hang out with my mates; same as I'd do if she were here. I just check in with granddad from time to time."

"So why couldn't you do that today?"

"He shrugs his shoulders. Ma says granddad's going to be too busy. Why? Do you see this as you looking after me?"

"Not really. It's a kind of *everybody wins* lad's day out isn't it? We just can't put it that way in front of your mother."

Another grin. "Why?"

I'm shrugging my shoulders now. "I suppose it's because mums see sons differently. No matter how old or how big you are, you're always their little boy."

"They do trust me you know. I get to fish here with my mates; it's just that Ma knows they're all away for a few days and granddad is busy."

"All of your mates are away at the same time?"

"The regular ones." He drops a handful of crisps into his mouth and crunches them down before continuing. "There are others; it's just that Ma's not so keen on them."

"Mothers are like that," I tell him. "She just wants the best for you."

A couple of beeps ring out and he digs into his bag and checks his mobile. "It's Ma. She says she's sending a text so she doesn't disturb the fish." He types out a reply and slips the phone back into his bag. "I told her we were having lunch and that you were more likely to catch a cold than a fish."

My own mobile signals a text message. It's from Shelley. Two words. Thank you!

Joel goes a little quiet and stares out into the river. "Can I ask you something?"

191

"Sure."

"You said the other day that your Ma was a single parent. So you never had a dad. Didn't that bother you?"

It's a question that sends a chill through me. He's asked it while still staring out into the river and I'm glad for that because I'm not sure I could have held his gaze. As it is I let my head fall and rub at the back of my neck. I feel him turn to look at me because I've taken too long to answer.

"I suppose it's different for everyone in that situation, Joel. I think you feel you've lost out, but I can't say I ever missed my dad. As far as I was concerned if he didn't want us then we didn't want or need him. I miss my mother every day; I never give him a second thought."

He nods, then a quizzical expression spreads over his face and I realise I've said more than I meant to. I know what's coming next.

"What happened to your mother?"

"She died." I wait a second or two then add, "it was a long time ago; I was twelve."

Joel' eyebrows lift for a second. "So, no dad, then no mum either. How'd she die?"

It's not a subject I want to go into, but for all Joel's streetwise savvy he still has a child's innocence; he can get away with asking awkward and personal questions and I feel unable to shut the conversation down.

"She had cancer," I tell him.

Joel stares out into the water. "I'm twelve," he says.

****

Chapter 18 ~ Shit happens ~

~ Mo ~

I park the Astra and hit the streets, asking after Boots at the doors of the pubs and clubs he used to hang in. But other than shaking heads and the occasional wary look, all I get is the name of a different haunt to try, and the impression that even that much is reluctantly given. There are no 'no-go' areas for me in Harlesden, but I'm reminded that there are places where respect exists though trust does not. The Harlesden of today is very different from my mother's time, changed even from when me and Harvey grew up here. The divide grows day by day. The Black and West Indian communities seem to shoulder the blame for the reputation the area has with a kind of pride, and there's no escaping the claim that they're responsible for the majority of the muggings and petty thefts that happen on their turf. It gets up the noses of the Yardies simply because they think Cornelius has a hand in organised crime in the area without ever getting his name blackened or his hands dirty. And, of course, they're right. But Cornelius backed away from the drug scene because he was smart enough to see that although it brought high rewards it would also lead us on a collision course with Sholto Carnie. And Sholto's probably the single most popular reason why half of Harlesden feel the need to carry a gun and why the likes of Gav Marsden make money.

I try a basement nightclub in the High Street suggested by someone a block further back. The large, bald-headed doorman here watches me as I descend the stairs and lifts his chin to look down at me as I reach him. I ask the same question, in the same manner that I have at the previous bars and clubs, "I'm looking for Boots. Is he here tonight?"

The doorman is a little wary. "Are you on the pre-approved guest list?"

"No, is he?"

He doesn't answer; I glance at my watch and try again. "Look, it's just gone nine, the place won't be busied up yet and I only need five minutes of his time."

"I don't want any trouble," he says.

"If I was here to make trouble you'd be in pain already."

He takes the hint, opens the door for me and I step inside. A couple of girls stand in a booth to the left of the door taking entry money and coats. I glare at them and while the doorman still has hold of the main door I tell them that if I'm not out in five minutes they can send 'him' after me for the entry money.

I pass through a set of double doors and I'm immediately slowed by people standing in small groups, drinks in hand. Chesterfield sofas are grouped in clusters but are already occupied leaving people filling the walkways in between. Did I say it'd not be busy yet? It's packed. They lean into each other to talk while rap, maybe it's hip-hop, pulses from wall-mounted speakers. I side-step my way through until I reach the bar. My intention is to ask one of the barmen, but with the queue two deep I place my hands on the shoulders of the girl in front and ask her if this is all there is to this place.

She points to the side of the dance-floor. "Upstairs, love, there's another bar, but it's even smaller than this one."

The upper bar is indeed much smaller, less crowded and the noise a little muted. The sofas are here too but it feels more like a private function area with a small flat-screen

TV by the bar showing the dance floor downstairs. It's maybe three years since I've seen Boots, but he's not the type of person you forget. He's as black as they come, has a prominent lower jaw and wears his hair in dreadlock style. He's a dealer rather than the chemist his nickname implies, but details like that didn't seem important at school, so the name stuck. These days it's like he's a cult hero in a perverse way; he sells drugs within his own community but has their respect because he refuses to sell any of the shit Carnie's lot try to push. It's like Cornelius getting recognition for regulating the area's organised crime.

I catch sight of Boots in the far corner of the room; small, square-rimmed spectacles sit on the bridge of his broad nose, but otherwise he's as my memory recalls him. He and his friends cut short their conversation to look up as I approach and in an instant I see a smile break across his face and he stands to greet me.

"Onion, what you doin' here, man? Did you done get yourself lost on the wrong side of town?"

I reach out my hand to take his as his friends push back to make space. "All of Harlesden is my side of town," I tell him. "I need to have a chat with you; can you spare a couple of minutes?"

"Sure thing, my friend, sure thing."

He makes to sit down again, but stops when I add, "In private."

The guy to his left leans in and whispers something into his ear and Boots looks at me and his lips part for a second.

I lift my hands to shoulder height, palms out. "I'm not carrying anything. You can check."

They pat me down and when they're satisfied I follow Boots into the gents to talk.

"Sorry about that," Boots says.

"Don't be. I came to buy but what I've seen has me worried."

"I don't follow you."

"It might be nothing," I tell him. "But I know Carnie has something big going down right now. It could go one of two ways."

Boots leans against the toilet wall and pushes his specs further up on his nose. "I'm not sure I get you yet, but I'm listening."

"It's an open secret that you irritate him, yeah?"

Boots smiles. "It's a free country, man. You don't want me to push his shit any more than I do."

"No. But I want you to be careful. Maybe what he has going on will mean he's too busy elsewhere. But if whatever he's into puts him under pressure for cash he could be forced to come after your cut of the market. And after what I've seen tonight you're vulnerable."

"Hold on. Nobody wants a war; not even Carnie would risk that."

"Oh, c'mon, Boots, he'd be cleverer than that. He'd use someone with no direct ties to him. Take me for example; the doorman let me know you were here. Did he get a message to you before I found you?" His eyes confirm it. "I didn't think so. And what about those guys around you? By the time they thought to frisk me I could have pulled a gun and blown you away."

"But they'd have killed you."

"Do you think Carnie would care? Whoever he'd send would be expendable too."

Boots rubs at his earlobe and stares at me long and hard. "What is it that's going down?"

"I don't know, Cornelius hasn't let on and I didn't set out to tell you. It just strikes me that if Carnie's under the same pressure then you might be in danger. Just be warned, that's all."

Boots straightens up. "I hear you." He's silent for a few seconds, as though thinking through what he might change. Then he lightens the mood. "Anyway, you came to buy. Didn't you get yourself burned last time?"

"Nothing heavy and not for me; for my girl. She likes to mellow out…afterwards."

He begins to laugh.

"What's funny?" I ask.

He's laughing so hard his eyes are watering. "It's just…" he wipes the tears from his eyes with the back of his hand. "Man, I seen you bust people up and not so much as flinch for the hurt you gave. But I never took you for shy and respectful in that way."

He's lost me. "How d'you mean?"

"That word, *afterwards*, like you was avoiding saying after you'd fucked her brains out."

He slaps me on the shoulder. "Nothing wrong, man. In fact, it's nice, courteous even. She must mean a lot to you.

C'mon, I've got some quality blues that'll kick in…
afterwards," he adds, laughing again.

I'm back in the Astra and heading for Calendar Girls
but I can't get Boots out of my head. Carnie's sure to have
markers on guys who'd be willing to do a job on Boots.
Even if it was a suicide mission there'd be those who'd risk it
to clear their marker and at worst set their family up for life.
I just hope Carnie has his mind on other things. My mobile
rings startling me for a second. I pull it from my pocket and
take my eyes from the road to glance at the screen, it's
Harvey. I push the button to accept the call.

"I'm driving, hold on a sec 'til I pull in." I toss the
phone onto the passenger seat and take the next left. All the
while I can hear Harvey wittering on, the stupid fuck didn't
listen. Once I've pulled over I take the phone to my ear.

"Did you hear what I said?" Harvey shouts.

"No. I just pulled over. I'm on my way to Calendar
Girls. What the fuck do you want?"

"Get yourself over here now. It's Ferris, I've fucking
lost him."

I'm silent for no more than a second taking it in
when he speaks again.

"Did you get that? The little bastard's bolted."

"Okay, stay where you are. I'll be as quick as I can."

"No, I'm going out look for the little shit. He won't
get far. Call me when you get close."

Harvey cuts the line and I'm speechless; I can't believe he's let the runt escape. I turn the car around and head back out of town. It's a fuck-up and no mistake. Cornelius will go crazy if he finds out, but for once it's not my doing. This job's been trouble from the start and the more I think back the more annoyed I get. This isn't a fucking game, if it goes wrong for Cornelius it goes wrong for Carnie. And if Carnie gets messed about then everybody suffers. How could Harvey let it happen?

About a mile from the lock-up my temper's up and the Astra's flying. I clip the occasional corner to the sound of screeching rubber. A few hundred yards from the lock-up I remember that Harvey said I should call when I got close. I reach for my mobile and hit speed dial but I let it slip and it falls into my lap and onto the floor. I fumble for it keeping my eyes on the road but I can't reach and have to glance down for a moment to get it. When my fingers find it I look up in time to see the headlights pick out a shape as it emerges from the bushes at the side of the road. He sees me, but he steps out anyway, his arms flailing. I turn the wheel and hit the brake but I know it's too late, I'm too close. I side-swipe him and in the mirror I see him spin like a rag-doll then crumple to the ground. The Astra comes to a halt about twenty yards further on, only fifty from the arches. I shift into reverse, back up quickly and bring her to a stop.

His chest rises and falls, though his breathing seems shallow. His left leg lies at an impossible angle and there's a little blood too but I'm not sure from where. This isn't good. I know I have to act quickly. I open the rear door of the car and bundle him in. He manages a low moan, my lifting him causes him discomfort, but it's the least of his worries, and mine. The housing scheme is only a short distance away and I check for any signs that we've been seen. It seems not.

The lock-up is open. I raise the roller door and drive the Astra inside before lowering the door again. I'm looking round when I hear the footsteps.

"I thought we agreed you were to call before you got here," Harvey says. "We need to find the little bastard."

I turn and glare at him, his shirt collar's tugged away from his neck and his face is red with effort.

"Panics over, I found him. Or rather he found me."

Harvey's brow furrows. "Where is he then?"

"In the back of the car, dying."

"What?"

"He staggered out in front of me not fifty yards from here. I couldn't stop. Poor bastard's all broken up."

Harvey moves to open the rear door and looks inside. "Ferris, can you hear me?"

When he gets no response he shuts the door and turns back to me. "Are you good to drive?"

"Don't try turning this on me, Harvey. You were meant to keep him under wraps."

"He was asleep. I went out for a fag, okay? I was less than two minutes."

"But you didn't tie him to the bed with the cable ties like I said."

"He was sleeping. I didn't think I needed to."

The damage is done; we're both of us quiet for a moment. Maybe they won't renew my licence next time around, but I'm not about to tell that to Harvey.

Harvey runs a hand backwards through his hair. "Look. I didn't think I needed to tie him up 'cos I'd slipped him enough sleeping pills to knock out a fucking elephant."

"What?"

"Don't give me that. It was you who gave me the idea. You suggested it yesterday and I brought some from home. I only remembered when you mentioned going to see Boots."

"That'll be why he hadn't got far and why he looked almost drunk stepping out in front of me. Poor bastard was fighting it." I scratch at my goatee. "So what do we do now?"

Harvey sits at the table. "Ferris was our insurance that Rosewood would do the job. Until it's done and we have the money he has to think we still have him."

"What about the runt?" I nod in the direction of the Astra.

"We have to dump him. He's not dead, but you said yourself he doesn't look far from it. And even if he wasn't we can't risk leaving him at a hospital and having him talk."

I nod in agreement, I can see the logic. It's why it pays not to get too close.

Harvey sighs. "We need to gather up everything that says he's been here, his bag, his wallet, anything that might ID him."

While Harvey goes to the car to go through the runt's pockets I pick up his rucksack and take a slow walk around the room looking for any other signs of his stay. When I walk past the boxes stacked in the corner behind the washroom I notice they sit askew. I ease them apart. The exit doorway they block is still padlocked but scores on its surface suggest someone has tried to force it.

"You all done?" Harvey shouts.

"Yeah."

"Then let's get out of here."

"Where do we take him?" I ask.

Harvey looks around at the figure slumped across the back seat. "Just drive for now, I'll think of somewhere, but let's put some distance between us and the railway arches."

"We could take him back towards Tannock Bar. That way it might look like he had an accident there."

"That sounds good for now," Harvey says. "Go for it." He flicks the radio on and we listen to some late night programme until it slips off the station.

A mile or two from Tannock Bar Harvey pinches the bridge of his nose. "I still can't work out how he got out you know."

"He hid behind the boxes," I tell him.

"Bollocks. How would that work?"

"When I looked around I noticed the boxes behind the washroom had been moved. At a guess he knew there had to be another exit and hoped to force it when you went for a fag break. When he couldn't break the padlock he pinned himself to the door and drew the boxes around. He'll have come out when you went out to look for him."

"You mean the little bastard was there all the time. Stop the fucking car."

I look at him, unsure if he's serious, but his face is scarlet with rage.

I pull over and moments later I'm bundling the runt into my arms then laying him in scrubland not thirty feet from the road and maybe half a mile from Tannock Bar.

A few miles down the road Harvey's rage is subsiding. "He's hanging in there," he says, "but the cold will finish him before morning." They're the only words that pass between us on the journey back to Harlesden.

****

Chapter 19 (Part I) ~ The lay of the land ~

~ Adam ~

It's Sunday. I've grown used to waking to the sound of birdsong and the sharpness of the morning air on the back of my throat. But it's still early so I prop myself up in my sleeping bag and read through a few magazine articles before heading for the shower block.

I let the shower run for a few minutes while I shave at the basin, I've learned that it takes those few minutes for the water to warm. Then I load my brush with paste and step into the shower already scrubbing at my teeth, old habits die hard. The water cascades over me; I close my eyes and turn to face the shower. A breeze passes under the door of the shower block and I have to beat the curtain off as it sweeps inward and clings to me. When I set my toothbrush aside and get to soaping myself I let my mind wander towards what the day might bring. I've not seen Joel since our day's fishing. We had a great time and I'd expected to repeat it before now. But the tentative offers that I left at the desk with Shelley were not taken up. In fact, now that I think about it, I realise that on each occasion Shelley barely spoke to me. I presumed at the time that she was just busy, but maybe there's more to it. I decide to be more direct and ask outright if there's a problem. Anyway, having had time on my hands hasn't been all bad news; it did give me the chance to do some homework on the local roads and find myself a few alternative routes. I took the chance too to pick up some things I'll need on the day – a ski mask and a set of jogging bottoms and top from a second-hand store. The thought leads me on and in my mind's eye I see myself taking those last few steps before crossing the threshold at the Post Office door. It reminds me that there's still something else I should check and first thing on a Sunday is as good a time as any.

Just over half an hour later I'm walking into the village, it's become almost a ritual; a daily trek for fresh milk, rolls and whatever else I need. But there's a little more to it this morning. Being a Sunday it's even quieter than normal. I walk three quarters way down the high street, squinting down the side streets until I find what I'm looking for. The only bank in the village is set off the main street, and its location means my route on Wednesday won't have me pass directly in front of it at any time. It's good news as any security camera focussed there won't pose me a problem. My walk back past the Post Office to the nearby newsagent gives me the opportunity to look at the surrounding buildings. Street surveillance cameras tend to be positioned high up on the sides of buildings where their wide angle lenses can capture street crime and traffic problems – but it seems that Mountebridge, thankfully, has had no need of these. There are two options; either I stroll from the car to the Post Office pulling on the ski mask at the last moment or dash from the car with the mask already in place. I prefer the former as the alternative risks alerting passers-by and this morning's reccy suggests it's safe.

I buy a couple of Sunday papers at the newsagent and begin to walk back. The next time I see the Post Office will be a few minutes before I point a shotgun at the old man behind the counter. It strikes me that I'd find the whole idea much easier if Ferris were here but, of course, if that were the case we'd not be in Mountebridge and no doubt we'd be facing a different kind of payback with the Scallion brothers. In the spur of the moment I stop in the street, take out my mobile and call Ferris's number. It rings out until the line disconnects. I try again; it's answered on the fourth ring.

"Rosewood, this better be good."

I recognise Harvey's voice and tell him I want to speak to Ferris.

"It's half past nine on a fucking Sunday. He's sleeping. Now piss off."

"How do I know you've even got him? Let me talk to him."

"You can speak to him when we have the money. Now fuck off."

Harvey ends the call. I'm no better off and might just have made the situation worse for Ferris.

When I get to The Huntsman I want to find the number for Ferris's work and find out if he's been in.

"Good morning, Adam, you're up early. Can we tempt you with a Sunday breakfast?"

I've forgotten all about Shelley giving me the cold shoulder, so much so that the breezy welcome doesn't surprise me the way it should. "Maybe later; do you have a Yellow Pages I could borrow?"

Shelley frowns. "It went awol I'm afraid. But if you give me the details I'll call direct enquiries for you."

"Mickelson's DIY in Tannock Bar," I tell her.

"Okay, now how about breakfast? They stop serving in fifteen minutes, so you'll catch them if you go through now. I'll bring you the number."

I take a seat and order the 'Full English'. A few minutes later the waitress serves it up as Shelley arrives with the number I need on a piece of note paper. She hands it to me and I thank her.

"Actually, do you mind if I sit for a moment?" she asks.

"As long as you don't mind me eating?"

"Of course not. I'll join you in a cup of tea and call it my break," she adds, signalling to the waitress to bring another pot.

"I was beginning to get the impression I'd done something to annoy you," I tell her.

Shelley breaks eye contact for a second to stare at the table then looks back to me. "That's what I wanted to say. I owe you an apology."

"How come?"

"I didn't tell Joel you wanted to go fishing again. In fact, I told him you were too busy."

I want to ask why she'd do that but my mouth's full and the waitress arrives with Shelley's tea.

"Thanks, Mary," Shelley says. When the waitress has gone she continues. "When Joel came back from the day's fishing with you he did something he hasn't done in years."

I set my knife and fork down, wipe my lips with the napkin and give Shelley my full attention. It seems to put more pressure on her, she looks around as the last few customers in the dining room begin to leave and the waitress reappears to clear the tables.

Shelley lowers her voice and leans forward. "He ran up to me and gave me a hug."

I'm waiting for more but she stops there, as if that's it.

"And?" I ask.

"His eyes were watery, as though he were close to tears and…" her voice trails away and she breaks eye contact again.

"Oh, God. You thought I'd… done something to him?"

"No. I don't quite know what I thought. It just made me a little uncomfortable." Shelley rests her elbows on the table and rests her head in her hands. "I'm sorry."

"But you must have asked him? I mean we had a laugh, I know we did. It was…"

"Of course," she interrupts. "Look, he said the two of you had a great day. It was just me who misread that initial hug and the look in his eyes."

I push my plate away, my appetite for the rest of breakfast gone. "I'm shocked," I tell her, "I don't know what to say."

"I'm sorry," she says, unable to look at me for a second.

"So what's changed?"

"He raised the subject himself last night, still hoping you two could go out again. He told me he liked you because you didn't treat him like a kid and because you understood what it was like to grow up without a father. But then he said you'd lost your mother at his age. It made him feel lucky and ashamed at the same time. I knew then what that hug was for. You made a connection with him and I jumped to the wrong conclusions. I'm really sorry."

"So what do I say to him now if I bump into him?"

"We can take care of that. Let me make it up to you," she says. "You picked up a leaflet earlier in the week for the Five Villages Festival. It's the opening day of Wingate's festival week. Joel and I are going this afternoon. Come with us."

****

Chapter 19 (Part II) ~ Chemistry ~

~ Adam ~

At one o'clock I meet up with Shelley and Joel on the gravel driveway outside The Huntsman. Shelley is dressed casually in jeans with a pale blue blouse worn under a thin jacket. She smiles at me then looks down to fish her car keys from her shoulder bag. Joel is in good humour but the first thing he asks is why we've not been fishing again. I tell him I watched him closely last time and decided I'd best read a few fishing magazines and pick up some tips before our next try.

"Watching what exactly?" he asks.

"Little things that show you really know what you're doing," I tell him. "Like how you grip the reel and the way you cast. I want to give you more of a contest next time."

It brings a smile to his face and in those last few strides toward Shelley's car I'm sure he walks that bit taller.

I sit in the back of Shelley's hatchback as we travel to Wingate and it's clear from the excited conversation passing between Shelley and Joel that both are looking forward to the afternoon. I'm left in no doubt that it's more than a fayre to them. Shelley talks of the bits and pieces she hopes to find among the stalls while Joel is keen on the games and the rides on show. Both are anxious to see what competition the Wingate Festival offers against Mountebridge.

We find a parking spot on the grass of the local sports field, its purpose altered for the week, and we join the numbers milling through the streets. For me it's a little like déjà vu. The village main street is cordoned off - along with several adjoining side streets - and from all around people converge on the makeshift stalls. We wander on, Shelley stopping to look at the bric-a-brac and buying a couple of small, framed pictures. We watch street artists draw caricature sketches for a couple of pounds then we queue to roll pre-decimal pennies onto a large expanse of coloured squares only marginally bigger than the pennies themselves. To win a prize the penny must topple inside the edges of a square and, of course, it's harder than it looks.

The stalls come to an abrupt end and we have a little more room to manoeuvre; the town square opens out before us but beyond we can appreciate now that the stalls are set out along Wingate's two main streets intersecting the square. It's clear though that this is the centrepiece of Wingate's festival effort. They have avoided the street-long bunting that filled Lower Weaton's Hope Street and concentrated on decorating just this focal point. Flowers spill out over baskets hung at height from the arms of the olde world corner lampposts and the square itself is a topiary garden, an oasis of calm amid the chaos, a sensory experience.

The tea shop overlooking the square has thrown open its doors and set up tables outside. Shelley casts an eye in their direction and suggests a cup of tea would be in order. Joel, though, is anxious to press on, so after agreeing to meet back here in an hour Shelley and I sit at a table.

"They've done the square up nicely," Shelley says. "It's really pretty."

"Yes, someone's taken a lot of care," I tell her.

Her hazel eyes search the square, then fall back on me. "You mean more than pretty though, don't you?"

"Yes," I say, as a waitress, dressed in black with a white lace apron presents us with a menu and waits patiently as we order tea, jam and scones.

Shelley looks to me, eyebrows raised. "Go on then, tell me what you see?"

"Well, firstly there's the visual impact, the vibrancy of the colours in the flower boxes hanging from the lampposts; and that contrasts nicely with the greens that dominate in the plants chosen to sit at ground level. But it's not just that, it's the use of space, shape and symmetry."

"Symmetry?" she asks.

"Sure. The corner lampposts frame the square and within topiary bushes and plants have been spaced evenly apart. It'd be easy to overdo it and lose the effect. But here, someone has understood that less is more."

"I never noticed a pattern," Shelley says, looking around again.

"I'd even go as far as to suggest they've thought about the sensory impact."

Shelley leans forward, places her elbow on the table and cradles her chin with the palm of her hand while her index finger rests pointedly on her cheek. Her furrowed brow conveys both interest and surprise. "Go on," she says.

"The colours I've mentioned, but then there are the topiary shapes, round and plump, tall and slim but always overall symmetry within the frame. Then there's the smell, the gentle scents from the flowers above are just enough to be noticed, to draw you in even, but they're not overpowering or it'd compete with the aromas here at the tea shop." Our tea and scones arrive. "There will be a textural difference between the plants chosen too, but that's getting too subtle."

Shelley gives a wry smile. "You're full of surprises," she says, uncrossing her legs before daintily dividing her scone and coating it with jam.

"Have I impressed you?" I ask.

Shelley's head is lowered over her plate but her eyes lift up and fix me in her gaze. "Twice in a short spell," she says.

"Twice? When was the first time?"

"That white lie over the fishing. You managed to cover my intervention and boost Joel's ego at the same time. He all but floated into the car."

"That wasn't a lie, he does fish well."

"You know fine what I mean," she says. "You seem at ease with kids."

I'm about to tell her I've no experience in that department but we are both distracted by a group of brightly attired men emerging from the tea shop. The four align themselves not six feet from our table and begin to sing. They're a barbershop quartet.

The singers are a magnet for the numbers at the stalls and draw them around us but Shelley and I have front row seats. After three songs they move off to loud applause and the crowd dissipates as quickly as it gathered.

"You enjoyed barbershop," I tease. "You had a smile on your face the whole time."

"Well, they were good," she says, "and it was unexpected and very different."

Shelley is beaming, contentment radiates from her and it's as though the last fifteen minutes were the most relaxing of her week. I realise she's not alone for there's a tingle running through me too. I'm seeing a different side to Shelley; she's unwinding and beginning to have fun. The breeze catches her shoulder-length hair and whips a few strands across her face; she peels them away and gives a shake of her head, causing me to smile.

"What is it?" she asks, grinning back at me.

"Nothing, it's just that I recognise that head flick. Joel does it too." She turns away, embarrassed and for a moment there's an awkward silence that makes me think I've said something I shouldn't have. But then she rescues me with a change of subject.

"So," she says, "how come you and Joel ended up chatting about you losing your mother?"

"Ah, not fair. Having impressed you earlier I can't answer that one without breaking your vision of me as one of the hardened tenting fraternity."

"I see," she says, still grinning, "and you're not."

"No. Joel wasn't particularly impressed with my attempts at putting up the tent. He sort of presumed that my dad would have taken me camping when I was young and shown me such things. He'd been so helpful it just felt easier to tell him the truth – that I never really knew my father, there was just my mum and me."

Shelley sighs. "Ah, there you go. You see, he assumes that all fathers do these things and that he's the only one losing out. But it gave you two a common bond, then."

"Exactly; but he raised the subject again when we were fishing and asked me how it was for me growing up without a dad. I sensed it was a big issue in his life but it hadn't been important to me and I said as much. I told him I missed my mother every day, but never my father." Just saying that aloud halts me for a second or two and when I raise my eyes to look at Shelley there's warmth in her returned gaze. It was also the kind of pregnant pause that begged an interruption, yet she didn't give in to it. She allowed me that moment, the sign of a good listener. I regain my line of thought and continue. "You said earlier that I was at ease with kids but I've no experience. I didn't think about my answer to Joel's question and shouldn't have let him realise I'd lost my mother too. I didn't appreciate the synergy between the age I was when I lost my mum and the age Joel is now. In fact, I took him to be a teenager; he's more switched on than I ever was at twelve."

"They grow up quicker these days; things were different when we were their age."

"I suppose," I say.

"You don't have kids of your own?"

"No."

"Well," Shelley says, "even if you did it wouldn't prepare you for situations like that. They put you under pressure and you don't always get thinking time."

"Well, I apologise if I made things worse."

Shelley stretches out a hand and places it on the back of my own. "You didn't, my imagination did that all on its own." She draws her hand back. "I know he feels it, especially when his friends talk of whatever they get up to with their dads; it's natural I suppose. His granddad tries so hard to be there for him, but I think he appreciated your openness, it helped him. I certainly can't remember when he last gave me a hug like that." She looks at me, sheepishly. "Can you forgive me for what passed through my mind?"

"Already done and dusted," I tell her.

"Good, then let's catch up with Joel."

I move to pay for our tea and scones but Shelley won't have it.

"No," she says, "I can't allow that and I owe you breakfast too."

I let my mouth drop open in mock surprise. "Well, you asked if you could make it up to me, and I was hurt, but I'd no idea you'd go that far."

She picks up on the double entendre and it brings a little colour to her cheeks, but just as quickly she fixes me with a stare, "Okay, I suppose I walked into that one. You're cute... but not that cute."

She has a sense of humour. I like that.

****

Chapter 20 ~ Worrywart ~

~ Mo ~

It's the small hours of Wednesday at Moods and the staff are preparing to close having tidied up long after sending home the last of the night's customers. I'm apprehensive and still a little angry. The Astra is in position; we changed the plates but have avoided telling Cornelius that one of his pool cars will be used in the heist; he's too tightly wrapped as it is. If it goes smoothly he'll never need to know. I drove the Astra to the lay-by myself over three hours ago with Harvey following on to give me a lift back. It's a stretch of road with very few turn offs and that too makes me uneasy; I don't trust Rosewood. I've had a bad feeling about this job from the start and nothing that's happened since has changed that.

There have been no reports of a body being found in the woods near Tannock Bar and as long as Rosewood still believes we have his friend then everything is cool. But I worry that, lying out in the open, the corpse will start to smell, attracting flies by the thousand and every passing fox or badger for miles around. We just need a few more hours. Harvey is relaxed about the whole thing but called Rosewood on the runt's mobile after we'd left the Astra. He said Rosewood was up for it and that I'm becoming a worrywart. I told him to go fuck himself and made a few insurance arrangements of my own. But Rosewood has made me wait and the tension has my head fit to burst. I slide a hand under my shades and massage my temples with my thumb and middle finger. It's time for me to head home too.

At the flat I undress and spend ten minutes laying waste to the punch bag; it's enough to clear the dull ache that had been settling over my brow. I shower and I'm about to slip a DVD into the player when my mobile vibrates and dances on the coffee table. I push the green button to accept the call and stretch out on the sofa. "How did you get on?"

"That's me just clear now. You called it right, Mo, the guy approached on foot, must've left his car at least half a mile away. I waited until he was well down the road before I dragged the bike out of the trees. Two and a half hours I sat in those fucking bushes and he turns up when I'm having a slash."

"Did he just drive off or did he check the car out first?"

"He rummaged around in the boot, but he didn't look keen to hang around."

"And you managed to follow him?"

"No problem, I stayed well back and kept his taillights in sight. I turned mine off when we hit the quieter roads so he'd have no idea there was anyone behind him."

"Where did he end up?"

"The middle of fucking nowhere; a place called Mountebridge a few miles off the M2. It's maybe twenty minutes from the lay-by, half an hour in normal traffic. He left the Astra in a side street and started to walk. So I had to park up and do the same. He disappeared in back of a hotel called The Huntsman, maybe he leaves a door or a window open at the back or something. That do you?"

"Good stuff, but remember, not a word about this to anybody. I'll leave your money in an envelope behind the bar tomorrow."

It's 2:25am when I end the call. Rosewood wouldn't have made the pick up if he wasn't going to go through with the job, so maybe Harvey can afford to be smug about my worrying, but I feel better knowing where Rosewood's hiding out anyway.

****

Chapter 21 ~ The lowest of the low ~

~ Adam ~

The last few hours before a job are always the worst, for me anyway. Colin was always cool; nothing phased him, he was always super-confident, but not me; never me. I stifle a yawn. I've been awake for most of the night, my mind too active for sleep. Instead I've lain in my sleeping bag, going over the plan in my head time and time again, visualising it happening. There should be no need - it's straightforward; not so much about what to do as what not to do. The physical requirements are all in place, now it's about concentrating, picking the moment, getting in and out fast and saying as little as possible.

I can't remember the name of the street where I left the car from the lay-by and it seems like the harder I try the deeper I push the detail. Not that it should matter, at worst it's two minutes further to walk. I've got to the point where I don't want to think about any of it. I'm confusing myself, creating doubt when I need to be positive. A glance at my watch tells me it's time to get up, I need routine. On the way to the shower block I glance at the two caravans opposite that arrived on site during Tuesday. I'd been extra careful not to disturb the occupants when I returned in the early hours and I'm keen to do the same now.

In the shower I turn the heat up higher than normal and let the water and the steam chase the tingling tiredness from my legs. All the time I'm trying to think of anything but what's ahead. The day at the fayre with Shelley and Joel comes to mind. I remember how relaxed I felt in Shelley's company, I see her crossing and uncrossing her slim legs as she sits with me at the tea shop and I recall the unexpected peck on the cheek she gave me at the end of the day. It almost felt like we'd been on a date, with Joel as chaperone. The breeze whips under the door and I lose the image as the cold plastic curtain wraps itself around my calf. I fight to think of Shelley again. She smiled yesterday when I booked to stay on site until Friday and said she was pleased I was staying a little longer. I convinced myself that leaving before the robbery might appear suspicious; that by staying I'll get a feel for the aftermath. Shelley has grown on me, I won't deny the attraction, nor the niggle that suggests I might be letting it cloud my thinking.

The Astra is where I thought it was. There are a few people milling about but I make sure it's clear before I climb in and move off. I drive a few hundred yards until the houses are replaced by open fields and it's safe to pull over. I take the ski mask from my trouser pocket and throw it onto the passenger seat. I've worn the baggiest trousers and jumper that I brought with me. The jumper comes off first then I undo my trousers and press my shoulders into the seatback so I can raise my hips and slide them down my legs, but I have to open the door to get them off properly. Underneath I'm wearing the thin dark coloured jogging bottoms and top that I bought the other day. I turn to throw my clothes in the back but I notice the seat is stained red. There's a sort of gamey smell that hits me too, as though someone's sat some road kill in back and the poor thing's oozed more than one kind of fluid. In daylight and fresh air this car really is a pile of shit. I climb out and open the boot, throw in my trousers and top and remove the draw string bag. Only once I've slid back into the driver's seat do I pull the short-barrelled shotgun out and check it over. It breaks open with a reassuring click, it's well-oiled and unloaded. Feeling its weight in my hands makes me hesitate for a moment. But then I remember the call to Ferris's work yesterday, hearing that he'd not been in at all the previous week and the sinking feeling hits me again. What choice is there? I have to do this. I snap back to now, time is getting on. There are shells in the bottom of the bag. I take them out and put them in the glove compartment and that's where they'll stay. There's no way I'd ever use this, I've just got to look as though I will.

I'm parked in a line of cars a little way down the street on the opposite side of the road as the security van draws up outside the Post Office. These guys are creatures of habit; they might vary their route but not their arrival time. I watch a crash-helmeted guard go in, a single metal box in one hand and a clipboard in the other. He emerges a few moments later still with clipboard and box, but by the way he swings it, I know it's empty.

Once the van has gone I check the street. A few strides away, a man walks along the pavement towards me while, in my wing mirror, I can see a couple in the distance walking in this direction, on the Post Office side of the road. I wait for a car to pass then pull out, drive past the Post Office and turn right into the side street just a few yards beyond. I stop as close to the junction as is reasonable, switch the engine off but leave the keys in the ignition. Now it's all down to timing.

My heart thumps against the wall of my chest in the few steps toward the shop. The black drawstring bag is slung over my right shoulder and my elbow tucks it tight to my side. The ski mask is scrunched into a ball in my left fist. When I turn the corner I'm only a few seconds from the Post Office and a last glance tells me how far away the approaching couple are. At the door, I duck my head down, draw the mask over my head in a single movement and step inside.

By the time I plant my first foot over the threshold I'm already pulling the sawn-off from the bag. The shop is empty. An elderly man stands behind a meshed counter at the far end; he's busy with something and doesn't even raise his head to acknowledge my entrance. I walk toward him between two aisles of greeting cards, calendars and stationery.

"Be with you in a second," he says.

I wrap the barrels hard against the mesh and he raises his head. "Fill it," I say, shoving the drawstring bag beneath the serving point. He doesn't even look me in the face; he can't take his eyes from the twin barrels facing him. Seconds go by, I'm suddenly aware of the exaggerated sound of my own breathing in the constraints of the mask, and still he does nothing. I rattle the mesh again and raise my voice telling him to fill it.

He's startled and jumps back; his eyes are wide with fright. I want to tell him I won't hurt him, but I can't. Finally he lifts his head to look at me. "The Post Office counter doesn't open until 10am; I've not even taken the money from the box yet."

Watch your time, speed up, I tell myself. "Fill it," I yell.

"It's on the floor…" he points to his feet, "can I?"

"Careful," I say, moving closer to the grill and straining to see that he's not pressing an alarm behind the counter. He takes another step back then bends first onto one knee, then two.

"Please," he says, "bear with me, I'm rheumatic; I can't get down any other way."

He reaches under the counter and I hear the metal box scrape across the linoleum floor. Then he gathers it in and goes through the reverse process to stand and heave the box onto the counter. I'm about to question why the guard left with an empty box when I realise it would be the one from the previous week. Without my having to ask he opens it and transfers the bundles of notes into the bag and slides it back through. I grab it and back away, he looks more nervous now than at any time before; his mouth hangs open, his breaths are shallow and his face is pale to the point of matching the wispy, white hair on his scalp. When I near the door I drop the shotgun back into the bag and sling it over my shoulder. I do this while still facing him, he's transfixed, he doesn't move a muscle. Then I'm out the door and tugging off my mask. I don't look left; I bear right and keep walking. Behind me I can hear the couple chatting, two women, and maybe only twenty feet from the shop. I turn the corner, my heart is racing but I resist the urge to run. Instead, I walk to the car; throw mask and bag onto the passenger seat then climb in, gun the engine and pull away.

I stick to the speed limit and keep an eye on my rear-view mirror expecting a commotion in my wake at any moment, but there's nothing. A few miles out into the open countryside I find a quiet spot in the road with trees either side and park-up. I grab the shells from the glove compartment and throw them into the bag along with the ski mask. I change back into my own jumper and trousers and leave the jogging clothes in the boot with the drawstring bag. The whole process takes less than a minute, and then I'm back behind the wheel and heading back to the rendezvous. I listen for news on the radio, but keep losing the station. In the end I switch off and just drive.

Less than an hour after stepping into the Post Office I'm walking into the outskirts of Faversham having left the Astra locked up in the lay-by with the keys tucked into the exhaust. I left the clothes and the ski mask in the boot with everything else. The Scallions are going to have the car torched so the mask and clothes will burn with it. I collect the Sportrak from the pub car park, picking the keys from the exhaust pipe – it saved me worrying about leaving them in the tent or, worse still, in the Astra.

The drive back to Mountebridge is uneventful and feeling perhaps less cautious than I should I decide to push things a little further and go in past the newsagents. An empty police car sits outside the Post Office, its blue light spinning silently around. Half a dozen residents stand across the street chatting in a huddle. I park the jeep and realise, like the old cliché, I'm returning to the scene of the crime. I keep my head down and move directly into the shop. Inside the assistant smiles from behind the counter, recognising me from what have become daily visits over the last week. I pick up a paper and a fishing magazine and pass it to him to ring up. "What's all the fuss outside?" I ask.

He shakes his head and tuts. "A right mess there. A robbery is what I've heard. In Mountebridge; can you believe it? They targeted the pension monies. Now, steeling from pensioners, that's got to be the lowest of the low, hasn't it?"

It's not the kind of question that seeks an answer, I hand him a fiver, and wait for change. "Anybody see anything?"

"Not as I've heard. Folk here walk around with their eyes shut at the best of times. But they'll slip up, they always do."

I slip back into the jeep and head back to the campsite. From my rear-view mirror the scene outside the Post Office is as it was when I drove up. Back at the tent I leave the paper and the magazine unopened on the ground, strip off and climb back into my sleeping bag. The nervous energy that's kept me going has evaporated; I feel as though I could sleep for a week.

****

Chapter 22 (Part I) ~ A job well done ~

~ Mo ~

Harvey and I collect the Astra from the lay-by just before 11am. There are sketchy reports on the local radio about an incident at a Post Office in the village of Mountebridge, but no more than that. We transfer the bag from the boot of the Astra to Harvey's XJS and then I follow Harvey back to the lockup. Inside it's still set up as though we were baby-sitting the runt. There's been no rush to change it back but we can still accommodate the two cars with ease. Harvey empties the contents of the drawstring bag onto the table and begins counting the money while I change the plates on the Astra. When I'm done I give it a last check and find some stuff in the back.

"He's left some shit in the boot," I call out.

Harvey sits at the table, his counting completed, enjoying a cigarette.

I wander across. "Did you hear me?" He's left some clothes in the boot. What should we do with them?"

"Yeah," Harvey says, blowing a plume of smoke into the air. "There was a mask in the bag too." He nods at the shells on the table, "shove those in a drawer and put everything else in the boot, the gun too. We'll send it all through the crusher."

"I thought we were going to hang onto the Astra to keep Rosewood in check?"

"We don't need it; he just has to think we have it. Besides, you're sick of it, aren't you?"

"Yeah, but what will Con say?"

Harvey taps the bundles on the table. "There's nearly twelve grand here; a bit more than we needed. Enough for Con to pick up another runabout at the auctions."

"Fair enough. So when do we tell Rosewood about his buddy?"

Harvey runs his left hand backward through his hair, and thinks about it for a moment. "Let's hold off on that one for a bit." He lets his cigarette stub fall to the floor where he crushes it with a twist of his foot, and then sweeps the bundled notes across the table until they tumble into the open drawstring bag that he holds at the edge. He stands, takes a step away from the table and gestures back to the sawn-off and the mask still lying there. "C'mon then, you're the one with the gloves on. Throw the rest of that crap in the boot, the plates as well, and then we'll go find Con. Let's see if we can't put a smile back on the old bastard's face."

~

Con is where he always is, behind the desk in his smoke-filled office at Moods. His eyes fall upon the bag in Harvey's right hand the second we walk through the door and his face lights up.

"Lads, come away in, and close the door behind you."

We take our seats in front of the large walnut desk and Harvey hands the bag to Con.

"It's all there?" Con asks.

"It's a little shy of twelve grand," Harvey says. "What we needed and more on top."

228

Con beams. "Grand so, grand so." Then he picks up the phone and tells whoever answers to find Rats and have him meet him out front. He hangs up and continues as though the call had never happened. "And it all went smoothly?"

Harvey shrugs. "As far as we can tell."

"Okay, but we can't have any more fuck ups. Remember, no loose ends. I want the two of you to keep an ear to the ground, make sure it *was* clean and more importantly that there's no come back on us. You know what to do, lose the gun; dump the motor, make sure Rosewood and his friend keep their mouths shut. Whatever's necessary; am I clear?"

"Sure, boss," Harvey says.

"Grand so," Con says, standing. "Get it done and we can celebrate some tonight. It's the end of a long fekken sweat, so it is." He ushers us out then overtakes us on his way to the stairs with the bag bouncing at his side. Harvey veers right to go into the toilets. He turns to snap his thumb twice against his closed fingers suggesting that we have to talk. Inside he checks there's no-one in the cubicles, then he removes his jacket and folds it over a wash basin before standing at a urinal to relieve himself.

I stand by the window. "You didn't mention the Astra," I tell Harvey.

"Well, you heard him. He took the surplus like it was expected, didn't give me a chance. But tell me. Are you comfortable with all of this? I mean, didn't that just feel a little rushed to you?"

I take my shades off and give them a clean. "None of this sits easily with me. Not since I've known Carnie was involved. But are you saying Con is holding out on us or are you just irritated that he's still using Rats?"

"I don't know," Harvey says. "I suppose I was just expecting to have a clearer picture of what's going on by now. And yes, I'd be happier if we'd seen the back of that little fuck." He gives it a moment's thought, then continues. "Ah, you're probably right. Forget it. Most likely he's just using the little shit to drive him to the bank."

Despite his words I can see the whole thing still gets to him, so I try to move things on. "What do we do about the Astra?"

Harvey zips himself up and moves to the wash hand basins. "Just what he said. No loose ends; let's get it to the scrap yard and make it a memory by teatime."

"Do we tell him about the runt?"

"Who Con? No way," Harvey says, drying his hands. "He'd only go off on one and it'd be another thing for him to worry about. Let's keep the peace. You and me can handle this. We're still doing what he wants, just achieving it a different way. Whatever's necessary, that's what he said and that's what we'll give him. Tell you what, you take care of the Astra and I'll make sure things are tidy where Rosewood's concerned."

"You gonna take him out?"

Harvey checks his look in the mirror and runs his hand through his hair. "There's no need." He throws his jacket across his shoulders, slips first one arm then the other into the sleeves and shoots his cuffs to settle it across his frame. "Rosewood is all sewn up. He just doesn't know it yet."

Chapter 22 (Part II) ~ Myrna ~

~ Mo ~

We give in to hunger and go for an Indian at nine o'clock. Con's idea of celebrating usually involves a meal, but no-one's heard from him since he left with Rats in the afternoon and it's a sore point with Harvey. He's used to being Con's right-hand man and I sense he feels a little humiliated to be left out of things. We each look at the menu but when the waiter arrives at our booth Harvey just picks out a main course, so I do the same.

"You shouldn't let it get to you," I say.

Harvey shrugs his shoulders. "It's that obvious?"

I nod and fold my shades into my top pocket, the lighting is low, I'll be comfortable without them.

Harvey shakes his head. "Why all the secrecy? We've been with him for years, doesn't he trust us?"

"Don't waste your time thinking about it," I tell him. "There will be a good reason, you'll see." I'm not sure I really believe this, but that's not what Harvey needs to hear. So I change the subject. "Hey, tell you what, I got a real kick out of this afternoon."

"At the scrap yard?" Harvey asks.

"Sure. Do you know how often I've had to sit in that piss-rotten pile of junk? Today was payback. I saw it - and everything in it - crushed into a two and a half foot cube. And as the magnet tossed it into the pile awaiting disposal I yelled *slip off the station now, you piece of shit.*"

My attempt at humour falls flat, Harvey hardly raises a smile. Instead he looks me in the eye and changes the subject himself. "How are your headaches these days?"

It catches me off guard a little. "They're okay; I mean no better, no worse. Why?"

"It just seems a while since we played a few frames, that's all."

"Well," I tell him. "There's been a lot going on. But you called it right the last time. I'm kidding myself if I think stretching my endurance is really improving things." His nod is one of acceptance, and, in terms of my photophobia, I realise acceptance is a place I've reached myself.

Our food arrives and we eat in relative silence; he's downcast right through the meal only perking up when his mobile rings.

"And?" I ask, after he clears the call. I don't need to ask who it was, I can tell from the instant change in his demeanor.

"Con's been in touch with Benny to arrange a table at Calendar Girls. We've to meet there at half ten."

"Who's all going?" I ask.

Harvey grins for first time all evening. "Just the home team: you, me, Con and Mickey.

~

We show at the club a little early. Harvey nods to the girl in the booth; she smiles, says something I don't quite catch and waves us through. My appearance startled her last time. I know she remembers; she won't look at me, even though I'm wearing my shades. We walk through the foyer and turn right, Harvey a stride ahead.

"We're in the Pole Room again," he says, turning his head to me. "Remember?"

"Every night," I tell him, and now he laughs.

We open the door to the anteroom and, almost in unison, three heads turn to greet us. Con, Mickey and Benny McGinn are flushed with laughter, their faces almost as pink as the stage behind them.

"Lads," Con says, raising an arm in welcome. "Come in why don't you. Now the party can begin. Benny, get the lads a drink."

Harvey and I take the last two seats at the table while Benny lifts a bottle from an ice-bucket I'd failed to notice and pours each of us a glass of champagne. I glance around the room, it looks bigger than before, but then I realise that Benny has catered to the size of tonight's get together. He's taken out the clutter of the redundant seats and instead arranged our chairs around a table near the glitter-pole.

"There you go," Benny says, in his gravel voice. "Get that down you, you've got a lot of catching up to do."

"The old man's well oiled," I whisper to Benny and tuck my shades into my top pocket.

Benny winks, "I think he was partying long before he got here."

Benny returns to his seat and Cornelius struggles to his feet. "Now that we're all here I want to make a toast." He gazes at each of us in turn, "well raise your glasses you dozy bastards."

To a man we do as he asks.

"Today I concluded a bit of business," Con continues. "A watershed is what it is. And each of you did your bit to bring it about. I give you a toast; to the future, to bigger and better prosperity."

A quizzical look passes momentarily between the rest of us. It's a bit of a mouthful and our hesitancy means we neither start nor finish the toast together. But we all manage to neck the champagne. Con gives a dismissive wave of his hand. "Oh, to feck with the fancy words, let's just have a drink and enjoy ourselves." He sits down as Benny refills everyone's glasses.

For the next hour and a half the drink flows. When the novelty of the champagne wears thin we settle on brandy, except for Mickey, who is given a bottle of malt to himself. The laughter has steadily become more raucous. We're smiling and joking but I can't help feeling it's more the end of something than the beginning. I think it's because Con's walking us through our past, entertaining us with the scrapes we've been through. One story leads to another and it seems they form an endless chain, most of them anything but funny at the time, but distance and hindsight lend them a sentimentality they don't really deserve. It's gone midnight when Benny calls a halt to the stories and tells us the girls will be getting restless. He leaves the room for a few minutes and when he returns he dims the lights a little and retakes his seat.

Slow, seductive music filters from every corner of the room and while the rest of us look on in anticipation I notice Mickey lift his glass from the table, swirl his whisky and lick his lips to taste the air. A wolf whistle refocuses my attention and it's Myrna who emerges from the curtained doorway to swivel and sway across the stage. Her two-piece costume is flame red, but there's nothing of it. The beat picks up and Myrna bends, struts, stretches and high-kicks. My ears pick up on the gasps and under-breath murmurs around me; I'm aware that none of the others can tear their eyes away from her. She has a presence not explained by beauty alone; an effortless in-built rhythm, a natural grace. Myrna owns the stage, and they crane their necks to follow her every undulation. She bears her breasts to a chorus of sighs. Across from me, Mickey swallows hard, the glass in his hand forgotten and hanging loose at an angle, its contents - precious to him moments before - spill out onto the table.

After Myrna comes Katya, a slim, high cheek-boned brunette. Benny tells everyone that she's from Warsaw, like it makes a difference. She's good, though her moves perhaps lack the seamless quality that flowed through Myrna's, but I'm more relaxed watching her. With the dances over we finish our drinks while Benny has someone arrange transport home. As we make our way back through the foyer Harvey tries to engage Con in more talk of the deal that's been done, but both of them are too far gone. Myrna stands by the booth at the entrance. She's wrapped in a long dark coat and smiles as I approach.

"Did you get my note?" she asks.

"Yes."

She raises her eyebrows, "And still you kept me waiting?"

I shrug my shoulders and try to look apologetic. "It's been busy; I tried to come see you. I wanted to but ..."

She lifts her index finger to my lips to shush me. "No matter, you're here now. Can we go to your place?"

"Yes," I tell her. I glance back. Harvey and Benny wave me on while Con and Mickey's mouths hang open in disbelief.

The taxi journey consists of small talk, I ask how she's been and she tells me Faith has moved on and that it's left her feeling lonely. I tell her again how much I wanted to see her and that work had got in the way, but it seems a feeble excuse, like something she's heard a hundred times before.

We reach the flat and Myrna loses no time in making herself at home, she knows where everything is. She fixes herself a tall drink and joins me on the sofa.

"Did you like my routine tonight?"

"You were great. Amazing," I tell her.

She takes a long drink from her glass and sits forward in her seat, taking care not to look at me. "Then how come you hardly watched?"

My chin drops to my chest, I thought she'd been too busy to notice, but she's caught me and a surge of shame runs through me.

"It happens," she says, raising the back of her hand to the corner of her eye. "Not usually this quickly, but it happens. Guys get what they want, and then they tire of me."

"Hold on. Who said I was tired of you?"

"You didn't need too, you couldn't watch. You were bored," she says.

"Not bored," I tell her, "jealous maybe."

"Jealous?"

I move to the edge of my seat and force her to look at me. "You come on stage and it's like no-one dare draw a breath in case it breaks the spell. You're beautiful, I've never seen anyone dance the way you do. I looked around that room tonight and knew everyone felt the way I did. I didn't like it; I didn't want them to feel what you made me feel inside. I wanted you all to myself."

"So you're not tired of me?"

"No, never."

Myrna leans forward to put her glass on the coffee table then throws her arms around me and buries her head in my chest. "Then I'm glad," she says. "I want someone like you. Someone I can depend on, I get lonely and I have needs."

"You don't have to be lonely," I tell her.

She pulls back for a second, places a hand on my chest to gently push me back, and then she swings a leg across to sit astride me. "I won't give you any cause to be jealous," she says, letting her fingers get busy unbuttoning my shirt. "Anyone can watch me dance, but no-one gets to touch." She bends forward, kisses my neck and works her way up. Her tongue flicks at my ear and she whispers, "no-one but you."

"Good," I manage to say, "and I got you a present."

She pulls back to look at me, her face beaming. "I love presents, what did you get me?"

"What you asked for; a little something for afterwards."

Chapter 23 (Part I) ~ Shelley ~

~ Adam ~

It's Thursday morning and it's raining so hard that it rules out walking to the shop. I drive down and pick up my regular newspaper and ask the newsagent if there's any coverage of what went on at the Post Office. He points out a local paper and I buy that too.

The heavy rain makes eating in the tent too awkward to contemplate; instead I opt for comfort and a leisurely read through the papers in the hotel's breakfast room. At reception I tell young Katy that I'll be eating in the dining room and ask if Shelley's around. She reminds me that it's Shelley's day off and says she'll try to track her down.

As I wait for my order to arrive I flick through the local paper and find the write-up on the robbery. It's not a lengthy piece but it leaves me relieved and not a little confused:-

Gun Crime visits Mountebridge

Postmaster, Stanley Oster, is said to have been traumatized by a lightening raid on the Mountebridge Post Office early yesterday morning. The raider surprised Mr. Oster shortly after he had taken delivery of monies intended for dispense as pension and disability payments to the many elderly residents within the community. Although Mr. Oster was confronted by a single raider Police believe the Post Office may have been under surveillance for some time and are not ruling out the involvement of an organized gang. Leading the investigation, Detective Welland, of Kent Police, added that Mr. Oster's personal safety was threatened by the armed raider but roundly praised his handling of a difficult situation. The raider is described as being approximately 6ft in height and of stocky build with a distinctive northern accent. Anyone with information is urged to contact Detective Inspector Welland at Faversham Police Station. Mountebridge Post Office is scheduled for closure in June despite an enthusiastic local campaign to reverse the decision. A Post Office spokesman last night advised that this incident was unlikely to hasten its demise.

Clearly I don't fit the description, I'm a good two inches short of six feet and I'm too thin to pass for stocky. But the weirdest part is the northern accent. I tried hard to say very little and when I had to talk I made sure I used the same words each time. It's possible that I slipped up, but I doubt I'd manage a convincing northern accent if I tried. Maybe the old guy really has been traumatized and has felt obliged to come up with something. There's no mention of the mask, or what I was wearing. Surely he'd have been quizzed on this by the Police? It leaves me feeling that this is either a somewhat desperate piece of reporting or they've very little to go on. But at least it looks as though I can walk the streets safely.

I had hoped to hear from Ferris by now. I assumed he'd need some space and time after the ordeal, to make sure he still had a job to go back to for one thing and no doubt he'd want to get in touch with Tina and explain his silence, though God alone knows what he could tell her. Of course, he could be sulking, believing that he has shouldered the brunt of all this and I'd probably agree that he has. If they haven't sacked him on the basis of his non-appearance he'll be making time up at work, so I pull out my mobile and send him a quick text asking him to call me when he gets a chance.

Shelley finds me long after I've finished eating but I've stretched breakfast to include a second pot of tea and a spare cup. I invite her to take a seat.

"Your day off I believe? Got any plans?" I ask.

"Nothing special, though my dad has asked me to cover in the bar for an hour before lunch. Why?"

I don't know why it hasn't struck me before, because Joel has mentioned his Granddad working in the bar, but I remember the old barman who winks at me as he gives me my change. "By any chance is your dad the guy who serves with a towel draped over his shoulder?"

She smiles. "Yes, that'll be him. And I've told him that image doesn't serve our best interests. I think he wants a word with you before you leave, did I tell you?"

"No. What does he want?"

"You'll have to ask him, I've no idea. Anyway, you haven't answered my question."

"What question?"

"You asked if I had plans. Why?"

"Because I want to ask you out."

Shelley almost smiles but stifles it, places an elbow on the table and leans forward to cradle her chin. "What form of 'asking me out' would this be? Define it for me."

I hold her gaze for a moment. Until that split second smile I'd not been sure if I'd be this plain but the combination of the news in the paper and the fact that it just feels right decides it for me. I lower my voice: "Oh, this would very definitely take the form of my asking you out with the expressed intent of getting to know you better."

Her eyes are locked on mine, she gives nothing away and her hesitation has me thinking that she's about to blow me out. But as she makes to speak there's a flicker, a hundredth of a second when her facial muscles make to smile until she overrules them and imposes a stony calm.

"And where does my son fit into this plan of yours?"

"Joel fits right in. You bring him along. We don't need to be alone to have fun and get to know one another."

She can't hold back the smile any longer. "When?"

"After lunch."

"And are you going to tell me where we're going or what we're doing?"

"No, it's a surprise."

"So how do I know what to wear, it's pouring with rain?"

"We'll be inside, dress casual," I tell her. She gets up to leave and as she turns away I raise the stakes a little. "Those tight jeans you wore the other day, they'd be good."

She throws me a look that tells me there's a fire in her and I get the feeling that when it burns hot I'll be dead meat.

~

Shelley and Joel are sheltering at the door of the hotel when I pull the jeep to a halt on the gravel driveway. I lean across, open the passenger door and Joel sprints out to tug the seat forward and clamber into the back. Once he's in Shelley dashes out and climbs in beside me.

"Where are we going, Adam?" Joel asks, barely able to contain his excitement.

"You'll have to wait and see," I tell him, and glance at Shelley as she snaps on her seatbelt. She wears her hair down and I catch a faint whiff of her perfume as she turns her head towards me. "Ready?" I ask. She's wearing her jeans and realises I've noticed.

"Because they're practical," she says, smiling, "and no other reason."

"Right," I say.

I turn the radio on low as we drive hoping the music will fill any awkward silences but it's soon apparent that I needn't worry on that score. Joel is desperate to know what we're going to do and when I won't tell him he tries to guess and it evolves into a game with Shelley joining in and demanding clues. I have to make them a little cryptic to keep the suspense alive. But the journey's a success; even the rain can't dampen our spirits. We park in a pay and display area in Faversham and as Shelley gets out she spots the signage along the street and all my clues fall into place.

"Oh, good grief," she says, "I think I see where we're going. I can't do that; I've no coordination, I'll fall flat on my face."

"What is it, Ma? Where are we going?" Joel asks.

I put a hand on Joel's shoulder and guide his line of sight toward a neon sign across the street. "Over there, Joel, Superbowl. See it? We're going ten pin bowling."

"Wow," he says. "I've never bowled. I don't know how."

"Then it's time you learned," I tell him. "C'mon."

~

I'm in the middle as we prepare to cross the road and, without thinking, I extend my arm to guide Joel across and do the same with Shelley on my other side. But she grabs my hand and it's only once we're safely across that, in mild embarrassment, we release each other. I feel a pang, a tweak of sudden disappointment. As though it happened so naturally that I didn't make the most of it.

Inside we climb the stairs and while I pay at the counter Shelley and Joel wander off to take in the twelve bowling lanes, the polished wooden floors with the pins lined up at the far end and the scoreboards overhead that flash cartoon bowling clips between plays. I explain to the teller that we're beginners and she offers to place us a lane or two away from the nearest other players. We busy ourselves changing into the red and white bowling shoes and Joel asks why we have to wear them. Shelley jokes about making them standard issue for the hotel staff.

The place is far from full with only half of the lanes in use. By the time we're ready the teller has kindly set up our game and Adam, Joel and Shel are loaded onto the computer screen. We start slowly, I show them both how to hold the ball and try to make sure they pick one that's lightweight, but I leave it at that. Predictably, each of their first few bowls are gutter balls and Shelley says it's harder than it looks. But when they take out a few pins their delight is almost euphoric. Joel is taken by the cartoon graphics on the scoreboard that greet every attempt. But he's trying too hard, and like all beginners places too much emphasis on trying to throw the ball as hard as he can. Eventually he wants to do better, as I knew he would.

"I hit a few then next shot I'm back to missing all of them again. What am I doing wrong, Adam?"

"It's like fishing, Joel, without the patience. Like the way you grasp the reel and prepare to cast. It's not how hard you throw it; it's about technique and timing your release." I leave my seat next to Shelley and step out beside him.

"Get the ball balanced in your hand," I tell him. And then I watch him slip his fingers into the ball then raise and extend his arm to take aim. "Use your left hand to steady it if you need to." He does this. "Now, only pull back when you're ready and try to make your swing a single, smooth, continuous movement, releasing as your arm begins to climb out of the forward swing, understand?" He looks at me and nods, his tongue protruding from his mouth in a show of concentration. I go back to sit with Shelley.

He goes through the routine again, taking aim, steadying himself. Then he takes a couple of tentative steps, drawing the ball back before releasing it as his arm lifts out of the swing. It's not his fastest bowl but it takes out eight pins, and he's delighted.

"Hey, that wasn't bad," Shelley says. "Can you show me?"

"Sure, but you have a different problem." We walk out to the lane and I have Shelley pick up a ball and make as if to bowl it. I stop her at the point where she's ready to release. "Now, do you see the position of your feet?"

"What's wrong with them?" she asks.

"They're together, so your right foot actually gets in the way forcing you to swing out and back across your body. Walk through it and time the release with your left foot planted forward, just as your right lifts off the floor behind you."

Shelley tries, but I've made it all sound so technical that it causes more confusion. So we end up walking it through together with me holding her at the waist and spooning in behind her. Her hit rate improves, but more importantly I feel it breaks that barrier of embarrassment at the level of intimacy passing between us.

With our game over I suggest we take a break before having another go. We grab a drink and a snack at the canteen. Joel finishes his drink quickly and asks if he can play the video game in the corner until we catch him up. Shelley waves him on. It gives us a chance to speak.

"So, are you having fun?" I ask.

"Actually, I'm having a great time," she says, "and I'm very impressed."

"With my bowling?"

She pulls a face in mock annoyance. "You know, I watched you with Joel, the way you explained what he needed to do. You're really good with him. He listened and it worked."

I nod, "he's a good kid."

"Don't put yourself down;" she tells me, "not everyone has your patience."

"There's no secret to it. He had to make his own mistakes. Once he'd recognised that, he was ready to listen."

"I worry," she says looking across at him as he plays the video game.

"About what?"

"He likes you and you're about to disappear."

"Who says I have to disappear? I'm only an hour or so's drive away. I like Joel, but I like his mother too."

"You hardly know me, nor I you," she says, teasing.

"Isn't that's how everyone starts off?"

"I suppose." She looks back across at Joel for a moment then turns back to me. "I don't feel I can afford to make any more mistakes, for his sake. It's been hard enough for him as it is."

"Okay, I'll make it easy for you. I'm thirty. I live in a small, rented flat in Tannock Bar and work for the Council Parks and Gardens Division. I'm single, have no dependants, like music, action movies and Indian food. But I don't like cooking. In fact, I plain can't cook. What else do you need to know?"

Shelley's mouth hangs open. "Wow. Well, I suppose that saved me some time, but it doesn't answer everything."

"Such as?" I ask.

"She bites her lip, lets her gaze drop to the table for a second, then looks back to me. "Well, what if I said I could tell if we'd get on if I knew what music you were into?"

"I'd have to say it sounds like a particularly ropey theory on relationships."

She laughs. "Oh, come on, you're meant to play along. Who's CDs would I find most of if I looked through those you have at home?"

"I think I've a pretty varied taste, but if you're basing it on who I've got most of then that might be some older stuff, maybe Crowded House, or Annie Lennox if you include her various incarnations."

"Incarnations?"

"The groups she was in previously; The Tourists and The Eurythmics."

"Hmm," she says, "that makes you sound a bit retro."

"Maybe, but only because you chose to look at quantity. I grew up listening to those two because my mother played them all the time. They're both still on the go, so I tend to pick up their new stuff and give it a listen."

"I see," she says. "And if I pushed you for a solo female artist?"

I grimace, and a satisfied smile flits across her face. "I'm struggling," I tell her. "I think I've got a couple of Rhianna CDs somewhere."

A look of incredulity spreads across her face.

"Okay, okay," I tell her, but in fairness she can sing too."

Joel rejoins us. "So are we going to play this second game?"

"Of course," Shelley tells him. "And Adam's just told me he can't cook. Do you think we should invite him to dinner tonight to say thanks for today?"

"Yeah, that'd be cool," Joel says.

Shelley throws me a sly grin. "Looks like you're invited then."

Chapter 23 (Part II)

~ Two and two makes five ~

~ Adam ~

It's gone 10:30 when Shelley waves me goodnight from the doorway of the bungalow behind The Huntsman. All this time and she'd been closer to me in the field than I realised. We'd eaten a great dinner, the three of us, relaxed in each other's company. Afterwards I spent some time playing with Joel on his Playstation before Shelley and I had some time on our own. She asked what I got up to in Tannock Bar and I told her of my nights out with Ferris; I described him as a cheeky git with a heart of gold. But we wound up talking music again. She's into stuff like Jay Kay, Maroon 5 and The Killers; and for me it's definitely a case of opposites attracting. We kissed in the hallway and she's left me tingling, wanting more. I walk toward the camping field, there's a song playing in the back of my head and I'm trying to think what it is as I push in my hand deep into my trouser pocket to retrieve my mobile. It's been such a fantastic day and I want to share it with Ferris and tell him how everything's coming back together. Then it tumbles into place, that song in my head. Annie Lennox, belting out the line '...feels like I'm seventeen again', and I do.

I find Ferris's mobile number in my directory and hit the call button. It rings and I'm actually excited at the prospect of speaking to the little bugger.

A voice at the other end says, hello. It's not Ferris, it's Scallion.

My disappointment expresses itself in a little bravado. "You've got your money, why am I not speaking to Ferris when I've dialed his number?"

"Ah, I wondered how long it'd take you to call. But you'll have to phone back on the land line, you still got the number?"

"No, but I remember it."

"Then use it." He hangs up.

There's a payphone in the hallway of the hotel, but I daren't go there, the way this conversation's going I can't risk being overheard. I take the long walk back to the square; I remember seeing a phone box there. The journey takes me a good five minutes but the box is unoccupied and thankfully there's a dial tone when I lift the receiver. The call is answered right away.

"Hello," Harvey says.

"Don't tell me you've still got him, that wasn't the deal."

"I have some bad news for you."

Simple words, but they send a shiver through me and I feel the hairs on my arms stand to attention. "What d'you mean?"

"I'm afraid we lost your little friend."

"Lost him? Lost him how?"

"He's dead. Ran out in front of a car. All very tragic."

I can't take it in. My heart pounds in my ear. Ferris, dead. It can't be. "You're lying," I tell him, feeling the panic rising in my own voice.

"No."

He offers nothing more, but it's like he's enjoying this. I can almost see him smiling into the mouthpiece. I lift my head to glance through the windows. The streets are empty and the light is fading. "Then there's no reason for me not to go to the Police and let them deal with you."

"Ah, that's where we differ. You spend your time avoiding Plod whereas you have to understand how he thinks. We didn't torch the car. It's wrapped-up nice and safe."

"You think I care about that now? I'll tell them myself," I yell.

"You're not listening," Harvey says.

His voice is cold, there's a calm detachment about it that chills me, and forces me to let him speak.

"Think about it," he says. "Plod find an abandoned car. In it are the shotgun and clothes used in an armed robbery. They check with the witness and he confirms it. The car will yield your fingerprints - the gun too if you didn't wear gloves – and the clothes will hold your DNA. Do Plod have your fingerprints on file, Rosewood? No matter, you go to them with your story and as far as they're concerned they've caught the thief."

"That doesn't bother me," I blurt.

"Oh, but it will," he says, annoyed to be interrupted. "They see only what's put in front of them. They already think you had an accomplice, so what do you think they'll make of the blood on the back seat?"

"I saw it; I thought someone had laid road kill there."

He laughs. "We did."

My stomach lurches as though an icy hand has reached inside and squeezed the air from my lungs. Ferris struck by a car. Road kill.

"Plod see it all the time, a squabble between the bad guys because someone got greedy. Right now you're ready to admit to armed robbery, but that won't be your problem. You'll be squirming to avoid a murder rap. They'll have all the evidence they need, it won't matter that two and two makes five."

He's silent and I'm too shocked to say anything.

"Don't panic when the body turns up; keep your mouth shut and the car stays out of their hands. I think we're done here, Rosewood. But I've got your mobile number, I may want another chat. You be careful now."

The line goes dead and I slump against the perspex wall and slowly sink until I'm sitting on the concrete base of the phone box. Ferris is gone and there's no song in my head that can match the emptiness I feel.

Amid the numbness I close my eyes tight and see Ferris in his suit, squinting over his shoulder at the dirty mark on the seat of his pants. I see him shining his shoes against the back of his trouser leg and the breadth of his smile as he dances ridiculously with Tina. I want to hold onto these, but I know I can't. I know that, however hard I try, my friend is lost to me. Bit by bit, time will pick my pocket of what little I have of him, until I can't quite picture his mannerisms; that's the way of it. When my head clears of these thoughts I find myself in front of the bandstand. Its joints creak in protest as the wind gusts and the ropes barring entry rattle in their metal hook and eye sockets. It's like I closed my eyes on the floor of the phone box and opened them here; I've no recollection of the journey. Harvey Scallion's veiled threat comes back to me ...*I may want another chat. You be careful now.* I still hold my mobile in my hand; I hit the power off button and as a surge of anger courses through me I take three steps forward and launch it as far as I can. It sails over the lawn and disappears into the trees and the embankment below. Let the bastard try to call me now.

****

Chapter 23 (Part III)

~ An offer and an exit ~

~ Adam ~

Friday morning, and Shelley's smile as I approach her at the hotel reception desk is hard to resist. I find myself smiling back for the briefest of seconds until guilt tears it from me; no doubt Tina had the same effect on Ferris.

"Whoa, you look a little pale this morning. I hope you're not about to blame my cooking," Shelley jokes.

A quick glance assures me there's no-one else to overhear. "I've not slept much. I've had some bad news. I'm afraid I have to leave early."

"You're leaving? When? What's happened?"

"Today. This morning, I suppose."

"But what's happened, Adam?"

I let my gaze fall to the desk; I can't look her in the eye. "After I left you last night, I had a call. It's Ferris; he was struck by a car."

"Oh, my God, is he okay?"

I want to raise my eyes to meet hers but it's just too hard. "He was killed."

"No!" She stands; I feel the light touch of her hand on mine as she leans across. "I'm so sorry, Adam." She pulls her hand back, lifts the phone and hits a few numbers on the dial pad. "Ray, can you come to the front desk right away, please?" Then she abandons reception, leading me into a side office. She sits me at a desk strewn with paperwork and unopened mail. "You sit there for a moment; I'll ask Mary to fetch you some sweet tea." She's gone before I can protest.

When she returns the grey-haired barman from the snug is with her.

"Adam, this is Ray, my father."

I give him a nod and manage a brief smile. I'm obviously not at my best and I'm still not sure there's a need for this level of fuss.

Ray extends his arm and we shake hands.

"I told Shelley I wanted a word with you before you left," Ray says, "but I didn't expect to be meeting you when you've had such dreadful news. A close friend Shelley tells me?"

"Yes. My last," I add. Then I realise how that might sound and feel forced to explain. "You know how it is, things change and take you away from the friends you grew up with, Ferris and I were the last of the group."

Ray nods. "But Shelley's right. You've been a help to us, what with looking out for young Joel. You look shattered, it wouldn't be right to let you travel in the state you're in. She tells me you've not slept."

"No, I'm fine, really. I mean I'm upset, but I'm okay."

Mary stands in the open doorway, gives a polite knock then comes in to place the sweet tea in front of me, and leaves again without a word.

"You drink some of that, lad," Ray says. "It's good

for shock. But I think we'd be a mite happier if you tried to get some proper sleep before you head off. Is someone taking care of arrangements for your friend?"

I take a sip of the hot tea; Ray's question seems too difficult.

Ray tries again. "I mean do you have to rush off to deal with this or are his folks handling it?"

"No, I don't have to do anything," I tell him. "In all honesty there's nothing to keep me in Tannock Bar, but right now I just feel I have to be there."

"I understand, lad," Ray says.

Shelley shakes her head. "A few hours won't make any difference, Adam. Shouldn't you get a little sleep first?"

"I'm packed and ready to go."

An exasperated expression settles on Shelley's face. She's about to argue further when the phone rings at the desk and she rushes out to the unmanned reception to answer it.

Ray watches her disappear then turns back to me. "Adam, if you've a mind to head straight back, then all well and good. Just take care." He gives a sigh and momentarily bites his bottom lip. "Look, now's not the time, but if you're looking for a fresh start I'm sure I could find a job for you here. That's what I wanted to speak to you about."

I set my tea down. "You're offering me a job?"

"Maybe not as fancy as the one you have with the Council, but if Tannock Bar holds too many memories, then moving to Mountebridge might help. We could work something out."

"Believe me, Ray, my job with the Council is anything but fancy."

Shelley returns and it seems to jar Ray a little. "You've got other things to cope with just now," he says, "but it's an option." He pats me on the shoulder, "I'll say goodbye for now." Then he leaves Shelley and I alone.

"So you're going?" Shelley asks.

"I have to."

"I feel terrible just asking but I need to know if I'm going to hear from you again."

I stand. "Give me a couple of days and I'll call you. I'll give you the phone number for my flat, don't use my mobile number, I've lost it."

"You lost your mobile?" she asks.

"Sort of; I threw it away after hearing about Ferris."

She pushes the door closed and gives me a long kiss. But this isn't the parting either of us wanted. Guilt ruins it for me and I'm sure fear of being cast aside does the same for Shelley.

****

The Power of 2

Book II

~

What's for you

won't go past you

~

Chapter 24 ~ *The great divide* ~

Harvey reaches the black Jaguar and opens the door. Mo lies slumped in the passenger seat, his arms are folded and his head rolls towards his chest then jerks up as though pulling back from a precipice, but he continues to doze. Harvey shakes his head and slips off his jacket. He removes the thick brown envelope from the inside pocket and tosses it across at Mo. It bounces off his chest and Mo wakes with a start.

"Sleeping in the afternoon, Myrna too much for you or what?" Harvey asks.

"Can't get enough of me more like," Mo says, sliding forefinger and thumb under his shades to rub his eyes.

"You want to watch that," Harvey adds, "she'll sap your strength."

"I could answer that," Mo says, "but it'd only turn you a deeper shade of green."

Harvey spins away; it seems he can't get Mo to bite as easily of late. He opens the rear door, folds his jacket onto the back seat and uses a little more force to close the door than is needed. He climbs into his seat. "Did you pick up the envelope?"

"What envelope?"

"The one I bounced at you to wake you up. It'll be on the floor somewhere."

Mo retrieves it. "It's pretty thin, how much is in there?"

"Less than five hundred," Harvey says.

"That's not gonna last."

"Tell me about it. Two whole weeks since this big deal and we're having to pull Benny's takings before he even gets to bank them. I think Con's done his money you know, I really do."

"I never liked the idea," Mo says, "and all this inactivity is getting to me. D'you think this is how it's going to be in this new business of Con's?"

"I don't know, but something has to change, we can't go on like this. I'm going to have it out with him when we get back."

"Good for you. You can drop me at the flat; I'm going to do an hour's workout to shake off this lethargy."

"Nice," Harvey says. "So you're leaving me to take it up with the old man myself?"

"Why not?" Mo says. "You don't need me to hold your hand. Besides, he listens to you."

~

When Harvey walks into Cornelius's office he finds him at his desk with his head bowed, wiping the sweat from the back of his neck with his handkerchief. The room is thick with tobacco smoke. A quick glance at the overflowing ashtray confirms he's been alternating between cigarettes and cigars for most of the afternoon.

Cornelius raises his head and beams at him. "Ah, Harvey, your timing's perfect. I was about to phone you when the lads downstairs told me you were on your way up. How are things with Mickey and Benny?"

Harvey had intended breaking the news gently, but when the moment comes he thinks *fuck it* and blurts it out. "No bad debts at Mickey's, but you know the score - he can't take on any new work. Benny's takings are minimal, and he was a bit lippy about handing them over. If you ask me he might need a kick up the arse before we do this again."

Cornelius dismisses the news with a wave of his hand. "I expected as much. But it doesn't matter right now; we've bigger issues to deal with." He pulls the glasses from his face and gives the lenses a cursory wipe. "I don't mind telling you, the past few weeks have been difficult, my nerves are shot but I've still got the balls for it, Harvey. We've bloody nailed it."

Harvey smiles. The phrase *not before fucking time* runs through his mind but he resists the urge to say as much. "So what's happening?"

Cornelius replaces his glasses, balls his right hand into a fist and waves it beneath his own chin. "It's on. Sholto's got the casino and we, Harvey, are riding the fekken gravy train. He's called a meeting of the stakeholders later today. We came through for him – so we're guaranteed a percentage. The good times are just around the next bend."

"Casino? What casino?" Harvey asks.

"That's the investment I was telling you about."

"But won't the money from that be a ways off yet, boss?"

"For sure, but we get a kick-back tonight that will see us clear. Just wait, Harvey, this is gold. Moods, Calendar Girls and Loan Solutions pay a pittance in comparison. Is your car fuelled?"

"Yes."

"Good, so." Cornelius checks his watch, "I want yourself and Mo with me at the meet, it's being held at a manor house an hour or so up the motorway. It might take a bit of finding, we should leave right away."

Harvey winces, "I've just dropped Mo back home; he wanted a workout to wake himself up. Do we have time to pick him up on the way?"

Cornelius stands. "No, I've waited long enough for this as it is. I'm impatient to be away. We'll go on us own, you and me. Sure, you can tell the lazy bastard what he missed out on tomorrow."

~

"So where exactly is this meeting?" Harvey asks as they buckle up.

Cornelius passes Harvey a piece of paper, the directions he'd jotted from his earlier conversation with Carnie. "Hockley Manor," he tells him. "Apparently it's some secluded country house off the A10 and to the north of Cambridge."

Harvey reads the note then sets it down beside his loose change in the stow area between Cornelius and himself. "Why there? What's wrong with the centre of London?"

"Eyes and ears I suspect," Cornelius says. "There's bound to be some faces in this crowd that don't want to be seen together. Anyway, Carnie said it kept things fair – everyone has some travelling to do and no-one is on home turf."

Harvey nods, appreciating the logic in that much at least.

They join a stream of queuing traffic. "Holy mother, from where did all this fekken lot come?" Cornelius asks. He sets his left hand along the trim at the window's edge and begins to drum his fingers.

"We're going to be fighting the Friday evening traffic for a while," Harvey says, "but it'll ease up after the first few bottlenecks. I can put some music on if it'll help pass the time?"

"Better still," Cornelius says, "why don't I fill you in on some details. You'll know everything soon enough, sure, but I can tell you now. Would you like hear about it, so?"

Harvey throws Cornelius a smile. "Haven't I've been trying to get you to tell me for the last few weeks?"

"I know, I know. But there's been reasons, Harvey, lad. That little feck, Rats, for one."

Harvey feels a little of his own tensions ease. This is more like it; the old man's more like himself.

"Yeah, where's he at anyway?" Harvey asks.

"Back where he came from," Cornelius says. "He works for Carnie."

"What?" Harvey says, taking his eyes from the road to glare at Con.

Cornelius pulls a cigar from his inside pocket and holds it up. Harvey waves him on and Cornelius begins to light up.

"That reaction is exactly why I couldn't tell you," Cornelius says. "You see this whole thing is so big it calls for different rules. Carnie's not daft; the stake money for a seat at this table isn't cheap and he knew I'd be pushed to come up with the necessary. He insisted on having a man on the inside and I had no option but to agree. Rats was a fekken cuckoo in our midst, ready to chirp, he was, if we screwed up."

"I can't believe it," Harvey says. "I hated the little shit; there was just something about him that made my flesh crawl."

Cornelius exhales a plume of cigar smoke. "I can always rely on you there, Harvey. You're a grand judge of character. Rats is more than he looks though, he's a shrewd little man with a dangerous reputation, as Mickey and Benny will find out."

Harvey frowns. "I don't understand, what have Mickey and Benny got to do with Rats?"

Cornelius taps ash from his cigar into his left palm and closes his fingers over it. He opens the electric window and disposes of it before answering. "You can't make the jump we're doing without making sacrifices, Harvey. Calendar Girls and Loan Solutions are sold; signed the papers two weeks ago, I did. Carnie owns them and effective tomorrow, Rats is in charge."

"Fuck me," Harvey says. "Do Mickey and Benny know about this?"

"Not an inkling."

"Fuck."

Beyond Cambridge the built-up areas become fewer with longer gaps in between, they give way to flat, open countryside. Harvey is able to ease the Jaguar into the outside lane and pick up the pace.

Cornelius checks his watch before looking again at the note in the stow tray. "Are we on the A10?"

"Hmm," Harvey manages, "heading for Ely."

"You're shocked?" Cornelius asks.

Harvey sucks air and blows out hard. "Just a bit. This casino you mentioned earlier, it must be some deal if you've sold the businesses and thrown in cash too. I mean, Mo and I couldn't understand all the fuss over a poxy fifty thou."

"It's a question of scale, Harvey. I told you I'd invested everything and I meant it. I even sold my BMW and leased it back."

"What?"

Cornelius nods. "That's how desperate I got for cash. We're looking for the Dilton Farm turnoff, remember – about six miles outside of Ely."

"What about Moods?" Harvey asks. "Is it still ours?"

"Yes, we need a base, but the others are gone."

Harvey checks his rear-view mirror and takes the slip road leading onto a single-track road in the direction of Dilton Farm. The road is bordered on either side by high hedgerow with passing places set out every few hundred yards. After a mile the hedgerow on the left comes to an abrupt halt.

"Ah, there's the farm," Cornelius says glancing again at his notes. "Set your trip meter, Harvey, Hockley's three miles from here."

"This must be some casino, then." Harvey says.

"You've heard of the plans for a super casino over the last few years?"

"Yeah," Harvey says. "Manchester got it and Blackpool kicked up shit."

"That's the one, so," Cornelius says. "Except it's not going to Manchester anymore. It's coming back to London either as a super casino or as one of a group of smaller regional casinos and we're part of the successful consortium – Carnie's consortium."

Harvey glances at Cornelius; the old man's face doesn't flinch. "Straight up?" he asks.

"There was a government team set up to decide who'd run it and where it'd go. Half of them were on Carnie's payroll. Didn't matter where the bloody thing went; it was always packed and wrapped for Carnie. But mark my words why don't you. When all the hoo-hah over Manchester dies down and the decision's announced, it'll be London gets it."

Harvey takes a hand off the wheel and runs it backward through his hair. "But, I mean, Jesus. Just how does someone as bent as Carnie pull that off?"

"Give the man credit now, Harvey. He's buried the true ownership of the consortium in so many Holding Companies and laundered them to the point that Her

Majesty herself wouldn't get a cleaner bill of health from the Revenue."

"Fuck me." Harvey says, scratching at this goatee.

Cornelius grins. "Now you begin to understand why I got so uptight, huh?"

Harvey shakes his head. "I'm completely blown away, boss. But we're almost there, how do we play this?"

Cornelius empties another handful of ash out of the window. "Don't fret, Harvey lad, we've come through for Sholto. He won't forget it, so let's you and me play it cool. At a guess there'll be about ten of the faces there, just make sure you're respectful and we'll come out of this high and handsome."

Harvey checks the trip meter; they're inside the last mile. Ahead, the road bends to the right and there's a solid outline on the left. As the bend straightens it becomes clear this is a large perimeter wall, the kind that surrounds stately homes and grounds. Harvey slows at the entrance, the black wrought iron gates are open; a brass plaque on the wall confirms they've arrived at Hockley Manor.

Gravel peppers the wheel arches as Harvey follows a central driveway flanked either side by a grassy lawn. The house is set well back from the road. It's an imposing two-story building in red brick. The main entrance is covered by a porch supported by two ornate pillars. Adjacent to the house is a further building; its wooden doors wedged open by a couple of bales of hay.

"Jesus, this is some place," Cornelius says. "Probably eighteenth century. Look, it's even got stables."

Harvey nods. "Yeah well, the gardener wants a hoof up the arse; the grass looks as though it's overdue a trim."

Several cars are already parked outside the main building. Harvey reverses into a space alongside them and cuts the engine. He looks to Cornelius, but he's already out of the car and striding towards the porch. Harvey hurries to catch up.

Cornelius drops his cigar butt on the gravel and steps on it. "Look at the doors," he says as Harvey reaches him, "they must be eight feet high. I'd love somewhere like this myself in a couple of years."

The twin doors open inwardly as they approach; each is attended by a heavily built man dressed in a formal dinner suit. The guy on the left smiles welcomingly. "Good evening gents, have you come for the meeting?"

"Yes," Cornelius answers. "We're here to see Mr. Carnie."

"And you are?"

"Cornelius Callaghan."

"Ah, you are expected, Mr. Callaghan."

They pass through the doors and wait in the hallway. Cornelius marvels at the wide staircase off to the left while Harvey points to the high ceilings and cornices.

Muffled voices and laughter filter from behind closed doors at the far end of the hallway. Cornelius looks back to the attendants. "Down this way, is it?"

"Yes, your meeting is in the drawing room but first, gentleman, I'm sure you'll appreciate that this is a sensitive meeting, no weapons of any description are allowed beyond this point."

"We wouldn't insult Mr. Carnie by bringing any," Cornelius says.

"Nevertheless, sir, all guests are required to undergo a check for weapons or wires."

The attendant moves forward and both Cornelius and Harvey raise their arms to be frisked. Satisfied, the attendant leads the way to the door at the far end whilst his partner turns to close both main doors. The sound of clinking glasses and general chatter grows as they near. The attendant stops short of the doorway and extends an arm to bid them onward. Cornelius nods his thanks and Harvey, practising respect, does likewise as he passes the attendant.

Cornelius opens the door and moves inside. Two steps behind Harvey sees Cornelius spin around open-mouthed, a frown upon his brow, his movements strangely half-paced. His lips move but Harvey strains to hear him, the words are lost in the howling gale that fills his head and makes thought an effort. Harvey stares into Cornelius's midriff and senses that he's on his knees. Only then is he conscious of the searing pain at the back of his skull and the tingle of pins and needles throughout his body. He falls forward. Through a tangle of legs he sees that the room beyond is an expanse of linen-draped furniture; there are no people, just a large black boom box in an ocean of white. Harvey's then suddenly aware of being spun onto his back; the face of the second attendant looms over him, contorted in a grimace, his teeth tightly clenched over thin lips, the nostrils flaring and the eyes wild. His right arm is fully extended and Harvey's eyes follow it out to see what looks like a piece of shiny pipe clasped in his hand. His arm swings downward in a long slow arc. Harvey is transfixed; the pipe glistens and sparkles as it cuts through the air.

~

Harvey's initial return to consciousness is fleeting. The sound of voices draw him from a deep place. He can't make out what they say; they're distant and bent out of shape, as though heard through a long tunnel. He tries to open his eyes but sees nothing, so attempts instead to raise his head and is at once enveloped in such pain as to lose consciousness again.

When he awakens it's as though he's edging toward the surface from a bottomless pool; his senses are dull, everything appears distorted, inexact. His left eye is shut tight; it feels egg-shaped and tender on the side of his head. His right eye opens only after his eyelashes break free from the sticky mass of dried blood binding them to his face. Focussing is difficult and his head throbs, his arms and shoulders too. He tilts his head back and feels his ears brush against the sleeves of his shirt. Only then do things fall into place; his arms are bound at the wrist by a heavy rope that chafes and irritates his skin. The rope extends to a pulley and beyond that is the thick wooden beam he's hanging from. "Fuck," he says, lowering his head again. He looks down, sees his legs are bound at the ankles by sticky tape, then realises where he is. *The stables, they've strung me up in the stables.* Something moves just out of his field of vision. He summons his strength and manages to wriggle and turn himself until it comes into the view of his good eye. It's Cornelius, stripped of his jacket and suspended a few inches off the floor from the same beam as himself. Cornelius though, is out cold.

"Ah, so you're back with us at last. That was a nasty head-knock."

Harvey turns his head too sharply to face the speaker and winces at the pain it causes him. He has to squint, but recognises the well-worn leather jacket and the ragged pony-tail.

"You?" Harvey says, unable to hide either his surprise or his dismay.

Rats stands inside the open doorway, flanked by the two attendants and two others, less formally dressed. "I thought you'd be pleased to see me. Not so high and mighty now though, are you?"

"What the fuck's going on?" Harvey demands.

"Did you think you could get away with it?" Rats says with calm authority.

"Get away with what?" Harvey asks.

"The money. The biggest fucking deal ever pulled in this country and you brainless morons risk it all by feeding in dirty money as part of your stake."

"I don't know what you're talking about. Ask Con, he told me you were the go-between. If anything's dirty maybe it's down to you?"

Rats paces back and forth. "Don't get smart, pretty boy. We asked Con; he can't help us."

"Wake him up," Harvey says. "We've nothing to hide."

Rats pulls a bottle from his pocket, holds it up to Harvey and rattles it. "Did you know he was on these?"

"On what?" Harvey shouts. "Spit it out will you? I'm in fucking agony here."

"Heart pills," Rats says through gritted teeth. "The bastard had a heart condition. He pegged out on us."

Harvey's mouth turns dry at the news. He kicks out, spinning himself around until he can look at Con. His head is slumped to the side, just as before, but there's no visible rise and fall of his chest, Cornelius has gone the way of Alonso. Who'd have thought the old man had a heart condition? He smoked and drank with the best and worried enough for all of them.

A phone sounds, not a fancy tone but a standard ring. Harvey watches Rats pull a mobile from his inside pocket and step outside to answer it. Harvey's thoughts turn to his own plight. Dirty money, would Con have chanced it? He recalls the sweat that poured from him, the amount of cigarettes and cigars he got through; he was certainly desperate enough in the run up.

Rats returns and gathers the henchmen together.

"How much money was dirty?" Harvey asks, as they come out of their huddle.

"The last nine grand," Rats says, walking toward him. "But no-matter. Sholto wanted us to make an example of you both. Give you a good going over and keep you in your place. But he's decided Con's death changes things." Rats gives a little laugh. "In gambling terms his share is forfeit to the house."

"Okay, so you've taken Con's stake and you've got his businesses too," Harvey says. "What now you little fuck?"

"And you're the smart one of the pair?" Rats grins. "Work it out pretty-boy. You guys fucked up and the cost is… well everything. Sholto can't leave you and your brother nursing a grudge, he'd be forever looking over his shoulder. Call it an Egyptian funeral. You know; the kind where they bury master and servants together."

"For the sake of nine grand, you've got to be

kidding?" Harvey says, hearing the panic in his own voice. "My fucking motor's worth more than that alone."

Rats gives a short laugh. "It's not the value, it's the principle. Sholto's big on principle. Tell me, I've heard your brother has fast hands, good with a knife too?"

"Better than anyone I know," Harvey says.

"That's not saying much though, is it?" Rats sneers. He juts his chin and one of the henchmen tosses him something. Rats unfolds the blade and lets Harvey see him do it. Then he steps forward and plunges it into Harvey's gut.

For all the lead up it's still a shock to Harvey. He lets out a cry as his breath rushes from him. He's aware, not so much of the pain but of the sensation of dampness in his crotch. His breathing becomes laboured and shallow. The rope holding him relaxes and Harvey feels himself lowered. His feet touch the floor and buckle, unable to take his weight, but the lowering stops as quickly as it began and he's held there.

Harvey watches Rats move in close, until his face is a few inches from his own. He feels weak, as though he's about to faint. His instincts tell him to fight it; he focuses on Rats' greasy, pockmarked complexion.

"You thought it funny to give me a sick little nickname; maybe it's fitting I tell you my real name."

Harvey feels his head jerk as Rats grabs a fistful of his hair and yanks him closer. Then a sudden pressure and a searing heat rip through him as Rats twists the knife in his gut. His breath is forced from him in a rasp as Rats' lips brush against his ear, "I'm Jack Muldoon, you won't forget now, will you?"

Chapter 25 (Part I) ~ Crossing the bridge ~

~ Adam ~

It's two weeks since I said goodbye to Shelley but it feels more like a month. I did the little things on my first full day back. I went around to Ferris's flat and spoke to his landlady; she thought it a little odd she'd not seen him, but she wasn't yet concerned. I telephoned his work and they again confirmed he'd not been in. I told them, that as a close friend, I was worried. They said they'd have their personnel department follow it up, but if they knew more they weren't saying. Since then I've half expected someone to pull me aside and tell me what I already know, but no-one has. It seems that, until Ferris is found, the weight of my certainty is mine alone to bear.

Work was no escape. Nigel made it clear he hadn't forgotten the imposition my hastily arranged vacation had placed him in and said it'd done me little good as I'd returned surly and distant. The only light in all of this was Shelley. I called her at The Huntsman and gave her my home phone number. She was pleased to hear from me and the warmth in her voice was the push I needed. By the end of my first week back my mind was more or less made up, but I waited until today to hand in my notice. In hindsight maybe I should have held off until Nigel was more approachable. But if sulking were a sport he'd have an array of international caps and what can any of us do but act on how we feel? He knew the job was getting to me; he wasn't to know that it'd been the case for quite a while or that things had now truly fallen over the edge. With a close friend already cold in the ground and another just waiting to be found, my work at the cemetery could never be anything but a gruesome reminder. I had to get away and Ray's offer, imprecise as it was, was worth checking out, but I knew there was more to it. When I told Nigel he kept calm, but told me to collect my things. They'd pay me what I was due and respect my notice period, but I'd not be expected to work it. That took the wind out of me; last point to Nigel.

It's afternoon when I pull into The Huntsman's gravel car park. I avoid the main entrance and instead go around the side to find the separate entry to the bar. I often went via reception during my stay but I decide it'd be best not to bump into Shelley before having a chat with Ray. When I push open the door and walk in it's much as I'd expected. What passes for the lunchtime rush has come and gone and the place has returned to a rather dark and quiet haven for the odd pensioner either enjoying a pint and a flick through the local paper or stopping off for a fly drink under the guise of exercising the dog. The bar area is empty and I prop myself up against it for a short while and wait. The old guy nearby lowers his paper and peers over the top at me.

"Anybody serving?" I ask.

"Ring the bell," he says, nodding toward the far end of the bar. "Ray's not on, but one of the waitresses will come through if they hear the bell."

I straighten and take a couple of steps towards him and he sets his paper down. "Ah," I say, "actually it was Ray I'd come to see, but he's not on you say?"

"He'll be at the village hall," he says. My expression must beg another question, without waiting for it the old man adds, "the festival's getting near."

"I see," I tell him. "I'll try to catch him there, then. Thanks."

After parking the jeep in the main street I cross the road and walk down the path towards the village hall. I can see there's activity ahead with several rows of chairs already stacked outside the hall. Folding tables and cardboard boxes too, in varying sizes, lie strewn along the grass. As I pass the notice board one or two of the flyers, now insecure, flap in the breeze and draw my attention. The board itself is as busy as before, only the faded thermometer drawing has gone. When I reach the hall, Ray emerges from inside and standing in the wedged-open doorway calls out, "that's the crap out of the way, Archer, looks like your kit was last in and first out."

Off to the right, a heavy-set guy wearing a black T-shirt and an unbuttoned corduroy waistcoat raises his balding head and yells, "Righto."

As Ray turns around his eyes settle on me. "Hi, Ray," I say, "have you got few minutes for a chat?"

He squints, adding a few more lines to his leathery face. "Adam?" When I nod in confirmation he adds, "I wasn't expecting to see you back so soon."

"I wanted to see if your offer still held good."

The heavy-set guy makes to pass Ray in the doorway, Ray glances at him, "I'm going to take break for a few minutes, okay? Just keep things moving, Arch."

"No problem," Arch replies.

"C'mon," Ray tells me, "we can talk in back."

Inside, the hall is crammed. Tables and chairs are stacked tight to the far left wall and extend to the middle of the room; the other half is littered with an array of boxes spilling bunting, streamers, raffle ticket books and coloured cards. "For the festival," Ray says seeing my reaction to the confusion. The heavy-set bloke Ray referred to as 'Arch' meanders around the boxes heading for an open storage room still piled high with equipment while I follow Ray toward what looks like a kitchen area. It turns out to be no more than a small annex with a sink and worktop with cupboards beneath. A microwave and an electric kettle sit on the worktop and there's a small table with two chairs in the corner.

"Fancy a brew?" Ray asks, gesturing me to take a seat at the table.

"Sure, why not?"

He pulls a couple of cracked mugs and some teabags from the cupboards under the sink and lifts the kettle to check it's full before throwing the switch.

"Milk and sugar?"

"As it comes is fine," I tell him.

"Just as well, I don't think anyone remembered milk," he says.

He takes a seat. "How'd things go with your friend?"

I shake my head. "Oh, you know, not easy." It's not a lie, but I don't want to talk about a funeral that hasn't happened yet. Or worse, why it hasn't. "But I've been thinking about what you said and I've decided the sooner I get away from Tannock Bar the better. You said you might have something here."

"Ever worked in the hotel trade?" Ray asks.

"No."

"What about bar work?"

I let out a nervous laugh, as this isn't going quite the way I'd hoped. "Sorry, it's got to be a no to that one too. I thought you realised I …"

Ray raises a hand to stop me there. "It's okay, I know," he says, lowering his hand again. "You worked in the Parks and Gardens side, a bit more creative. But that kind of thing is seasonal from a hotelier's perspective, so I was thinking you could cover other areas too."

"I see," I tell him, though I'm not sure I do yet.

"To be honest, it's probably better if you haven't worked behind a bar before. That way I can show you how I want it done." He smiles and taps the side of his nose; "and you won't be clued up on some of the skimming that can be done."

"So, just what would the job entail, Ray?"

The kettle boils and Ray stands and moves across to pour water onto the teabag in the first cup. "Well I'm short-handed in the bar at present, so you could start there, but with the summer just a few months away I thought you could help bring some life to the gardens and make the campsite more attractive, it's no more than a field right now." He transfers the teabag to the second cup with his fingers and pours the water after it.

"Whoa," I say, "watch you don't burn yourself."

"No problem," he says and gives a short laugh, "I've been doing that so long it's like I've got asbestos fingertips." His face turns serious again. "You see, I've got some ideas for the hotel, we need to diversify and give the place a higher profile, but I need help to turn some of my ideas into reality, I can't do it myself. I don't have the skills or the energy if truth be told."

"What kind of ideas, Ray? And why me?"

"Well, I thought you could re-design the campsite like I said, maybe you could develop some specialist breaks for anglers and the like. Then there's the hotel itself, you could spruce up the rooms and the breakfast area with some floral decorations – give it a whole new look and perhaps widen our appeal. How does all that sound?"

I scratch the back of my head as he sets the tea in front of me. "Well it's different," I tell him. I don't want to appear too eager, although the fact I'm here at all tends to give that away. "I need to ask what it pays, Ray. I'll need to find a place close by."

"What are you on at the Council?" he asks.

"Nothing spectacular," I say, mentally rounding up the numbers and giving him the figure. "But there's a progression plan and a pension on top of that."

Ray sits again. "And then there's the hotel side."

"Hotel side?"

"Progression," he says. "Over time you'd be getting familiar with the whole business, a proper grounding; set you up that would." He sips his tea and stares into the table.

"And the money?"

He blows on his tea, takes a sip and hesitates as though considering further. "Okay, I'll match what you're on at the Council and you can live-in at the hotel until you find something local. Sound fair?"

"Fine," I tell him. I know we haven't discussed things like hours and time off. I sense it's not Ray's style and to be honest they're not important right now.

He extends a hand and I take it. "Deal done," he says. "Now when can you start?"

"I'll need to give up my flat but I suppose I could commute until that's sorted."

"Or go back over the weekends and move across piecemeal like," Ray suggests.

"Yeah, I could do that," I tell him.

"So when can you start?" Ray asks again.

I take a gulp of tea. "As soon as you like."

"But what sort of notice do you need to give?"

"I already quit and I've got a backload of vacation days they didn't want to pay for so I'm free right away." I feel a flush of guilt saying this but I don't want my new employer thinking I've left under a cloud. He might wonder what kind of trouble he was taking on.

"Great," Ray says, "just one last question." I steady myself for it. "Now that you're working for me do you still intend seeing Shelley?"

I stare into Ray's lined face for a second or two trying to see where he's coming from, there are no winks this time; I can't read him. "Can I be honest?" I ask.

"Always."

"Being closer to Shelley is a significant part of the attraction in coming here, Ray. If you're suggesting that I can't work for you and still see her then I'll have to find work elsewhere."

Ray grins. "On the contrary, you've put a smile back on her face. I've a good feeling about you, Adam, but I suppose I needed to hear you say where you stood with Shelley. C'mon, the others will think I'm slacking; I'll introduce you."

We leave the kitchen and go back outside. "Arch, Vernon," Ray yells. The bald guy is in the process of placing a large wooden panel against the side of the building with the help of someone I've not seen before, he's older, maybe mid-fifties and thin as a pipe-cleaner. They steady the panel and walk across to us.

"Adam, let me introduce you to Archer and Vernon." Each in turn extends his hand to take mine. Archer's grip is strong while Vernon's is clammy, but their smiles are warm enough.

"Adam's going to be working with me at The Huntsman," Ray continues. "I've nicked him from Tannock

Bar Council. He's got experience in the planning of parks and gardens; everything from general aesthetics and layouts to floral designs. And he's not afraid of getting his hands dirty either. If it's not too late I'm hoping he might be able to give us an idea or two before this year's show."

The guys nod in unison and the stick-thin Vernon says, "That'd be great. Welcome onboard." I smile back but I'm a little lost for words.

"The three of us are part of the local Roundtable," Ray adds. "And as the younger and fitter of the bunch it falls to us to get the festival kit out from cold storage. Arch here runs an outdoor pursuits programme. Vernon is our events coordinator and organiser; he does everything from arranging the bunting to running the raffle."

"So are we going to see you at tonight's meeting, Adam?" Archer asks. "You could take a look at what we've got going where."

Ray jumps in before I have a chance to speak. "Too soon, Arch. He's got details to sort out. But he'll be a real asset to us down the road a bit."

Ray walks me back down the path and I wave goodbye to the guys. "Don't mind my little embellishment, Adam. I know you've got great deal to offer and I want these guys to feel a real boost at having you on the team."

"You've certainly given me a bit of a billing to live up to, Ray."

"You'll be fine," he says, patting me on the shoulder. "Now, does Shelley know of your decision?"

"No, I though it best to see you first."

"Then go tell her your news and she can sort you out with a room in the hotel just as soon as you need; in fact, the sooner the better. I'll expect you when I see you."

I sit in the jeep, roll the window down a little and give some thought to what's just happened. Nigel's decision to release me straight away actually looks to have worked in my favour and it'll help me cover some of the inevitable costs of moving. Ray though, has been more than reasonable and I like the idea of learning about the hotel trade. I'm not sure what he expects me to bring in terms of planning but he mentioned the hotel gardens and the campsite. I've helped in the digging and maintenance of so many council parks that I don't even need to think too hard about what works best where; I know I can do this. More importantly, Ray seems genuinely encouraging of my relationship with Shelley. A tingle of excitement runs through me. Is this what it feels like to have someone believe in you?

When I walk into the hotel reception Shelley is busy dealing with some customers. She sees me and beams but I have to wait until she has finished booking in the new arrivals before we can speak. "What are you doing here?" she asks.

"Is that any way to greet a new employee?"

A look of incredulity spreads across her face. "What do you mean?"

I take a deep breath, I suddenly realise I have to present this properly or I stand to blow it before I get any further. "Can we talk in the office for a moment?"

Now she looks worried. "Okay," she says.

I follow her into the office and close the door as she spins to face me. But then I get lost in those large hazel eyes, I hesitate and my mouth turns dry. I have to break eye contact or I'll never get the words out.

She beats me to it. "You said something about being an employee, has my dad offered you a job here?"

There's a tension in her voice and already I can feel this slipping away. "Listen;" I tell her, "this is difficult for me but will you let me try?" She relaxes a little and I grab my chance. "There are plenty of reasons why starting afresh somewhere feels so right for me just now. Losing Ferris means Tannock Bar holds too many memories and, yes, I'd got to the point where I'd grown tired of my job. That last day, your father said he might have some work for me if I fancied a change. The truth is a fresh challenge would do me the world of good, but it's more than that, Shelley. I've thought about you every day, I've missed you like I've never missed anyone before."

"Like a holiday romance?" she says, folding her arms. "And my father offering you a job to entice you down, like I'm a charity case. What am I to think?"

"Shelley, it's not like that. You knew I was attracted to you during the two weeks I was here, you felt it, I know you did, and I've been miserable every day since I left."

"That's grief, Adam; you've just lost a close friend. You're feeling lonely, nothing more."

"No!" I tell her. "I know what lonely is and this isn't it. Guilt stopped me from telling you how I felt. How could

I be happy at finding you after what happened to Ferris?" I take a deep breath; I know I've gone about this all wrong. "Your father asked me if I expected to continue seeing you after I took the job," I tell her. "I thought for a horrible moment that the job was to be his way of keeping us apart."

"My dad's not like that," Shelley says.

"I realise that now. But I had to tell him that you were the reason I was coming and that I'd find other work if accepting his offer meant I couldn't see you. He was testing me Shelley, he wants you to be happy, he loves you and so do I."

She looks at me, her eyes full, round and watery. "And Joel? We come as a pair you know."

"Joel's a credit to you and he and I can be great friends." I let that hang for a second, "but it's his mother I've fallen for."

She swallows hard. "And you think this can work?"

"I know I want to try," I tell her. "That is, if you'll let me?"

She won't look me in the eye, her pride won't let her. She makes me wait then utters quietly: "Okay, but I should get back to reception now."

She makes to pass me, but I shake my head and let my hand gently catch her by the waist. "No, not good enough," I tell her, pulling her close. I hold her tight, breathe in the delicate smell of her perfume and feel the softness of her hair against my cheek. Then we're kissing and, for a moment, we're like two teenagers who can't keep their hands off one another. Her arms reach for my shoulders, find the back of my neck and draw me into her. My own hands settle in the small of her back then fall over the curve of her backside.

When at last our lips part Shelley calls a halt to it. "Wait, this isn't right, I'm supposed to be working."

"I'm sorry," I say, doing my best to look sheepish. "I've missed you so much."

She straightens her clothing and throws me a cheeky grin. "My shift finishes at four; you can have dinner with us tonight."

A telephone enquiry comes in just as she settles herself back at reception. I make my way out but feel compelled to glance back at her from the hotel doorway as she deals with the call. I blow her a kiss and smile thinking how beautiful she looks; she shoos me away in mild embarrassment, and in that second, just as I turn away from her, something inside me breaks. It's like I'm crossing the bridge that holds two halves of me together; I'm leaving the past where it lies. Shelley's my future; I know she's the one.

****

Chapter 25 (Part II) ~ Hawaii ~

~ Adam ~

By the time I roll up outside the bungalow to the rear of The Huntsman it's gone five and I half expect a frosty reception. Joel opens the door and is surprised to see me, his eyes drop to the flowers and the bottle of wine I've brought.

"Adam," he says with a grin. "What are you doing back?"

"Your mum didn't mention she'd invited me to dinner then?"

"No," he says, standing back to let me pass.

"Where is she?"

"Kitchen," Joel says, wandering back to the living room and waving me on.

I stick my head around the door and see Shelley busy chopping vegetables at the sink. "Sorry, I'm late," I tell her.

"You're not," she says, "dinner won't be ready 'til nearer six. Those for me?"

I hand her the flowers and the wine having all but forgotten I was carrying them. "I thought when you said you finished at four you were implying I get here early, only I got held up in the village."

Shelley puts the wine in the fridge to chill then opens a couple of cupboards before she finds a vase for the flowers. "I thought you could use the time to talk to Joel."

"I just spoke to him, he let me in."

She fills the vase with tap water then sprinkles in the contents of the sachet that came with the flowers. "I mean talk to him properly."

"I thought I had. We get along fine," I tell her.

Shelley sets the flowers on the worktop, ready to arrange in the vase, walks across and plants a kiss on my lips. "My father knows you and I are seeing one another and he seems happy with it, but have you spoken to Joel about it?"

I didn't realise I had to, but now Shelley's mentioned it I can see where she's coming from.

"We come as a package," Shelley reminds me. "Joel and I don't have secrets and I'm not about to encourage any. I'll get on with dinner; you'd best go through and explain that his fishing buddy wants to date his mum."

"You're kidding?" She stops what she's doing and just stares at me. "Okay, you're not kidding. Just how do I broach that?"

She smiles, "you'll find a way."

When I reach the living room I'm in something approaching a cold sweat. What do I say? It feels as though I'm about to ask for his permission. He's bound to feel a little apprehensive about change and protective toward his mum. But I gather it's been just the two of them for quite a while, what if he really doesn't like the idea?

I take a seat next to him on the leather sofa; he's watching some quiz show on the TV. Before I've settled he hits me with a question.

"Hey, you any good at general knowledge, Adam?"

"Average," I answer, though his obvious enthusiasm tells me he likes quizzes.

"Give us a game then," he says, flicking his fringe from his eyes. "See if you can answer the question before they do. We'll take alternate questions and see who wins. Quick, you first."

I'm immediately under pressure. It's that Anne Robinson programme, The Weakest Link. She fires the question at the contestant, but they answer before I can.

"Too late," Joel shouts, then he's on the edge of his seat to listen to the next question and quick as a flash he shouts out the right answer. The contestant follows a second or two behind, and Joel's already proclaiming a one, nil lead.

This goes on for over twenty minutes. It's mad, it's frantic; the little bugger's so competitive and he's giving me a beating. When Shelley shouts us through for dinner it comes as a reprieve.

Joel takes his place at the kitchen table and as I sit he says, in Anne Robinson style, "Adam, you are the weakest link, goodbye."

Shelley looks at me. "He just thrashed me on a general knowledge quiz show," I tell her.

"Oh, showing off were you?" Shelley asks Joel. He lowers his head and gets on with his meal.

"And you spoke to him, did you?" she says turning back to me.

I swallow a piece of boiled potato then try to explain. "Ah, well I didn't quite get around to that; the show was already underway." But I can see in her face that no excuse is going to do. So I turn back to Joel who is busy chewing and playing head-tennis between Shelley and I. "The thing is, Joel, your mother and I have been getting on really well since we met and we wondered how you'd feel if we started... well, started seeing each other?"

It's over. I didn't really think about it, I just said it and now it's out both Shelley and I look down the table for Joel's reaction.

He shrugs his shoulders. "Cool," he says, then carries on eating like it's no big deal.

I look back across to Shelley hoping his answer satisfies her.

"It means Adam will be around more often," Shelley adds. "Your granddad offered him a job at the hotel so he'll be looking for a flat here and moving down at some point."

"Great," Joel says. "We'll get to go fishing again."

"Sure," I tell him. "That'd be good."

"But you'll have to sharpen up," Shelley tells me.

I don't catch her meaning, but a knowing look passes between mother and son, then they smile at one another.

"C'mon, then. Share the joke?" I ask.

"Not five minutes before you arrived," Shelley says, "genius here was complaining because that quiz show was a re-run and he'd seen it before."

I shake my head in disbelief, it never crossed my mind. Not for a second.

Joel shrugs his shoulders again. "It kept you occupied," he says, as both Shelley and I look on. "Well, I'd have had to be deaf not to hear you two talking about it in the kitchen and I didn't really need it explained." Another shrug, "It's cool."

Shelley's lips turn up at the corners for a split second, but it's enough. It tells me that a potential hurdle has been overcome. This can really work.

****

In the living room after dinner I notice for the first time how relaxed I am. The room itself has a warm, lived-in feel, tidy but not overly so; welcoming I suppose you'd call it. I get the impression too that Joel would normally be off to his room to play computer games or pushing to go out with his friends, I think he's holding off for a short while to be sociable. But it's more than that, there's something in the atmosphere of it all; the way Shelley leans toward me on the sofa, drawing her legs up and pulling a scatter cushion to her that just says we're all comfortable in each other's company. It just feels … it just feels right somehow.

"So what was it held you up earlier?" Shelley asks me.

"Just the goings on at the village green," I tell her. "They were erecting an enormous marquee; it was a feat of organization seeing them set up the support poles, then laying out the guy lines and canvas before bringing the whole thing together. I must have watched for almost an hour."

"That'll be for the spring festival," Joel says. "You'll be here for that now won't you, Adam?"

"When is it?" I ask.

"It opens on Sunday afternoon," Shelley says. "We've used that marquee company before and they do put it up unbelievably fast. They must do it so often that it's second nature to them."

"The festival goes on all week though doesn't it? I probably need to use the weekend to tidy my flat and get a few bits and pieces together so I'm ready to start at the hotel on Monday."

Joel moves forward in his seat. "You can't miss the opening day though, Adam, you should be there at the start. Tell him, ma."

"Oh, it's not quite the Olympics, with an opening and closing ceremony," Shelley says. "I like to see both the start and the end though, it feels special, but you're right, you have other things to be getting on with."

Joel's brow furrows. "No, you have to be there if you can, Adam. It'll be fun."

I weigh it up for a second. I can see it's important to him and I don't want to let him down when things have started so brightly. "Fair enough," I say. "I've got all day tomorrow and might even manage to make a start when I get back later tonight."

The telephone rings in the hallway. Shelley groans and heaves herself up from the sofa to answer it. Within a minute she returns with her coat and smiles apologetically at me. "That was Ray; they're having a meeting of the Roundtable and think you might be able to help with an idea that's come up. Do you mind?"

"Of course not, but isn't it a bit late in the day for ideas if it starts on Sunday?"

Shelley sighs. "Oh, this is fairly typical I'm afraid, but hopefully it'll be straightforward. You can come too, Joel."

We take the Sportrak and pull up across the road from the village hall; behind it, dominating the green, is the white marquee. Joel sees some friends hanging out by the chess boards and Shelley recognises the look on his face. "It's okay," she says, jutting her head in their direction, "go on, we'll come get you when we're done, just don't disappear."

Shelley knocks at the hall door and enters. Inside and to the left a group of people sit around a wooden table but I'm a little taken aback at the apparent emptiness of the rest of the room. I'm still looking over my shoulder at the vacuum when Ray's voice bounces off the walls.

"Ah, here's Shelley with the young man I spoke of. Adam, you're looking a little lost," he says.

"Sorry," I say, as I turn back towards the table, "only I was here earlier in the day and it was filled to overflowing with tables, chairs, boxes and what like."

"They've all been moved to the marquee," Ray says. "Sit yourselves down and I'll make the introductions."

Shelley nods to the people round the table as we each take a seat.

Ray continues. "Moving from my left we have Audrey Perry, Chair of Mountebridge Community Council, David Heston, incoming President of the Mountebridge Traders Association, Stanley Oster, our village postmaster, and the two chaps you met earlier, Vernon Tutt of the Resident's Association and Robbie Polson of Mountebridge Outdoor Pursuits."

I nod to each in turn and feel the hairs on the back of my neck rise as I'm introduced to the postmaster. He smiles back at me and although there's no sign from him that he recognises me I'm now feeling decidedly uncomfortable. So much so that it doesn't immediately register that Archer was introduced under a different name.

"As you know, Adam, the Mountebridge Spring Festival begins this weekend and coming last in the running order this year we've been caught out a little by the apparent introduction of themes by the other participating villages. The Roundtable has, as always, arranged the usual mix of stalls, family entertainment and fun but we don't actually have a theme. However, Vernon has put forward a suggestion from the Resident's Association and we'd like your thoughts on feasibility given the lateness of the proposal. I've taken the liberty, again, of explaining your background, Adam."

I'm still feeling a little exposed but manage to nod calmly.

"Vernon," Ray says, "would you like to explain the request?"

Vernon is a little startled at hearing his name and seeing everyone turn in his direction. "Ah," he says. "Well, very simply, given the proliferation of themes evident in the festivals of our competitors this year I asked the Residents for their ideas. I'm afraid Mrs. Ollenshaw's idea won popular support, even if it was something of a sympathy vote. She's an unfortunate soul, not been in the best of health you see and …

"Yes, yes, Vernon," Ray chirps in, "but cut to the quick. Adam doesn't need her life story."

"Of course," Vernon says. "Well, Hawaii."

"Hawaii?" I ask, beginning to loosen up a little.

"Apparently she's always been smitten by the place, ever since seeing Jack Lord in that old TV show. She was all set to go there on vacation two years ago until her stroke stopped her. Of course, the poor dear will never pass fit to fly now, so it'll never happen."

Ray rescues me, the confusion must be written in bold type across my face. "We want a Hawaiian theme, Adam. You know, girls in grass skirts, flower garlands, palm trees, that kind of thing. We've only got tomorrow; do you know where we can we get hold of these things in a hurry?"

"Wow," I say. I let my eyes drop but my mind's thinking. It strikes me that there are a few things they could do relatively quickly even though it would mean a bit of running around.

"If it's too much just tell us straight," Ray says, taking my silence for bad news.

"How authentic does it have to be?" I ask. "Because you might just get away with it if we can take the odd liberty."

"What exactly do you mean?" The rather crusty Audrey Perry asks.

"Well," I say, "Hawaii is synonymous with all the things already mentioned plus limbo dancing, surfing and a whole lot more besides; if we need to be accurate then we just won't have time to get what we need. But we can suggest Hawaii and more importantly the Hawaiian Party atmosphere if we replace what we can't get hold of with look-a-likes or close alternatives."

"Such as?" Audrey asks, still not fully satisfied.

"That depends on what's readily available," I tell her. "But say for example we had to go for inflatable palm trees, or cutout versions of surfboards that we had to paint. You could also consider asking people to wear loud Hawaiian style floral shirts and maybe look at getting a steel drum ensemble to give the whole event a Caribbean flavour."

"That's brilliant," Ray says, "I'd never thought of limbo dancing or the steel drum idea. It's beginning to sound as though this idea could be a real crowd drawer. There are bound to be plenty of steel drum bands playing out of London."

"Won't they all be booked up?" Stanley asks.

"Maybe, but you never know until you try," Ray says.

"I'm sure you could offer food in a Hawaiian style too," Shelley adds. "The girls at the hotel could check the internet and we could prepare something almost authentic."

"This is great stuff," David Heston says, "very positive."

"Then let's put it to a vote," Ray says. "All those in favour?"

Six forearms are lifted in unison; it's unanimous. Ray beams at Shelley and I. "Okay," he says. "If you two can give us a few minutes to discuss budgets and close out the meeting I'll see you outside."

Once outside Shelley and I decide to walk back toward the jeep to afford them a little more privacy. It's then I remember my initial discomfort with the postmaster and my confusion over Archer. "Your dad introduced me to Archer this afternoon but in there he said his name was Robbie something."

Shelley smiles, "Robbie Polson. It's a little cryptic but I suppose you'd have to add all the clues together to make the connection. He runs various outdoor pursuits, white water rafting, mountain biking, hill walking; that kind of thing. But his favourite sport is archery and every year he runs an arrows stall at the festival; it's very popular."

We lean against the jeep and look out toward the chess boards where Joel stands chatting with his friends. "All you had to say was it was a nickname," I tell her, and get a playful dig in the ribs for my trouble.

Ray marches up the path from the hall, his arms pumping. "Right, Adam, can you deliver on those ideas; the garlands, the palm trees, grass skirts and whatever?"

"I can certainly try, Ray, but we either find them tomorrow or not at all."

"Then let's go for it," Ray says. "I'll look for a steel band and have the girls at the hotel see what they can dream up in the way of a Hawaiian menu. But I want you to think about how it's all laid out too."

"Dad," Shelley says. "Adam was going to use tomorrow to tidy his flat and get his things together for moving down, you're taking that time away from him."

"It's okay, I don't mind." I tell them both. "This sounds like much more fun."

"Thanks, Adam," Ray says. "I'll make it up to you, but it might be best if you stopover at the hotel tonight. You and Shelley can search out the stuff using the phone and the internet from first thing, no doubt you'll have to run around picking up what you can't have delivered."

****

Chapter 26 (Part I)

~ The trouble with Carnie ~

~ Mo ~

It's a little after 1am when my mobile rings. I'm set to give Harvey a blast for leaving me behind but it's Myrna's name that appears on the screen. I push the green button and tell her hello.

"Mo, where are you?"

"I'm at Moods. Waiting for Con and Harvey to get back. Why?"

"I'm heading home. I wanted to come by the flat."

I check my watch again, "Isn't it a little early, don't you have another set to do?"

"Not tonight, there's been a bit of a commotion. I'll tell you about it later."

"Okay, get a taxi. We're ready to shut-up shop here anyway. I'll be there in twenty."

I find the keys to Cornelius's X5 in his office sitting next to the ashtray on his desk. Darren, Moods Bar Manager, is still tidying up when I get back downstairs.

"Con and Harvey are probably celebrating somewhere," I tell him. "I'm taking Con's Beamer in case I have to go get them."

For a second he almost questions it, but I halt him in his tracks. He wouldn't have given it a second thought if it'd been the Astra. Of course, neither Con nor Harvey deserve the concern I'm showing but it's not them I'm thinking of. Taking the car means I don't have to mess about getting a taxi myself and I can save Myrna standing outside in the cold.

Con's silver X5 sits in his parking bay in the street behind Moods. It unlocks with the press of a button and the lights give a solitary flash in acknowledgement. I open the door, slip my shades off and put them into my top pocket before sliding into the driver's seat. The beige leather is cold and I have to hit the vanity light so I can adjust the seat and get comfortable. It's not often any of us use Con's motor; not that he minds, more that the need seldom arises. Anyway, it's an automatic, a lazy man's car.

It takes a little longer than planned to get home. When I pull up outside the flat I can see Myrna standing in the shadows by the stairway, her arms folded against the chill night air. Harvey's flat is in darkness, but no surprise there.

"I didn't realise you could drive," Myrna says as I reach her.

"I'm light-sensitive not fucking blind." I say it without thinking and immediately regret it. Her reaction tells me I've hurt her and I didn't want that.

"You should give me a key," she says, changing the subject. "Then I can warm you when you get home."

"You know that's not a good idea," I tell her as we climb the stairs, "for lots of reasons."

She slides her arm through mine and smiles. "But I'm your girl, aren't I?"

"Of course," I say, opening the door so she can step inside.

"Or maybe you want me to prove that to you all over again," she says, with a wicked grin. "I'm going to go for a shower, then I'll show you."

I lock the door behind me then move into the living room, turn the lights on low and throw the car keys on the coffee table. I close my eyes and quickly massage my temples with the middle finger of either hand. It's great having Myrna around but she hasn't understood why she can't have a key and I worry that my relationship skills are too clumsy to make this work. Harvey would be able to handle this and the bastard should have called by now.

The dull whisper of the running water filters through into the living room and shortly after I hear Myrna humming to herself in the shower. It's tuneless but, to me, beautiful nonetheless. I find Harvey's number on speed-dial and make the call. An automated voice tells me the number cannot be reached and may be switched off, then adds the familiar 'please try later'. I try Con but get the same response. No doubt they've decided to get completely pissed and will emerge as though it was always part of the plan.

"Are these what I think they are?" Myrna asks from the doorway. She's draped in a bath-towel and the low light picks up her blonde curls and glistens off her still damp shoulders. She's peering into an envelope in her left hand. The last of the pills Boots gave me a few weeks back.

"Your 'little something for afterwards', yes."

She pops one into her mouth.

"You've not even taken your jacket off," she says. "We can't make magic with you fully dressed."

In the time it takes me to remove my shades from my pocket and set them and my mobile next to the car keys, Myrna closes the gap between us. She leaves the envelope on the table and pulls my head down to kiss me, her tongue darting into my mouth then pulling back so that she can suck and bite at my lips. I make to take my jacket off and she stops me.

"Uh, uh," she tuts. "You had your chance for that. It's my turn now."

She eases my jacket from my shoulders, throws it on the couch and slips a hand inside my waistcoat to rub at my chest through my shirt. All the time her eyes never leave mine; it's like she's teasing me, feeding off my reaction. And just the heat from her hand is amazing. When she's bared my chest and had me step out of my trousers, shoes and socks she lets her bath-towel fall and stands naked before me. But I'm not allowed to touch. Instead she invades my space; lets first her fingers roam full length across my body, moving to within an inch, making to caress but never quite touching. She does the same with her lips and her tongue, kissing and licking the air above my flesh, so close that I feel the warmth of her breath on my skin and ache for her soft, moist lips to fall upon me. Finally she uses her breasts, running them across my chest, circling my groin, never touching herself but enjoying too the sensations of close proximity and denial. The torment is almost more than I can bear and several times I rise to meet her, desperate for her touch, only for her to move away. When at last she lays me down, climbs on top and allows me to enter her I know that she's as aroused as me. I don't last long.

Myrna returns to the bathroom and on her way back she collects the envelope. "These are good; I can feel it building. Want one?"

"I can't," I tell her. "They don't mix with photophobia."

She climbs back into bed. "What's that? I thought you were albino?"

"I am. Photophobia is just a complication meaning my eyes are all the more sensitive to light; I get bad headaches. I can't use that stuff."

"Why, wouldn't it make you relax?"

"It's just a bad idea. Anyway you never told me why you didn't complete your set tonight. Was it a rowdy crowd?"

Myrna smiles, "I'd forgotten. You see, you're good for me. I was upset but you took my mind off that and got me onto other things." She giggles, and stretches out on the bed. The pills are kicking in.

"So what was the problem, Myrna?" She's staring at the ceiling and I have to lean over her and ask again. "Myrna, what made you leave the club early?"

Her face hardens and a frown spoils her pretty forehead. "I went to see Benny to change my music. That horrible little man was arguing with him and threw me out and Benny didn't raise a finger."

"Who threw you out?" I ask.

"I don't know his name; he's a greasy looking guy with a pony-tail."

It takes me a second to take in what I'm hearing. It could be nothing but why would Benny argue with a customer then let him push one of his girls around. The description is familiar too, but what would Rats be doing at

Calendar Girls? I check my watch; the club will be closed by now, there's little point in going over. I leave Myrna in bed; she's in a world of her own now anyway. I move back to the couch and hit the mobile again. Con and Harvey are still unobtainable, I look up Benny's number and call him too – but it rings out. I'm beginning to feel uneasy, why can't I get hold of anyone? Finally I call Mickey, he answers on the third ring.

"Mickey, thank fuck for that."

"Mo, is that you? What the hell time is it?"

"Never mind the time. Have you heard from Con, Harvey or Benny tonight?"

"Not since yesterday?"

"I can't get hold of any of them, Mickey. Con and Harvey haven't come back from their meeting with Carnie and it seems as though Rats, or someone like him, was arguing with Benny at the club earlier. Now I can't raise Benny either."

Silence. "I don't understand," he says. "This is the meeting Con's banged on about for weeks. And you're worried 'cos you've not heard from him in what, four or five hours?"

"More like ten, Mickey."

"Yeah, but you wouldn't expect them to be in touch before or during the meeting so you can only work back from the point the meeting was likely to break up, and you don't know how long it was going to take. It might be going on through the night for all we know; and if it's as bloody important as Con made out don't you think they might have a drink afterwards?"

As soon as he's made his point I can see that I might be overreacting, but it doesn't stop me trying another tack. "Possibly, Mickey, but Benny too; and what about Rats?"

"Benny's probably had a rough night and wants to sleep. All the more likely if he's had a run-in with that little wanker. Go to sleep, Mo, it'll sort itself out in the morning."

I sigh. "You're probably right, but keep your ear to the ground, eh?"

"No problem," Mickey says, "get some sleep. I'll be in the office early; I'll get back to you if I hear anything."

When the line clears I wander across to set the mobile on the bedside table and climb in beside Myrna. She's spaced out, staring at the ceiling, her pupils twice their normal size. I snuggle up to her, I'll watch her 'til one of us falls asleep.

When I awaken shafts of sunlight poke through the gaps in the curtains and streak across the room to smash against the far wall; I realise I've slept much later than normal and come around quickly. Myrna is still sound asleep. I check my mobile, there's a text from Mickey. One word... Takeover.

~

Takeover, I'm thinking about that word as I park in Horton Square and look up at the offices of Loan Solutions...and it aggravates me. What the fuck did Mickey mean? Is it an instruction or a warning? Mickey's mobile has joined the list of those I can't reach and I've tried them all, over and over.

Loan Solution's offices are on the first floor but the door is locked at street level. I buzz the intercom but there's no comeback. I've a key for Moods but not for here, there's never been the need. Then I remember something in among Con's car keys that doesn't belong; it's a key with a 'P' scrawled onto it in black marker pen. I try it anyway, but it doesn't fit. I'm left with nowhere else to go; I climb back into the car and head for Moods.

A nightclub bar is a quiet place with no-one else there. I've let myself in, unset the alarm and locked the door behind me. For a few minutes I wander around in the semi darkness just wondering what to do next. I find myself back in Con's office looking for any clues as to where he and Harvey went for their meeting. But there's nothing on his desk pad and the waste paper basket has been emptied. There could be something on his computer but I won't go there – the screens are always too bright. For no particular reason I glance through the vertical blinds onto the street below and the rear of the building where I've parked the X5. A few feet from it sits a vehicle that wasn't there when I arrived, I recognise it and the figure behind the wheel, it's Mickey.

Five minutes later I sit Mickey down in the darkened bar having helped him from his car. He's bleeding from the corner of his mouth and has a large swelling over his left eye. He hasn't answered any of the questions I've asked, insisting instead that I get him inside first. I sense he's ashamed, he won't look me in the eye; maybe he didn't put up much of a fight. He takes a sip of the whisky I've poured him, winces and sets in back down. Then he picks up the bar towel I've loaded with ice cubes, shuts his eyes and holds it to the side of his face, wincing again.

"So what happened?" I ask him.

"Carnie happened." He doesn't bother to open his eyes and his speech is a little slurred, then I realise he's just trying to avoid working his fat lip.

"What the hell's going on, Mickey?"

He doesn't answer right away and it's beginning to piss me off, like he's annoyed it was him and not me and perhaps making a point that he's taken one for the team. Finally his eyes open, he pulls the towel from his face, takes an ice cube from inside and runs it across his lip.

"Bastard, that burns," he says, and runs his tongue around his swollen lip from inside his mouth so that, for a second, it looks even worse than it is. "They were waiting for me when I opened up this morning; they laughed and showed me the documents to show it was all legal and above board."

He's loosened off the fat lip and sounds more like himself, but he's still not making sense to me. "What the fuck are you on about?"

"Carnie owns Loan Solutions, Mo. Cornelius sold him the business, Calendar Girls too."

"No way!"

"I saw the papers, it's fact; and that little prick, Rats, is going to run them for him."

"Rats? What's he got to do with Carnie?"

"All I know is they had me log them into the system," Mickey continues, "and then some long-haired streak of piss they brought along runs some programme that copies all our records, access codes, the lot. I sent you a text but they took my mobile and my office keys then beat the crap out of me." He rubs at his jaw as though reminding himself of the blows.

I feel myself grinding my teeth. "They can't do this, they'll start a war."

Mickey hangs his head for a moment. When he raises it his eyes are watery. "They've already won, Mo. Con sold the businesses and Carnie has them; and there's something else."

"What?"

"Something Rats said."

He hesitates and I don't like it. I don't like any of this. "What Mickey?"

"I don't know how to tell you," he says. "Con and Harvey are dead. The little bastard laughed about it." Mickey swallows hard and when he speaks again his voice is cracked and broken. "They killed them, Mo. Lured them in and fucking killed them."

"They're winding you up," I tell him. "Harvey wouldn't let that happen." But even as I say this Mickey's shaking his head. An image burns into my mind; Con's face, his colour drained and his eyes bulging in their sockets. It could happen, too much good living has softened Cornelius and these days his bark is worse than his bite. But Harvey? No, not Harvey, that's a leap too far for my imagination. He's too sharp, too strong. I look back at Mickey, and even in the half-light of the bar his actions begin to make sense. He's not ashamed, he's been trying to cushion the blow; he's not beaten, he's buckling under the weight of the news he brings. His whole manner says he believes what Rats has told him is true.

"Dead?" I ask. "Both dead?"

Mickey grabs his whisky, gives it a swirl, then nods, but he doesn't look up.

There's tension in my gut. I'm aware that I've started rocking back and forth in my seat. "I don't believe it, not for a minute."

He lifts his head enough to peer at me from below his eyebrows. "They were pretty convincing. I'm sorry, Mo, I liked Harvey."

I'm not having it. "It's bullshit," I tell him, and slam a fist into the table. "Where are they now?"

He looks at me, confused.

I push my chair back and stand. "Carnie's guys? Rats and whoever?"

Mickey sits up in his seat and raises both hands, palms up. "No. Don't you see? The only reason they let me go was so I'd tell you and you'd react. They want you to go after them."

"Then I'll try not to disappoint them."

"For Christ's sake, they'll kill you too. You have to think this through, Mo. Like Harvey would have done."

I glower at Mickey; half of me wants to smack him just for the sake of it. But he's right about Harvey and that's enough for me to catch myself and begin to calm. I retake my seat. "What do we do?"

"I've no idea," he says.

I look hard at him, I had hoped for more spine but I remember telling Harvey that Mickey wasn't like us and it comes back to me now. Mickey can help, but maybe not with those kinds of questions. I have to deal with those myself and I have to think like Harvey.

"Do we still have this place?" I ask.

"As far as I know."

"Then your new job is here, you run it."

"I don't know anything about running a bar or a nightclub," Mickey protests.

"We've got people to do that, Mickey. You're a money man; you set the prices, authorise the spending and make sure the books balance."

~

When the Bar Manager arrives to open up I pull him aside and let him know that Con and Harvey will be gone longer than expected, there's no need to say anything else at this point. I tell him Mickey's in charge until further notice and leave it at that. Then I let Mickey get acquainted with Con's pc, I need space to think.

In the early afternoon I give Myrna a call. She's in town shopping. When I tell her there was more to the ruckus she witnessed the previous night she readily agrees to stay away from Calendar Girls for a while and suggests maybe I take her out tonight instead. I tell her I'll be at Moods when she's ready – it's the easier option for now and maybe by then I'll know what's really going on.

The snooker room is cold and quiet. I set the table up to knock a few balls around but when it comes to it I'm not in the mood. Instead I sit at one of the tables and try to decide what to do, or rather, try to think what Harvey would have me do. If what Mickey said is right then they see me as a hothead, prone to react first and think later; most of the time they'd be right, it's what I do. So they'll expect me to turn up at Loan Solutions or Calendar Girls when it opens later, but I'd be walking into a trap. So, maybe I should look to do what they've done? Stop the war before it starts; cut off the head – Carnie himself? It's an idea not without appeal. But he surrounds himself with hired muscle; I'd never get close enough. I pick up a piece of chalk from the table and absent-mindedly pass it between the fingers of my right hand – a dexterity exercise I've long outgrown. Harvey would look at this problem in a different way I'm sure, he has a way of standing problems on their head. It nags at me, that thought, and then I see it. Carnie won't drop his guard and he'll always be stronger on his own territory. Harvey wouldn't go to him and neither will I. The only way to get close enough is to get him to come to me.

It's strange seeing Mickey sat behind Con's walnut desk. He's engrossed in the computer screen; I'm almost at his side before he notices me.

"I can only get so far," he says, "everything's password protected."

"Then get your own streak of piss," I tell him.

He gawps at me open-mouthed. "A programmer who can find a way in," I tell him.

"Oh, I see," he says.

"Anyway, I want to speak to Carnie. Con must have his number, have you come across a contacts list?"

"No, but like I said, I can't access his personal files."

"Try to find something; I'll be down the corridor." I make to leave but Mickey stops me.

"Are you sure that's wise?"

I shrug my shoulders. "You said it yourself, Mickey. There's no war to be won. I might have to settle for bringing this down to a one on one."

Downstairs the bar is open for business, but attracting only passing trade. I grab an OJ and head back to the snooker room, realising I've eaten nothing all day, but I've no appetite anyway. I mull over the options but it's not long until I realise I've nothing that will tempt Carnie into the open. There's a knock on the door and Mickey sticks his head around before coming in.

He passes me a thick black filofax. "Look under 'C'," he says.

"Even I could have worked that out," I tell him.

"Not 'C' for Carnie," he says, "'C' for casino."

I flick through the pages and find what he's talking about, scrawled in pencil beside the word 'Casino' is a telephone number with Sholto in brackets beside it. I look up to see Mickey's hesitant smile. "What's the problem?" I ask. "This has to be it."

"I had to bust into the old man's desk to find it," he says.

"I don't think he'll mind, Mickey."

"So what are you going to do?" he asks.

"Get him to agree to a meet."

"But what's in it for him?"

"Me. If the casino is the real deal he won't want any distractions. We each walk away; he calls off the dogs, gets on with his plans and doesn't need to watch his back."

"But he'll try to kill you anyway," Mickey says.

"Yeah, that's the trouble with Carnie, you can't trust the man."

Mickey shakes his head. "Doesn't sound much of a plan to me."

"Well, it's all I've got. I'll use Con's office to make the call."

"Do you need me?" Mickey asks.

"Better if you're not involved, Mickey."

~

I dial the number. A gruff male voice answers, "Yeah?"

"Let me speak to Sholto."

"This ain't his number," he says.

"It's the number I have for him."

"Who is this?"

"It's Maurice Scallion."

There's a muffled delay then complete silence. I'm beginning to think I've be cut off when I hear the sound of someone clearing their throat and I have him, or he has me.

"Maurice, what a surprise, to what do I owe the pleasure?"

I ignore Carnie's sickly-sweet tone and cut to the chase. "You know why I'm calling. I think you owe me an explanation."

"You may speak freely Maurice, this is a secure line. And you have my sympathies; it went beyond what I'd sanctioned, but I had to act; my backers would expect it of me."

His early acknowledgement ends any hope I had that Mickey might be wrong. It throws me and any pretence I have of calm. My hand tightens around the telephone and I wish it were his throat. "You had my boss and my brother murdered? You know I can't let that pass."

"No-one was supposed to die, Maurice, but if you must blame anyone, blame Cornelius, he made the mistake. He put our entire plans at risk by feeding in dirty money. He paid a heavy price, yes, but the mistake was his. It's the business we're in. Cornelius would understand that."

His calm annoys me, more so because the conversation's taking turns I didn't expect and already my plan feels shot. Dirty money? I'm confused.

"Why did they have to die if you didn't order it?" I ask.

"Someone took things personally. I'll take care of it, Maurice, I promise you."

"Not good enough," I tell him. "If you didn't order it then I want whoever did."

"I can't help you."

"If they disobeyed you, Sholto, you don't owe them any loyalty. Isn't that the business we're in too?"

There's a pause; I've got him thinking and while I have his attention I push my luck a little further. "I know about the casino, Sholto, and you know I can cause trouble you don't need right now. But I'm ready to make you a deal. Give up my brother's killer; send him to me, that's all I ask. Do that and I'll stay out of your way."

The line is silent. I hear an angry exhalation of breath; mentioning the casino has made him uncomfortable.

"I could do that, Maurice, but I like to clean up my own mess."

"You'd be doing just that by sending him to me."

"Hmm, I don't know, he may be more of a handful than you realise."

I sense he's wavering, he sees something in this for him that he's not admitting to.

"Him or me, either way all you lose is trouble." I tell him.

"Let's say I agree," he says. "Where do we do this?"

"The offer is good for my patch only; midday tomorrow at Moods; him alone."

"On a Sunday?"

"It'll be quiet, I want to talk; I need to understand. But perhaps he'd feel safer in public?"

"Don't flatter yourself Maurice. He's good at what he does; you'd do well to be wary of that. But then you've already met him. That unfortunate little nickname you gave him really pissed him off. You see he craves notoriety and found it very disrespectful."

Any momentary elation I feel at having won him around dies. "You're talking about Rats? He's no match for Harvey."

"Which one of them's still breathing, Maurice?"

"Okay, Sunday," I tell him through clenched teeth. "Tell Rats I'm looking forward to seeing him again. One last thing. What did you mean about feeding in dirty money?"

"The last nine grand, Maurice. It was useless."

"My boss and my brother were murdered for nine grand?"

"Not for nine grand, Maurice. For the tens of millions they put at risk."

"I know where that money came from," I tell him. "When I've finished with Rats I'll put an end to the source. You can have that one for free."

"If you're still around, Maurice," Carnie says. "If you're still around," then he cuts the line.

I slam the handset back into its cradle and try to take in what's just happened. Harvey and Cornelius are dead. Even Carnie wouldn't suggest it unless it was fact. To do so only for it turn out differently would make him look weak. My teeth are clenched tight in my mouth; I suck and expel air noisily through flaring nostrils, it's the only sound in my head. Then I feel the heat rise in my gut and it ignites me; I grab the first thing that comes to hand, launch it at the wall letting out a yell at the same time. Con's ashtray gouges out a chunk of plaster then clatters to the floor, unbroken.

In my head I hear Harvey whisper, *feel better?*

Chapter 26 (Part II) ~ Only me ~

~ Mo ~

There's no consolation to be had from Mickey when he gets his nerve up and comes back into the office. He doesn't bother to ask why I'm angry. But then he'd believed the message all along hadn't he? It was only me who doubted, only me who thought Harvey too strong and too shrewd to be caught out. Instead he asks how it went.

"We have a meet," I tell him, "here tomorrow afternoon."

"I'm surprised he agreed to it."

"Not with Carnie," I say, "with Rats." Mickey's face contorts in confusion. "They weren't supposed to die, Mickey. Rats went further than Carnie ordered."

"Rats killed them?" Mickey asks. "And Carnie's agreed to send him to the meet?"

"Yes."

"And that doesn't strike you as a convenient way for Carnie to get himself out of the firing line?"

I ball my fist and slam it onto Con's desk. I don't want to think that Carnie's fooled me. "Don't come across fucking clever now, Mickey. I didn't get the answers I expected, I had to think fast."

Mickey sighs heavily then sits in one of the chairs the other side of the desk from me. "What did he say?" he asks.

"He talked about cleaning up his own mess; only gave Rats up when I mentioned the casino. That's what makes me think he's genuine."

"Rats isn't the meek little guy he was while he was here, I've seen another side to him," Mickey says.

"I've glimpsed that side too and if he killed my brother then it's him I want."

"But he'll come knowing you're after him. What are you going to do?" Mickey asks.

"I don't know. I'll have to think it through. But whatever I decide, it's probably better you don't know."

~

I spend the next hour in the snooker room with just the light over the table turned on, but I don't play a game. Instead I alternate between pacing the floor and sitting at one of the side tables. Carnie's words dance around my head, teasing and taunting me. Thinking about it gives me a headache and every now and then when I turn around I can almost picture a column of smoke at the far end of the room billowing up from Harvey's cigarette. Dirty money, dirty fucking money, my brother murdered for a poxy nine grand and the bent ego of some twisted little bastard. I pull a cue from the rack and feel its weight in my palm, run my fingers down its smooth tapering stalk before I grip it like a golf club and smash it against the heavy wooden lip of the table. The cue splinters and shears, the free piece catapulting into the corner. I throw what's left in my hand across the floor. *Feel better?* I didn't tell Mickey about the money and I won't. It's disrespectful, firstly because nine grand is fuck all.

Nobody gets killed for nine grand; and secondly, well secondly I don't want anyone thinking we fucked up and got turned over by some trumped up little thief. Rosewood will get what's coming to him when I've finished with Rats.

I pace the floor and sit, pace the floor and sit. My shades sit squarely on the bridge of my nose yet still my head buzzes with all the discomfort of being stuck in a whiteout. What if Mickey's right? What if Carnie is setting me up? I bet he's lining Rats up to hit me before the meet. What should I do? There's no-one left I can trust. Harvey would know, but he's not here, there's only me. We've a club full of employees but none with any balls, at least not for this – a consequence of going legit. I pace the floor. This is Con's fault, all Con's bloody fault. I fucking told him. Harvey fucking told him. You can't deal with Carnie. I grab another cue from the rack. It goes the same way as the last.

My mobile rings, it's Myrna saying she's on her way so we can go out like I promised. But it's way too early; I put her off; tell her something's come up. So now I've upset her and I get the 'aren't I your girl?' routine again. I tell her I'm working, that she should go for meal with one of her girlfriends and come past Moods when the nightclub opens. It buys me more time to think.

There's a tentative knock at the door; then Mickey's voice. "You okay in there?"

"Sure," I call.

The door opens. In Mickey's arms are a couple of thin cardboard boxes bearing a delivery pizza logo. "Holy fuck," he says looking around.

My eyes follow his gaze, broken cues litter the floor and the edge of the snooker table is scored and indented. "I lost my temper."

"We heard, well the whole bar heard," Mickey says.

We sit down at a table and Mickey opens the boxes. "You must be hungry by now, I thought it wouldn't go amiss to get something on the off-chance."

"You did right," I tell him. "I've not had a bite all day."

We eat for a few minutes before he manages another question. "Have you decided how to play it?" he asks.

"If Carnie didn't see Rats as something of a loose cannon he wouldn't have been quite so happy to set him up," I tell him. "But I can't be sure which one of us poses a bigger threat to his casino deal."

Mickey nods and rubs at the side of his face; he's finding chewing a little uncomfortable. "So what will you do?"

"I haven't decided, but like I said, you're safer not knowing."

****

Chapter 27 ~ Teamwork ~

~ Adam ~

Shelley and I spend the best part of Saturday morning in the office behind reception. She's dressed in tight jeans and a casual top and looking as good as I've seen her while, despite my morning shower, I'm dressed in second-day clothes and feeling more than a little grubby. We use the hour or so before the shops open to trail through various internet sites searching for ideas under the heading of Hawaiian parties. Neither of us realised that the possibilities were so wide; within an hour of starting we've added Tiki totem poles and masks, leis, table skirts and room decorations to our burgeoning list. But the real bonus comes when we find a supplier in Hemel Hempstead, a couple of hours drive away but close enough to give us a shot at getting something together today. Shelley gives them a call and it sounds as if they can meet most of our needs. But before we finish with the internet there's one other thing I want to check.

"What was it that led the old lady to think of a Hawaiian night?" I ask Shelley.

"Sounded like she had a crush on the actor in a TV show," Shelley says.

"That's right, what was his name? I was thinking if we found out a little about him or the show it might give us some more to play with."

"Jack Lord," Shelley says, "I'm good with names."

"So it would seem," I tell her.

She types his name into the search engine and I look on over her shoulder as a handful of sites emerge. We pick out one which one lists his hit TV show – Hawaii Five-O – though it seems poor Jack passed away a number of years ago. Shelley finds a link to the show's theme tune and a video runs the titles and an upbeat, pacy tune.

In the video huge waves break along the beach and spark an idea. "Do you get lots of kids coming to the festival?" I ask her.

"Why? What are you thinking?" Shelley asks.

"I'm thinking about our theme and how popular a surfboard simulator might be. I think anyone who uses a skateboard would love it, and if we managed to hook up the waves breaking from that clip on a big screen behind them with the TV theme tune playing it would really draw people to it. It'd be a nice fun item and I bet it would bring back memories of the show for the old lady."

"Mrs. Ollenshaw," Shelley says, wide eyed. "That's actually a good idea. It's the type of thing you'd have to levy a small charge for though, just enough to cover the hire costs. I even know someone who could put the waves and the music on a repeating loop."

We get back on the internet and find a hire company advertising a surfboard simulator seventy miles away. Shelley gives them a call; the machine's available but she stalls on ordering. For a full week's hire she wants it before noon on Sunday with delivery and collection charges included. The Sunday delivery seems fine but the free delivery and uplift look to be a stumbling block, but Shelley holds her ground. Eventually they offer to split the difference and Shelley readily agrees. She'd have settled for much less.

"Remind me not to bargain with you," I tell her.

We stop off at the Village Hall but find Ray and Joel busy in the marquee. Shelley tells Ray about the simulator and the supplier we've found for the party accessories and he's delighted. Then she has a few quiet words with Joel before we bid them goodbye and head for Hemel Hempstead.

It's gone three when we find the supplier. It's more of a warehouse than a shop; I suspect most of their business comes from telephone or internet orders rather than people turning up at the door, but the bespectacled assistant makes us welcome. Shelley identifies herself as the lady who called earlier and we're encouraged to wander around the store to see what they have. In Hawaiian party-planning terms they prove to be something of an Aladdin's cave. I can't imagine there's anything more you could ever need for a beach style party. Shelley delves into everything from boxes of single coloured leis and multi-coloured flower garlands to paper plates and cups with luau imprints. She scribbles prices and quantities into a notebook taken from her handbag.

I ask if they have any Tiki totem poles and masks and I'm shown an array of ornate, hand-carved, wooden poles and face masks.

"The poles are beautiful for a permanent display," I explain, "but too expensive just for a party and not nearly tall enough for what I have in mind."

"Oh, we do have six foot inflatables," the assistant says, walking me down another aisle to a Tiki with the standard carvings printed onto a heavy-duty, but bright yellow, plastic. "They give the impression of the real thing although the colours are a little garish – they're meant to be fun and attract attention. Is the party being held inside or out?"

"Inside a marquee for the most part," I tell her, turning my attention to the palm tree behind, "but there will be some things outside."

"The palm trees and the totems each have a weighted base," she says, "but you may want to secure them if there are likely to be high winds."

I thank her and tell her I'll want two each of the inflatable palm trees and the totem poles and that we're building a list for her.

"No problem, just shout when you're ready," she says.

I head back down the aisles to find Shelley. I hesitate at the Tiki face masks; they would look good decorating the internal walls of the marquee, but maybe they too would be a little extravagant.

When I find Shelley we talk over what we've found individually and score off anything we have doubts about, but it's still a healthy list. We call the assistant back and go through it together. There's all the tableware, a thousand paper cups, plates and napkins all bearing luau imprints. There are half a dozen skirt dressings for the tables, boxes of leis and boxes of garlands. Then there are a dozen hula skirts in pink hemp with matching head and wristbands, three large wall murals depicting sea, sand and tropical islands, some banners and numerous packets of tropically decorated balloons. Finally, there are the inflatables, the palm trees, the totems, a couple of plastic parrots and a limbo stick.

Shelley negotiates some discount on the final figure and the assistant assures us we can have more supplied on a next day delivery should we run out of anything. I load everything into the back of the jeep and we start back.

When we hit the late afternoon traffic Shelley calls Ray on her mobile. She tells him she's shattered but that we've got everything we need to pull off the Hawaiian party theme and asks how things have gone at his end. They chat about the menu and then about Joel. She bites her lower lip then I watch the corners of her mouth turn up. It's clear how much she loves him and it's nice to see. She has the same relationship with Joel that I had with my own mother, until I ruined it.

"Did Ray manage to sort out a menu?" I ask her when she clears from the call.

"Yes," she says. "The girls checked luau menus on the web and we can make up something close to authentic without being so different that people will be scared to try it - a sort of chicken-in-a-basket version complete with sweet potatoes sprinkled with coconut."

"Sounds good," I say.

"Let's hope the girls think so too when they see what they'll be wearing," Shelley says.

"Are the hotel waitresses serving food at the marquee?" I ask.

"Some of them, yes. And in the pink grass skirts I've bought."

I pull a face. "I'm sure they'll take it in good spirit."

"I hope so, or I'll be forced to wear one myself," she says.

"Now that might not be a bad idea," I tell her. "I could just fancy you in one of those."

"Well now, there's a thing," she says. "When I told dad we'd got what we needed he suggested we chill out, go for a meal and spend some time together. He'll look after Joel." She stares at me until I take my eyes from the road for a second to meet hers. "We don't need to be back until tomorrow morning," she says.

I glance back at the road then again to Shelley. "What, stay over at my flat?" I ask.

She nods.

"I always knew Ray was a good bloke," I tell her, and she smiles. I let my eyes linger on her and she begins to blush and looks away.

****

Chapter 28 ~ Not for nothing…~

~ Mo ~

Mickey fucks off home for a few hours after we've eaten. Not the best policy if he wants to learn how the club runs but it's been a difficult day for us both. Left alone again my doubts return; what should I do? Who can I trust? It was Harvey who people liked; I'm the one they put up with for his sake, I'm the sideshow, the scary one, the freak.

I sit in the half-light at the table with the empty pizza boxes staring back at me. Their lids, peeled-back like open mouths, remind me of loose talk and overeager tongues. I may already have said too much to Mickey. It's not so much that he could be in with Carnie; more that he's weak and it'd take little to make him talk. Think: *What would Harvey do?* The question burns inside my head; I take my shades off and massage my temples to ease the building tension. Without thinking, I start to rock back and forth in my seat. *What would Harvey do? What would Harvey do?* and my subconscious finds an answer. He'd minimise the risks and prepare for the meet. I remember Pinchbeck; home itself isn't always the sanctuary we imagine it to be. Maybe it's best I stay away from the flat tonight; if Rats or Carnie plan to hit before the meet then the flat would be the place to do it. I put my shades back on and start to pace again. Con's car keys jingle in my pocket as I walk and now that I've noticed it, it annoys me; it breaks my concentration. I pull them out and throw them onto the green cloth of the snooker table. Under the light the shiny key with the letter 'P' scrawled on it in black-marker catches my attention, like I should remember it. It comes to me; it's a spare key for the lock-up – 'P' for Paxton's. My headache dips a notch.

Saturday afternoon and I'm in Harlesden. Going back to the flat wasn't part of the original plan; it's not what Harvey would do. *He'd minimise the risks and prepare for the meet.* Part of me wants to run into Rats, but if I come across him now he won't be alone, I'll lose any advantage I have. Harvey would want an edge for the meet and I've had an idea that might just give me that. I won't find it at the flat, but I decide to go there anyway. After driving past a couple of times I'm satisfied that there's no-one watching the house from a parked car, at least no-one I can see. I pull up in a nearby street, cut through the gardens to reach the stairs to the maisonette and then climb the steps two-at-a-time. Once I've slipped inside I stand by the door, listening. There's no movement in the flat and no sound of footsteps scurrying up the stairway outside. All is well and good so far. I set the snib on the door, slip off my shoes, and carefully check each room. The flat is empty, but that means nothing. Harvey had his keys with him, so I'm alive to the possibility that someone could be listening from his ground floor flat. I change into jeans and a tee-shirt and take a leather jacket from my rail. Then I quickly throw a few things into a holdall: clothes, scissors, my electric shaver. But no more three piece suits; Harvey's idea of style made us stand out – right now I have to blend in. A moment of panic, my mobile sounds off and I have to thrust my hand into my inside breast pocket to silence it. I catch Mickey's name on the screen as the light on the set winks out. I hold my breath and listen; in this quiet those tones were certain to be audible from Harvey's flat. I hold still and feel with my feet for any sense of vibration signaling movement below. I wait a full minute, nothing. But it's possible someone there is doing the self same thing, and if that's so then it becomes a case of who blinks first and I've no time for that. I leave as quietly as I arrived and make my way back to the car. Only after changing direction several times am I convinced there's no-one tailing me. It's a timely reminder to think of everything; one slip is all it takes.

The local gym is a little exclusive and uses a member card entry system. That makes it an ideal stop; free use of the facilities and no-one at the door to verify comings and goings. Thankfully though, Saturday evening isn't the busiest at the gym, too many other things to be doing I suppose. When I walk in there's only the one guy in the locker room; he looks up from tying his trainers to acknowledge my arrival. I drop the holdall on the bench and begin to undress; he hits the gym before I've got far.

I stand in front of the long mirror above the washbasins and start to shave. Not my normal shave, far from it. First, I take out the stubble then I remove my goatee and finally, after starting with the scissors, I shave my head, taking care to wash the cuttings down the sink. Then I strip and take a long, hot shower. When I'm finished, dried, dressed and back at the long mirror I slide my shades on and check my look. My eyes and eyebrows are hidden, and though my pallor is still pale, I pass for normal – whatever that is. The guy from earlier returns as I'm about to leave.

He's a sweaty mess and heaving as though he's breathing through his backside. He does a double take and I tell him the sauna made a new man out of me. He manages a smile and a nod, but I doubt the penny quite dropped.

Before I start the car I give Mickey a call. He answers on the first ring.

"Mo, I've been trying to reach you for ages. I was beginning to panic."

The similarity to the situation with Con and Harvey hadn't struck me and I can see how it might have looked, but I set his mind straight. "It's okay, Mickey, I was busy was all."

"Where are you? I assumed you'd stay at Moods today."

"You don't need me at Moods, Mickey, there are plenty people there who can help you get to grips with how the place runs. You have your job and I have mine."

"But for how long?" he asks. "This place is in Cornelius's name. We can keep it going, but pretty soon he'll have to be declared dead and this place will be wound up. What do we do then?"

Mickey's not a fighter, not in any sense of the word. I can hear it in his voice, but I don't have any answers for him. "I don't know, Mickey. You figure a way round it. That's what we're all doing isn't it? Trying to take care of business."

"Is the meet still on for tomorrow?" he asks.

"I've not heard different," I tell him.

"Do you need me there?"

"No, Mickey, you leave that to me. If it goes my way, I'll call you."

~

It takes longer than before, but this time I don't ask at the doors. I keep a low profile and wander through the clubs and bars like I was anybody else. I stick to the High Street to begin with, and then I move on to Manor Park and Craven Park. I'm mindful of the time and it's getting late when I find him, tucked away in a cosy corner of some bar I'd never heard of, not far from Willesden Junction. He's surrounded by the same entourage as last time. None of them look too handy, but that's his look-out. The man of the people is deep in conversation with someone, the deal is struck and they embrace. But there's no exchange, not yet. Boots won't sully his hands with that; he'll have one of the hangers-on pass the pills and accept the cash.

I lift my shades as he looks my way and he stares for a second, pushing his square-rimmed specs up the bridge of his nose, before jutting his chin in recognition. He pushes his way past his own minders to get to me.

"Onion, back so soon, how you doin', man?"

"I need your help," I tell him. "Is there somewhere we can talk?"

Boots throws an arm around my shoulder and starts to walk me away, "nowhere in here, man."

We stand out on the street corner with the traffic driving by. Four or five of Boots's minders follow us out but they hang back by the doorway when he tells them to give him some space. I doubt he's ever been comfortable with the need for them; it's a wonder he's lasted this long.

"You look different; the word must be true?"

"Depends what the word is," I tell him, folding my shades into my breast pocket.

His brow furrows, his serious face. "I heard Carnie took over Cornelius's patch."

I shove my hands into the pocket of my jeans and look off down the street, like I don't want to look him in the eye and tell him the biggest threat to him just got stronger.

"Con and Harvey are dead, Boots. I've set up a meet with the guy who killed them. I need you to give me an edge."

Boots nods then glances at the guys huddled around the doorway and makes a quick couple of circles with his index finger and one of them disappears back inside.

"Ain't nothing moves faster than bad news," he says, looking back to me, "I hoped you'd tell me it wasn't so."

"I didn't believe it myself," I tell him.

"How did you arrange the meet?"

"I spoke to Carnie and he agreed it." I watch Boots' jaw drop a little and know an explanation is called for. "I thought Carnie was behind it. It was him I wanted. But it seems he'd set Harvey and Con up for no more than a slap on wrist."

"And you believe him?" Boots asks.

"Strangely enough, I do. There was some bad blood between Harvey and the guy responsible. It fits and I suspect Carnie thinks he's taken a few liberties or he'd not have been so keen to give him up."

"So who is this guy?"

"I never found out his real name. Harvey called him Rats and it stuck. A little guy with a ponytail and a bad skin. Carnie rates him; thinks he's a bit handy, I guess I'll find out."

"I don't know him, but even so, you know it won't end there with Carnie?"

I give a shrug. "I know it."

A car draws up alongside us and Boots waves three fingers at the guys in the doorway then gestures me toward the car. "We'd best see if we can find you that edge then, Onion."

Five of us squeeze into a dark-coloured Volvo that has seen better days. Boots reads my mind; he turns around from the passenger seat. "She's comfortable enough on the inside, huh? This neighbourhood don't appreciate no posers." He raises a palm to say hold-off for now and returns his gaze to the front. I appreciate that, not that I'd have been keen to continue our conversation in front of his minders. We drive only a few blocks and pull up outside a tenement block; Boots has two of the guys stay in the car bringing only one with us and once we get to his flat he has him wait outside the door.

It's a modest flat, with a dingy hallway and what I glimpse as we pass the living room suggests it's not the tidiest. Boots takes me to the kitchen and has me take a seat at a rectangular wooden table while he takes off his heavy overcoat.

"So tell me," he says, "where's the meet and what kind of edge do you need?"

I look up at him as he slides his coat over the shoulders of the chair. "At Moods," I tell him, "and I was hoping you could suggest something."

"No sweat, man. But do you want to slow him down, kill him quick or what?"

"Any of the above, Boots. I thought it'd depend on what you had available."

"Okay," he says, "but I'm a dealer, man, all I got is stuff he needs to swallow, unless you can get close enough to stick him?"

"He'll know I'm handy with a knife, so I expect he'll keep me at a safe distance."

Boots pushes his glasses further back on his nose, and then begins to rifle through a few of the wall-cupboards. He pulls out various bottles and sets them on the worktop;

some are liquids but most are pills. He checks the labels and one by one returns them to the cupboard. Something in my expression gives me away; he looks back at me and smiles as he opens the next cupboard.

"Don't worry, Onion, this ain't no ordinary kitchen. I don't keep a lot here but maybe I have what you need. Does your man drink spirits?"

"Sure."

"You're meeting at a bar, d'you think you could persuade him to take a drink?"

An image comes to mind of Rats lifting a glass from the overhead rack at Moods Bar and helping himself to a brandy. "It's not like we'll be in public and I don't expect he thinks he's coming to a party, but maybe he'll take one."

"Ah," he says, checking the label on his latest find. "This could be the one." He sets a bottle on the table, then pulls a pair of plastic gloves from a drawer and slaps them down beside it.

To me it looks like a bottle of cough mixture.

"What is it?" I ask.

"Croton oil. It dissolves in alcohol. Keep the mix right, he won't even taste it."

"And what does it do?"

"It eats, man; it'll eat him from the inside out. This stuff blisters the skin on contact but dilute and digest it and it burns through your gut; you'll get a reaction in maybe ten minutes. Then you either end his misery or let him suffer, but he's gonna have too much trouble of his own to be givin' you any."

"So how much does it take and what reaction do I look for?"

"Onion, a spoonful of this could kill a horse, but don't use too much or it won't dissolve properly."

"And the reaction?"

"Hell, man, I don't know. What does anyone do when their insides is dyin'?"

I tilt the bottle and watch the thick liquid roll slowly around the neck. Blisters the skin on contact and a spoonful enough to kill a horse, yet it's off the shelf in his kitchen cupboard. Not for nothing is he called Boots.

"I'll take it. What am I due you?"

"Nothing, we go back, man. You, me; Harvey too. Just make sure you take this bastard out. I don't know the guy but already I don't like him."

"Thanks." I check the top is secure then place it in my jacket pocket.

Boots grabs my wrist. "Take the gloves," he says.

****

Chapter 29 ~ Together alone ~

~ Adam ~

"So this is it?" Shelley says as she checks out the living room of my second-floor flat in Tannock Bar. I follow her into the room, having stopped to pick up the pile of mail behind the front door.

"Don't say it," I tell her. "A typical bachelor flat, untidy and in dire need of the feminine touch."

"Well, now that you mention it," she says.

I flick through the post, junk mail mostly but I recognise the Council logo and rip the envelope open to find my P45.

"Here," I say handing it to Shelley; "you might as well hang onto that, I'm liable to lose it." I watch her put it in her handbag then tell her I'll give her a quick tour.

From the hallway I push open the door to the kitchen, we don't go in, being a galley kitchen it's small and what you see is what you get. "The bathroom's next door and the last one's the bedroom."

Shelley sticks her head around the bathroom door. "Just a shower, no bath?"

"Saves space," I say. "You do get used to it. But I know what you mean. Every now and again it's nice to have a long soak."

"And this is the bedroom?" she asks, pointing to the final door. "May I?"

"Sure."

"It's actually nice and light," she says, as though surprised, "and I like the picture mirror, it makes the room look bigger."

"I can't claim any kudos. I haven't done a thing with the place; it's as it was when I moved in."

Shelley sees the picture on the corner of the dresser and picks it up for a closer look.

"That's Annie," I tell her.

"Your mother, the Annie Lennox fan?"

"Yes."

"She was pretty," Shelley says.

"Yeah, you two would have got on really well." There's an awkward silence; as though neither of us knows quite how to move on from there. Shelley sets the picture back down. "What kind of food do you fancy?" I ask. "There's a terrific Indian restaurant close by if you like curry."

"Another day," Shelley says, "I'm in jeans and a top and right now I'd prefer we go somewhere casual, somewhere we can just relax and be ourselves, if that sounds okay."

"No problem, there's an Italian diner with a decent offering in pasta dishes if you prefer; but it's close to the cinema and busies-up before and after showings."

"That'll be fine."

"All right, give me five minutes to get out of these second-day clothes and scribble a note then we can head off."

"What's the note for?" she asks.

"Notice for the landlord," I tell her. "If I drop it in with the neighbours on the way out they'll pass it on."

~

"Tannock Bar looks a nice little place," Shelley says as we leave the flat.

"Mention it outside a radius of ten miles and no-one's ever have never heard of it."

"Same with Mountebridge," she says.

"It was new to me," I admit, "but that's not saying much."

We reach the first floor and I knock on the door. A few seconds later fuzzy-haired Barry opens up and I ask him if he can pass the note to the landlord for me.

He takes the envelope with a grunt, his eyes look over my shoulder towards Shelley. "Not seen you before," he manages.

"No, it's my first time in Tannock Bar," Shelley says. "I'm from Mountebridge, do you know it?"

Barry looks to me, but I'm not going to help him, he then returns his gaze to Shelley. "Where's that then?"

~

"I was famished when I came in, but I'm not sure I can finish this," Shelley says, pushing back her plate and the last of her mushroom lasagne. "I could feel myself filling up after the starter; I should have gone for the bruschetta, like you."

"You found the soup too much?" I ask.

"It was delicious," she says, "but more than enough." She sits back in her seat and glances at the pictures on the cream-coloured walls, letting her eyes flit from one fifties picture of American-Italian diners to another. "This was a good choice, busy enough to talk and not feel that your conversation's too readily overheard."

The waitress clears our plates and asks if we'd like anything else?"

"Cappuccino, Shelley?"

"Hmm," she nods.

"Two cappuccinos, please," I tell the waitress and once she's gone I turn back to Shelley. "So, how has Joel got on today?"

"Dad says he's been a real help."

I look into her hazel eyes, waiting for more, but none comes. "You're being coy."

Shelley gives a flick of her head, reminiscent of Joel himself. "What do you mean?" she asks, trying not to smile.

"It's what I said earlier; what my mother would see in you. It was in your expression earlier when you spoke to Ray about Joel this afternoon, that you love him is clear but there was something else."

"Go on," Shelley says.

"I don't know exactly, warmth, pride maybe?"

There's a flicker of a smile on Shelley's face. "You saw all that?"

I nod.

Shelley leans forward, rests her elbows on the table and makes a bridge of her hands. "I'm not supposed to tell you, so you have to look surprised when you find out. I told Joel about your idea for the theme tune and the background waves running on a loop. He got hold of the person I told him could do it and now it's all done; they've been testing it this afternoon."

"That's great," I tell her. "I'll do my best to look surprised but the appreciation will be genuine enough."

"He likes you and he's anxious to impress you," she says.

"He's a great kid and he's already impressed me," I tell her. Then we fall into another pocket of silence.

Our cappuccinos arrive. "Tell me about Annie," Shelley says.

"What do you want to know?"

"She died when you were twelve, you said."

"Cancer," I say, stirring my cappuccino. "I knew she was sick, after all, she was in hospital. But she didn't really look ill, you see. So it was a shock; I wasn't ready for it."

"But she knew how bad it was?" Shelley asks.

"Yes, she'd have known. Afterwards, I was taken into care. I suppose she hoped I'd be adopted by some caring family. It just never turned out that way."

"That's horrible, but you turned out okay; it's nice that you still have her picture."

"It's the only thing I have of hers."

Shelley frowns, "that's so sad. How come?"

"A long story," I tell her, "maybe one for another day. C'mon, there's somewhere I want to take you."

~

The chalkboard in front of The White Hart advertises a nineties disco; I take Shelley by the hand and we side-step through the bodies inside until we find a space near the bar.

Shelley is wide-eyed and a little tense, and watches me gaze around. "It's a young crowd," she says.

"Not unless you've been lying about your age."

She pats her elbow, reminding me of a previous dig in the ribs. So I get the drinks in and we just stand for a while and listen to the music. But before long she can't help herself and her upper body begins to move to the beat.

"C'mon," I tell her, "you've nursed that drink for long enough; it's time to take the plunge."

"But I've not been dancing in years," she says.

"Don't worry, you won't have forgotten how."

Shelley's confidence flows back as we dance and she relaxes; her eyes sparkle with energy, life and fun. I watch her smile and can't help but return it. I lose track of how long we stay on the floor, but it doesn't seem to matter what the DJ plays; we dance. Then it all winds down with the first slow record of the evening. Shelley buries her head into my neck and I slide my hands to her hips to pull her close. The heat of her body sets my fingers tingling, a sensation that courses through me and seems to heighten my awareness. Her hair, like silk against my cheek is sweet-scented and wonderful. She lifts her head and looks into my eyes, neither of us need to say anything. Our mouths find each other in a deep yet gentle kiss that stretches on and on until eventually she pulls away, her chest heaving, then she nestles her head back into my neck. We sway to a nineties song I'd long forgotten; frankly the kind I'd normally dismiss without a second thought. But now I have reason to think fondly of *Stand By My Woman*.

At the flat I search through my rack of CDs in the front room and find a copy of Lenny Kravitz's Greatest Hits. The track we danced to is on the CD so I programme it into the player along with a few other chosen tracks, hit repeat and leave the living room door ajar so the sound will filter throughout the apartment. By the time I've freshened up Shelley is already in the bed. I undress and slip in beside her; she looks a little nervous. Under the covers I run my fingers lightly over her arm in an attempt to reassure her. I feel the goose bumps on her skin.

"Listen," I say. "You will be gentle with me, won't you?" She laughs and the tension in her evaporates. We kiss, softly at first, but then with a hunger. My hands explore her body and I kiss and caress every inch of her, building to the point where neither of us can wait any longer. But for all the heat and urgency of it all, our love-making remains caring; tender like Lenny's velvet voice in the background as he sings the intro to Let Love Rule. It's the most exhilarating and emotional sexual experience of my entire life. When it's over I roll onto the free half of the bed and stare into the darkness below the ceiling.

"When you get your breath back you'll have to turn the music off," Shelley says.

"Thank God," I manage. "For a second I thought you were about to say when I got my breath back you were ready to go again. I don't think my heart could take it."

I catch her smile in the half light and it's as though her whole face is aglow. I hug her to me.

"You're forgetting the music, Adam."

"In a minute," I say, kissing her. I don't want to let her go. Not now, not ever.

****

Chapter 30 ~ Demons ~

~ Mo ~

It's gone 10pm when I return to Moods nursing a building headache; Myrna has been there for the last hour. She's had a few drinks and isn't best pleased, but I get her another drink and suggest we go to Con's office. She complains loudly on the stairs and along the corridors about having to leave the bar, telling me that if I can't take her out then surely I can at least let her enjoy the atmosphere and the beat from the club next door.

Once we're inside I close the door behind us. "There's something you need to hear," I tell her.

Myrna sits on the edge of Con's desk, her eyes wide, and her tongue still for a moment. The straps of her bag slip from her left shoulder and she transfers her glass to her left hand to haul them up then switches her glass back to her right hand. She's seven parts to the wind and I wonder how many it's taken to bring her to this state.

"Do you remember the grey-haired old guy with the thick glasses the night you danced for us at Calendar Girls?" I ask.

She smiles, but the drink has it a little crooked on her face. "The night I made you jealous?"

"Yes, that's the one."

"Vaguely," she says. "But I do remember you saying how special I made you feel."

I ignore her attempt to steer the conversation back to us. "That was Cornelius, my boss; Harvey's boss. He owned Calendar Girls; this was his office, his bar, his nightclub."

Myrna takes a sip from her glass and shrugs her shoulders. She doesn't see the relevance, doesn't pick up on the past tense. I'm no good at subtlety, either.

"Cornelius and Harvey are dead, Myrna. My boss and my brother. I wanted to…"

The glass slips from Myrna's hand and falls to the floor, the colour has drained from her. "What happened?" she asks, suddenly altogether more sober.

"I don't know for sure," I tell her. "I think a business deal turned sour. It looks like they were murdered."

Myrna lets out a gasp and pulls her elbows to her chest. Her balled hands press at her cheek, her shoulders shrink inward and she cowers into herself. I've seen this a hundred times, it's a defence mechanism; the forearms drawn up to deflect the blows. I've frightened her and I'm suddenly ashamed. I move to hold her close.

"You see why I couldn't take you out, don't you? Something bad is going on, Myrna." She's shaking but I feel her nod her head as it's buried against my shoulder. "It's not safe for you to work at Calendar Girls just now and we can't go to the flat either. But I know where we'll be safe tonight."

I drive the X5 into the lock-up and leave Myrna sitting inside until I close the roller doors and hit the lights. It's cold and the air is stale. Myrna steps tentatively from the car as I turn on the portable gas heater. There's been barely a word from her since I told her the news, she's in shock, but I don't expect she'll stay that way when she realises how basic the lock-up is.

Myrna's head lifts and I see her take in the red brick walls, the high arched ceiling and the suspended strip-lights. She glances at the workbenches and the stack of boxes at the far wall, then across to the bed. "What is this place?" she asks.

I set the heater to full and watch the three burners catch. "Just a disused warehouse," I tell her. "It used to be a security firm."

"But there's a bed and ... stuff."

"Not quite the comforts of home, but we can lie low for a day or two. No-one knows about this place. Con used it to keep his cars off the streets."

"Why the bed then?"

"For times like this," I lie. "Look there's a TV and a fridge, the loo's at the far end and there's running water and a kettle so we can make a brew. It's not too bad."

Myrna takes a seat at the table. Her cheeks still have no colour; I'm worried she's going to puke.

"How about a coffee?" I ask her, "It'll take my mind off my headache and you look as though you could do with one."

She nods. "I'm sorry about Harvey," she says, "Faith liked him."

When I come back with the coffees Myrna is digging around in her bag. She snaps it shut a little hurriedly as I near but I can see she's been touching up her make-up and doesn't look so bad now. I set the coffees on the table and check the fridge. But it's a pointless exercise, the power has been off and the milk in the fridge has turned. "I'm afraid it's black or nothing."

She manages a smile. "How long will we have to stay here, Mo?"

I take a seat at the table. "Hopefully just tonight, it'll all be sorted tomorrow." I take a drink from my mug. "It doesn't taste the same without milk," I tell her, "but it'll warm you up."

We're content for a minute or two quietly sipping our coffee until she breaks the silence. "So if we spend the night here can I go back to my flat during daytime? I'll need to wash and change."

"You stay away until I sort things," I tell her, and the fright returns to her eyes. I sigh, remove my shades and for a second or two make circles on my temples with my thumb and middle finger. "Look, it's not worth the risk, Myrna. It's me they want, but I can't take the chance that they might hurt you too. Do you understand?"

She sniffs back a tear; opens her bag and rummages inside until she finds what she's looking for. She throws her head back, pops the pill on her tongue and swallows.

"You brought those from the flat?" I ask.

"Just as well too, given that we can't go back. My nerves are shot, I need one. You too, make you forget your headache."

"I can't take them, Myrna. I told you; they're bad for me." Her face is ashen again and her eyes fall away from me. For the first time she's suddenly reacting like everyone else, unable to look at me. Her eyes linger a little too long on my drained coffee mug and I recall her rooting in her bag before I set it down. "Tell me you didn't slip one into my coffee, Myrna."

Her eyes well up. "You've been through so much. I thought it'd make you feel better. One can't hurt, can it?"

I lift my hands to claw at my scalp as if it'll make a difference.

"What will it do?" she asks, tears now making her mascara run.

"It'll be all right," I tell her.

"But what will it do?"

"They might calm you down, Myrna, but to me they're a stimulant, they make the pupils dilate, open wider." I sense she's not getting it. "My eyes are sensitive to light," I tell her, my voice raised more in frustration than anger. "I need to shut light out, not open up to it."

"I'm sorry," she sobs.

I turn the fire off to buy a second's composure; I don't want to sound angry with her. "It'll be okay," I manage, "let's just put the lights out and go to bed."

~

Myrna's not asleep, she twitches and every now and again a soft sigh or a pleasurable moan escapes her lips; she's in a peaceful place. I lie beside her, my head pounding, almost fearful of opening my eyes. There's no sense of elation, perhaps nothing will happen. I wait for sleep but it doesn't come, the thumping in my head won't let it. I think of Harvey and Cornelius, I wonder about the end, how it came to them and if it could have been prevented. I think of the bottle of croton oil lying in the holdall in the back of the Beamer, and what I plan to do with it and then it starts, slowly at first. It's like the membrane of my eyelids sizzles against my eyeballs then thins. Little specks of light break through and begin to join up, but there's no pain - the room beyond is in darkness. The sensation continues until I'm seeing clean through my eyelids. I can make out the pitch of the ceiling arch and the metal framework that supports the strip-lights. With no real effort or conscious will on my part I'm suddenly staring close-up at the brickwork ceiling. There's no untethering of muscle, no tearing of fibrous tissue, none of the things I practice, I'm just there, twelve inches from the ceiling. I turn to look down at the bed. It's strange to see another lying next to me.

I move down until I float above my own empty shell and begin the self-same operation I've performed a hundred times or more; knowing it will bring me the inner peace I need. I tug the sheet away then draw a scalpel down from the breastbone to the navel, pressing firmly; cutting through skin, muscle and the sinewy fat beneath. Thin red beads break to the surface to form a line in the scalpel's wake. My hand probes the wound, forcing its way in, groping blindly through a sea of warm filth for that which ought not to be there. My first pass is unsuccessful. I withdraw my hand, adjust my position, and then plunge in again, attacking from a different angle. The yawning cleft swallows my arm. My fingers, coated in tepid sludge, brush against bone, slide along stomach wall and creep into crevices between animated organs; but I don't come upon anything cold, nothing inorganic. I lower myself still further until my chin lies hard against my own hip and extend my reach by an extra few inches. A putrefying stench leaks from the crimson gash and fills my nostrils. It's the smell of decay my old aunt warned me of. She said it was a gauge to the infection of my soul. If that's true I'm beyond hope.

I try to ease out so I can start again but suddenly I'm held fast. My free hand grips the side of the bed giving me purchase and I pull back for all I'm worth. My hand emerges from the blood-red maw but another grips me at the wrist. I cry out in shock and the fingers open to release me then disappear back into the incision.

I watch, rooted, as the belly inflates and the lips of the wound part giving birth to a rising black mass. Harvey's blood-drenched head breaks free and his eyes spring open and fix me.

"He-lp me," he pleads; his words no more than a staggered whisper.

A heavy hand smashes down and forces Harvey back into the bloodied pit. The shock startles me once more and I look up at the now sitting figure; it's no-longer me. Rats' greasy, pockmarked face stares back at me; wild-eyed and grinning he tells me I can't help Harvey now. Harvey is his forever.

I fly at him. We become a tangle of flailing limbs, but I'm heavier and stronger, he can't throw me off. His fingernails gouge at my face but I sweep his hands aside and land a punch, sending blood and mucus spilling from his nose. He squeals in pain and I hit him again. He killed my brother and all that matters is that I make him pay. My hands are around his throat, my thumbs pressing into his windpipe. He convulses; a rasp escapes his throat in a cough and I almost lose my grip. So I squeeze all the more. His mouth opens, desperate for air, while his hands claw at mine. His eyes betray his panic, they plead but they'll find no pity in me. I feel the strain at my biceps and my arms begin to tremble with the effort. Through gritted teeth I squeeze harder still. His eyes bulge; his resistance is fading. A sudden noise ends it, like the snapping of a dry reed underfoot, his windpipe gives way, the cartilage crushed beneath my thumbs. He lies still and I roll off of him, satisfied. Grinning.

~

It's still seems dark when I awake and prop myself up on my elbows. My head's clear, I've slept well and it takes a second or two for the stale air and the shafts of daylight breaking at the edges of the roller doors to remind me where I am. I slide out of bed then curse the cold concrete floor as I pad across to hit the lights. The strip-lights stutter into life before I've reached the gas heater and I kneel to depress and turn the ignite switch. I catch my reflection in the heater's shiny aluminium facing; not a sharp image but enough. I lift my hand to my face and trace around both cheeks. Stubble; a day's growth, but beneath it I'm cut and scratched, the backs of my hands too. In my mind I have a vague recollection of a fight with Rats, him reaching up at me, his fingers clawing at my face. I stand and start to move back toward the bed. Myrna's still asleep; her right arm outside the duvet, her head turned away from me. I call her name as my mind replays the sound of Rats' windpipe collapsing beneath my fingers.

I know it. Somehow I know it even as I climb onto the bed, but it doesn't prepare me, not nearly. Myrna's head lies to the left; when I lean over her I see the dried blood on her right cheek and at the rims of her nostrils. Her eyes are open, unseeing and a bloated, purple tongue lolls from her slack mouth. I let my gaze fall to her neck, peppered in a rage of red and purple bruises. Finger marks; mine. There is no doubt.

I pull the duvet up to cover Myrna and to hide my shame. Then I sit on the edge of the bed and hold my head in my hands. I didn't cry for Harvey and I can't cry for Myrna, I think I've forgotten how. But I do feel something. I feel empty: empty and utterly alone.

I think about freshening up but decide to wait 'til I get to Moods. Everything has changed and at the same time it has all become very clear. I'm at peace with it and with myself. I once asked Harvey where we'd fit in this new enterprise of Con's. I didn't really get an answer. The truth is

Harvey would have fitted right in; he had the looks and the chat, the ambition; even a little of the sophistication needed. It's me who wouldn't have fitted; and I don't fit with what's left behind now. Even when I kill Rats, Carnie will feel he has to look over his shoulder, which makes me a loose cannon he can't afford. He'll send someone and then another and they'll keep coming until I screw up. The clock is ticking but I'm not sure what my future can be, or if I have one at all. For now, I'll settle for making sure Rats has none either and then Rosewood for his part in this.

****

Chapter 31 ~ The imperfect past ~

~ Adam ~

I awake to the feather-light touch of lips on mine and open my eyes to see Shelley's smiling face.

"You're an angel and I've died and gone to Heaven," I say.

"No such luck," she tells me. "It's 7am and there's a lot to do, we need to get moving."

"Okay," I tell her, "you take the first shower; I'll get us some breakfast."

"Cereal and a cup of tea will do," Shelley says.

"It's probably all there is," I tell her.

"Off you go then," she says.

I realise then that she's waiting for me to get out of bed first so I don't see her naked in daylight.

"You're not shy are you?" I ask, seeing her blush again. "Because I thought maybe I'd sit back and congratulate myself on the beauty I'd caught. I might even drag you back into bed and ravish you again."

Shelley slides out of bed and I let out a roar of appreciation. She grabs a pillow and belts me with it as she walks past.

"I was going to ask before borrowing your toothbrush, but I think you owe me now," she says, grinning.

I pull on a pair of boxers, dig out a bag and pack a week's clothes and a few essentials then get a couple of bowls of cereal ready in the kitchen. I've eaten mine before Shelley comes through.

"My turn for second-day clothes," she says.

"You could always borrow a shirt or tee-shirt of mine if you'd prefer."

"Can I?" she asks.

"Help yourself; I'll leave your tea and cereal on the table in the front room."

I load my toothbrush with paste and jump into the shower letting the jets refresh me while I brush my teeth. I hear the door open and Shelley asks me to stick my head out. I tug back the curtain. She's wearing my blue, cheesecloth shirt, gathered at the waist and tied.

"Looks better on you than it ever did on me."

"Okay?" she asks, seeking reassurance.

"Sure," I tell her.

"Hang on," she says, narrowing her eyes. "Are you brushing your teeth in the shower?"

"It's called multi-tasking."

She gasps and bites her lower lip in fake shock. "You've been on your own too long."

When I've shaved and dressed I wander through to the living room, a smile still fresh on my face. Shelley's been quiet and I'm unprepared for what I find. She's on the sofa, tears streaming down her cheeks. In her hand is a crumpled sheaf of papers. The smile slips away from me and I sink into the chair opposite. I've not seen them since the night I wrote them, but I know what it is that she holds in her hand.

She raises the letter; it quivers in her trembling fist. "Jammed in the corner of your sofa, Adam. I've a vulnerable young boy to consider, please tell me I've not got myself involved with a thief."

I raise my hands palms up to placate her. "It's not what you think, Shelley, honest."

But as soon as the words are out of my mouth I know I've headed down the wrong path. It's her eyes, so big and so round. They're like search lights, ready to cut through any smokescreen I dream up. They peer into my soul and implore of me, don't lie. If I'm not honest with her now, she'll know it and I'll never have her trust again. I let my eyes drop from her.

"Actually, that's not true. It is what you think and worse besides. But there were…" I correct myself, "… there are reasons."

Shelley wipes her tears with the back of her other hand. "I've read the letter, Adam. I know you went through a hard time, but you grew up long ago; the frightening part is that this reads like the present."

I shake my head, "It's the past," but then I add, "but it's the recent past and I'm done with it, I swear. But let me explain, because I want to be honest with you and there are things you need to know."

Shelley nods, but her body language has changed. She's stiffened, like I'm the enemy trying to wear her down and she's already set against me. But I go ahead anyway, I tell her about Colin and how it started out as a way to a hit back, then snowballed.

"So you're blaming Colin?"

"No, Colin might have been the instigator, but Ferris and I could have said no. I'm not ducking responsibility."

"Ferris was involved too?"

"Latterly, yes; but you have to understand that Colin was a real character, a good friend, the type you didn't like to let down. He had a taste for it that Ferris and I never aspired to. We helped only because we knew he was crazy enough to do it alone."

"So the money had nothing to do with it," Shelley says, a sarcastic undertone in her voice.

"It didn't as it happens. But I don't expect you to believe that."

"Fine, are we done now?" Shelley says, making to rise from the sofa.

"No," I tell her, and lift a hand to signal for her to sit back down. "You've judged me already but you might as well hear the worst."

Shelley retakes her seat, her expression further hardened against me. I use both hands to rub at my temples but, of course, I feel no better after it. Rather than see Shelley's contempt for me I look toward the floor as I speak.

"Colin was killed in a car accident in the lead-up to a job, so it never went ahead. But it had been sanctioned by some real heavies and they wanted their cut, it was like they were desperate for it. They got hold of Ferris and made it clear what would happen if they didn't get their money. I had to rob the Mountebridge Post Office to get it for them."

"YOU?" Shelley gasps, crumpling the letter as she draws her hand to her mouth. "How could you?"

I shrug my shoulders, "How could I not? Ferris was the only friend I had left."

"You stole from pensioners, Adam."

"Wrong," I tell her, raising my voice for the first time. "I stole from the Post Office, the old folks were still able to cash their pensions; just a little later than normal." I walk over to the window, feigning interest in what's outside because of the shame I feel in defending the indefensible. "But you're right," I say quietly, "it's stealing whichever way you cut it and I wish I'd done things differently because they killed Ferris anyway."

From the corner of my eye I see Shelley turn her head in my direction.

"They killed Ferris?"

I nod. "Ran him down and joked about it. I hoped to see his girlfriend, Tina, at The White Hart last night, it's where they met. I wanted to tell her how much she meant to him. He'd want her to know."

"Wasn't she at the funeral?"

"There was no funeral, Shelley, he's a missing person. They mowed him down with the car I used in the robbery. It's covered in my prints and his blood. If I go to the cops, they'll make sure I take the fall."

"This is absurd," Shelley says.

I sense her rising to leave. But instead she walks around and comes up behind me. "Is everything that comes out of your mouth a lie?"

I spin around. "That's enough," I tell her. "Do you have any idea how difficult it is to be this honest with nothing but bad news to tell? It took me nearly twenty years to write my mother the letter you're tearing me apart with."

She swallows hard. "Okay, I could have put that better. What I meant was are Joel and I part of your lie?"

I stare at her; it never occurred to me that she could imagine me to be that callous. "I'm not that good a liar, Shelley. Everything that passed between Joel and I and between you and I was honest, heartfelt and unplanned. If you didn't mean something to me I wouldn't be telling you any of this."

She breaks eye contact, like she's weighing up what I've said. "What is it that you don't believe?"

I shake my head, I don't understand.

"The letter," she says. "You say your mother said something that you didn't understand at the time and now that you do, you don't believe it."

I let out a sigh. "That's not important right now."

"No, tell me," she says.

I take a deep breath. "Her last words to me: *Don't worry, it'll be okay. What's for you won't go past you.*"

"And things haven't been okay?"

"Nothing was ever the same again. Years of waiting for something better tends to knock any optimism out of you. Let's just say I think we determine our own fate. Some of us don't carry the luck that others do."

"Now you sound bitter."

I gesture to the letter, "I was; now I'm just realistic."

Shelley glances at her watch. "We'd better be going."

"We're still going? Is there still an 'us' or was I a little too honest for you?"

Shelley gathers her jacket and handbag. "A lot of elderly people – the same ones you inconvenienced not so long ago – are counting on you. I think the least you can do is finish what you've started for them. I won't tell anyone what you've done, but I think you and I end here. I need a man I can trust; my son needs a role model. You're neither of those."

The drive back to Mountebridge is subdued with hardly a word passing between us. I replay our conversation in my head wondering if somehow I could have changed the outcome. Our relationship came out of nothing and has dissolved just as quickly; and I'd been so sure that it's hard to accept. But after my thoughts have gone round in circles for a while I shake my head clear of them and switch on the radio to break the silence. The unmistakeable voice of Annie Lennox belts out 'When Tomorrow Comes' and a look passes between Shelley and I, but we say nothing. I reach out and turn the radio off. A few miles further on I take the exit slipway and turn onto the Lower Weaton road. The hedgerow rise on either side of us blocking the views of the open fields and I'm overtaken by a sudden feeling of déjà vu. The narrow road tapers into the distance and I feel like we're thundering down the stem of a spout with the wind at our backs, knowing that we're about to be spat out into God knows what and powerless to stop it. I give my head another shake causing Shelley to look at me strangely. "I don't believe in fate."

"So you said," Shelley says.

Only then do I realise that I'd said that out loud.

~

We slow to pass over the hump-backed bridge and I drop into second gear to take the steep incline before turning sharp left at the top into Mountebridge's main street. Bunting runs above the shop fronts on the right while people mill around on the grassy lawns to the left, they even occupy the wooden benches, scattered along the outer edges.

"You wonder where they all come from," I say.

"It's a big day for them; they want to see it all come together." It's the first time I've seen Shelley smile since this morning's shower.

"Shall I stop by the marquee so we can take these things across?"

"Yes," she says. "No point in getting changed just yet with all the work that's to be done. And remember to look surprised when Joel shows you the video clip and soundtrack. He's had his share of disappointments."

We unload the jeep in three trips taking the boxes into the village hall. When we're done we wander over towards the marquee, there's a new gazebo erected adjacent to it and under its shade the surf simulator is being set up.

Ray is on hand and comes over to plant a kiss on Shelley's cheek. "Everything Okay?" he asks.

Shelley smiles at him. "Fine, wait 'til you see what we've got. It'll just pull the whole thing together," she says, sweeping a hand across her chest to emphasise her point. "Where's Joel?"

"He's helping Archer set up his stall," Ray says.

"Okay, we'd best get to work too," Shelley says. "I'll get the girls to give me a hand with the party plates and table dressings. You two can discuss where the other things fit in."

Ray waits until Shelley is out of earshot, throws an arm around my neck to rest his hand on my shoulder, and walks me in the other direction.

"You two had a falling out, Adam?"

"Is it that obvious?" I ask.

"I know my daughter," he says.

"It's my fault, Ray, not hers."

"Work at it," he says, pulling his hand from my shoulder and patting me twice between the shoulder blades. "She'll get over it." He changes the subject and asks me if there's anything else we need to be doing.

"Where are all the stalls going?" I ask.

"They're all on the green." He points ahead, "look, they're setting up now. The fun things like shove ha'penny and target shooting are closer to the simulator to keep all the activities together. We've put the brick-a-brack and the food stalls at the far end and that way they don't feel they're competing so much with the food on offer at the marquee."

I stop him, "target shooting?"

He waves a hand dismissively. "That's Archer's crossbow event. Don't worry; he'll set up by the trees. If they miss they'll be firing into the woods."

"Can we sketch this out so I can see how it all looks?"

"Sure," he says.

We walk to where the nearest stall is being set up and Ray borrows a pen and draws out a map of the green on one of the stallholders' paper bags.

"The hall is here and behind it is the marquee with the simulator and gazebo close by. A little further down - just beyond the bowling green - we have the activity stalls, then the brick-a-brack, the old bandstand and the food stalls. Beyond that, we have the end of festival bonfire."

"No-one mentioned a bonfire."

"We have one every festival," Ray says, "but we don't even put the stuff out 'til later in the week."

"Okay, now that I know the layout let me get started with what we've brought and I'll come find you when I'm done."

"Sounds good," Ray says. "But don't stray too far. Joel's been working on one of your ideas; he'll want to show you once the simulator's ready. You'll need to make out I haven't warned you."

~

I set to work with the inflatables; but I don't waste time blowing them up. The surfboard simulator sits within something resembling an inflated paddling pool minus the water, presumably so that anyone falling off has a soft landing. The guy assembling it has one of those rapid inflators and I have him sort the palm trees and Tiki totems in seconds. Thereafter it's just a matter of positioning and securing the palm trees near the village hall and the Tiki totems between the last activity stall and the simulator. Each pair is weighted and tethered to the ground. I fit some wooden stakes to the 'Aloha' banners and sit them alongside, together they act as a gateway channelling the visitors and alerting them to the fact that they are entering the themed area.

In the marquee light filters through the white canvas roof giving it a spacious and airy quality. Tables and chairs, set out for diners, take up half the room while the profusion of coloured balloons conveys a party mood. At the front, the serving tables look smartly dressed with grass skirts and laden with luau imprint paper cups and plates. Commercial catering equipment hums quietly by the tent walls and although various people rush here and there Shelley is nowhere to be seen. In her absence I fit the three large tropical murals to the walls high above the catering equipment and suspend the two inflatable parrots from the ceiling. By the time I've finished Shelley returns followed by six youthful waitresses resplendent in pink grass skirts, with matching head and wrist bands and pink T-shirts too.

Shelley sees the murals. "Looks good," she says, almost grudgingly. "What do you want to do with the leis and garlands?"

"They're giveaways aren't they? Have the girls take turns in handing them out," I suggest.

"Hmmf," she says, "we'll give them to those buying meals; a little incentive."

I shrug my shoulders at her tone, so she's commercially astute, big deal.

Ray appears at the entrance to the marquee and shouts for everyone to come outside, they're going to run the surfboard simulator. Shelley passes me, arms folded and throws me a look, "surprised, remember!"

There are a couple of hours until the official opening but already people are beginning to gather. A small group of elderly folk crowd near the simulator and I recognise Vernon among them. But my attention is taken by Joel as he climbs onto the surfboard and Ray throws a few switches at the back. The projection screen behind Joel shows rolling wave after rolling wave breaking over calm waters and the surfboard begins to undulate with Joel onboard, arms outstretched. Then a solo drumbeat kicks out from the speakers and the Hawaii 5-O theme tune plays. It's like there's a unanimous intake of breath. Ray stops the ride as the speed picks up and threatens to throw Joel off, but he's given an ovation as he jumps down.

There's no pretence in the smile on my lips and I half expect Joel to run over to me given that he's done this as a surprise, but he doesn't. Instead he pushes his way into the crowd at the side and yells, 'okay, play.'

The crowd part as the steel band break into a Caribbean lilt and I'm truly taken aback. I never asked Ray if he'd managed to track one down. Ray and Joel walk over to me beaming from cheek to cheek.

"You found one," I say, nodding toward the band.

"No," Ray says, "everyone I tried was booked up. Those are kids, Adam. Joel suggested we try a school band."

I ruffle Joel's hair then lift my hand for him to high-five as Ray is pulled aside by Vernon. I hear him introduce Ray to Mrs. Ollenshaw and see her give him a hug.

"See that?" I tell Joel. "That's the old lady who wanted a Hawaiian theme. Your granddad's getting the hug. But it's what *you've* done that's made her day."

Shelley coughs from behind me. "I need to go home and change, but my handbag's still in your car."

"I'll take you," I tell her.

Shelley sits in jeep and looks out of the side window as we drive to The Huntsman.

"Can't you just be happy that it looks to be coming good?" I ask.

"You're feeling pretty pleased with yourself aren't you? Everybody's happy and you look the hero, if only they knew the truth."

"Just what do you want Shelley? I can't win."

"Oh," she says, sounding exasperated. "I'm just so angry at you."

When I pull up behind the hotel she jumps out of the car, slams the door and marches towards the bungalow. But she gets halfway before turning back and yanking the door open again.

"I take it back," she says. "You've done your part for the old folks; you've made it up to them. I think you should leave."

For some time I sit in the Sportrak and wonder how things could get so bad so quickly. I consider heading back to my hotel room and collecting my bag, it's the reaction I'd have given to any previous girlfriend expressing her feelings so bluntly. But this is different so it's a thought I give credence to for all of two seconds. I understand Shelley's disappointment; I know she feels let down, but I can't just walk away. Instead I decide to give her some time on her own, maybe she'll have calmed down once she's had a chance to change her clothes and freshen up. I head for the snug telling myself things might look better after a coke and a sandwich.

Chapter 32 (Part 1) ~ Legend ~

~ Mo ~

I fold my shades into the pocket of my leather jacket and sit in the shadows with my back to the wall at the far end of Moods Bar. In front of me is a bottle of OJ, as yet untouched. From here I look across the scattering of empty tables and chairs towards the windows and the glass-fronted doorway. The lights are on above the bar, but the rest of the room is lit only by what light filters through the windows and reflects off the polished wooden surfaces. There's nothing to do but wait and I try to stay focused but it's more difficult than I imagined. The stillness and the quiet eat away at me; this place is full of memories, none of them quiet or still. I shift my foot and kick something from beneath my chair, a button. Loose threads hang from my jacket, it's mine, I pick it up and place it on the corner of the table.

His head and shoulders appear at the window, pressing close, he's early. He arcs both hands between his forehead and the glass to shut out the glare and peer in. I stand and the weight of the closed knife in my breast pocket shifts as it falls against my chest. It's my fallback if all else fails. My movement draws his attention and I retake my seat as he comes through the door trying, I think, to look calm while checking the shadows left and right. He stops about ten feet away.

"You're safe enough, there's no-one else here," I tell him, "just you and me, as agreed." I catch a flash of his teeth, not a smile, more of a leer; and for all that his clothes are more up-market and his posture altogether more confident it's his poor complexion and greasy, tied-back hair that draw attention.

"You look different," he says.

"Funny," I say. "I was just thinking that you looked much the same." I take a swig from my bottle of orange juice. "You and I need to chat."

"Really," he says. "Why don't we just cut to the chase? We both know where this is going."

"Because I need an explanation. I need to know why. Carnie understands that. That's why he agreed to it."

"Yes," he says. "Mr. Carnie does like to set me little tests now and again. But then, I always come through."

My palms are sweating, I want to wipe the smugness from his face and beat him to a pulp. But it's like Harvey's sitting by my side, urging me to hold back, telling me that my time will come. I gesture to the bar:

"Relax, grab a drink if you want, then pull up a seat."

He looks at my OJ. That's not a drink," he says.

"I drink as I choose," I tell him. "It's early, but you suit yourself."

He walks to the bar, being careful to keep an eye on me. "That's a good example of why you're in the wrong job, Mo." He pulls a tumbler from the overhead rack. "This is a thinking man's business these days; looking the part's not enough anymore. People don't trust those who won't share a drink with them. You have to be clued-up, be able to handle

yourself and to be able to do it even if you've had a drink."
He fills his glass at the brandy optic and downs it in one.
Rasping a little, he pours himself another before taking a seat
at a table a few feet away from me. "Naughty," he says,
setting his glass down. "You've been replacing the good stuff
with cheap substitutes, that one was still rough round the
edges."

"It's Con's booze you're drinking, show a little
respect."

"He's dead, your brother too, get over it," he says,
swirling his brandy while his eyes remain fixed on me.

I feel the heat rising in my gut, I want to lash out
but he's taken the bait, I can afford to wait.

"Carnie said it was meant to be a wrap on the
knuckles. What changed?"

"He said that did he?" He gives a little laugh, "no
matter, they had it coming." He takes a sip of his drink and
smiles at me. "The likes of you have no place in this
business; you're a dinosaur, a meathead, too stupid to be
capable of anything more than minding the doors. They say
you're good with a knife though. Fast hands I hear."

I try to slow things down, make him wait but he's
playing a different game; there's no fear in his eyes and I
can't work out whether it's confidence or just arrogance.
Either way, he sees the silences between us as an opportunity
to take charge and I'm left fighting the urge to tear at him
and rip the head from his shoulders. He's trying to pick a
fight but if the oil does its work then all I have to do is wait.

I lift the button from the corner of the table, and place it on the back of my right hand. I hope the dexterity trick will put a little doubt in his mind, I don't even need to look, instead I watch for his reaction. Just by raising and lowering each finger in turn I pass the button at speed from finger to finger and back again.

He shakes his head, "shit like that can get you killed." He holds up his right palm and with his eyes fixed on me reaches into his inside pocket using his thumb and forefinger. "I like to use a knife too." He makes a show of opening the blade then extends his arm to slam it into the table in front of him. "I don't have any fancy tricks, just accuracy, I never miss."

His eyes are still locked on mine, he's knows what he's done is yet another insult, he's set on provoking a reaction and I so want to give it to him. But there's a flicker, a brief second when I can see his annoyance and I grab hold of that, I bite down on my anger.

"Tell me why you killed Harvey," I insist.

"He deserved to die. When I do a job," he says, pounding his bony fingers into his chest, "it's done right. Then and only then do I put my name to it. My reputation demands respect; my work commands a high fee."

His casual dismissal of Harvey irritates me; he's too full of himself. "So you don't take sides? Instead you prostitute yourself to the highest bidder."

"Call it what you like," he says through gritted teeth, "but my name is whispered by people who matter. Jack

Muldoon will be legend," he says, spraying spittle angrily from his lips. "Fucking legend."

I manage a smile back, "but Rats suits you better."

He composes himself. "Time for you to do your bit knife-boy, killing you can still enhance my reputation. I hope you're better than your brother. He cried out like a girl when I stuck him with this," he says, pointing to the blade on the table.

Ten minutes have come and gone, they must have. Either the croton oil has failed or I've not used enough. I've sat past the point where I should have reacted. What stops me is my realisation of the mistake I've made in letting him get his blade drawn and set out on the table, if I make a move for mine now I'll be slower.

Rats' pock-marked face can't hide his puzzled expression. It's like he knows he's got the drop on me but wants me to act first so he can talk up his success later.

"Since you raise the topic of prostitution, did you like Myrna?" he asks.

I feel my jaw drop, could Benny have told him about Myrna and me?

"You looked shocked, Mo. Surely you can't be that stupid? You must have realised a girl like Myrna wasn't with you for your looks or sparkling personality?"

It's when he starts to laugh that I lose it. I reach into my inside pocket and the moment I do he rises to grab at his own knife. A twist of my wrist flicks open the blade almost as soon as it's out of my pocket but as I turn to throw it I see it spill away from me, the thud in my chest causing me to lose my grip at the vital moment. I fall backwards into my chair with Rats' knife embedded high in my chest. I look up expecting to see Rats coming for me but he's sprawled across the table having some sort of convulsive attack.

I scramble to retrieve my knife from the floor then manage to get to my feet. Rats is slumped over the table, saliva tendrils stretching from his mouth to the pool of bloodied vomit that's spilled from his guts. He's breathing heavily, his knuckles white as they grasp the edge of the table to ride out the spasm rippling through him. His mouth opens wide in reflex and he wretches, although there seems to be nothing left for him to bring up. I don't waste time or chances; I move around the table to come at him from behind pressing his face down into his own puke and ignoring the pain it causes me. I thrust the knife deep into his side; he lets out a muted cry and curls up; it's a wound that might prove fatal, but not immediately. I fetch the bottle of croton oil from a low shelf behind the bar and return to Rats. I roll him onto his back and his hand reaches up to grab at the knife still sticking from my chest, but he has no strength and I brush him away.

"This stupid meathead coated every glass in that fucking rack." I hold up the bottle so he can see it. "There's some left, but a man like you can hold his drink. You ought to finish it." I upend the bottle and ram it into his mouth. He struggles and I get some on my hands. Boots was right. It burns.

Rats is close to his end; his lips and tongue are swollen in a mass of angry blisters, bloodied drool spills from his mouth and judging by the smell he's lost control of his bowels. I wipe my knife on his lapel then tilt his head to sever his ponytail, his eyes follow me, I know he can hear me.

"When you're dead no-one will give a fuck." I drop the ponytail on his chest. "But you'll be found like this, de-mystified, emasculated. The only part of legend to you will be the stinking pile of puke and shit you've shed on your way out." I let my blade rest against his throat. At last there's real fear in his eyes, there's no fight left in him. I make him wait for a second or two, just long enough perhaps for him to think I won't do it. "This is for Harvey," I tell him. Then I push the knife home and hold it there until his last breath gurgles in his throat.

Moods' first aid box doesn't quite have what I need, but what there is I can use. I take it to the loos together with a lighter I find in the staff kitchen, then I brace myself before pulling the knife from my chest, and still I almost pass out. I'd not done it earlier for that very reason and, of course, because the blood loss would then increase. It's a bad wound, aimed at the heart and not far from its mark. It's in a difficult place to work on, too close for me to focus on it properly. Instead I get as near to the bathroom mirror as I can and work from my reflection.

The wound looks clean, the skin around the entry point has contracted a little making it seem smaller than the width of the blade, but it's the depth that worries me. I can't know what damage has been done, but I do know I need to stem the blood flow. I know better than to waste time looking for a needle and thread in this place, so I break one of the larger safety pins from the first aid kit and knot the loose thread from my lost button around the end. Once I've heated the pin's leading edge under the lighter flame I pull back the skin a little and try to stitch up the inside. The knot holds, though the stitching has only limited success; the thread isn't nearly long enough. I heat the tip of my knife as I'd done with the pin and touch it to the exposed flesh of the wound; the sizzle is followed by a loud cry, my own. It takes me a minute or two to find the strength to continue. I should stitch up the outer skin too but I've no thread and no heart for it. I settle for taping a sterile dressing over the top and covering that with a wrap around bandage. It's not the best, but it'll have to do. I wipe myself down and pull my last fresh T-shirt from my bag.

I call Mickey and tell him he'll have to arrange for both Moods and Paxton's to be cleaned; he knows what that means. He wants detail but I tell him just to get it done and hang up. Before I leave I do two things. I use a broom to knock every tumbler from the overhead rack, smashing every one on the floor. Then I rip Rosewood's address from the bar's telephone directory.

****

Chapter 32 (Part II) ~ Afterglow ~

~ Mo ~

I slip my shades on for the drive to Tannock Bar but it passes me by; my head swims with all that's happened. That part of me that lives for the thrill of the fight, the adrenalin-induced rush, is elated that I've overcome an opponent I'd clearly underestimated. But I don't dwell on that; I don't want to offer any credit to Muldoon, because he'd clearly underestimated me too. Instead I concentrate on the debt due to Harvey and Con – a debt I'll pay in full when I slit Adam Rosewood's throat. At least I want to concentrate on that, only I can't. Every now and then I experience a warm tingling sensation running through me, like pins and needles – yet it's not. Maybe it's my body's response to the pain in my chest or the amount of blood I've lost. I can't be sure but it makes me want to find Rosewood all the more quickly.

Some of what Rats said sits uneasily with me, it robs me of a little of the euphoria I should feel. I proved I'm not a meathead, I won through, but when he spoke of the future, he mirrored my own thoughts; the likes of me don't fit, Carnie will see to that. But if my place is with Myrna then I'm content with that, because no-one can tell me what passed between us was false. Beneath it all Myrna was a frightened young girl but she did me no harm – she wanted to be my girl; she was my girl.

In Tannock Bar I find Rosewood's address, pull the X5 in to the kerb outside his flat and take a moment to get my strength up. Then I step outside and try the communal door; it's locked but his name on the intercom system at least confirms I have the right place. If I hit every bell I know the chances are that someone will buzz me in without checking. I'm reaching for the intercom when the door opens and a frizzy-haired teenager walks out. He stares at me as I catch the door, his expression blank but clearly expecting something of me.

"It's okay," I tell him. "I'm a friend of Adam Rosewood."

Recognition brings a softening to his expression. "I'm not sure he'll be back," he says, "he's giving up the flat."

"Where is he meantime?" I ask.

"His girlfriend did tell me," he says, "long name, Bridge something."

That strikes a chord with me and I let my gaze fall to the pavement while I try to remember. He hid out somewhere before pulling the job, a hotel, not far from where we dropped the Astra. It comes to me.

"Mountebridge."

"That's it," the frizzy-haired kid says. "How did you get it from that?"

"He did tell me," I say, "but I'd forgotten until you mentioned it."

****

Chapter 33 ~ Sunday girl ~

~ Mo ~

I've been feeling out of sorts long before I get to Mountebridge; I can't remember if I ate this morning, although I'm sure I gulped down some milk from the staff kitchen at Moods. It's a warm day to be stuck in the car, my body's running on empty, I'm dehydrated; I don't want to think that I've already lost too much blood. I've tried to remember the name of the hotel Rosewood stayed at but it takes all my concentration just to drive; it won't come. It doesn't help either to find that the circus is in town, with people and traffic choking the high street. I thump the steering wheel and curse in frustration; when I finally get clear of it I pull into a service station in the square at the end of the road.

The garage shop is empty and the eyes of the young counter assistant burn a hole in my back as I pick a few items from the shelves. A teenager, a Sunday girl.

"Nice day," she says as I set a bottle of still water and a couple of high glucose energy bars on the counter. "Wish I was out enjoying the festival with everyone else."

"Is that what this is?" I ask.

"Don't you just love it. It's on all week," she says with boundless enthusiasm.

I shrug and force myself to respond. "To be honest I'd rather avoid it."

She rings up the items. "Careful then, we meet our destiny on the road we take to avoid it."

"What does that mean?" I ask handing her a twenty.

"Oh, it's just a saying, something my dad often says." Her eyes linger a little longer than necessary as she takes the cash. "Are you okay? You look a little pale."

I lift my shades for a second and watch for her reaction. "I'm an albino, I always look pale."

Her mouth drops, just a fraction. "I'm so sorry," she says. "I didn't realise."

"No problem," I tell her, "but maybe you can help me? I'm supposed to meet a friend at a hotel here, but I've forgotten the name."

"It's a small place," she says. "There's only The Crown or The Huntsman and they're both only a few hundred yards from here. If you came past the green then you've already passed The Crown and if you follow the road round you'll find The Huntsman on the left-hand side."

"Thanks, that last one sounds right. One last thing, is there a rest room I can use?"

"Sure, outside and first on the right."

When I make to leave she calls out saying I've forgotten my change. I tell her to spend it at the festival when she gets to it.

The rest room is a little dowdy and the mirror is polished aluminium rather than glass. I set my purchases in the sink and slip off my jacket to check my wound. I'm not sure what to make of it; I'm not the bloodied mess I anticipated; a small strawberry-shaped stain has leeched through the bandage onto my dark T-shirt, but it's not readily noticeable. Searing the blood vessels looks to have helped; the dressing is coping for now. But the girl had a point, my skin wears the sheen of a fine sweat, yet I'm cold; clammy to the touch.

The Huntsman is only a short drive away and the car park at the front is full forcing me to move to the overspill at the rear. I plan to ask for Rosewood at the reception, but it'll keep for a minute or two longer. I wash an energy bar down with a few large gulps of water, I'll feel better soon. Across to my right, a guy paces back and forth crunching gravel beneath his feet, breaking into my concentration. I squint thinking I'm imagining it, but my luck has turned.

****

Chapter 34 ~ The hurt we do each other ~

~ Adam ~

I knock on the door of the bungalow and pace on the gravel drive, there's movement inside, a door slams, it doesn't sound encouraging. I walk back to the jeep, climb in and wind down the window to wait for her. When she appears, she's immaculate in a floral dress with a short cream coloured cardigan covering her shoulders. Her brown hair shines in the sunlight and is pulled back as she would wear it to work.

I lean out, "Jump in," I tell her. She stares at me for a second or two, as though deciding whether to bother, then comes across.

I make to start the jeep but change my mind and instead I turn to her. "Can we sort this out?" I ask.

"I don't know if it'll sort," she says quietly.

Her eyes are a little red, she's been crying. "Have I hurt you that much?"

"I've had enough lies to last me a lifetime," she says.

I reach out cupping my hand to her cheek. "Everyone has a past, Shelley. I'm not making excuses for mine, but I've not lied to you. I've been honest with you because you mean so much to me. You and Joel don't have secrets, I don't want there to be any between us either. I think we have something, I feel it." I pull my hand back. "Now if we're through, then it'll be your decision, but I'm not going to make it easy for you. You won't be able to say I walked away because I'm not going anywhere."

"I need to think," she says.

"Take all the time in the world," I tell her as I gun the engine. "I'll be right here."

Parking anywhere near the village hall proves impossible, but I find a space in one of the side streets opposite the green. At the main street we're forced to wait before a break in the traffic affords us the chance to cross. My hand finds Shelley's, it's an automatic response, a natural response but she pulls her hand away when we reach the other side as though I was purposely encouraging an intimacy she was no longer prepared to share. I recall the first time we held hands on our day out with Joel. My touch was welcome then, it hurts to see it rejected now.

"Ray will be in the marquee," Shelley says. "I'll pick up an extra box of paper cups and plates from the hall and meet you there."

"Can I help?"

"Not with one box," she says, "but Ray may need you. I won't be a minute."

I tell her okay and push my way through the growing numbers towards the marquee.

****

Chapter 35 ~ What I've always known ~

~ Mo ~

Rosewood climbs into a green Daihatsu and I pat myself down suddenly panicked that I may have left my knife behind, but it's folded safely in my pocket. The car park is quiet; I consider whether I could sneak up on him without being seen. A door slams and a woman exits the house Rosewood paced in front of. He calls out and she climbs in beside him. I slink down a little in my seat, ready to follow them, but instead they talk. I watch him reach out and caress her cheek – his girlfriend, then. Sweet irony.

I sit three cars behind them in the queuing traffic heading back through the village. They turn off into a side street and find a spot to park up; I'm forced to drive past them and double park the Beamer. Perspiration gathers at my temples as I try to catch up with them; they're not too far ahead, I can see them waiting to cross the road, but my heart races inside my chest and I feel lightheaded, I have to slow. They disappear into the crowds on the grassy embankment as I wait to cross the road. But I won't lose him now. I step out only for the screech of rubber on tarmac and the whine of metal on metal to jolt me out of my frustration. I ignore the yelling and the gesticulations of the driver and tell myself I'll find him if I stay calm. I move among the rabble on the embankment, people wander in all directions, half-paced and smiling. There's a carnival mood, a constant chatter rising over the sound of Caribbean music, a happy atmosphere that I'm at odds with. Then I see her, barely twenty yards away, the floral dress helps me pick her out, but where is Rosewood? She enters a wooden clad building and I follow her in.

The building is an empty shell; a spacious room lies open to the left, all wooden floorboards and frosted windows, while some tiny rooms sit off to the right. The girl is not alone, another figure, that of an older man, stands alongside her. They have their backs to me as they empty things from cardboard boxes onto the table at the far end, too intent on their business to notice me.

I pull the knife from my pocket and pass it to my left hand, the whole arm feels weak, but they're not to know. I come up behind them and sweep my right arm around the girl's waist hauling her tight to me.

"Not a sound," I tell them, letting both see the knife.

"What's the meaning of this?" the old man asks. "There's no money here."

I move to the other side of the table, dragging the girl with me; I want to keep an eye on the door.

"We're long past worrying about money, old man. You know Adam Rosewood, don't you?" I say to the girl. Her eyes are fixed on the blade, she nods slowly.

"We both do," the old man adds.

"Then go get him," I say. "Bring him here."

"Okay," he says, "don't do anything silly." Then to the girl: "Shelley, stay calm."

We are alone, the girl and me. I need to conserve my strength, so I fall into a chair and pull her down onto my knees, my strong right arm still wrapped around her.

"My hands are full," I say. "Take my shades off. I don't need them any more."

She sets them on the table. She's rigid with fear, yet her inner trembling passes to me through the closeness of our bodies. It relaxes me to know that she's uneasy. People have always been uneasy around me; it's what I've always known. And right now that gives me comfort enough to accept what's really happening. I'm losing blood, bleeding inside, not out. Rats has killed me after all, I just need time to take Rosewood with me.

****

Chapter 36 ~ The Revival Committee ~

~ Adam ~

Ray stands with his arm on Joel's shoulder looking on as the steel band play in the corner opposite the Hawaiian food counter. The marquee itself is packed with barely a table free.

"Looking good?" I ask.

Ray turns, "we've never had an opening like it, Adam, it's just stunning. Look at the faces, it's a hit."

"I thought you were going to have the band play outside."

"I was but I thought having them start inside would draw people in and get the food sales off to a good start."

"It's worked," I tell him.

"Yes. We'll move the band outside for their next set. I notice the ground in the corner is taking a bit of a pounding. I'll order some boarding to put down so we can protect the ground a little."

"People love the flower necklaces," Joel shouts.

"Your right, Joel," Ray says. "It's the little things, the detail."

Just then a garlanded lady passes, laden with her pineapple drink and her plate of chicken and sweet potatoes, she calls out to Ray: "Fantastic having the school band; nice to see young faces having so much fun."

I lean over to Joel. "Hear that? That was your idea."

"Too right it was," Ray says. "You three make a great team you know."

I wink at Joel and he smiles back. "Mountebridge has its own band though, doesn't it Ray? I remember seeing it on the board outside the village hall."

"We did have," Ray says, "they're defunct now, ran out of money and couldn't find sponsors. But we'll sort that and get the bandstand re-opened too. By the way, where's Shelley at? People have been so complimentary about the girls in the pink hula outfits."

"She stopped off at the hall to bring down more plates, said she'd only be a minute," I tell him.

Just then Stanley arrives, a little flushed. He cups a hand to Ray's ear and whispers something. Ray looks at me and for a split second I wonder if Stanley's remembered something and somehow rumbled me.

"Take Joel, and find Arch," Ray tells Stanley. "Joel, we'll need you to look after Arch's stall for a bit, take bookings or whatever it is he does."

Stanley heads off with Joel, still looking worried. "C'mon," Ray tells me, "we've got a problem."

"What's going on?" I ask as we get outside.

"Some bloke's asking for you at the village hall. He's got hold of Shelley and he has a knife."

~

I'm half a stride behind Ray as we walk into the hall and turn to the left. At the far end a bald-headed figure sits at the table facing us, half hidden behind Shelley who appears to be perched precariously in his lap. It takes a second for my eyes to find his face, so readily am I drawn to the shiny blade he holds at Shelley's throat. But his ice-cold, neon-blue eyes give him away. It's the guy who clobbered me at The White Hart, the guy who threatened and probably killed Ferris. It's Mo Scallion.

"What's all this about?" Ray asks.

"This has nothing to do with you, old man," Scallion spits. "Me and Rosewood have a score to settle."

"You're wrong, son," Ray says. "That's my daughter you have there."

Shelley's forearms are pulled tight to her chest; a fright-induced defensive response, but useless when your assailant already holds a knife at your throat. Scallion looks a little different, he wore a suit when I saw him last and his cropped white hair and goatee contrasted with his brother's. Now he wears a loose-fitting leather jacket and the hair and goatee are gone. He's sweating profusely, not a good sign. I know what he's capable of, I have to stop this. I put a hand on Ray's shoulder.

"Ray," I say, in as calm a voice as I can muster. "This is Mo Scallion; he works for Cornelius Callaghan, who I believe is a London gangland boss. Is that right, Mo?"

"No, it's fucking wrong," Scallion roars.

I swallow hard. I thought Ray was likely to irritate him but I've managed to do that all on my own.

"Past tense, Rosewood. Past fucking tense," Scallion says.

He takes the knife from Shelley's throat and points it at me. "Cornelius is dead, my brother Harvey too; and they were murdered because of you."

Everyone's eyes are upon me, Ray's too, his eyebrows raised as though he's unable to take it in.

"Mo, I don't know what you mean. I did what you asked. I got you the money so you'd let my friend go. But you killed him anyway. Don't do this, please."

"The money was dirty," Mo shouts. "Do you know what the mob does to people who fuck them over?" He presses the point of his blade to Shelley's throat and she lets out a cry.

"No, don't," I shout. "I swear I don't know what you're talking about, Mo; but we can sort this."

He lifts the blade from Shelley's throat and points it at me again and a thin trickle of blood runs from where he's nicked Shelley's skin.

"There's only one way to sort this. People are dead because of you; my girlfriend included. This is your girl isn't it? Maybe you need to know what that feels like?"

I glance at Ray, he's ashen, his whole posture sags under the weight of his concern for his daughter. I can't stand back, I have to act. I raise my hands.

"No, please, Shelley has a young boy. There's no need to hurt her, we're not together anymore." I take a step forward. "It's me you want isn't it?"

"I want you to feel what I feel."

"I'll make you a trade," I say. "My life for hers."

Scallion lets out a short laugh. "You'd love that wouldn't you?"

"I'm just trying to sort this; Shelley has no part in it."

"Okay," he says, returning the blade to Shelley's neck, "but try anything and I'll slit her throat in front of you."

"I'm coming around," I tell him.

"Wait, Adam," Ray says. "This isn't a good idea."

"Ray, I'm getting Shelley out of there." I step slowly around the table.

"That's far enough," Scallion shouts when I'm two steps from him. "Shove both hands into your trouser pockets and get on your knees."

I do as I'm told then he has me face Ray and edge backwards to him on my knees. I watch Ray's eyes for a signal, a moment when Scallion lets his guard down, but none comes. When the blade slips under my chin I realise he's switched hands. Shelley is free but almost too scared to move, he has to push her off his lap before she finds the power in her legs to scamper back to her father while I replace her on Scallion's lap.

The door opens at the far end and Stanley enters with Archer following, his crossbow at the ready.

"What is this, a fucking circus?" Mo asks. "Who are all these people?"

"They're my people," Ray says, consoling a distraught Shelley.

"I've told you before old man," Mo says, "this is between him and me."

"And I told you that you were wrong," Ray says.

I watch Archer raise his crossbow and take aim but I'm in the line of fire. Scallion's left arm lies limp around my waist but his right arm is clamped to my chest while the point of his blade sits tight to my chin.

"We switched the money," Ray says.

"Who did?" Scallion asks.

"Us," Ray says, making a circle with his hand linking Archer, Stanley and himself; "The Revival Committee. Adam was duped just as you were."

Scallion snorts. "You expect me to believe that?"

"Believe what you like; but it's true," Ray says.

I can't believe what I'm hearing and by the looks of her neither can Shelley. She gawps at Ray. But then I realise he's trying to get Scallion to lower his guard to buy me an inch away from the blade so Archer can loose a shot.

"Tell him, Stanley," Ray says.

"I'm the Postmaster," Stanley tells Scallion. "That money box sat gathering dust under my counter for three years waiting to be robbed. Didn't know it was Adam here, but he got the worthless stuff nonetheless."

Now I'm lost, I squint at Stanley. "You pulled a switch?"

"Sure," he says. "The money from the security guard went directly into the safe, but I told you I'd not even had a chance to open the box, remember? That gave me the chance to just hand over the box from the floor."

"Fuck me." I hear myself say.

~ Mo ~

I'm getting weaker by the minute; a searing pain settles behind my eyes, I should have kept my shades on, but it'll soon be over and Rats will have claimed me. Rosewood is on the point of my blade just as I'd hoped. I'll bet when this kicked off he expected to be the hero; I certainly planned to make him a dead one. I thought he was to blame, but now it looks like even he didn't know what went down. We've been turned over by a bunch of bloody farmers. I can still kill Rosewood of course, but where would be the satisfaction in that? I've had enough scheming bastards squirming at the point of no return to know the difference; and I'll be free of my pain soon enough whether I kill him or not. Rosewood's been the soft touch these guys were waiting for. Even now he's busy watching them talk back and forth, still lost at how they've played him. He should be looking into his girl's eyes the way I am, then he'd learn a simple truth.

What the Sunday girl said was right. In a few minutes I'll pass out; Rats will have killed me, while Rosewood has found purpose in the place he chose to hide from the end I'd planned for him. Yet even now he looks set to blow it. My options are few, but it strikes me that maybe I can do us both a favour.

I smile, summon the last of my strength and lift my left hand to Rosewood's forehead. I whisper in his ear as I yank his head back at the same time opening my right palm to let my knife spill onto my fingertips. A quick flip then I draw it across his throat. I hear her scream.

~ Adam ~

It happens quickly, one moment I'm listening to Stanley explain how he put one over on me and the next Scallion is pulling my head back with a strength I was convinced he no-longer had. My eyes see only the wooden rafters and the suspended strip lights as he whispers in my ear. The cold metal of the blade zips across my neck and my breath freezes in my throat. There's a jolt and the room spins, we're tumbling backwards and across the dusty floorboards. Shelley is screaming. I clasp my hand to my neck and wait for the pain to come and life to spill through my fingers. Everyone is above and beside me. I hear Ray say Archer's bolt has hit Scallion flush on the forehead, he's dead. I'm still clutching my hand to my throat to stem the flow of blood when they realise the knife still clenched in Scallion's hand holds the dull side of the blade uppermost. When I pull my hand away I'm told there's no more than a red score across the skin.

A few people have overheard Shelley's screams. Stanley wards them off at the door as I'm helped to my feet; he forces a laugh and tells them Shelley saw a mouse.

Archer finds a dustsheet and covers Scallion's body, then, together he and Ray carry him into the storeroom and lock the door.

Shelley holds me tight, "I thought I'd lost you," she says.

"It looked like he was dropping the knife," Archer says. "He suckered me. If he'd caught the knife properly he'd have cut your throat for sure."

"Do we call the Police?" Shelley asks Ray.

"Shelley," Ray says, "it's gone too far for that, we'd all be implicated."

"What do you mean?" Shelley asks. "We have a dead man in the storeroom, what do we do with him?"

"The bonfire," Stanley says, "douse him in petrol and cremate him in the bonfire."

Ray rubs at his chin, "that's not a bad idea. Arch?" Arch stares at the floor and gives a nod. "Okay," Ray continues, "let's arrange that tonight and bring the bonfire forward, we can come up with an excuse later."

"Just hang on," Shelley says. "Is anyone going to explain what all this is about?"

"It's a long story," Ray says.

Shelley folds her arms and waits.

"Do you remember Vernon's brother, Bernard?" Ray asks.

"Of course," Shelley says. "Everyone knew Bernie Tutt; he passed away two years ago this summer."

"He ran a company called Risley and for years they handled Government contracts to dispose of old out of date notes. Money."

"He stole the money?" Shelley asks, narrowing her eyes.

"Bernard was as straight as a die," Stanley adds. "He didn't steal it, he just didn't destroy it."

"In the end I suppose he bent the rules a little," Ray says. "He was something of an amateur historian too. You know the problems we've been facing for years, an aging population, more and more local businesses going bust; a slow death for the village."

"It's the way of things," Shelley says. "Little you can do to stop it."

"Maybe not," Ray answers, "but it annoyed Bernard. He delved into the village's history in an effort to find something we could use in a positive sense to reinvent ourselves and keep the village alive. Mountebank was another name for a trickster or swindler and he discovered this area was originally named Mountebank for that very reason; it was frequented by conmen and fraudsters. It broke his heart, he'd hoped to find something in our history to help revitalise the community and instead found something that could bury the place."

Stanley then takes up the story: "When Risley's eventually lost their contract to a Government owned establishment Bernard gave me a box containing the money. He explained we could never spend it; it was no good any more. He was fed up seeing Mountebridge 'fleeced' and 'passed over' as he put it. He thought if our past were anything to go by then we'd find a use for it and maybe turn the tables for once. I kept it as a promise to his memory; I never expected to actually do anything with it."

"None of this was planned," Ray adds. "But when Stanley handed over the old notes we saw the chance to help the village. We've all had our eyes well and truly opened. People have died, this ends here."

"So who else knows about this?" I ask.

"Just us, and Vernon, of course." Ray says.

"But wait a minute," Shelley says, "How deep does this go? Who decided what to do with the real money?"

"The Revival Committee; Vernon, Arch, Stanley and myself," Ray says.

"But isn't it fraudulent?" Shelley asks.

"Yes," Ray says, "I suppose it is."

The room falls silent. "C'mon," Stanley says, "there's still a festival to oversee."

"How do we return to normal after this?" Shelley asks.

"As best we can girl," Ray says. "As best we can."

Stanley and Archer make their way out, then Shelley and I, but I catch Ray at the door.

"Ray, now that you know about my involvement, what happens?"

"Adam," Ray says, "as far as I'm concerned you're one of us and I know Stan and Arch feel the same. This village needs incomers; it needs young people like you." He turns to Shelley, "We all make mistakes, Shell. There's none of us perfect. This man risked jail to save a friend and would have died for you back there. If you think you'll find better qualities than that then best of luck to you, but I'd say it's time you came down from that pedestal you've climbed onto."

Shelley looks stunned, but links her arm through mine. We join the numbers passing between the inflatable palm trees intent on heading for the marquee.

"Are you okay?" I ask.

Shelley gives a shudder. "It's surreal, either of us could have been killed back there yet we're acting like everything's normal. Then there's this *committee* business and the bonfire. I don't know how I'm going to get through the rest of the day."

"I'm sorry your father had a go at you back there," I tell her.

She gives a nervous smile. "It's his way of saying he's worried for my future and telling me that I'm too quick to judge, that I expect too much."

"And do you?"

"Probably."

"I don't want to lose you either," I tell her.

Shelley nods. "We've only known one another for a few weeks and today's been a shock on so many levels. Let's take it a day at a time."

I give her hand a squeeze as someone taps me on the shoulder. When I turn the girl smiles, she's petite, her long red hair glints in the sunshine and her face is vaguely familiar.

"Excuse me," she says, "but would you be Adam?" She smiles again, "only, there's someone who's eager to see you." She looks back to the road and I follow her gaze. Struggling in ungainly fashion towards us is a slim man with his left leg encased in plaster. I feel my jaw drop and I'm frozen to the spot, it can't be.

"Told her you'd be the one with the scrawny arse," Ferris yells as he gets within range, "and she picked you out right away."

It's really him and I run to close the yards between us and hug him tight.

"Careful," he says, "I'm just out of the bleedin' hospital."

"Ferris, I can't believe it, they said you were dead."

"Should've been," he says. "They found me in the woods; busted leg, broken wrist and a fractured skull. Spent a couple of weeks in traction, out of it most of the time, thankfully. Tina here phoned all the hospitals until she found me. She's a keeper this one."

"Thank God she did. How did you track me down?"

"Well, seeing as you don't answer your mobile these days we had to ask everyone in your block this morning. Barry said you were here and had a nice bit of skirt in tow."

"She's chatting to Tina," I tell him and we make our way back down to the girls.

We make the introductions and in no time Ferris is doing what Ferris does best, making us all laugh; even down to the story of how he came to be found in the woods by the dog walker who explained to the medics that he'd found his red setter trying to hump Ferris's leg. Laughter, it's the best therapy.

"C'mon," I tell them, "there's someone special I want you meet, his name's Joel."

****

~ *Epilogue* ~

~ *Adam* ~

It's after midnight and a light drizzle falls as I walk down the pathway toward the village hall. Archer's stocky frame is visible by the door, hands in pockets and kicking his feet together to stay warm. His smile is too brief, it's the first indication I've seen that he's finding this harder to deal with than he's let on. When I reach him we fall into the same stride and walk on towards the marquee.

"Everything's laid out as you asked," he says in a stage whisper.

"Good, then don't worry, it won't take long."

"It's good of you to do this," he says.

"After what you did for me, don't be silly."

We slip inside the marquee and close the flap behind us. At the far end where the steel band had stood I can see a small lamp set on the ground, we walk towards it. The spade and the tarpaulin sit by the lamp.

"What about the wheelbarrow?" I ask.

"I've left it leaning against the hall for now. I thought I could use it to bring him down."

"Good thinking," I tell him.

"Adam," he says, "Thank-you for doing this. I know I couldn't."

Even in the half-light I can see in his eyes that he's

close to tears, he's taken a life and regardless of the circumstances it's a hard thing to come to terms with. I give his shoulder a squeeze.

"I should be thanking you, Arch. I owe you."

"The bonfire would be too risky. I'd never feel good about another one; and in any case it's just not right."

"It's okay," I tell him. "I've discussed it with Ray. The boards for this corner will arrive tomorrow, no-one will see that the ground has been dug over for the remainder of the festival and thereafter no-one will bother. We'll get permission to plant a garden here later in the year, somewhere the whole village can use. He'll be in a peaceful place, Arch. Somewhere you can come to if you feel the need."

He nods, "I know he wasn't a good person, but…"

"No need to explain, I understand. I'm going to get started, all right?"

"Can I ask you something?" he says.

"Anything."

"I saw him whisper to you. What did he say?"

"I think he was already slipping away, Arch. It didn't make much sense." He looks on though so I tell him. "He said, shit like that'll get you killed. Don't fuck it up."

Arch rubs at his balding head. "I don't know what it means either."

I work with an energetic rhythm and when the perspiration gathers on my brow I wipe it away with my sleeve; and that's how it goes.

ABOUT THE AUTHOR

'The Power of 2' is John Holding's debut novel. He lives in Ellon, Aberdeenshire, in the North East of Scotland with his wife, youngest daughter and two energetic Irish Red and White Setters. He is currently working on his second novel – 'The Waiting Place'.

Made in the USA
Charleston, SC
19 July 2011